BY THE SAME AUTHOR

No More Sea, Book Guild Publishing, 2010
Out of the Depths, New Generation Publishing, 2012
Place of a Skull, Thames River Press, 2013
Sisters of Fury, Book Guild Publishing, 2015
The Eye of God, New Generation Publishing, 2016
Evil River, Book Guild Publishing, 2020

KEITH JACOBSEN

SHADOWS OF FURY

The Book Guild Ltd

First published in Great Britain in 2022 by
The Book Guild Ltd
Unit E2 Airfield Business Park,
Harrison Road, Market Harborough,
Leicestershire. LE16 7WB
Freephone: 0800 999 2982
www.bookguild.co.uk
Email: info@bookguild.co.uk
Twitter: @bookguild

Typeset in 12pt Adobe Jenson Pro

Printed and bound in the UK by TJ Books Limited, Padstow, Cornwall

ISBN 978 1914471 360

British Library Cataloguing in Publication Data.
A catalogue record for this book is available from the British Library.

AUTHOR'S NOTE

*S*hadows of Fury is a heavily revised version of my first novel *No More Sea*, published by Book Guild Publishing in 2010. It is shorter, more concentrated and narrated throughout in the first person. The intention is to provide a more intense and focussed experience for the reader, one which reflects my developing experience as a writer in the intervening years. The similarity of title with an earlier novel with Book Guild, *Sisters of Fury*, is deliberate. Though independent of each other in terms of plot and character, they share the same focus on the psychological aspects of crime, vengeance and retribution.

Originally from Liverpool, I read French and German at St Catherine's College, Oxford, in the late 1960s, an unforgettable experience to which I pay affectionate tribute in the opening chapters of *Sisters of Fury*. I joined the civil service, specialising in international health relations. Since taking early retirement I have divided my time between music and writing, taking qualifications in pianoforte performance and music teaching in private practice. I taught piano privately for a number of years. I now do so on a voluntary basis as local piano group leader and national subject adviser for the University of the Third Age. As well as fiction I have written poetry, short stories and articles on music.

PROLOGUE

I have at last decided to tell Madeleine's story. Or rather to
let her tell it, in her own words.

When she swore me to secrecy I did not know she was
writing it all down. I now know that she did it only to help her
recover her memories, not to leave a record for posterity. That
was the very last thought on her mind. So why did she not
destroy what she had written, once all the demons prowling
in the dark recesses of her mind had been dragged forth into
the light? It would have been so easy in those final moments
just to drop the book over the edge and let the waves embrace
it and caress it into oblivion. But no, she kept it, clung to it,
knowing I would find it. It was her way of telling me it had all
changed. Now she wanted her story to be told, when the time
was right.

In unveiling her secrets I must also tell my own, inviting
the judgement of all into whose hands these pages pass. I am
long since reconciled to that. For many years I have sat in
judgement on myself, my actions and my omissions. I have

often wondered, since Megan departed, why of all those who inhabit this story only I remain, I who of them all had the least claim to life. I know the answer now. It is because once my role as agent of so many tragedies was over I was the one appointed by time and circumstance to be their historian. It is the only atonement I can make. That task done, I too will take my long-overdue leave.

Brenda Rogers
April 2007

ONE

May 1995

I emerged at last from the path through the woodland and began to follow the trunk road, which, after a further ten miles, would reach Land's End. At the top of a rise I could see a strip of sea on each side of the land that stretched ahead. It was late afternoon and the strip seemed to surround me with silvery light. The large cultivated fields had given way to small fallow ones with untidy drystone walls. Houses were few and scattered. It was as if a skin of modernity had been peeled back to reveal the ancient landscapes beneath. In deference to their venerable age the modern road wound around rather through those old fields, forcing cars to a moderate, respectful pace. I was grateful for that. I knew I would never have the strength to walk all those miles. A car passed me, slowed down and stopped. The young man behind the wheel had noticed my stumbling steps and, assuming I was a frail old woman, for I surely gave every appearance of one, offered me a lift.

1

We drove on in silence. A few miles before Land's End he stopped by the turning down to the coastal village of Porthhella, the destination I had given him. I thanked him, got out of the car and watched him as he drove off towards Land's End. I began the long, slow walk down. A wide sweep of sand lay to the right, to the left the outline of the village crouching beneath a steep hill. The water was a placid lake of ruby and gold beneath the setting sun. Of the day visitors to the beach, only a few stragglers were left: irritable parents, fractious children, making their way to the car park. Nobody gave me as much as a glance. Why would they notice an old lady on her own wearing an over-long torn overcoat and carrying a scuffed leather overnight bag? The inn was still there where I remembered it, on the corner as the road turned to run along the sea front. I entered and rang the bell at reception.

The manager frowned when he saw me. I clearly did not strike him as a promising customer. But it was still out of season and they had plenty of free rooms. How long for, he asked me, brusquely. I'm not sure, I said. A week at least. Maybe a few. That seemed to cheer him up.

The next morning I walked on along the sea front, through the old fishing quarter and on to the coastal path. I struggled up to the first headland, crowned by the observation point, castellated and circular, now little more than a ruin. Beyond the building the ground was level, easy on lungs and legs still weary from the previous day's walk. I reached the massive granite cliffs, pink from the surface of the water up to the point where they began to slope landwards. There the lichen gave them a green tinge. At a junction where the main path turned inland, a narrow side path led on to a Bronze Age fort whose stone outlines were still visible, clinging precariously to the cliff-top. Beyond it, towards the horizon, a lighthouse

2

marked the end of a string of tooth-like rocks projecting from the water like the scales of a partly submerged dragon.

Between two headlands the path turned back towards the sea and the cliffs. I came to a rope slung across the path between two metal posts, barring the way. Beyond the rope the disused path was still visible, though an overgrowth of grass and gorse bush was beginning to claim it. My eyes followed it for a few hundred yards to a point where it almost brushed the cliff edge. Far too dangerous now. Once it had been a safe distance away. That was before the earth had fallen. By the rope was a warning sign, diverting me to a newly cleared path which led back safely inland. I followed it between dense, bright yellow gorse bushes. Stonechats, a haze of brown and orange, flashed and darted among the bushes, sometimes taking noisy and assertive possession of the sharp top of a branch.

After half a mile the new path rejoined the one which had been roped off. I passed several small inlets before reaching one just about large enough to be called a bay, embroidered with a narrow strip of dark yellow sand. The path led downhill towards this mini-beach and rose again on the other side. The land behind the beach was a gentle rise, in contrast to the surrounding cliffs. The lake-calm water in the bay was turquoise at the mouth and dark green closer in to shore.

I was looking for the house. Was it still there? Had wind and waves finally swept it away, as was surely its destiny? But it had to be there. Megan had written to me from it only a few weeks before. As I rounded a sharp corner there it was, set solidly enough on a plateau about halfway up the hillside. It was as I remembered, faced in grey stone, with two large downstairs French windows and four upstairs bays. Sunlight flashed into my eyes, reflected from three skylights set into the sloping slate roof. All the windows on the first floor were shuttered, giving the impression that the whole building was wearing a severe frown.

I had seen enough for one day. I turned back along the path. I had to prepare myself. The next day I would go to see Brenda.

She was locking the door of the tiny art gallery on the sea front. Silver-haired now. She stooped a little. But I had changed much more than she had. Would she even recognise me?

'Hello, Brenda,' I called out.

She stared back. 'Good God, it is you. I heard they let you out. I never thought you'd come back here.'

'And it's good to see you again, Brenda.'

'How long has it been? Six years? Now look at us. I've become an old lady, and you look like a departed spirit. No point in our scratching each other's eyes out, I suppose. I'm not going to pretend I'm pleased to see you. But I've had time to get over the way I used to feel about you. Even my hate can't survive six years of not seeing you, of trying not to think about you. I'm too old and tired. Have you gone back to live at the house?'

I shook my head. 'I'm not going to live there again. I only came back to see Megan. But I can't face going up to the house yet. I don't know if I could handle the memories. Me being arrested, Megan screaming at the police to leave me alone.'

'Where are you staying?'

'At the inn.'

'Come and have a cup of tea. I've closed up early today. Hardly any customers. Still a few more weeks to the high season.'

Brenda's home was only a few yards away, a pink-washed picture-postcard conversion of an old fisherman's cottage. The door opened straight into a spotlessly clean and tidy lounge.

A large, beige three-piece suite with neatly embroidered antimacassars over the backs of the armchairs took up most of the floor space. I wondered why she thought she needed so much furniture. I was sure I was the first person she had ever invited over the doorstep.

She served tea in tiny china cups, with shortbread biscuits. I remember how nervous I was. I stared at my cup as if unsure what to do with it. When I picked it up I held it tightly in both hands. Would she notice the tremor in my fingers and wrists?

'So, when was it we last spoke to each other?' she asked. 'Let me see. It must have been that time you came round to see me about Michael's will, a few weeks after the funeral. I refused to let you in and I told you to get lost.'

'You used stronger language than that. In a very loud voice so the entire village could hear. You said I was a scheming bitch... I'm editing now... who had wormed her way into Michael's affections just to get my hands on his money, and you wouldn't take any leftovers from me to save your life. That wasn't fair, Brenda. I had only come round to see if you were all right. To check that you and Michael hadn't come to any understandings he had not put in his will and which I didn't know about.'

'I know. I knew it wasn't fair when I said it. If you had been a gold digger, Michael would have realised. He would never have let you stay. I wasn't in the mood to be patronised by you of all people, that's all. Michael and I had come to a mutual arrangement years before. He had made the gallery over to me. I never wanted or expected anything more. How long have you been out?'

'I was discharged a year ago. I had to live in a hostel for a year, under supervision. Relearn my daily living skills.'

'I'm surprised. I thought... after what you did...'

'Come on, Brenda. Out with it. You're surprised they let me

out so soon. You expected me to do at least twenty years. You expected and hoped it, didn't you? It's all right, I understand.'

'All right. I admit it. I am a little surprised.'

'They decided I was crazy. I had no motive for what I did. So I was detained at Her Majesty's pleasure for as long as I was thought a danger to myself or to others. I was in a secure hospital, not a prison.'

I thought of the scrap of paper I carried in my handbag, the passport to my early discharge. I wondered how she would react if she knew. I would certainly not have been drinking her tea from one of her cups. I would never have been allowed within a hundred yards of her cottage.

'And how are you now?' she asked, an unmistakeable tone of suspicion in her voice.

'Well, I'm out. So that must mean I'm no longer a danger, you'll be relieved to know. When I was discharged I had no idea what to do. I asked them at the hospital whether there was anybody connected to Laura, anybody I could apologise to. Make it up to them in some way. But there isn't. Her sister-in-law died. There were no other relatives. She was about to die anyway. It was the most pointless killing in history. I sometimes wonder if it was my way of killing myself. I was too cowardly to do what David did. Jump off the cliffs. Make a nice clean job of it. So I killed someone in a way that caused minimal damage. Somebody who had no husband or children, who was dying anyway. To make sure I would be put away.'

'Who was she, Madeleine? Who was Laura? The papers only said she was a friend of Michael's. One of the journalists was convinced she was the main beneficiary of Michael's will. But you had looked after him all that time so you thought you should get everything.'

'But she was dying anyway. And killing her wouldn't have made me the beneficiary. No, there was no doubt about his will. Everything came to Megan and myself. You really don't know who she was?'

'No idea.'

'She was David's mother...' I shuddered.

Brenda leaned forward and shook my arm. 'Madeleine, are you all right? You shivered as if a goose just walked over your grave. Do you remember what you just said?'

I shook myself and forced a smile. 'Yes, yes, I remember. I'm sorry. I get like that sometimes. Don't mind me. All those drugs. Sometimes I lose concentration. I said she was David's mother.'

'David's mother? But David's mother was that French woman who was killed in a car crash. The one who married Michael's brother, George.'

'That was what Michael wanted the world to believe. He passed David off as his orphaned nephew. He never had a nephew, as far as I know.'

She leaned back in her chair. 'So Michael really was David's father.'

'You don't sound too surprised, Brenda.'

'I'm not. I did wonder from time to time. How did you find out?'

'Find out what?'

'That Laura was David's mother and Michael was his father. Did Michael tell you?'

'Good Lord, no. It was his great secret. I can't remember how I knew. It just came to me one day in the hospital. I knew it had to be true. I'd been there for months, all the time trying to remember who she was. Hoping that would help me remember why I killed her. Only it didn't. That's all still a blank. I may have seen some papers Michael had left in the house somewhere. He could be forgetful at times towards the end.'

'But assuming you're right, why should you want to kill David's mother?'

'Exactly. There's no possible motive. I gained nothing by it. It proves I was crazy. I'm a paranoid schizophrenic, apparently. We can't always distinguish between dreams and reality.'

'I have read about schizophrenics killing total strangers, imagining they're CIA agents or God knows what. But Laura wasn't a total stranger to you, was she?'

'I didn't know her. I have a vague memory of her coming to the house to see Michael, a few weeks before his final stroke. He let her in. He thought I was asleep upstairs. I didn't meet her then. I saw her from the landing. She never saw me.'

'But you knew who she was and where to find her. You went all the way to Portsmouth to see her.'

'Maybe Michael had left an errand for me. Something he wanted me to give her or tell her. But if so I can't remember anything about it. I certainly didn't leave anything with her, or with her sister-in-law. I remember her name was Naomi, the sister-in-law, that is. What Naomi said to the police was… let me see if I can remember. Yes, she told the police that I had told her Michael was a mutual friend and I wanted to give her the news of his death in person. Perhaps that was it. Michael just wanted me to visit her, check out how she was, see if she needed anything. Feeling guilty, perhaps.'

'Guilty about what?'

'I never knew about her. Neither did you, obviously, though you had known Michael for much longer than I had. So where was she all that time? After their affair he must have sent her away somewhere, until he was ready to take David from her. Gave her money, I suppose. On condition she kept out of his life, out of both their lives.'

'If you're right, he would have had his reasons. He would have wanted to protect Celia.'

Celia. Michael's wife. Poor Celia. 'Yes. But after Celia died he didn't take Laura back into his life. Only her child.'

'I suppose he might well have felt guilty about that. Again, assuming you're right. Neither of us knows for sure.'

'It might explain why I went, and it fits in with what I told Naomi.' I paused, carefully reassembling what I could of my memories of that day. 'I went to see Naomi first. She took me to the hospice. Laura was in a private room. There was a nurse outside at a nursing station. Not directly outside, about twenty yards up the corridor. Naomi told her I was a friend who wanted to see Laura. Then Naomi looked into the room to see if Laura was awake and ask her if she minded another visitor. She came out and nodded to me. Naomi left me there because she had already been in to see Laura earlier that day. I went in on my own. Laura was there in bed, very sick, only a few days to live, so Naomi had told me. I left the room an hour later. I knew that, because while I was waiting for Naomi to come out I had noticed the clock on the wall in the corridor and I looked at it again when I left. I found my way home, in a daze. The strange thing was that I couldn't remember why I had gone or what we had talked about. I couldn't remember anything that had happened in that room during that hour. I still can't. The police came the next day. They had traced me through Naomi. She told them I had mentioned Michael. Maybe she had heard of him. Or maybe I had said he was a famous artist and I had lived with him. They got the address from the Royal Academy. They showed me photographs of Laura, dead, with purple bruising around her lips and cheeks. Apparently I had pulled the pillow from underneath her head and pressed it down on her face. She was too weak to resist. It didn't take long. There was no doubt I did it. Nobody else could have. It was just the two of us in that room.'

Brenda said nothing. My cup rattled slightly as I placed it slowly on the table. I was relieved not to have dropped it or spilled any of the contents on her immaculate carpet.

'Thanks for the tea, Brenda. I've said what I came here to say, about me not being after Michael's money. There are plenty of reasons why you should think badly about me, but I didn't want that to be one of them. Oh, there was something else I wanted to ask you. About the cottage. I haven't been back there yet. I just wanted to have a look. Is anybody living there now?'

'Not the owners. They live in Truro. They rent it out in the high season. It's empty at the moment. But you can go inside if you want. I have the key. I do some cleaning jobs around the village. It keeps me occupied when the gallery's closed. And I find the extra money useful.' Useful for what, I wondered? 'Here you are. You can drop it back here through the letterbox when you've finished.'

She took a tarnished Yale key off a hook near the door and handed it to me. A cardboard label identified it as the key to Cove Cottage. My hands grasped clumsily at it. I shuffled towards the door, painfully aware of how old I must have looked and sounded. Brenda closed it firmly behind me.

All that is true, every word she has written above. Yes, she was the first person I had ever invited in. Yes, I had too much furniture, as if filling the spaces in the cottage could compensate for the void within. And yes, I would never have invited her in if I had known then about her condition. Yes, I did think she had aged. How old was she? Forty-five? Forty-six? About the same age as her mother when she died. But Madeleine looked more my age. She shook like a leaf. She had a terrible cough. She doesn't mention that.

After she had gone, I went over to the sideboard and took out a slender gold bracelet from the back of one the cupboards. I opened it out and looked at the words engraved on the inner rim. To Ceridwen with love. I wondered whether I should give it to Madeleine. But she knew nothing about it. I decided to keep it. I had earned it. It should have been mine from the start.

I sat down again and thought about what she had just told me. I remember those thoughts as clearly as if it were yesterday she had first visited my cottage. So David really was Michael's son. And now she had cleared up the mystery of who his mother was, assuming she was not just imagining it. Poor Laura! What had Michael done to keep her out of the way? Had she given David up to him willingly or did he have to force her? And Madeleine couldn't remember why she would want to kill her. Perhaps I could have helped her out there. Jealousy was always good for a motive, in my book. I knew all about jealousy. Why shouldn't Madeleine have been jealous of any woman Michael had known in his prime, any woman he had made pregnant? After all, by the time Madeleine finally decided she wanted to be with Michael he was old and sick. I saw them together sometimes, watched them from the coastal path, going out for walks together. He leaning on her arm, stopping every few yards to catch his breath. What sort of relationship was that for a woman who was still young and attractive? A very frustrating one, I would have thought. Yes, she could well have been jealous of Laura's past. But jealous enough to kill her? Not in cold blood, perhaps. But in the heat of a quarrel, if she had rejected Madeleine's offer of help and sympathy, taunted her with her passionate past with Michael?

Go on, Brenda, confess it. Those were my thoughts.

And worse, much worse. What if she had had a motive, one she could remember, one which she had been proud to confess, one which made her clearly guilty in the eyes of the law. Then maybe she would still have been locked up instead of coming back to haunt me.

B.R.

TWO

I had seen the three fishermen about the village, when I first went to live there. They were long since retired now, and spent their days on a bench by the sea front and their evenings in the bar of the inn. I had never spoken to them but I knew their names. Charley, George and Samuel. When I went back to the inn that night they were there. And I knew they were talking about me. I sat in the reception area, out of sight, and listened.

'And I'm telling you, it's her! I recognised her as soon as she walked past me to get her key, when I were going through the other bar to take a leak. Her picture were in the papers again only a couple of weeks ago. She looks much older now but it's her.'

'Well, I suppose she signed the register, so let's ask John. John, over here!'

John was John Foster, the manager.

'Finished those beers already, gentlemen? I only pulled them ten seconds ago.'

'No, we don't need filling up. We wants private information. Not shouted across the room. So do us a favour and get over here. Your legs are younger than ours.'

John was new, or at least he had not been there in my day. He was not a local. I could tell that from his voice. I had known many like it, during my years in the City. He might have been a lawyer, or an accountant, or, like me, a financial whiz-kid. Unlike me he had dreamed of spending his time with real country people, people of the sort he had never met in his entire life, people who were wise in the ways of the land and the sea, stoic in the face of storms and natural disasters, fixed in the traditions handed down by their ancestors, real people, the salt of the earth.

And here they were. Charley, George and Samuel were now the centre of his universe, enough to make him long for the past he had only recently escaped. And yet these men fulfilled all the criteria of his dream. Each of them had faced death on the high seas, night after night, year after year, for a pitiful living. They had survived the flooding of their homes, the sinking of their boats, the loss of sons and nephews swept from the decks in storms which had risen without warning. From their early teens to the threshold of old age they had lived a way of life which would have killed people like John and myself within hours. But somewhere along the way they had forgotten to read the script. Their hardships had not nourished their spirits. They did not sing local ballads in obscure dialects, or send chills down the spine with ghost stories about haunted tin mines and shipwrecked sailors told so convincingly that they had to be true. They did not dispense folk wisdom and remedies which had been tried and tested down the centuries. They drank and gossiped. That was all.

'That woman as is staying here,' said Charley. I will attribute the words to him, though I cannot be sure.

'What about her?' asked John.

'Samuel here reckons as she were the one used to live up in the big house on the bay, along the coast towards Land's End. The one as went out of her head and killed some poor old lady in Portsmouth. She had a cottage here before she moved up there.' So they knew all about me. Hardly surprising, for a village that small and eyes and ears with nothing else to occupy them. 'What was her name? Reed, weren't it? Madeleine, that were it. Madeleine Reed.'

Nothing wrong with his memory. Unfortunately.

'Can't be her,' said John. 'That's not the name she's signed in the register.'

'So what name were that then?'

'Russell. Mary Russell.'

All three of them clapped their hands with a simultaneity of which any orchestra would be proud. I imagined them taking long draughts from their mugs with equal precision.

'There's the proof then.' Shall we say that was George?

'Proof of what?' John sounded utterly bewildered.

'That it's her. Mary Russell. Madeleine Reed. Same initials. Must be her. Going under a nom dee ploom.'

'Don't be daft,' said Charley. 'You mean a pseudo-name. Didn't they learn you anything at school?'

'Well, what if it is her?' asked John.

'You can't let her stay, that's what. She's killed somebody. We're not safe. Might be murdered in our beds. She's crazy. That's what the judge said. She were sent to a loony bin.'

'Well, if she's here, that means she must have recovered. They wouldn't have let her out otherwise.'

I did not expect them to be convinced by John's logic. I was right.

'That's as may be,' said the third one. That would be Samuel. 'But her sort only ever brought us trouble here. It weren't just her. He started it all. The rot. That Michael Wallace. Artist chap.' If he had said 'serial killer' he could not have pronounced the words with more venom. 'The last thing we needed around here. This were a proper working community before he came. Farmers, tradesmen, fishermen like us. Over at St Ives they'd been going all poncey and arty for years. But not us. Then he came. Did up the old capstan house as an art gallery. That were a working building for the boats in my young days. He brought that Brenda Rogers woman in to run it. So all the arty types would come and look at the pictures and then look around and see how quaint all the little cottages were. And then they bought them all up and drove up the prices so none of us as had given our hearts and souls and the sweat of our brows to this place could afford to buy them. She never fitted in either. Came from up north. Funny accent.'

'But he never lived here, did he, that Wallace chap?' said Charley.

'No, that were the trouble. He were too high and mighty for the likes of us. So he lived in that big old mansion up the coast. But the damage was done. He planted that gallery here. In a few years' time it'll be like St Ives here.'

'After him came Madeleine Reed's mum,' continued Samuel. 'Bought Cove Cottage. Real stuck-up city type, she were. Never fitted in, either.'

'But she were worse than that Brenda Rogers, though,' said George. 'Madeleine's mum… she had a fancy Welsh name I could never pronounce… she were what you call a fatal femme. In her late thirties, on her own, quite a beauty. When she were walking about the village my Susan wouldn't let me out of doors. Not that she would have honoured any of us with so much as a glance.'

'Well, she did the decent thing in the end,' said Charley. There was a long pause.

'What was that?' asked John. He sounded interested at last.

'Walked off the cliffs. Killed instantly. Mind you, I've never been sure as it were an accident.'

'What, then?' asked John. There was no reply I could make out, only murmurings and mutterings. He was clearly not yet worthy to share all their secrets.

'Then that Madeleine Reed came along,' said Samuel.

'I don't suppose she fitted in, either,' sighed John.

I knew what answer to expect.

'Too right she didn't. She were like her mum to look at. On her own as well. Next thing she were at it hammer and tongs with Michael's young nephew. Disgusting it were. So I heard. I never saw them together.'

Another long pause. For God's sake, how could they possibly know so much?

'So what happened?' ventured John at last, his voice sounding timid, as if the next revelation might be too much for him.

'Oh, nothing much. The young nephew went mad and fell off the cliffs as well, old Michael died of grief, Madeleine Reed went mad in her turn and killed that woman so they took her away.'

I could never have imagined it could all have been condensed into a single throwaway sentence like that. But I could not fault his description.

'Anyway,' continued George. 'We wants to know what you intends to do about it.'

'About what?' replied John, testily.

'About that Reed woman, of course. She can't stay here. I mean, as you know, we are as open and welcoming as anybody. But my Susan would never allow it. And as the man in the house she'd expect me to do something about it.' The others choked audibly on their beer.

'Well, gentlemen, it's a free country.' They grunted in response, clearly unimpressed. 'She's entitled to stay here if she wants.'

'We're only asking you to speak to her,' said Samuel. 'Make it clear she's not exactly welcome here. Find out when she intends to move on. For her sake. We wouldn't want any harm to come to her. Not from us, of course. From those with less understanding and toleration.'

'And if she still wants to stay?'

'Well, I hate to say this but you may find as your most loyal customers takes their custom elsewhere.'

There was no elsewhere, of course, and John knew that. But he would not want to alienate his regulars, however tedious he found them. My stay in the inn would be shorter than I had anticipated.

'I'll have a word with her. I promise.'

I slipped out of my hiding place and went up to my room.

Cove Cottage stood on the steep hillside behind and overlooking the village. The only access to it was from a narrow lane, too small for cars, too steep for bicycles, lined with giant fuchsia bushes. The cottage itself was rather too large to deserve the label and it was neither pretty nor quaint. It was not thatched. The garden on the landward side was so steep that the gate, almost hidden by fuchsia shrubs, was on a level with the roof.

I clambered down the path, now barely visible beneath the encroaching weeds. There was the familiar brass doorknocker in the shape of a smiling man's head. I stepped into the hall. It had been painted in chocolate brown in my day. Now it was hung with garish wallpaper of yellow flowers against a pink background. The kitchen and the bathroom on either side of the hallway near the front door had all been refurbished in stainless steel and pink and yellow ceramics. Bright, modern and functional. Perfect for a holiday let. I walked through into the main living room. Through the two wide bay windows the panorama of sea and sky spread across the bay to the right, down on to the village below and over to the rocky headland to the left.

I looked at the wall above the huge iron stove, a feature which the new owners had obviously thought quaint enough to retain. To my intense surprise the picture was still there. That picture. Impartial observers would see only an ink drawing of a nude woman, her face out of sight, a broad sweep of back, hips and buttocks. They would not see what I saw, the ghosts that moved towards it, through it and beyond.

I descended the steep staircase which had been cut into a corner of the room near the window. The new owners had installed a safety gate at the top. For children or drunken adults or both. The main bedroom was downstairs. This had been the original cottage, a single low-roofed storey built into the side of the hill so the only windows, ill-fitting sashes, faced out to sea. The room clung on to the damp from the rain and sea, and never caught enough of the afternoon sun to dispel it.

I touched part of the wall on the land side. Some flakes from the thin layer of whitewash came away in my hands. Nothing here had changed. The iron bedstead, the solid oak cupboards and chairs, were the same. The moveable full-length mirror was still in its place in the corner, silent, heavy with the secrets of everything it had witnessed. I shivered. I hurried back up the stairs, through the living room and out through the front door without a backward glance.

On my way back to the village I lingered only to drop the key through Brenda's letterbox. A few minutes later I found myself outside the main door of the inn. I was about to enter, then stopped myself. Why go back up to my room now? The narrow, bare walls would crowd in on me, stifle me, like those of my hospital room. But then I had had no choice. Now I was free. I could go where I liked, return when I liked. I was still not used to the idea. I walked slowly along to the bend in the road and on to the empty beach.

In high season the beach would be noisy and crowded by mid-morning, though the village was barely affected by the daily invasion. The cars and motorbikes would crawl in a patient queue down the steep approach road descending from the main route between Land's End and Penzance. The beach and its large car park would beckon to them, siphoning off the flow of humanity before it had a chance to notice the village, tucked out of sight around the corner. The few who drove on would find themselves passing the sea on the right-hand side, and, on the left, a row of spacious houses built in Edwardian times for visitors taking the fashionable sea air. The road finished abruptly. Just before the end, opposite a lifeboat station, was a turning space for the local bus which visited once a day. The space and the double yellow lines which ran along the entire sea front were a stern invitation to the unwanted cars to turn around and go back. Few casual visitors would ever find the old fishing quarter, with its jumble of thatched cottages, looking as if they had been cast up there at random by a particularly high wave. Hardly anybody would ever find the way to the narrow lane behind Cove Cottage.

Today was not a day for visitors. The breeze was strengthening by the minute. An inlander would not hesitate to call it a wind, though the locals would scoff at the idea. For them, a wind was what caused the waves to rise over the sea wall and strew spray and foam across the road. I had lived for months in Cove Cottage, and then, for a much longer period of time, in the far more exposed house on the bay two miles up the coast. But I had never become acclimatised. I was still an inlander at heart. What I was feeling now was definitely a wind. Not to mention the sand which penetrated my thin loose shoes and irritated my toes and the soles of my feet.

I turned round, walked past the inn again and on towards the fishing quarter.

The gallery over which Brenda Rogers presided was one of the oldest buildings in the quarter, perfectly round in shape and sited just by the harbour. It had once been a capstan house, for drawing boats up the harbour beach when the water was low. Now the ebbing tide would leave the flotilla of tiny boats which comprised what was left of the inshore fishing fleet forlornly on the sand until the sea returned to refloat them. At night they would slip out unobtrusively into the bay, slinking back at dawn before most inhabitants were awake. Nets and lobster pots in various states of disrepair lay strewn around the edge of the harbour. The sea wall, the only protection against the Atlantic breakers, was just a few yards long.

As I threaded my way through the cottages to the end of the village I found myself once again at the start of the coastal path, looking up at the first headland, on the far side of which were the sheer cliffs where my mother, and then David, had perished. I had already walked up there, the day of my return. Now, in this wind, the path would be much too dangerous. I turned back, facing the sea, gripping the rail on top of the sea wall, letting the moisture-laden air beat into my face.

So why had I come back to this bleak, lonely spot I had always hated? I had lied to Brenda, partially at least. It was of course true that I had come to see Megan. I was desperate for the kindness of Megan's eyes and voice. She was the one person who would not judge me, would not ask me why I had done what I had done. But there was another reason. I wanted to recover my memories of the killing. I wanted to know the worst before it was too late.

I had forgotten because I had remembered. That was what the therapist at the hospital had told me, a few weeks after I had been detained. On the advice of the lawyer appointed to handle my case I had pleaded guilty to manslaughter on grounds of diminished responsibility. The psychiatrist who had prepared reports for the court had diagnosed paranoid schizophrenia with severe long-term and short-term amnesia. He had recommended therapy to help me recover my memories. So for a few weeks I had therapy sessions, twice a week. They were a complete waste of time.

He had asked me about my childhood. I had expected that. So I told him I had had a very happy childhood, been very close to both my parents, been saddened by their early deaths. So, he asked me, why had I been compulsorily admitted to hospital at the age of fourteen with cuts on my arms which I had inflicted on myself? A misunderstanding, I had told him. I was clumsy, cut myself accidentally. Perhaps I was still upset about my father's death a few months before. But I never deliberately harmed myself. My mother overreacted. So if there had been nothing wrong, why had I had myself admitted four years later to a rehab clinic for drug addicts? Okay, I experimented with drugs. Didn't everybody at that age? Hadn't he? I was only at that clinic for a few weeks. The treatment worked. I never relapsed. Well, not onto the hard stuff anyway. By then my mother and I had gone our separate ways but there was surely nothing unusual about that. As for my father, he and I were always close. I helped him with his research for his books, sat in with him when he gave tutorials. I was grief-stricken when he died.

The therapist listened to all this, then accused me of idealising my childhood. He told me I had serious gaps in my early memories which I had filled with images of the childhood I would have liked. He even had a word for it.

Reconstruction. It's quite common, he said. We all do it to some extent. He suggested that some of my early memories had come back to me momentarily at the time I had killed Laura. He questioned me closely about her. Had I known her before she had come to the house to see Michael? If not, was it possible Laura reminded me of someone I might have known in my childhood, someone who had frightened me? If my early memories had returned without warning, then the shock of what I did to her had caused them to be suppressed once again, along with the memory of the killing itself. Amnesia is a learned reaction. We use it to protect ourselves, and when another threatening situation occurs we use it again. But it is dangerous because the emotions of terror and loss associated with the memories are not suppressed. They stay with us until we recover and confront the memories, until we know them for what they are. Then we need no longer fear them.

I listened patiently but I did not believe him. Yes, the moment of the killing had been erased from my mind. But the rest seemed nothing more than an elaborate fantasy designed to fit in with his own jargon-ridden theories. I had forgotten because I had remembered. What nonsense! Thank goodness they had stopped the sessions. But I did want to remember the killing. I wanted to know what had been going through my mind. Nobody but a psychopath could see into the mind of a psychopath. And if that was what I was I had a unique chance to see what the workings of such a mind looked like. I was sure I was now harmless. I had no fear of repeating my crime. I had no fear of knowing the worst of what I had been, not now I was just a shadow, waiting to join the others who had already passed beyond the grave.

Like my mother. Like David and Michael. I had plenty of memories about those. And if thinking about them helped me towards the secret door in my mind behind which the lost memories might be hidden, then I would think about them. And to do that the best place to be was here, where they had lived and died.

I would start with my mother. At the age of thirty-seven, for reasons she had never explained and about which I had never asked, she had come to a run-down cottage right at the edge of the country. She had followed the road to the point where the narrow, tapering land finally tumbled over the cliffs and into the sea, leaving only a scattering of black, shiny rocks at the surface still clawing at the air, until the waves at last closed over them. Had she then simply waited until it was time to follow the road to the end, to complete her journey? Seven years later she had done so, quickly, dramatically, decisively. Had she come at last to the point where she realised that there was only one thing left for her? There was no way back to the life she had left. And the only way forward was into the sea.

My first thoughts had indeed been that she had killed herself. But I was wrong. The truth was much simpler. She had been walking on her own along the cliff-tops. She had lost her way in torrential rain and pitch blackness. She had stumbled to the edge and fallen over. That was what the police had told me, when I went to identify the body.

I have to go back to that time now, over twenty years, to that interview at the police station, the inquest and the funeral. And to do so I must confront the repulsive coldness of myself at twenty-five.

THREE

June 1973

'I f it's any consolation, we believe she died instantly,' said the inspector. 'Her head hit a sharp rock.'

'Who found her?'

'A couple of climbers. They use that cliff for training quite a lot. It's very dangerous. The rescue helicopter gets called out regularly.'

'Can I see her things?'

'We've got the clothes she was wearing when we found her. I can show you them if you like. I can't release them until after the inquest.'

I glanced inside the carrier bag he handed to me. 'Is that it?'

'That's it, Miss Reed. Everything she was wearing when we found her.'

I took the items out of the bag and examined them, one by one. A voluminous brown tweed skirt, thick woollen jumper unravelling in several places, oversized off-white underwear from a cheap high street chain, tights with several holes in them. All had brown stained patches.

'There wasn't much blood,' said the inspector, following my thoughts. 'Except from the head. So that wouldn't show in her clothes. Her body was badly bruised. A lot of broken bones.'

Was he testing me, trying to find my breaking point? I turned my attention to the bag once again. It was not yet empty. I took out a pair of flat, thin-soled water-stained shoes with worn heels and a thin, badly crumpled raincoat, torn and spattered with dried mud.

'Nothing else? No watch? No jewellery?'

'Nothing at all.'

Suddenly I started to giggle, unable to help myself. Then I put my hand to my mouth.

'What is it, Miss Reed? You find something amusing about the clothes your mother was found dead in?'

The inspector was in his late fifties, I guessed, balding, unshaven, grown careless in appearance and manner as he whiled away the time in his last job before retirement. His voice was flat, with traces of south London. Cynicism had grown into his features from beneath the surface of his skin and hardened them into the face which would now stare at him, unchanging, from the bathroom mirror every morning for the rest of his life. What had he done to deserve a posting to this backwater as the climax to his career? My mother's death was probably the most exciting thing to have happened round there for years. And he was too hardened, too lazy or too bored to get any enjoyment out of it.

'I'm sorry,' I said, shaking my head. 'I was just thinking that I wouldn't be seen dead in these things. Then I realised it wasn't an appropriate thing to think. In the circumstances.'

'If I may say so, Miss Reed, you don't seem too upset by what has happened.'

'I can't say that I am, really. I haven't seen my mother for some time. We had grown apart. She came down here to live and I left Oxford to work in London. Christ, was she really wearing this stuff? She used to have such a good dress sense. We were the same size. We could borrow each other's things. But this underwear is hideous. And this skirt... it's like a tent. She must have put on weight. Was this really everything? You said she was out walking on the top of the cliffs. It was very wet and windy. She had nothing else? Not even a headscarf?'

'That's it, Miss Reed. No headscarf, no handbag. Nothing we could identify her from. Everything else is still at the cottage. What there is. A few clothes in the wardrobe. A suitcase. A few books. Romantic novels. Not my sort of stuff. My wife likes it. I'm not a reading man myself.'

'It shouldn't have been her sort of stuff. She used to have a brain. Gave it up when she married.'

'You can claim it all after the inquest.'

'How did you find out who she was?'

'We sent the uniforms down to Porthhella to make house-to-house enquiries.'

'Porthhella?'

'Yes, that's where she lived. You didn't know that? You never went there to visit her? Never wrote to her there? It's the nearest village to where it happened. In one of the first houses they came to, the wife of an ex-fisherman told our chaps about a lady who lived in a cottage nearby who answered the description. Said she had gone to live there a few years ago. She didn't know the lady's name. Said she kept herself to herself. They went round to the address. There was no reply. They knocked at the cottage next door. Retired accountant from Bristol. He didn't know your mother's name, either. Had seen her around and said good morning sometimes. He confirmed the description as well. He said the same thing, that she kept herself to herself. They went back to her cottage and found a key under a pot plant near the front door. That's how she would have got back in. It explains why she had no key on her when we found her. They found her handbag inside. That's here as well.'

He pushed the bag over to me. I thought I recognised it. It had to be at least ten years old. It was in black leather, coming apart at the seams, the silver buckle tarnished and loose. It was empty.

'We took everything out. You can have it all, including the key—'

'I know. After the inquest.'

'Not that there was much. No letters, no receipts, no credit cards, no passport. No photographs. Only a few pounds in cash. Nothing with her name on it.'

'Make-up?'

'No mention of it on this list. Tissues. Cough sweets. That sort of rubbish. Not what I would have expected. Now take my wife's handbag, for instance. That has her whole life history in it. A whole forensic team would need a week to go through it. I'm sure yours is the same. All they found was a card with the address of a Mr Wilson. An office in Oxford.'

'Yes, that's our solicitor.'

'I rang him. He told me who she was. Said she had one surviving relative. He promised to pass the message on to you. He didn't think it was strange that we found nothing on her or in her cottage which mentioned you. But, speaking personally, I find it just a little bit strange.'

'Do you?'

The inspector shuffled in his seat and leaned forward. I was uncomfortably aware that he had suddenly become interested in the case, if for no other reason than the scope it gave him to embarrass me. I braced myself.

'Miss Reed, can I ask you a personal question?'

'I know you're going to, with or without my permission.'

'How old are you?'

'Is that it? That's the personal question? I'm twenty-five.'

'And when did you last see your mother?'

'I suppose it was about seven years ago. Yes, that was it. When I went to London to work and she came down here.'

'And she never told you where she was living?'

'Our solicitor had the address.'

'And you never told her where you were.'

'I told our solicitor—'

'Your solicitor. I see. Miss Reed, I've heard of divorced people only communicating through their solicitors, but a mother and daughter? Doesn't that strike you as a bit odd?'

I shrugged my shoulders.

'So what did you fall out over?'

'We never fell out. We were good friends. We just drifted apart, that's all.'

'So you had a good relationship until you were eighteen, then you went to London, she came down here and you never had sight nor sound of each other from that day since. That's more than drifting apart if you ask me. That's one bloody great falling-out if you ask me.'

'But I'm not asking you. You asked me. And I told you. I'm sorry if you don't believe me.'

'Before you and your mother separated, was she ever depressed?'

'Depressed? No, of course not. She was always full of life.'

'Were you like her? I mean, I can see you look like her. But you said you and she were good friends. So were you full of life as well? Did you enjoy the same things? Shopping, conversation, you know the sort of thing I mean.'

'I'm not sure I do know. But yes, we enjoyed the same sort of things.'

'But she came down here to live. In a little village in the remotest part of the remotest county in England. You would never have wanted to come here, would you? What do you do for a living?'

'I work in a merchant bank. What exactly are you getting at?'

'I'm getting at this, Miss Reed. She was full of life and the two of you shared the same interests. But she came and buried herself here. Then one night she went wandering up on the cliffs in the wind and rain with the sort of clothes that wouldn't get you through a damp afternoon in Hyde Park. In the meantime you're living the high life in London. She dies, aged only, what...?'

'Forty-four.'

'Thank you. She dies in a tragic accident, only forty-four. Just half an hour ago, you saw her for the first time in seven years, all laid out cold on the slab. Then you see her clothes and giggle about not being seen dead in them. What I'm getting at is that your mother was depressed, and one reason she may have been depressed is that her daughter had turned into the cold-hearted bitch I'm talking to now. That, Miss Reed, is what I'm getting at.'

'So you think she killed herself? And you think I may have had something to do with it? Even though I hadn't seen her for years. For reasons which are none of your business.'

'Actually, no. I don't think she killed herself. But after meeting you I can imagine she might have had reason to. Where are you staying?'

'Hotel in Penzance High Street.'

'Did you bring anybody with you? Husband, lover, girlfriend? Anybody to help you through this difficult time? No, I bet you didn't. You're very independent, aren't you, Miss Reed? Very self-sufficient. No, as I was saying, I don't think it was suicide. Not that you would give a damn anyway. There was no sign of a suicide note, either at the spot or in the cottage. Have you seen her will?'

'Not yet. Mr Wilson told me she left everything to me. She was a widow. I'm an only child. You're not going to suggest I murdered her for her money, are you? Laid in wait for her at the top of the cliffs?'

To my surprise, he laughed. 'No. I'm afraid not. Though God knows it would be interesting to have a murder round here, just once before I go. I'd think more of you if you had done that, you know. It would show you cared passionately about something. And that you had a sense of the dramatic. But sadly, neither is true, is it? No, it's all very clear, unfortunately. Those cliffs are dangerous even for experienced walkers in daylight in good weather. Anybody who did what she did needs their head examining. She was crazy, in my view. But suicidal? No. She would have found an easier and more comfortable way, don't you think? Of course, it's not for me to decide. That's for the coroner. The inquest will be in a few days. You'll need to be there. He may want to ask you some questions. Probably he won't. It'll just be a formality. You don't mind if we release her name to the local press, do you? They've been on at us ever since it happened and we like to keep them sweet.'

'Is that all you intend to release?'

He grunted. 'You're worried in case they come knocking at your hotel room door, asking about the rift between mother and daughter which drove the mother to throw herself over the cliffs. It makes a good story, you have to admit. And round here the press are desperate enough for those. No, I won't say anything about you. I'll just tell them she was a widow, came to the area a few years ago, tragic accident, well-known danger spot, all that sort of stuff. They might spot you at the inquest. Just ignore them. I will.'

The inquest took place in a stuffy office near the town hall in Penzance. A very thin, bearded young man in an open-neck check shirt sat at the back, scribbling into a notebook. I assumed he was from the local paper. To my relief he ignored me. Apart from the inspector and the police doctor there was only one other person present, a tall, distinguished, fair-haired man in his late forties. The coroner, an elderly, bald man with a distracted air, listened to the witnesses, nodded and pronounced a verdict of accidental death. The witnesses, the journalist and the other man hurried out without a glance at me.

I stood outside the street entrance, wondering what would happen next. I would need to arrange to claim the body. Then there would have to be a funeral. Christ, how would I go about organising that? I knew nobody there. I did not know if she had made any friends who would want to attend. I would need to go to the village where she had lived and contact the local priest. But she had never gone to church in her life, as far as I could remember. The priest would probably have never met her. And how was I to find the place? I could not even remember the name of the village the inspector had mentioned. I would need to get the full address from him. I shuddered at the prospect of another interview like the one I had already had. Perhaps the desk sergeant could get me all the information I needed, without referring me upwards. Or I could ring Mr Wilson and ask him. That would be embarrassing enough. He would remind me that he had had my mother's address all those years and express surprise that

I had never been interested enough to ask him for it, not until she was dead. But at least he would be civil.

Through my rising sense of panic I was aware that the distinguished-looking man who had been at the inquest was still in the street, standing a few yards away and staring at me. Now he stepped up and spoke to me.

'You must be her daughter.'

I realised too late that I had taken his proffered hand. I pulled it back sharply. 'I'm sorry, you're not a journalist, are you? I saw you in there but I assumed the young chap was the only one from the press. I don't really want to talk about it. The police said they wouldn't tell you she had a daughter.'

He laughed, heartily. 'Good lord, no. I've been taken for a few things in my time but never a journalist. Michael Wallace. I knew your mother a little. Please accept my deepest sympathies. Dreadful thing to happen. But those cliffs have claimed quite a few lives in their time. I was wondering if there would be any family here. She never mentioned anybody to me. She said she was a widow. That's all I knew about her. If there had been nobody else I would have volunteered to arrange the funeral. As a mark of respect. Spare her the indignity of a local authority funeral.'

'I'm sorry, Mr Wallace. What an insult, to be taken for a journalist. No offence meant.'

'None taken.'

'My name's Madeleine. Madeleine Reed.'

We shook hands again.

'Reed, you said? I knew your mother as Ceridwen Williams.'

'Williams was her maiden name.'

'Were she and your father divorced?'

'No. He died of cancer when I was fourteen. But, Mr Wallace, how did you know—'

'Michael, please. You're very like her indeed. You must have been told that many times.'

'I have heard it said. I suppose you read about it in the press.'

'Yes, but I didn't know who it was, of course. All it said was that an unidentified woman had fallen from the cliffs. Could have been a tourist or a day-tripper. They tend to be the ones who don't treat the cliffs with the respect they deserve. Then I saw her name yesterday in the same paper. It was quite a shock, I can tell you. The police had released the name, so that meant somebody had identified her. If possible the police prefer family to do the identification. So I thought I would come down and see if there was anybody here. I'm sorry if I scared you. It must be something of a shock to be approached in the street by a strange man, right after the inquest into your mother's death. I came on my own because my wife is ill. Is it just you? Are you the only surviving relative?'

'Yes, I'm afraid so. You said you knew her a little. Were you a neighbour?'

'Yes, I suppose you could say that. I don't live in the same village. I have a house a couple of miles along the coast. But that counts as neighbour around here. Come and have a coffee and we can discuss arrangements. You're a stranger to these parts, are you?'

I walked beside him as he moved briskly along the pavement.

'Yes. And I'm afraid I was rather a stranger to my mother as well in recent years. We got on very well before I went to London. When it's just mother and daughter you get very close. Like sisters. But since she came down here we seemed to grow apart...'

To my relief he did not press me further. I had had enough of that from the inspector.

'Please let me help you in any way I can, Madeleine. You'll be able to claim the body when they've done the paperwork. I'll get my housekeeper to ring them about that, and keep ringing them until it's sorted. After we've had coffee I'll take you along to see an excellent funeral director I know, here in Penzance. Very discreet and sympathetic. Then we'll collect my car and I'll drive you round to see the minister at St Olave's. I'm sure he'll be happy to conduct the service and have her buried there. I have a family burial plot in the churchyard. Plan to be buried in it myself when my time comes. Lovely little church, in a very peaceful spot. It's by the sea but sheltered. I can't imagine a better place to be laid to rest. I'm sure the minister will agree. Unless, of course, you have other plans. Or you know anything else about her wishes.'

'No, I talked to our solicitor before I came down. There was nothing in her will about wanting to be buried anywhere special or have her ashes strewn over the Welsh mountains or anything like that. What you propose is fine by me.'

I returned to London the next day, already anxious about the time I had missed away from the office and the effect it would have on my next bonus. The next day Michael rang my home number while I was at work, leaving a message that the funeral would be two weeks hence. He had arranged for the body to be reclaimed and deposited with the funeral director. I rang back to thank him and agreed I would meet him outside the church.

The day before the funeral, I took a couple of hours off and caught a taxi to Bond Street. I was painfully aware that I had nothing to wear. I had never dressed myself for a funeral before. I could not remember my father's, but presumably my outfit then had been arranged for me. If I had gone at all. I had only been fourteen, after all.

After searching through numerous boutiques, I at last found something which I thought would be suitable. It was a black knee-length woollen dress with a wide collar edged with grey fur. I also bought a matching overcoat, a few inches longer than the dress. I could wear it open so that the dress would not be completely hidden. I would need something to cover my head but I detested hats. After long deliberation and numerous suggestions from the endlessly patient member of staff I chose a black silk scarf. The overall effect was in my view dignified but not overdone.

The tiny old church was just outside the village of St Olave's, though the single row of miniature terraced cottages barely deserved to be called a hamlet.

Michael was waiting for me outside, as arranged. He looked as dignified as when I had first seen him at the inquest, but with an added measure of solemnity in his demeanour. A plain black suit, white shirt and black tie. How much easier it is for men to dress for this sort of thing, I thought. Next to Michael was a stout, middle-aged woman. Her loose overcoat, scarf and feathered hat presented a haphazard mixture of dark browns and faded greens. I was surprised to see that Michael and the woman seemed to be together. They made a bizarre couple. Surely this was not his wife? She seemed much older than he was. She looked in good health, though he had told me after the inquest that she was ill.

I clambered out of my car with as much dignity as I could muster, suddenly aware that a low-slung red sports car was not exactly calculated to go with either my outfit or the occasion. I should have left it somewhere and taken a black taxi, but it was too late now. Michael and the woman came up to me. He shook hands warmly.

'Hello, Madeleine. Good to see you again. What a beautifully co-ordinated outfit. I'm sure your mother would have been proud to see you today. She must have been proud of you, full stop. I wonder when she was going to tell me about you. What a pity she didn't have a chance to see what you had become. Oh, this is Megan, my housekeeper. Been with me for years. A real treasure. I couldn't do without her. She never met your mother, but I didn't want to come on my own. And I thought you would appreciate an extra person. My wife is still not well, I'm afraid.'

Megan smiled and stepped up to shake hands. 'Very sorry about your poor mother's sudden death, my dear. Must have been such a shock, and you being so far away.'

Megan spoke in an unfamiliar accent and I had some difficulty in understanding her. But I sensed a warmth in her manner which I did not find in Michael's carefully worded compliments. I decided Michael had made the right decision in bringing her.

Apart from four pallbearers only the three of us followed the coffin into the church. She was here for seven years, I thought. Did she make no friends at all, apart from this Michael? And even he had been at pains to stress that he had not known her well. Did she not invite people from her village round for coffee, go to their cottages for afternoon tea and exchanges of gossip? Where were they all? Then I remembered what the inspector had told me. It seemed nobody in Porthhella had known her name.

The minister, the Reverend Colm O'Brien, was young with a musical Dublin accent. He seemed unsure what tone to set for his address. Only three mourners and nobody crying. I had been unable to tell him anything useful about her life in Porthhella. He struggled with some opening platitudes, then with visible relief found in the manner of her death a theme he could develop. He warmed slowly to his subject.

'Ceridwen Williams was still a young woman in the prime

of her life. She had a sense of adventure. Sometimes that brings danger with it. She fell to her death, falling into the arms of the sea that she loved. But we who are left behind must not hate the sea because of this tragic accident. The sea brings forth life and sometimes by the will of God it brings forth death. I love the sea. I lived near Dublin Bay as a boy in constant sight and sound of it. There is a passage in the Book of Revelation with which I have to confess that I have always had some difficulty. It says that one day there will be no more sea. Well, I for one do not want to see that day, if it literally means the sea will disappear. But I do not think the author of Revelation, in his divine inspiration, really meant that at all. He was referring to the sea which divides people. We may all have friends and relatives over the sea. I meet many people round here who do. But to them we may be close in our hearts. Others may be only a few miles away, or in the next street, or next door, or even in our own homes with us. But between us and them there may be a whole raging ocean. An ocean of suspicion. An ocean of lovingly nursed grievances for past wrongs. And how lovingly we nurture our grievances, watering them, giving them a place in the sun, watching them grow from seeds and tender shoots to tall, sturdy plants and trees, which then take pride of place in the inner landscapes of our hearts. Those mighty oak-like grievances might, when they were still only seeds or saplings, have been consigned to oblivion for ever through a word of regret or the offer of a hand of friendship. But we never spoke that word or offered that hand. So there they stand like the sea between us and those we love. No more sea. Well, in that sense I for one will welcome the day when the events foretold in the Book of Revelation come to pass, and there is indeed no more sea.'

As the address unfolded, I felt my face redden. I bit my lip. I was sure his words were aimed at me. It must have been obvious to him from our conversation that my mother and I had been estranged. Now he was condemning me for that, publicly, in a church of all places, where I had every right to expect words of understanding and forgiveness. At least the inspector had attacked me in private and been discreet with the press. What business was it of the minister's, anyway?

In my embarrassment I looked round. There were two more people in the church. They must have arrived after the start of the service. They were sitting right at the back, in shadow. One was a woman. She wore a black veil across her face. By her side sat a very young, dark-haired boy. He could only have been five or six. I glanced across at Michael, who was standing in the front row on the opposite side of the aisle to me. His gaze was fixed where mine had just been, on the woman and the boy. I had the distinct impression that he was nodding in their direction. Then he turned back to face the altar. After a few more minutes I looked round again. The woman and the boy had left.

I began to feel sick. I rose and made my way outside. I felt the eyes of the others on my back as the final cadences of the minister's address echoed up into the beams and rafters of the low wooden ceiling. I stood just outside the door, gulping in the sharp air. The woman and the boy were standing a few yards away behind a tombstone, staring at me. The boy smiled and started to move forwards towards me. I was too surprised to smile back. The woman, her features still concealed behind the veil, restrained him. Then, without a word, the woman turned away, pushing the boy gently but firmly in front of her. As they moved up the path towards the gate the boy looked back at me over his shoulders. The woman quickened her pace and tightened her grip on his arm.

Had they just been passing by and dropped in to watch the service? No, St Olave's was not a place you just passed by.

And they had been dressed for a funeral. I was sure Michael had known them and made some sort of communication with them. So who were they? His wife was ill. Was the woman his girlfriend, with their love-child? That had to be the explanation. His girlfriend had known my mother and had wanted to attend the funeral. But Michael had not wanted her to meet me or Megan. Perhaps Megan did not know about her, and Michael did not want Megan to find out and say something out of order to his wife. Well, it was their business. Nothing to do with me.

I turned back towards the church. The coffin emerged, followed by Michael, Megan and the minister. Michael came up to me and put his arm round my shoulder. Instinctively I pulled away.

'Sorry about that dramatic exit,' I said. 'Very stuffy in there. I felt a bit sick. I'm better now. I needed the sea air.'

'I understand. And all that business about sea and trees. Like one big mixed metaphor. I couldn't follow it at all. Colm's a nice chap but he does get carried away sometimes. Imagines he's preaching in St Paul's to a congregation of thousands.'

After the coffin had been lowered and the final words of the service spoken, I thanked the minister, concealing my anger with him behind a taut smile, and turned back to Michael. Megan had withdrawn to leave us on our own, no doubt in accordance with prior instructions. I walked round the churchyard with him.

'Michael, I wanted to speak to you about her cottage.'

'Well, of course it's all yours now. You're the only surviving relative. Unless she left it to an animal charity or something.'

'Oh, no. Everything comes to me. I'm sure it's very nice.'

'Not really. It's very run-down.'

'But I thought you said you didn't live in her village.'

'I don't. But I go down there sometimes. There's a nice

little art gallery. That's where we met. We had coffee a couple of times, on the sea front. She told me she had bought the cottage on an impulse. It was almost derelict. I walked back there with her on one occasion. I could see from the lane that it was rather run-down. I never went inside.'

'The thing is, I've no use for it myself. I'm not into all this rural idyll stuff. I've no time and it's too far away. Could you sell it on my behalf?'

'Well, yes, I could. But there's another idea you might want to consider. There's always a demand for holiday cottages round here. Your mother's cottage has superb views over the bay. It has real potential. I could have it done up for you and rent it out. It would be something to keep me occupied. I'm retired now, you see. You wouldn't need to bother about it at all. You can leave everything to me.'

I was uneasy. I had already left everything about the funeral to him. Was I imposing too much on him? But he seemed willing, almost anxious, to receive this further commission from me. What else was I uneasy about? He had been sympathetic. He was not to know that I did not need sympathy. He had not tried to pry into the reasons why my mother and I had not seen each other for so long. His conduct had been impeccable. It was just that there was something about his eyes. I had noticed it when we had first met. They never met mine. They seemed to be looking around constantly, for something or someone. But that was no reason to reject his help. He was offering to take responsibility for the cottage off my hands. I would be foolish to refuse.

'Well, if you really don't mind. All right. It's agreed.' I fumbled in my handbag. 'Here's the key. And my card with my London address. You can clear out all her personal stuff, if you wouldn't mind. Clothes and books and all that. You won't find anything of value there, I'm afraid. Then you can do what you like with the place. Just keep the rent cheques yourself until you've covered your costs. Talking of costs—'

'The funeral? Leave that to me as well.'

'No, I couldn't do that. But take the cost out of the rent as well. Or send me the bill. Well, thank you for all you've done, Michael. I really was at a loss, and you've seen me through it. Thank Megan for coming, as well. I did appreciate it. I really have to be off now. I have to be back for work in the morning.'

We shook hands.

'Well, it was very nice to meet you, despite the circumstances,' he said, a little too cheerfully. 'Do keep in touch. You must come and inspect your property. I'll let you know how I get on with the renovations. Goodbye for now.'

As I slipped into the seat of my car I was conscious of his eyes focussing intently on me. Why only now, when I was leaving? I looked up at him and waved. Megan had returned and stood behind him, waving and smiling. As I drove away I thought about the parting expression on his face. Was it really one of relief? Or was I reflecting my own feelings onto him?

FOUR

May 1995

Megan opened the door and peered through her horn-rimmed spectacles at me, her familiar feather duster in her hand. Then she dropped it, put her hand to her mouth and squealed.

'Lord bless us, it really is you, Miss Madeleine.'

'Hello, Megan. Yes, it really is me. And it really is good to see you. Come here.'

We had never hugged before but neither of us was embarrassed. Perhaps Megan had prepared for it as I had.

'You haven't changed a bit,' I said. 'And don't tell me I haven't because I would know you were lying. And please call me Madeleine. Miss Madeleine is a bit young for me now, and makes me feel like a character in an eighteenth-century novel.'

'And no harm in that, either. They had proper respect in them days. But Madeleine it is from now on if that's what you want. Well, come on in and let's get you a cup of tea. You're really out for good? Not just on... what do they call it... probation? They're not going to take you back?'

'Yes, Megan, I'm out for good. Now where's that tea you mentioned?'

'Have you no luggage with you, Miss... er, Madeleine? You will be staying, won't you? It is your house, after all, and it's been so empty and lonely without you.'

We were sitting in her little parlour near the front door, where she did her knitting and from where she could look out for visitors. She had made tea on a miniature Belling stove she always kept there, to avoid having to go through to the kitchen.

'To tell you the truth, Megan, I don't think I could ever live here again. I'm staying at the inn in Porthhella.'

'Yes, I do understand.' She bent her head, a look of disappointment on her face. We sat quietly for a few moments.

'You don't mind me being here, do you, Megan? After what I did?'

She looked up and shook her head vigorously. 'Of course not. Don't be so silly. And I'll tell you again what I told the police the day they came for you. You never did it. Nothing will ever make me believe you did. Not to my dying day. Either she died naturally or it were someone else. That's what I think and what I'll always think. I know you wasn't yourself at the time. But that doesn't mean you could ever kill someone. And you're not the first person to be driven out of their minds in this awful old house. There were young Master David before you. That time he were away for a week and we didn't know where. When he came back he didn't know Mr Wallace from Adam or me from Eve. Then he wandered off the top of the cliffs that night. Dreadful. Mr Wallace were like a shadow of himself after that. When you came and looked after him, it were like the sun rising again in this house. Then he died and you… well, you did start acting very strange. You went away without a word. I knew you had something on your mind you couldn't tell anybody about. And when you came back and wouldn't say anything… I were so afraid the same thing might happen to you. Only thank God they took you away and they looked after you. We should have done that with him. Not let him live here and go out on his own like that. But Mr Wallace wouldn't hear of it, his being sent away, I mean. And in your case the loneliness of living here after Mr Wallace's death would have been enough to drive anyone over the edge, if you ask me. This great big pile, out on its own, looking out into the Atlantic. Fine, if you're used to it, like me. But not for someone like you, used to all that fast living up in London. If you want to know what I think, I think you should sell it. Get somewhere nice and warm and modern and light. No need to worry about me. Mr Wallace were very generous to me in his will. Best housekeeper in the world, he used to say, just to tease me. I'll be all right. I can find a nice cottage somewhere near here. I've lived in Cornwall all my life and I've never been outside it. But you've travelled. You can choose to go anywhere you like.'

I coughed. It was time to remind her. 'Megan, that other thing you wrote to me about? You remember? In your last letter?'

'What was that, now? My memory's getting worse all the time.'

'You mentioned a notebook.'

'Oh yes. I remember now. Well, it were like this. You know those locked rooms upstairs in the attic? Well, when Mr Wallace were in hospital and I were paying him a visit, it were just the two of us there, and I were doing some knitting because I thought he were dozing, he called me to lean closer to him so he could whisper in my ear. He told me where I could find the keys to the upstairs rooms. The rooms where Master David used to have his studio, and Mr Wallace before him. As you know, after Master David died he kept the whereabouts of those keys a secret and he wouldn't even let me go up there to dust and tidy round. Did all that himself, until he were too feeble to get up the stairs. Now he were telling me that it were his dying wish that I should take everything out of those rooms and destroy it. Made me promise. Said he would have done it himself except he realised too late that he would never have the strength.'

She leaned forward and whispered in a conspiratorial tone of voice, though the nearest living soul had to be miles away. Her eyes were shining.

'Luckily there were no Bible near at hand so I didn't have to swear on the Holy Book because that would have made things a bit difficult for me as it turned out. Anyway, I did promise but then I went and forgot all about it. The thing that puzzled me were, why didn't he ask you to do it, because you was far more likely than me to remember. But he didn't. He asked me. And what's more, he made me swear not to say anything about any of this to you. Well, I didn't say anything, did I? Because I went and forgot all about it. He died the next day and that put it right out of my mind. Then there were the funeral and you being preoccupied and then all that business with you being taken away. I never thought about it until it came back to me one day, about a year on, when I went to change the flowers on his grave. It were like he were whispering to me from the grave to remember what I'd promised. Luckily I remembered where he had told me the keys was. So I went up there to have a look around. I found there were things I couldn't destroy. A lot of drawings and paintings by Master David, done when he were a boy. I don't suppose they were great art, but I couldn't bring myself to burn them. And there were other drawings, by Mr Wallace himself, wonderful things, I thought, though I'm no expert. It would have been vandalism to have destroyed those. There were some papers I got rid of. Old bills, estimates for building work and the like. Though I can't imagine it were those he were bothered about. The funny thing is that I didn't find what he'd told me I would find. That was a blue folder, sealed, with very personal papers. I weren't to look at anything inside, I were to burn it right away. Well, I searched high and low and never found that blue folder. But something I did find, lying on the floor. An old notebook. I had a quick look at the first few pages and decided I couldn't destroy that either. It were nothing to do with Mr Wallace, and for the life of me I can't imagine what it were doing up in that room. I brought it down here and left it in the bureau.'

'And the other stuff that you didn't want to throw out?'

'It's all still up there. The police had a quick look round there after you'd been arrested, but obviously they didn't find anything of interest.'

'And the notebook?'

'I forgot about that as well. Then, I suppose it were a year ago, I were tidying up in that bureau when I found it again. I wondered why I had kept it. Then it came back to me. I had seen your name in it.'

'On the cover?'

'No. Your name were there among the words written inside. On the first page. I never read beyond that. The impression I got were that your mother had written it. So if it belonged to anybody it belonged to you. It were not for me or Mr Wallace to decide to throw it out. So I wrote and told you about it and asked if you wanted me to send it to you. You said, you hoped to be out soon and would come and see me and pick it up then. I've got it here for you. Nicely wrapped up.'

She picked up a parcel from a table by the side of her chair and handed it to me. I turned it over in my hands and waited, as if somehow it would speak and explain its mysteries without my needing to open it.

'So if it was my mother's,' I said at last, 'what on earth was it doing in this house, and locked away upstairs at that?'

'Well, that's the real mystery. I never met your mum. Mr Wallace knew her a bit. Enough to want to go to her funeral. You remember we met there for the first time. He were very insistent on me coming with him. Said he would feel very strange there on his own. And there would be so few people there that just one extra person would make a big difference. So I went, though I weren't very keen on the idea. Some people enjoy them but I'm not really a funeral person. They remind me of my poor Fred's. He were so young when he died. Not yet thirty. I'm glad I did go, as it turned out, because it became my first memory of you. I felt we were friends right away, even though it were another thirteen years before we met again. Anyway, Mr Wallace said as you and she were like peas in a pod. Those weren't his words exactly.'

I felt a tingling in my palms as if the parcel were burning my hands. I had to get it back to the inn and open it up. I put down my teacup and smiled.

'Thanks for taking such good care of it, Megan. And thanks for the tea and the welcome. You don't know how good it is to see your smiling face again. But I need to get back now. I'll come again soon.'

'And it's been so good to see you again. You have no idea. Sorry I couldn't come and visit. But when you've never been out of Cornwall in your life, it's too late at my age to start gallivanting around foreign parts.'

'I understand, Megan. I know you were always with me in spirit. I was going to say that that thought kept me sane. But what was I doing there if I was sane?'

I put my hand over my mouth. She did the same, neither of us really knowing why we should suddenly want to giggle. By the time we parted on the doorstep we were both laughing like schoolgirls.

FIVE

There could be no doubt about it. It was my mother's handwriting. The pages were yellow and the ink had faded but not yet enough to render it illegible.

June 1961

So it's come to this. I'm having to write to you. Even though we still see each other every day. I cannot talk to you anymore, Madeleine. I was getting desperate. Then I had a brainwave. It's a long time since I had one of those. I went out to buy this nice new notebook, specially. I'm not going to write anything else in it. Only the words intended for you. When I've written enough, I'll give it to you. Maybe weeks, months or years ahead. Then you'll understand.

What's happened between us? You ignore me. I start to talk to you and you turn away. You go off to do your homework, so you say, even though I know you've

already done it. Or you go off to be with him. In his study.
The two of you are so close now. You're shutting me out.
I don't blame you. I've been so distant from both of you,
so wrapped up in myself. When I go away I try not to be
away for too long. But sometimes I can't bear the thought
of coming back to a house where I'm a stranger. So I'm
away for days at a time. And I know neither of you needs
me anymore. You have each other. Don't be too hard on
me. It hasn't exactly been easy, paying for the mistakes
I made when I was so young. I'm still young, for God's
sake, only thirty-two. I wasn't in love with him, though I
thought I was. I married him because I thought I needed
someone to keep me calm and steady. I thought I could use
him to make myself complete, to give myself the qualities
I lacked. It didn't work, of course. I felt my soul drying
up. I ended up hating him for his calm and self-control,
for the very qualities I thought I had needed for myself. I
married him because I was wild and he was steady. Then
I wanted him to be like me. Not wild and out of control.
Just enough like me so he would understand me. Enough
so we could share a love of life and beauty. I knew he
had his loves, of books and poems and ideas and history.
I should have been able to share some of those with
him. There was a time when he tried to teach me about
them, when I was his student. But I didn't pay enough
attention. I've forgotten it all now. I was so obsessed with
imagining I was in love with him that I never really tried
to understand what he was trying to tell me. Now he is
teaching you. The two of you are so enclosed. The way
you look at each other, and whisper so I cannot hear.
So now I am on my own. Perhaps it could never have
worked, even if I had agreed to try to learn patiently from
him. I just don't have the gift for it. At least I can do the

things I do have a gift for. The things you're now just old enough to be disgusted by. Yes, Madeleine, I can see it in your face. Maybe one day you will make a mistake in your life which will haunt you for the rest of your days. Then perhaps you will judge me less harshly.

What was this? She hated him? I was cold-shouldering her? Well, maybe it looked like that when he was still alive. How old was I then? Thirteen. I suppose she and I had grown a bit distant from each other. But I couldn't remember taking sides with him against her. And what did she mean, 'the things you're old enough to be disgusted by'...?

The ink in which the next entry was written was less faded.

May 1964

I really don't know what's happening to you. I don't understand you. You're sixteen now, nearly seventeen, looking more and more like me every day. At your age I was an outrageous flirt. Everybody told me how attractive I was. When I try to tell you how attractive you are now I feel a little ashamed because I know I'm talking about myself as well. Or myself as I was. So why haven't you any friends? Why are you so controlled and distant, obsessed with your studies? I did try to talk to you about sex, just that once. You remember? All you said was that you would be careful. I wanted to say that there was a bit more to it than that but you just turned away. I wanted to give you the benefit of my experience. That's the problem, isn't it? My experience. You're still disgusted with me, even though I no longer have affairs. It's like our hearts are dying. But at my age, after a failed marriage, that's perhaps to be expected. But you have barely begun to grow up. Why have you closed yourself off in this way from everything life has to offer? I want you to be like me, but better, happier, more successful. If you can't talk to me, I hope and pray you meet someone you can talk to.

So she was having affairs. That was her business. But all that stuff about me being distant and closed off? We were very close in those days after my father's death. Like sisters. I told her about everything. What about those shopping trips we did together? And of course we talked about sex. And I had lots of friends.

I went over to the table and took out a notepad from the drawer. It had the name and address of the inn on each sheet. I had decided to make a list. Of the names of my friends, of the places my mother and I had visited together.

After half an hour the sheet was still blank. Those damn drugs they gave me. They said they were to calm me down. But they stopped me remembering. And all that time that stupid therapist was supposed to be helping me get my memories back. He probably never even asked what drugs they were giving me.

That was before they found out, of course. Then everything changed. At first, I had been with other female patients on a large Victorian ward. Not that anybody took any notice of me. Each of us was locked into her own private world: some buried in silence; others sitting on the edge of their beds, rocking from side to side and moaning; others telling their story out loud, at length and repeatedly, to the unheeding space around them.

Then without warning I was moved to a high-security wing. I had a room of my own, furnished only with a hard, narrow bed, a chair and a table. I was locked in, day and night. When I wanted the toilet, I called out through an aperture in the door for the duty nurse to escort me.

On the main ward they had only given me tranquillisers. Now there was a new regime of frequent drug injections. At first I resisted. A burly male nurse entered the room and stood by the door. Then a female nurse, almost as large as the male, came in, carrying a small white box. The male nurse took hold of my arm. When I tried to pull it away he jerked it behind my back and pressed upwards towards my shoulders. Slowly, casually, ignoring my screams, the female nurse took out a syringe, filled and tested it, and injected the contents into my still-imprisoned arm. Only when the injection began to take effect and I went limp and silent did the male nurse release his hold. Taking an arm each they half-carried and half-dragged me towards my bed.

That night, before lights out, the female nurse returned to watch me as I undressed, and to search through my clothes and bed for sharp objects which I may have somehow found and hidden away during the day. I had been assessed as being at serious risk of self-harm, she explained. When she had very slowly and carefully checked every inch of my body for any recent marks I was allowed to put on my night-clothes and get into bed.

Not that there was much chance of hiding anything dangerous. My meals were served with plastic cutlery, and even then I was watched closely as I ate. I was not allowed a pen or pencil. I dictated my letters to Megan to a clerk, who came to my room once a week for the purpose. I was allowed to see the letter and check it but not to sign it.

The routine was the same every day, except that after the first day I decided I would no longer resist the administration of the injections. The agony in my arm and shoulder persisted for a week. I was allowed out into a courtyard for exercise for an hour a day, heavily escorted and at a time when no other patients were there.

Though nobody told me, I knew the reason for the move and the new routine. It was all because of that examination, a couple of weeks after my admission. What was that doctor's name, the one who specialised in genitourinary medicine? Dr Simms, that was it. I had liked Dr Simms, at first. She was not like the nurses. She was young and pretty and smiled reassuringly. She told me to undress and lie down on the bed. We just need to check you over, she told me, just a quick check. It was not at all like that. The examination was long, thorough, intimate and often painful.

A few weeks later I was taken back to the same room to see her again. She asked me if I had ever used contraception. Not since I was seventeen, I had replied. I had had an abortion then, and there were complications. It meant I could never have children. Barely attempting to conceal the disapproval in her voice, she read out a list of the various venereal conditions she had found in the examination. Most were not serious. They would treat them with drugs. But there was something else. Something very serious indeed. I know, I said.

She was furious about that. She thumped the table and demanded to know why I had not informed her of the diagnosis. Because there was no diagnosis, I replied. I just knew. It was a stranger. A one-night stand. She then demanded a list of everybody I had had sex with since that night. The answer was simple. Nobody. She stared at me, then decided to believe me. She gave me that piece of paper I have kept with me ever since. Then she told me she would recommend me for early discharge, on compassionate grounds. The following day I was removed to the high-security wing.

I had learned my lesson from the time I had resisted the nurses' efforts to give me the injections. After that I was a model patient, always quiet and docile. I asked, patiently and repeatedly, to be allowed to send for some books from home.

Eventually they agreed, subject to the consultant in charge of my case approving of my choice. I sent Megan a list with directions on where to find them in Michael's library. They arrived within a week. I chose three favourites which I read and reread constantly, refusing to discuss them with the nurses whenever they asked about them. They were a volume of plays by Aeschylus, Sophocles and Euripides, and some books by my father on the Greek myths.

One day, months after my interview with Dr Simms, after I had gone to bed and heard the familiar clunk of the heavy key in the lock, it came to me, like a voice from another world. *The woman I had killed was David's mother.* I did not know how I knew but I had never been so sure of anything in my life. I was elated, though I hid the change in my mood, not wishing to draw any further attention to myself. Despite the withdrawal of the therapy my memories were returning. I waited. Now others would follow. Eventually I would remember why I had gone to see Laura, why I had killed her. Maybe there was a reason of sorts. It could never have been a rational act. But maybe there was a sort of twisted logic to it, a logic which might make sense to me, which might prove to me that at least on my own terms I was not crazy after all, that I had not committed a totally random act of violence. I continued to wait. No other memories returned.

After a few months, I began to suffer from increasingly serious bronchial conditions, with outbreaks of sores in and around my mouth. The infections spread to my kidneys. I spent more and more time under treatment in the infirmary, the last time for a total of six months. When I began to recover from my symptoms they told me I would be discharged within a week, though under supervision. It was not on grounds of compassion. My recovery was temporary. They knew I did not have much time left. It would be an embarrassment for them if I died in their care. There would be difficult questions to answer, suggestions that I had caught my condition there, criticisms of the circumstances which had allowed that to happen. Far better for them to be rid of me, to let me take my chances on the outside. There would be no public criticism of my early discharge. I was no longer violent, no longer a danger to anybody else. There were no surviving relatives or friends of the woman I had killed. Nobody would make a fuss. Nobody would remember my case at all.

I turned my attention back to her notebook. Three years between the first two entries. What happened during those years? He died. Not even a mention. It was cancer. Did my mother tell me that? What type of cancer was it? He smoked a lot. Lung cancer, probably. I couldn't remember visiting him in hospital or going to the funeral. Perhaps I didn't go. They thought it would be too traumatic for me.

A year later I was in hospital myself. No mention of that, either. She had a problem with sickness. She couldn't write about it. So for three years the notebook was silent.

Hesitantly, I started to write. A name. John Carey. Of course. My English teacher. I had mentioned him to Dr Simms. Not by name, of course. I had forgotten his name. In fact I had not mentioned him at all. I had only mentioned the abortion and the consequences. Now more of the detail was coming back to me. That was good. It showed that my memory was improving at last. The talks with Brenda and Megan, the visit to the cottage, my mother's notebook, my thoughts about my time in hospital, painful though they were, were all helping.

I was seventeen at the time. He was nearly fifty. I planned it meticulously. I went to see our family doctor. I had heard about this new pill that stopped you having babies. I persuaded him to prescribe it without telling my mother. That was what

I meant when I had told her I would be careful. She didn't ask me what I meant. She must have assumed I meant I would avoid sex. Another of her sad illusions, that her seventeen-year old daughter could still be a virgin! I asked Mr Carey if I could talk to him privately after school, about what subjects I should apply to study at university. We did talk, briefly. He told me English would be a very good subject for me. I would probably get a grade A in my A-level if I continued to work as hard as I had been doing. But you knew that already, didn't you, he said. I shrugged my shoulders. I followed him as he left the classroom. Outside the school gates I asked him if he could give me a lift home. I lived only five minutes' walk away, whereas his house was five miles in the opposite direction. He knew that and knew that I knew it. But he nodded and opened the car door for me. He took a route that led to neither of our homes, turned up a side road into some woods and parked in a clearing. It was over in less than a minute.

That wasn't the first time. He asked me that, immediately afterwards. Of course not, I said. But who was the first? Another teacher? Not a boy of my own age. I had always treated them with the contempt they deserved.

Mr Carey drove me back and dropped me off just outside the school. Neither of us said a word during the journey. We met at the same time every week outside the school gates and went to the same place, for four weeks. Once I tried to start a conversation. I asked him if I was special to him. He laughed. It was the end of our affair. I did not mind. He was certainly not special to me.

A few weeks later I found out I was pregnant. My mother knew nothing about it. I had told her I would be careful but I wasn't careful enough. Several times I forgot to take my pill. I had enough money of my own from my father's will to pay for an abortion. I told her I was staying with a friend in London.

The abortion had gone successfully, I was told. Except for certain complications. Irreversible ones. I did not mind. I was never the maternal type.

I lay down on the bed, still fully dressed, and closed my eyes. After a few minutes I sensed that I was about to doze off. There was a low whispering sound in my ear. I could not make out any words. Then I heard a different voice. My own. Insistent, desperate. *David's mother. It was David's mother I killed. I know that. I don't know why I did it. But I know it was her.* Now the other voice was laughing, a harsh, mocking sound. Then it whispered a word, very close to my ear. *Special.*

I woke up with a shout, rushed to the bathroom and was violently sick.

SIX

I sat at my dressing table, staring into the mirror. Behind me the grey shadows floated, shifted and pointed. I ignored them. I was used to them now. I had had years to get used to them. I wondered what had made me sick. I would not use the restaurant in the inn anymore. There was a café on the sea front. I would go there in future.

My face stared back at me. It was sallow, thin and deeply lined. My limp hair was a mixture of grey and white. 'Thank God you never lived to see me like this, Mother,' I said out loud. 'Anyone seeing us together now would assume I was your mother.'

I shuddered, stood up, undressed slowly and put on my pyjamas. They were the first things I had bought after my discharge. They were grey, made of a thick woollen material which eased the discomfort of my pressure sores.

I awoke again in the early hours and could not get back to sleep. I put on the light, picked up the notebook and resumed my reading at the third entry.

April 1965

After what happened yesterday you will understand that I have no choice. I have decided to leave Oxford. I've always hated it here. I only stayed here up to now because of you. At least you used to try to conceal your disgust with me. Now you scream it into my face. In front of everybody. You don't need me anymore. On the contrary, I seem to be making matters worse for you. The doctor told me you should be out soon and that you intend to go to London to find work. He expects you to make a full recovery. So long as I don't try to visit you again. He didn't actually say that, but I could tell it was what he meant.

You don't even need me for money. You have your allowance from his estate. I'll sell the house and buy something smaller, somewhere a long way away, in the country. Cornwall, maybe. I don't want to go back to Wales. I want to forget everything about my past. I'll be comfortable enough. The house should fetch a lot of money. I'll pay your share directly into your bank. I will have the royalties from his books to live on. They still sell well, even better than they did when he was alive. You remember Mr Wilson, don't you, our family solicitor? Let him know where you will be living and each time you move. In case anything happens to me. You'll inherit everything, of course. But he'll need to know where you are. I will ask him to contact you from time to time to see how you are getting on. He will let me know. And if you need anything, tell him and he will pass on the message. I will send you this notebook through him, when I have finished it. And should you wish to contact me directly, for any reason, he will give you my address. But if you do not, I will understand.

I wish you every success and happiness. I know you will be successful. You have that determination about you. As for happiness, I think you may find it a bit harder to come by. And it will not come unless you make some difficult decisions. What I mean is that you must try to get over your father's death. And when you get this notebook and have read here what I have been unable to say to you, if you cannot understand me at least try to forget about your hard feelings towards me. I do love you, Madeleine, and despite our coldness to each other I know I will miss you terribly.

At last, a mention of my father's death! But what was all that about me screaming at her?

I couldn't remember that, but I remembered the clinic where it was supposed to have happened. That nice big house out in the country. It must have cost quite a chunk out of father's estate to send me there, even if only for a few weeks. I had developed a little problem with drugs. It started at school, quite soon after I had gone back after that time in hospital. There were drug-dealers outside the school gates every day. We all knew they were there. They mingled with the pupils and parents in the mornings and evenings. Some were only children themselves. They approached me. They seemed to realise I needed their services. They could tell just by looking at me. It was only soft stuff, of course. But they put me onto other dealers near the council estate. In case I needed anything harder. Which I did.

The police caught one of them in the act of selling to me. He got two years. I got probation, on the condition that I attended a clinic. I had been expelled from school by then, just before I was supposed to take my A-levels. Not that I would have been in any state to take them. Whenever I managed to stagger into school it was straight into the toilets to inject. I did not mind going to the clinic. I had nothing else to do. And I wanted to kick the habit. The doctors were pleased with me in the end.

So, she and I had a serious quarrel, did we? I told her I was disgusted with her and never wanted to see her again. Really? And she took me at my word. But if I was disgusted with her, what gave me that right? Maybe I had found out she was having affairs. But I was hardly in a position to judge her for that, a seventeen-year-old drug-addict schoolgirl seducing her teachers.

He and I were close, no doubt of that. I was so proud of him, watching him becoming famous as his books sold more and more, appearing on radio and television. He was working on a new book when he died. About the Myth of Narcissus. I helped him with it, reading the proofs, looking up references for him. He never finished it. *Beauty in the young is a curse. It awakens evil.* I remembered that bit, from the opening chapter. I never knew what it meant. I wanted to ask him but I was afraid he would think I was being stupid. He thought I understood everything he said and wrote. That's all I remember. Nobody could find the manuscript afterwards. He must have destroyed it.

July 1965

I started very early in the morning. It was late June, the longest day. I wanted to get there before dark. I hated the entire journey. It was hot and dusty. There were long queues of traffic. Petrol fumes choked me when I opened the window. At last it was evening and I had the road to myself. It was nine o'clock and the road had only a few miles to go.

I don't know why I took that left-hand turn. I suppose it was the red sky. I wanted to see the sun going down, the dying sun marking the end of my life. In the car park near the beach, a few tourists were taking photographs of the sunset. I wanted to avoid them, though they were too preoccupied to notice me. At the end of the car park I found a path which led across the side of the hill above the beach. I could see the whole bay. I walked along for about half a mile.

It was on the way back along the path that I saw the dolphins. It was ten o'clock but still light. The tide was low. The water was calm and silvery. There were three of them, only a few dozen yards offshore. They were circling playfully around each other. Sometimes they jumped clean out of the water. They call that breaching, or so I have heard. When I was a child I often saw dolphins in Cardigan Bay. Perhaps they were the same ones. After all those years when I hardly ever saw the sea they had come to find me again. Or I had come to find them.

It was nearly dark now. I did not want to drive on. I did not want to go anywhere. I had heard voices from the sea telling me to stay. Just over the road I saw the inn. They had one single room left. I brought in my bag, much too heavy for its size. Wouldn't they have been surprised to know it contained only some of my books? I could have left them in the car but I wanted to give at least the appearance of having luggage. I would have to buy some clean clothes and a toothbrush the next day.

In the morning I looked around the village. I found the lane behind these cottages. There was a For Sale sign in the lane but I did not know to what it referred. I could see no houses. I was about to move on when a young lady arrived from the estate agents. She asked if I had come to view the property. Something made me say yes, though

I nearly asked which property? I followed her through a broken-down gate, which was nearly hidden by the dense foliage, and along the overgrown path. I gasped with shock and delight when I saw the cottage. She admitted it was in a bad state of repair and needed a lot of work. Nobody had lived in it for years. I did not care. I had already decided to buy it. It could not be expensive. After a quick look round I made an offer at just below the price she had named. I would have gone higher. She accepted immediately. I sometimes wonder what happened to the people whose appointment I had usurped. I am sure they would not have liked it. It was meant for me.

It really was a case of love at first sight. I was drawn to its dishevelled appearance, its melancholy air of neglect and its defiant inaccessibility to modern forms of transport. Did I see it as a reflection of myself? It is so oddly put together. There are two floors, but the upper one seems to have been added at a later time, with no internal connection to the ground floor. To get downstairs I have to go outside, down by the side wall and in again by the back door. I would like to make my bedroom downstairs, but first I will need to get an indoor staircase installed. There's damp downstairs and draughts everywhere. There's no electricity connected yet. I'm using candles. But I love it. It's all mine. The views are heavenly. I love to sit and watch the sea, especially when it's raging against those rocks out in the bay.

April 1966

I've just had a letter from Mr Wilson. He says he spoke to you last week. You've got a good job in a merchant bank now. On the bottom rung of the ladder, of course. But you couldn't really expect any more, could you, not without any qualifications, not even A-levels? You type, you take messages, you do odd jobs for the brokers and the analysts. But I know you do more than that, don't you? You watch, observe, listen and learn. You take any opportunity to show you can do more than they expect you to. You take any chance to surprise them, to make them remember you. One day an opening will come. Just a tiny one, a little crack, a chance to really shine. And you will be through that crack like lightning. And then you will be up and away. Nothing will stop you. Somehow I know it will be like that for you.

She was right about that. That's exactly how it was. She knew me better than I thought.

This week, spring has finally arrived, thank God. What a long, lonely winter it has been. I had the chimney cleaned so I could keep warm with wood fires, like the ones we used to have at home in Wales. There is a store on the sea front which sells firewood. I get my groceries there as well. I walk down there every day in all weathers, and struggle back up the path with the burden of what I have bought. The man in the store told me that he could deliver my purchases, for a small extra charge. I told him I was not on my last legs yet. I hope I didn't sound rude. I didn't mean to. He still smiles at me when I go in, but I can't get him to chat to me. Other customers, the ones who have been there for years, get all the gossip. I wonder how long you have to live here before they accept you? Not that I want to hear the gossip exactly. I just want to feel I belong.

My usual pastime, now the weather is better, is walking along the cliff-top path. My favourite spot is between the two headlands. Once I am up there, away from the village, I really feel that I do belong. I love all wild places. The other day I met a hiker there who was walking the coastal path all the way along to Porthcurno. He warned me that the cliffs between the headlands are particularly dangerous. People have been killed in falls there, he said. I am not afraid to go close to the edge. I love to look down at the water boiling and hissing below. Offshore there are huge rocky formations which were once part of the cliffs. The sea has cut underneath them and behind them. Their shapes are fantastic, like prehistoric monsters who have looked upon the Gorgon.

Many of the cottages round here are only occupied in summer. There are some nice old folk who retired here. I say good morning to them. I don't invite them to come round and they don't invite me. Why is that? Am I afraid of growing old? Do I think it might be infectious? There is a woman in the art gallery who is about thirty, I would say. I look younger than my age, so I thought we could be friends. We might have some things in common. We've said hello already. I don't know her name yet. I have to say that she doesn't look at me in a very friendly way when I go in. She's very reserved. I ask her questions about the paintings. I'm not really that interested in them. She tells me what she thinks I want to know. But I really want to know about her. I can't draw her out. She goes back into her shell. It's as if she's a little frightened of me. I think she's rather sad and lonely underneath.

So that was how she first met Brenda. Obviously her efforts to make friends didn't exactly work out. By the time I met

Brenda she still hated my mother, even though she had been dead for thirteen years. She had so much hatred in her she was only too delighted to redirect it towards me.

No more entries. All the later pages blank. So why did she stop writing? And why did she never send me what she had written? And why, oh why, did this notebook end up on the floor in a locked room, two miles along the coast, in the house of a man she barely knew?

SEVEN

A fter the funeral it was another thirteen years before I went to Cornwall again, before I finally saw the cottage. What made me go there? The inquest and the funeral were enough to put me off Cornwall for life. I had vowed never to return. I kept telling myself I should write to Michael and tell him to sell the cottage. I never got round to it.

Then everything changed. I got the sack. Can't blame them, really. They found me slumped in the ladies. Combination of alcohol and an overdose of coke. They found supplies of both in my desk. I had kicked the hard drugs habit years before, but coke was different. It was part of the culture. Everybody there was at it. Only I couldn't handle it. Not with my history of addiction.

The writing had been on the wall for months. Unauthorised absences, increasing signs of poor judgement, slurred speech at meetings, even at seven in the morning. Luckily they gave me a generous pay-off and didn't involve the police. Didn't want the publicity, I suppose. I went into voluntary rehab (again!) for the drugs and joined AA for the other little problem. I stayed off all drugs after that. I carried on drinking but managed to keep it under control. Most of the time.

So why did I return to Cornwall? I still had contacts in London. I could have set up on my own account. But I knew the business was no longer for me. I no longer had the energy or the stamina. I could not keep up with youthful, ambitious rivals who pretended to be friendly, who asked for advice only so they could learn from me and then trample over me on their way to the top. No, I needed a clean break from it all. A week or two where I knew nobody would help me get some ideas together for my future. But why here? That was easy enough. I owned the cottage. My retreat was there waiting for me. It was far enough away for me to resist the temptation to keep in touch with my former life, with colleagues and… I was going to say friends but in that walk of life you don't make friends. Only fellow lunatics addicted to making money, always ready to share a drink and a line of coke with you before stabbing you in the back. The sea air would do me good. Clear my mind. I had enough money to buy a business of my own, something very different, free from all that stress. Abroad, maybe. France, or Italy. For the first time in my life I would take time to dream.

So what if I had not returned? Did I unwittingly unleash my pursuers the moment I unlocked the door to my mother's cottage? If I had stayed away, gone elsewhere, would I have lived something like a normal life? Would that have been remotely possible? Or were my demons already prowling inside my head, preparing to assume their hideous forms wherever I went and whatever I did? Only my memories can tell me, if I can find them again.

I will start with what I can remember. Like the day I first met Brenda.

EIGHT

March 1986

I walked down to the general store on the sea front to buy some groceries for my evening meal, a packet of cigarettes, a bottle of red wine and a bottle of single malt whisky. I was used to a lifestyle in which coffee at the desk was a permanent feature. I was already suffering severe caffeine withdrawal symptoms. I also regretted the weight of my purchases and did not relish the prospect of dragging them back up the lane to the cottage. I struggled with them into a small café next to the store and ordered a cup of black coffee. I sat down and lit a cigarette.

I was on my second cigarette and coffee when I noticed that a stout, severely dressed white-haired woman at a nearby table was staring rudely at me. I looked away. After a few seconds I looked back. The woman was still staring. Out of habit I found myself sizing her up. Late forties or early fifties. Unmarried, living on her own. Owns a dog or a cat. Probably goes to church. Methodist or Presbyterian. The woman stood up and walked over. I stubbed out my cigarette quickly. Perhaps she objected to my smoking. If that was the case she only had to ask. There was no need to stare, no need to approach me so aggressively. She stopped, a few feet away. A look of embarrassed relief swept across her face.

'My God,' she said. 'You're just like her. I thought you were somebody I knew. Then I realised it couldn't be. Unless you were a ghost. I'm sorry I disturbed you.' She turned round and walked away.

'It's all right,' I called after her departing back. 'Maybe I am a ghost. Did you know my mother, perhaps?'

The woman seemed to freeze. She turned round, very slowly. My smile faded under her gaze. A sort of smile seemed to form on her face, but it could well have been a sneer.

'Ceridwen Williams?' She pronounced the syllables slowly, one by one, as if sipping a bitter-tasting medicine.

'Yes. She was my mother. My name's Madeleine Reed. Williams was her maiden name. Would you like to sit down?'

She took a chair from the next table and half-turned it towards me. She sat down. She had gone pale.

'Well, well, well. I never knew she had a daughter. Fancy that. She kept that a secret. But then nobody around here knew much about her. She kept herself to herself. My name's Brenda Rogers. How long are you here for?'

'Oh, I'm not sure yet. Not long, I should think.'

I was acutely aware of her hostility. She made no attempt to hide it. But then I was an outsider. I could not expect to be welcomed right away. Perhaps the atmosphere between us would improve with conversation. It was worth a try.

'Actually, the truth is that I lost my job in London, so I've come here for a break. To take stock. Decide what to do. What do you do here?'

'I own the little art gallery over there near the harbour.'
She nodded vaguely in the direction of the sea wall.

'Oh, that's interesting.' I tried to sound enthusiastic but her
expression was not encouraging. 'How did you come to buy it?'

'It used to belong to Michael. Michael Wallace.'

'Yes, I met him at my mother's funeral. And he's been
managing the cottage for me.'

'I ran the gallery for him. Got some of his former students'
work on show there at the moment. Feeble imitators, all of
them. They couldn't hold a candle to him.'

'Oh, so Michael's an artist? I didn't know. He never told me.
I had him down as a sort of local businessman or an architect.'

My surprise was genuine. Artists don't have such a
distinguished and business-like manner. Artists are raffish.

'He's very eminent, a member of the Royal Academy. I'm
surprised you didn't know.'

'He did tell me he'd retired. But he didn't say from what.'

'It's true. He hasn't done anything new for ages and
probably never will now. His wife died, you know. A year or so
after your mother. She'd been ill for years.'

'I suppose that's why he stopped. He never told me in his
letters that his wife had died. Did you know my mother well?'

She pursed her lips and her speech became more clipped.
'No. She wasn't here for long. She used to come into the gallery
sometimes. I met her there.'

'I suppose it depends on what you mean by long. I would
have thought seven years was quite a long time.'

'She was never here all that time. She sort of came and
went.' She seemed to want to change the subject. 'I suppose
this place must seem very dull and provincial after London.'

'I think that's what I need, for a while, anyway.'

'Not much high life here. No glamour and glitter. It's really
very quiet.'

'I never really had time for high living. Just work and sleep, mostly. I assumed it was the only way to live. I'd like to see if there's another way.'

Throughout our conversation she had sat rigidly in her chair, staring at me. Now the stare had hardened into a glare. 'But you said you weren't staying for long. Why should you, when there's so little here for you?'

We were clearly not going to be friends. And she obviously expected me to be the first to leave. I stood up.

'Well, it was nice to meet you.' I tried to sound as if I meant it. 'I've got to be off now. Lots to do back at the cottage. Goodbye for now. Perhaps I'll see you over at the gallery. I might want to buy something for the cottage.'

She made no response. She did not even look up. I picked up my shopping bags and went out, feeling my face redden. I made a mental note to avoid the art gallery. When I got back to the cottage, I was out of breath and my arms and shoulders were aching.

Was I really so rude and obnoxious? She had done me no harm, other than to be the living image of a long-dead woman I had hated. No, I had no cat and did not go to church. She was wrong about that. But she was right to see the emptiness in my life for which such things might have compensated.

B.R.

Michael came round to see me the next morning at eleven o'clock. I was just emerging from the shower when I heard the knock on the door. I slipped on my dressing gown and pulled back the heavy door. He smiled at me.

'Sorry, not too early, am I?'

'No, of course not. Come on in.'

He wore a dark grey suit, white shirt and red bow tie. He looked scarcely different from the time I had first seen him. Only his hair, a little whiter and thinner, betrayed the passage of thirteen years. He had the same upright bearing. He gave the same impression of pent-up energy, though this time I found it less threatening. I invited him straight into the kitchen and made us coffee. We sat down at the table. He had brought with him a flat parcel in brown paper. He pushed it to one side while he picked up his cup.

'So you found the place all right?' he asked, after a pause during which each of us seemed uncertain how to begin.

'Yes, thank you. That map you sent me was exactly what I needed. It was so neat and precise. It must have taken you ages. I'd like to thank you for looking after the place so well. You've spent so much time and money on it.'

'Pleasure. I enjoyed it. It kept me occupied. And it was your money I was spending. The conversion of the roof space was the biggest item. But it paid its way. It means we can accommodate quite large family groups. I'm glad you approve. Visitors really do seem to like the place. We've had several people come back more than once. What about you? How do you find it?'

'I don't think it's my style, really. I find downstairs a bit creepy. The old bit. I'm not sure about the village either. Not really my sort of place.'

He looked me in the eye constantly as I spoke. I found it a little disconcerting but preferable to the evasiveness of his eyes when we had first met. He seemed suddenly to become aware of my discomfort.

'Forgive me. I noticed the resemblance last time we met. But now, well, you've grown just like she was when she first came here.'

'Funny, I heard that yesterday. But it wasn't meant in a friendly way. From Brenda Rogers.'

'Oh, don't mind her. She's a bit odd these days. I don't see much of her now. Her gallery used to belong to me but I have nothing to do with it now.'

'I didn't know until yesterday that you were an artist. Brenda said you're famous.'

'I used to be quite well-known in some circles, but that was a long time ago.'

'So you sold Brenda the gallery?'

'Sort of. An arrangement. Payment for services rendered, I suppose you could say. How long were you planning to stay? I mean, I'm assuming you'll be here a while but you may have other commitments. In your letter you said a few days.'

'Actually, that was a bit misleading. I have no commitments. I lost my job. I got a good pay-off and I'm taking some time here to think about things. I may be here a while.'

'I'm so sorry. What a shock it must have been. I can well understand you not wanting to mention that in your letter.'

'Oh, it's probably for the best. Things were getting very uncomfortable for me. I was getting too old for that way of life. I was tired of making money and never having the chance to do anything with it. Oh, by the way, I was sorry to hear about your wife. Brenda told me.'

'Yes, it was a tragic illness. Multiple sclerosis. A particularly severe form, with no periods of remission. But that was many years ago now. I've got over it. Look, you must come over to the house some time. You could drive up there. I've brought a map. This is how you get there by road.'

I looked at the piece of paper he handed to me and smiled.

'You and your maps! Is that all you draw these days?'

'Yes, I'm afraid so. No more high art for me. Just useful stuff like this now.'

I studied the map for a minute, a little disappointed with his response, then folded it and put it down on the table.

'Or you could come by the coastal cliff-top path,' he continued. 'It's much shorter as the crow flies, but it can be a bit strenuous if you're not used to that sort of thing. And don't stray from the path. Those cliffs are very dangerous. As you know, of course. Your poor mother.'

I was surprised to feel a sudden stab of curiosity. 'About my mother. Where exactly did it happen?'

'It was very near here. Just the other side of the headland you can see from your front window. She must have been walking up there at night. Even in daylight it can be dangerous. It had been raining, so the edge would have been slippery.'

'Did she ever say why she came down here to live?'

'She never told you?'

'No. As I said when we met before, we had sort of drifted apart.'

'Perhaps it was because it's as far as you can go. She was desperate to leave her old life far behind her. For her it meant an end to that life, and the beginning of a new one. What a tragic shame that the new one was so short-lived.'

'Did she tell you all that? About making a new start?'

'Oh, no. We never talked that much. Just seems the most likely reason for coming down here, that's all.'

With a sudden movement that made me jump he slapped the table.

'Well, it's good to have you here, Madeleine. Please stay as long as you want.' He laughed. 'Sorry, of course you will. Silly thing to say. The cottage is yours. What I'm trying to say is, as far as I'm concerned, I'm delighted you're here, and you're always welcome up at the house.'

We stood up. At the door he turned back to me.

'Oh, I brought something with me. I left it on the kitchen table. It's a picture that used to hang above the stove in the living room. Nothing special. A little one of mine. I put it in there when I was doing the place up. I took it down to repair the frame. If you like it, you can put it back up. I'll leave it to you. Goodbye for now.'

I returned to the kitchen, made myself another coffee and lit my first cigarette of the day. I had not liked to do it while he was there. I was sure he did not smoke and did not approve of the habit.

I had to admit it. I now liked him much better than when we had first met. Something had mellowed him. Or somebody. Perhaps he'd remarried and was keeping it from me as a surprise for later.

I picked up the parcel and, without opening it, put it in a cupboard next to the cooker. I had not dared to tell him. But the fact was that I had no interest in pictures and preferred my walls to be uncluttered.

NINE

June 1995

Charley, George and Samuel were seated on a bench on the sea front by the lifeboat station. Unlike other benches along the front this one faced towards the village. I assumed they had no wish to look at the sea from which through the years they had wrought their precarious livelihood. But they did want to look at and maybe comment on passers-by. As I approached, the sound of their voices came into focus. I was not surprised to discover that they were talking about me, even less so that they obviously intended me to hear their words.

'He's done nothing about it,' said George. 'Even though he promised. She'll bring nothing but trouble here. Some folks just don't seem to know as when they're not welcome. Folks as can kill others in cold blood.'

His voice rose as I crossed over and passed on the other side of the street. I looked straight ahead.

'There's some sorts as we don't want here,' he continued, in an even louder tone. 'And that includes murderers.' His voice spat out the final word as I turned the corner towards the gallery. Once out of sight I paused to listen.

'Murderesses,' muttered Charley.

'What?'

'Murderesses. She's a she. So she's a murderess. A murderer is masculine.'

'Well, that's as may be. But I don't suppose there's any chance of her mistaking that I were speaking about her, not about some masculine murderer who just happens to be here as well.'

'Who's that?' asked Samuel. 'Is there another one? What in God's name is this place coming to?'

'No, of course not,' said George, irritably. 'We were talking about her. Only her.'

'Well, I still says it were that Michael Wallace as started it all,' said Samuel.

'Well, I would just go a bit easy, that's all,' said Charley. 'She might put a spell on you. And the rest of us. Close our mouths. Stop up our eyes. Make us lame.'

'You're lame already. Your eyes are hardly any use either. And I wish someone would close your mouth.'

'Remember that old woman who lived in the cottage up by the turning with the main road? She were a witch. Had a black cat, she did.'

'That were one hundred and fifty years ago. Of course I don't remember.'

'I didn't mean remember personally. The stories about her.'

'Anyway, this one's a murderer... all right, murderess. Not a witch.'

'Maybe. But I'll swear that Brenda Rogers is a witch. And it looks to me as if those two are forming an alliance. I bet that's where she's headed. To see Brenda.'

I smiled and moved on. If they were so ready to argue among themselves they were unlikely to be a serious threat. Still, the sooner I moved out of the village the better.

Apart from Brenda, the gallery was deserted. Brenda looked up as I entered.

'Oh, it's you again. To what do we owe this privilege? You've never been in here before, have you?'

'No. I was never an art gallery person.'

I looked round. Dozens of paintings and drawings had been crammed into the narrow space. Because the few windows were small and high the room was naturally gloomy, but Brenda had skilfully deployed artificial lighting to highlight details of the pictures. Six different artists were represented, mostly from St Ives, Newlyn and Penzance.

'Nothing here of Michael's?' I asked.

'I keep a few small ones of his at the cottage. I hang some of them here every now and then, to help keep his memory alive. But he never intended this place as an outlet for his own work. He wanted to use it to give young artists a chance to display their stuff and get noticed. I try to stick to that. Michael did quite a lot of large canvases. They need space. You have to be able to stand back from them. Get the overall impression and then move in to study the detail.'

'I know. After his death a number of galleries rang me and asked me to take back their stock of his works. They said they didn't have room for them anymore. They must still be up there at the house. I suppose they had decided he was too old-fashioned for them.'

Brenda snorted. 'Usually a painter's work goes up in price after his death, when people realise there isn't going to be any more of it. That didn't happen in Michael's case. He had stopped painting years before he died. There had been a short-term hike in the prices of his work when word got round that he had retired. Then his reputation began to decline. It's a cycle that happens to quite a few artists. Unfortunately Michael was still alive to witness the decline. He was always very painstaking. Would take months, sometimes years, over one canvas. Did he talk to you about his early career, when you lived with him?'

'He only told me about the time after he moved to Cornwall.'

'He was a late developer, not a young, spontaneous talent like David. He never even went to art school until his early thirties. He was in the army before that. Rose quickly through the ranks. Served in Greece and Cyprus. He was a major by the time he left.'

'I knew he was in the army. He never told me he was so senior.'

'He had done a lot of drawing and painting in the army. A lot of map work as well. That's why his draughtsmanship was so refined. He went to art school to consolidate and broaden his techniques. He hated it. Found himself out of sympathy with almost everything he found there. He never believed you could be original just by challenging traditional ideas and media. He always maintained that an artist should find his inspiration in the beauties of nature and the human face and form. Nobody could produce vital or lasting work if their sole purpose was to imitate others or to react against them. There would always be scope for new techniques, but they needed to be founded on established ones which had to be thoroughly mastered first. For many, that was enough for him to be labelled old-fashioned. So, how are you settling in?'

'Oh, wonderful. The locals are friendlier than ever. The landlord keeps asking me how long I intend to stay. I'm the only resident at the moment so I thought he'd be pleased to have me. He was welcoming enough at first. Now he's positively hostile. Last night I tried to get something to eat in the café, but the lady refused to serve me. I can't blame them, I suppose.'

'That would be Susan Croft. She's the wife of one of the chorus of three ex-fishermen you see hanging about the place. They're not exactly rays of sunshine.'

'I've come across them. They know who I am. One of them called me a murderer as I walked past just now. I'll have to move out soon and go back up to the house. I don't want to cause you trouble, just by speaking to you.'

'Don't worry about me. I can look after myself. You still haven't said why you're here. Can I help you with anything?'

'Maybe. I have a question. Do you think Michael and my mother had an affair?'

I sensed her stiffen. 'What makes you ask that?'

'I don't know.' I was not going to tell her about the notebook and where it had been found. 'Michael always said he knew her only slightly. I wondered... what with being at the inquest, and helping me arrange the funeral, and looking after the cottage—'

'That hardly amounts to evidence of an affair. Michael had time on his hands. He wanted to be helpful. And you lived with him up at the house all that time, before his death. Presumably he never mentioned it then. So why would he keep it a secret from you of all people? Anyway, the answer to your question is that I don't know and I don't care.'

'It was just a thought. One more thing. Could I borrow the cottage key again?'

'Another trip down memory lane? All right. Here's my front-door key. The cottage key is on a hook on the back. You can drop the cottage key through the box and return the door key to me here.'

I stepped out into the street, relieved that the three old men were not waiting for me. As I was turning through the gate leading down to the cottage, I stopped to watch a figure a hundred yards ahead of me on the lane. It had been there when I first turned into the lane, stooping, shuffling along, staring at the ground. Even at that distance I could see he was very shabbily dressed. An old tramp, I decided. I had expected to catch up with him but to my surprise he maintained the distance between us. I shrugged my shoulders and stepped down the path.

Once inside I stared again at the drawing hanging above the stove. One of Michael's many models, so I had thought when I first saw it. But even then I felt strangely drawn to it. Now I could see that it was much more than an exercise in line and perspective. There was a story here. These limbs were warm, relaxed, flushed. This was a woman who had just made love. Even though her face was hidden, the aura of satisfaction, of pleasure in her own body and her lover's, was unmistakable. Her lover was off-picture, just to the right. She was pushing herself into a seating position so she could reach a nearby glass of champagne, so she and her lover could toast each other. Michael had caught all of this in a few strokes of the pen. No wonder he was pleased with it. No barely remembered model could have inspired this, I was sure of that now.

Was it my mother? That would account for David's mistake. What was that phrase Megan had used? Like two peas in a pod. It would not explain how her notebook came to be up at the house. But it might explain why she had stopped writing in it and then forgotten about it. Living once again in the present, believing herself in love, she no longer needed it to probe the past or stave off the loneliness of the now.

I walked down to the bedroom. It was here they would have met. But Brenda's question troubled me. Why had

Michael always kept it a secret from me? Why had he always claimed that he had only known my mother slightly? By the time I moved in with him Celia had long since died. Both her grief-stricken parents soon followed her. There was nobody left alive who could be hurt by the knowledge. Not me. I would not have resented the thought that my mother had found at least distraction and possibly some happiness before the end of her life. Not Michael himself. My mother would not have been the only one. There was Laura. He had given her a child, one he did not publicly acknowledge as his son. Maybe there had been others. But why had he continued to keep them all secret right to the end of his life? No elderly artist's reputation is ever damaged by the disclosure that he had affairs. It was almost expected.

I walked slowly back through the hallway towards the front door. Then I spotted the envelope. It was not there when I entered. I was sure of that. I picked it up. My name scrawled on it. Inside a single sheet of paper, heavily dirt-stained. The words, printed on it in the same red felt-tip ink as my name on the envelope, screamed at me.

I can tell you about their deaths. St Olave's Church, tomorrow at noon. Front pew. Left-hand side. Don't look round. Or you will find out nothing.

TEN

April 1986

I sat by the bay window with a cup of coffee and my third cigarette of the day. I would not bother with breakfast. The weather needed my undivided attention. In London I had scarcely noticed the passing of the seasons. Now, dark or light, foul or fair, sunny or stormy, windy or rainy, weather streamed into my consciousness from the moment I woke up. The cottage seemed to be saturated with it from all sides. Out to sea there could there be one sort of weather, and, to the land on the right in the direction of the sunrise, yet another. I found myself attempting to predict changes by looking at distant cloud patterns and estimating where the wind might take them. One morning, when the air was still despite huge waves that were bringing the surfers crashing into the shallows in a swirl of foam, I predicted gales from off by the sea by evening. I was delighted to find myself proved right. The main advantage of my new pastime was that I did not need to leave the cottage. I could see it all from the windows in the front room or from the lawn.

It wouldn't do, though. I would have to take some exercise. I was sleeping very badly. My system was continuing to produce the addictive adrenaline which over the years had seen me through the highs and lows of my eighteen-hour days, the dizzying risks, the euphoria, the despair, the ecstasy of sudden huge profits and the sickening lurches into nerve-wracking losses. I wondered how long it would take for my system to realise it was no longer required. Perhaps it would help if I cut back on the coffee.

At last a day came when I felt a perceptible increase in the temperature. Heavy winds over the preceding few days had given way to mild breezes and dark leaden clouds to ones of the whitest cotton wool. I put on my trainers, a light, close-fitting jumper and jeans. I soon found the start of the coastal path but was dismayed to see that the initial slope was very steep. I would have to build up my stamina slowly. It would be some time before I could manage the walk to Michael's house. At last I struggled up to a small fort-like building where I stopped to catch my breath. It was still intact, but the windows and doors were missing and a dank smell exuded from the interior.

'Dates from the war,' shouted a bearded man in a green anorak, striding past me, a huge pair of binoculars dangling from his neck. 'Observation point for enemy ships.' He had come up the path behind me and was not even slightly out of breath.

'Thanks,' I managed to gasp. 'Very interesting.'

From the observation point the path was reasonably flat and I felt sufficiently recovered to walk on. There was another headland beyond. The path followed the top of the cliffs between the two headlands. This must have been where she fell, I thought. In places along the sides of the inlet, grassy slopes dropped away from the path leading to a low cliff for a final plunge into the water. The most dangerous section was where the inlet reached the point furthest away from the open sea. Here the cliff started very close to the path and fell vertically away for several hundred feet.

I left the path and headed inland. I soon came to an area of grassland where the soil, though thin, was still able to support some bluebells and wild pink pansies. A girl with her back to me was sketching in a large pad on her knees. She had dark hair falling almost to her shoulders. As I came past I saw that she was wearing a large loose brown pullover and jeans. The face turned to look at me. I stopped and caught my breath. It was not a girl. I guessed he was about nineteen or twenty. He stared at me. I had to say something.

'I'm sorry. I thought you were someone I knew,' I stammered.

He frowned. His eyes were deep and black, glowering at me. They were telling me I had intruded, that I did not belong there. But I could not pull my own gaze away. The seconds ticked by. At last, he looked down and carried on working. I walked around him and looked over his shoulder.

'Gosh, that's brilliant,' I said, with genuine warmth and surprise. With nothing more than pencil strokes of differing angles and thicknesses he had captured the sweep of the land in front of us as it tilted down towards the sea, the outcrops of rock near the edge, and the shimmer of the horizon where sea and sky met.

'It's a sketch for a watercolour,' he muttered.

'How long did it take you to do it?'

'I've been doing this one for about twenty minutes. But it's my third or fourth attempt at this view. I think I'll paint this one and see how it looks. I can do that back at the house. Look at the paper. Feel it. It's a special granular surface. You get an alternation of light and half-light. I could show you how it works when I've added the colours.'

A slight local tang beneath a public-school drawl. I felt the paper between my fingers. The surface created a tingling sensation. My hand was nearly touching his. I shivered, unexpectedly. The breeze up here must be colder than I thought.

'I'll leave you to it. Sorry to interrupt.'

He continued to work as I moved away towards the village, my presence already forgotten. I glanced back at him several times. His head remained motionless, his eyes fixed on the sheet in front of him, the pencil working furiously.

The next day I decided to take a walk in the other direction, along the sea front, past the inn and along the beach. Just before I reached the inn I changed my mind. Day-trippers, surfers showing off, screaming kids, sand in my eyes and shoes. Definitely not my scene. Much better to go the other way. Only a few hikers and bird-watchers ever got up to that headland. And the occasional artist, of course.

Not that he had been exactly sociable. Positively surly, in fact. I was sure I did not want to see him again. But we did have a sort of arrangement, didn't we? Even though we had not put a day or time to it. He had promised to show me how watercolour worked, after he had added the colours to the sketch he had been working on. It would be rude not to go back to see him and talk to him. Though he would probably have forgotten what he had promised. He would not even remember he had met me. If I hurried I would get there at about the same time as the day before.

It was as if he had not moved. I stood a few yards from him, taking care not to obstruct his view. He seemed to notice me without seeing me. He put the pencil down.

'I'm sorry. I didn't mean to disturb you.'

'That's all right. I'm getting a bit tired of this one.'

'Are you an art student?'

'Yes.'

'You're very talented.'

He shrugged his shoulders. 'My uncle's a painter too. That's where I live. With him. Along the coast that way.'

'Your uncle?' In a moment I understood. I wondered when Michael was planning to tell me.

'May I join you? I'm a bit tired from my walk. I'm not very fit, I'm afraid. What's your name?'

'David.'

'Mine's Madeleine. I'm staying in Porthhella. In one of the cottages there.'

'A holiday let?'

'No, the cottage is mine. I can stay as long as I want.'

'Are you here with your family?'

'My family? No, I don't have a family. My parents are both dead.'

'No husband?'

I laughed. 'No, no husband. Not even a boyfriend. I'm on my own.'

He stared at me. I felt naked in his presence. I had already admitted far more than I had intended to. I was a woman of thirty-eight on my own, with nothing to do with my time. Already I sensed his disdain.

'I like to be on my own. I can't concentrate on my work otherwise.'

'I can take a hint. I have to go anyway. Shopping to do back in the village. Before they close.'

The good weather did not last. The next day, heavy grey clouds scudded across the bay. Rain rattled against the windows.

Confined to the cottage, I watched from the window as the waves crashed against the black rocks at the base of the headland. The sort of weather in which my mother had been out walking when she fell. But who in their right minds would go walking up there in conditions like this?

Several days later, the sun reappeared. I put on a short-sleeved top, khaki shorts and my trainers, which now had a used, dusty appearance which their designers had never intended. I made for the headland. A few white clouds hung motionless in the light blue sky as if painted on it. From the sea came only the gentlest of breezes. David was there, sketching as before.

I sat down opposite him, waiting for him to notice me. After ten minutes he stopped and flicked back several pages in the pad. He looked up.

'Do you want to see this?'

I walked over to him. The pad was open at the landscape he had been sketching when I had met him. He handed it to me. I gasped. It was transformed. Little of the pencil outline remained. From foreground to background hues shaded into each other from emerald to dark green to purple to azure to an ever-lightening blue with patches of dazzling white. It was difficult to tell where land, sea and sky met.

'I think it's fantastic, David. I know nothing about art. Until today I thought I didn't like pictures. But I really do like this. It's all so different now.'

I thought about the space on my wall where Michael had once put one of his pictures, the one he had returned after repairing the frame and which remained unopened in my cupboard. Perhaps it would be a good idea to have something in the space after all. Already I could see David's watercolour there, greeting me each morning with its joyful kaleidoscope of colour, lifting my dull spirits. I would offer to buy it from him, then get it framed. Brenda would know a good local framer. Perhaps Michael would do it himself, proud of this example of the talent of the nephew he had not yet thought fit to mention. But before I could open my mouth David had torn the picture out of the pad and ripped it into tiny pieces. Some fluttered to the ground while others were borne away on the breeze. I gaped at him.

'What did you do that for?'

'Best way of making sure my uncle doesn't see it. Not his style. He doesn't think it should be mine. Anyway, it was trivial. All landscapes are trivial. No resonance, no symbolic meaning. I have much more significant work to do.'

He turned to a fresh sheet and started to sketch, ignoring my presence. After ten minutes I turned away. It was some time before I realised that he had packed up his stuff and was following me.

'David, I have a small confession to make.'

He was sitting on my sofa, drinking coffee, occasionally glancing out towards the bay. I sat opposite him. He had not said a word since following me into the village, up the lane and into the cottage and my living room. I was sure I had not invited him. I had not spoken to him since he had told me why he had torn up the picture. I wondered if I had unwittingly given him a gesture which he had misinterpreted. Well, it could do no harm to offer him a coffee. And there was something I had to say to him.

'I have met your uncle already. We met for the first time thirteen years ago. He knew my mother. This was her cottage. Since then he's been managing it for me. I met him again very recently. But he didn't mention you. I think he's keeping you back from me as a surprise. He said he was going to invite me over.'

'I knew he was looking after some property for somebody. I didn't know it was this one.' He sounded supremely uninterested.

'How long have you lived with him?'

'Since I was about six or seven. My parents were killed in a car crash when I was a baby. My father was his younger brother, George. My mother was French. That's what my uncle tells me, anyway.'

'You don't look French.'

'I don't feel it either. I was lousy at French at school. Look, we'd better not tell him we've met. He likes to control who I meet and where and when I meet them. He's very protective.'

'That's because he knows how gifted you are. I wouldn't blame him too much. Okay. We'll keep it a secret. When he introduces us, we'll pretend we've never met before.'

He stood up and wandered aimlessly around the room. He stopped in front of the wall above the stove.

'Looks as if there was a picture there,' he said. 'You can still see the outline where the frame was. And the hook's still there.'

I was on the point of telling him that Michael had had one of his own there but something stopped me. There were obviously artistic differences between nephew and uncle. And from the tone of his voice when he had mentioned them and from what he had said about Michael's protectiveness I suspected there were deeper, more personal differences as well. Michael was clearly a sensitive subject. Best not to mention him again, not yet. I decided to improvise.

'Somebody renting the place must have disliked it and taken it down and hidden it.'

'Or maybe somebody really liked it and took it with them.'

'Yes, that's a possibility.'

He returned to the sofa, where he slouched as before.

'So, David,' I said at last, sitting down and forcing a tone of normality into my voice. 'Who are your favourite painters?'

'Not the ones my uncle thinks I should like. His favourites are the old masters of the Italian Renaissance. He wants me to model my techniques on them. Titian, Bellini, Tintoretto. They were the Venetians. Then Raphael and Michelangelo. I suppose you've seen the Sistine Chapel.'

'Actually, I haven't. I did go to Rome once. It was for a conference. Some ugly modern building miles outside. That was all I saw.'

'Uncle sent me to Italy last year with a group of students from different countries, to study art on location, as it were. Venice was the first stop. He told me to spend time in the Church of the Frari. Make a copy of a famous painting there by Titian. It's called *The Assumption*. Just sketch it and then work on it when I got home. I have been working on it, but not exactly in a way of which he would approve. I'm keeping it hidden. I take it out and work on it when he's away from the house. My own favourites are the ones he most hates. Munch. The German Expressionists. I must get back now.'

He stood up, walked straight to the front door and shut it noisily behind him.

I drove much too fast down the driveway, the house looming up at me suddenly as I rounded a bend. I pulled up before the main door. I stood back to register my first impressions. The windows were narrow, with cramped Gothic arches. All of them were shuttered. Five wide stone steps led up to a broad porch beneath a flat granite slab roof, supported on four pillars in a Doric style which clashed harshly with the windows. Set into the wall beside a massive, iron-studded oak door with a ponderous round iron latch was a small window of opaque glass stained dark red.

The door opened and Megan stood there, smiling.

'Hello, Megan,' I called out. 'I remember you from my mother's funeral. You haven't changed a bit.'

'Neither have you, Miss Madeleine. Not a day older. Come in. Mr Wallace is expecting you in the front room. Go on through. I'll bring in the tea in a few minutes.'

The hallway was dark and cavernous, with a lingering trace in the air of lemon-scented furniture wax. Against one wall stood a manual wheelchair, in grey metal with a dark brown leather back. As I passed it I smelt oil and metal polish. From an ornate grandfather clock against the opposite wall came a slow, muffled click. Megan pointed to a door at the far end of the hall. I opened it gently. Late afternoon sunlight flooded through the French windows. My eyes blinked as they adjusted to the change. The room was spotlessly clean and furnished like the lounge of a seaside hotel. It was as if I had moved from one film set to another.

Michael had rung the previous evening to invite me to the house the following afternoon for tea. I had thought of attempting the walk via the coastal path but had thought better of it. It was another warm day and I wanted to arrive looking fresh and smart, not exhausted and covered with dust and sand. I had put on a low-cut floral cotton summer dress, incorporating a belt of the same pattern. A trim white leather handbag and a pair of light-brown high-heeled shoes, and the effect was complete, or would be once I had got into my Porsche, lowered the roof and fastened a chiffon scarf loosely about my neck.

Michael rose nimbly out of a deep armchair, walked up to me and kissed me on the cheek.

'Madeleine, good to see you again. You look lovely. The air here must be doing you good. Can I introduce you to my nephew, David? He's lived here with me since my wife died. He's an artist too, but much more gifted than I ever was.'

David sat slouched in another armchair, his legs dangling over the side. He made no attempt to move, and barely glanced in my direction.

'Hello, David,' I said, remembering just in time that officially we had not yet met.'Pleased to meet you.'

He was smartly dressed this time, in grey trousers and open-neck black shirt.

'Sit down, Madeleine,' said Michael. 'Make yourself at home.'

There was a third armchair opposite the other two. I sat down. Michael smiled at me, then beamed at David, apparently oblivious to David's rudeness.

'So what do you think of the house? Quite a setting, eh? You get fantastic sunsets from this room. Worth it for those alone. A local landowner bought the land in the last century. He had it levelled and built a house on rather flimsy foundations. It soon fell into disrepair and they knocked it down. The family had run out of money by then. This house was built just before the war. An industrialist from Bradford, would you believe? He sank really solid foundations, thank goodness. Then an American bought it on impulse. He read about it in a magazine and learnt it was for sale. He hated it from the start. I don't think he took the weather into account, especially the winters. It fell into neglect. I got it fairly cheaply.'

Michael spoke mainly to me, occasionally taking in David with a glance. David continued to ignore both of us. I decided I had to make some attempt to draw him into the conversation.

'So, you're an artist as well, David. Have you been to art school?'

'Not yet,' Michael replied for him. 'He's going to my academy in September. I set it up in Portsmouth to teach traditional methods and techniques. I don't want him going to one of these places where all they do is mess around.'

David glared sullenly at him. I wondered what the chances really were that he would go to his uncle's academy.

'So, what sort of things will he do there?'

'Landscapes, still life,' said Michael. 'We have life classes as well.'

'You mean nude models?'

'Some.'

'Something to look forward to, David,' I said, turning towards him in a desperate effort to lighten the tone and elicit even one word from him.

David caught my eyes and held them for a few moments. Then slowly, deliberately, his eyes travelled down my body and back up again to my face, his features distorted into an unmistakable sneer. My cheeks burned. I pulled my eyes away and turned to Michael, wondering whether he would say anything to his nephew about his behaviour. Michael seemed to have noticed nothing amiss. He was smiling.

'I'm afraid I'll have to disappoint you there, young man. Most of the models in the life classes are old men like me.'

We all laughed, Michael heartily, David coldly, I with relief. At that point, Megan, with perfect timing, brought in the tea. David suddenly sprang into action, unwinding his leg from the side of the chair and standing up awkwardly. He muttered something inaudible and left the room.

'He doesn't like tea,' said Michael in a tone of confiding awe, as if this were another of David's special qualities which only a select few were entitled to know about.

'I'm sorry I didn't tell you about him,' he continued. 'I wanted it to be a surprise. I wanted to see how the two of you got on.'

'I don't think he likes me,' I said. And I certainly can't stand the obnoxious little shit, I almost added.

'Oh, I think he does. He's always very withdrawn at first

with new people. I know he was a bit quiet today. But it's only an act. He discovered the sulky teenage thing a bit late. He only has a few months left until his twentieth birthday. So he's trying to get as much out of the role before it's too late and he has to grow up. He was always a very polite, well-behaved child. His parents died in a car crash in France when he was only a baby. After Celia died he came to live with me. He's been such a joy and consolation to me. He has a wonderful natural talent. He'll be up in his room working now. Sometimes a bit modern for my taste. I was always on the old-fashioned side, so my numerous critics said.'

'You sound very proud of him.'

'Yes, I am. And I know his father would have been too. I paid for his education at boarding school. The trouble is… well, I never remarried, so there was no feminine influence on him at home. Perhaps I should have. Remarried, that is.'

'I'm rather surprised you didn't. I'm sure many women would have been interested.'

'I suppose after Celia… nobody else could mean so much to me. Well, maybe the three of us can get together some time again. Now that the ice has been broken, we can all start to get to know each other gradually. I'm sure you and David will begin to appreciate each other in the fullness of time.'

'Yes, I'm sure we will.' And pigs will fly. 'I'd better be off, now, Michael. Thank Megan for the tea.'

'Thank you for coming, Madeleine. I have enjoyed having you here.'

Not half as much as I'm enjoying leaving, I thought as I walked through the hall.

I drove back at an even faster pace than the one which had brought me there, often barely seeing in time the sharp bends as they loomed out of the shadows of the roadside walls and trees. I was furious with myself for not complaining straight away to Michael about David's behaviour. I was furious with Michael for being so besotted with David that he could or would not recognise his rudeness to a guest. And above all I was furious with David. It wasn't that we had formed a friendship exactly. But I had thought we at least had an understanding. I had admired his work, accepting the individuality of which Michael had disapproved. And had he shown any gratitude? On the contrary. The work I had praised he had torn up before my eyes. Despite that impulsive churlishness, I had hoped he would see me as an ally if he needed one to assert himself against his uncle's will. Well, whatever we might have had was in the past now. He had ruined everything. The next morning I would go up to the headland to see him. I would demand an apology. And I would tell him that whatever troubles he had with Michael that I might have been able to help him with, he was now well and truly on his own.

ELEVEN

June 1995

I called at the house the next morning at ten o'clock. There was no reply. Megan was probably out shopping. I had asked the taxi to wait. I returned to it, paid the driver and told him I would not need him anymore. I would take the coastal path to St Olave's. There was plenty of time. My appointment there was not until noon and I was sure I still had the strength for the walk if I took it slowly.

The path wound across the tops of cliffs which were much lower and of gentler gradient than those between the house and Porthhella. They led gradually away from the Atlantic and into the Channel, where the coast was sheltered from the harsh winds and high seas. The sun beat warmly onto my back as it ascended the sky. The path sank towards sea level, the air growing stiller and hotter and the vegetation increasingly lush. The sea was now out of sight, though I could hear its muffled crash and swish on the other side of giant sand dunes covered in coarse grasses.

I took a side path which led inland through dense woods. Midges and mosquitoes whirred around my eyes and ears. Deep blue hoverflies darted along the path in front of me. A miniature wooden bridge crossed a narrow stream splashing playfully over mossy stones. Huge Brazilian rhubarb plants closed to form a canopy overhead. The sun filtered through the translucent leaves. Beyond the woods the path led between fallow fields. I saw the squat Norman tower of the church rise slowly from the sloping green earth. Near the church, at the side of the path, a Saxon cross, the carved inscription weathered almost to invisibility, marked the route of an ancient pilgrims' way. I crossed a stone stile to enter the churchyard, where derelict gravestones pointed up from the ground at every angle like the crooked teeth of giants.

I went up to the stones which were most familiar to me. I read my mother's. *Here lies Ceridwen Williams, 1929–1973, who sought peace by the vastness of the sea and sky. May she rest in the arms of the Almighty.* I had left Michael to choose the wording. Nearby was a white smooth marble stone large enough for three more inscriptions. *Here lies Celia Wallace, 1930–1974, beloved wife of Michael, remembered for a life devoted to others in spite of pain and sickness.* Beneath that, the one I had read most often. *In loving memory of David Wallace, 1967–1986, beloved son of George and Sandrine, beloved nephew of Michael, to whom he was as a son.* Finally, Michael's. *Here lies Michael Wallace, 1926–1988, in his immortal art and devotion to wife Celia and nephew David he gave the best of himself.* My own choice of words. No more space beneath Michael's. Nobody to follow him. The end of the line.

It was ten minutes to twelve. I looked around the churchyard. It was deserted. I entered the church, blessing the cool and dark which greeted me. Front pew. Left-hand side. I sat down. Don't look round. Whatever happens.

I smelled a presence before I heard anything. It was a not unpleasant fusion of damp hedgerow and coarse fabrics thickened by sweat and dirt. Then laboured breathing, very close to my ear. The kneeler immediately behind me creaked.

'I've seen you, haven't I?' I said. 'Yesterday. You're that tramp. You were walking along the lane leading to the cottage. You came back and left the message. Okay, so you know who I am. Who are you? How do I know I can trust you?'

I was aware of whispered sounds in the air around my head but could not form them into words. I let my body slump down to bring my ear closer to his mouth. His breath smelled of damp, hand-rolled tobacco.

'You don't. Yet.' A harsh, laboured whisper. 'We have to go back. Start at the beginning.'

'Beginning of what?'

'Your mother. And Michael.'

'You knew them?'

'Not your mother. I knew Michael.'

'Have we met before? I took care of Michael for over a year, before he died. Did you ever come to see him then?'

'Oh, I saw him all right. But he never saw me. Neither did you.'

'Wait a minute. How old are you? When I glimpsed you yesterday I thought you were an old man. But there's something about your voice. Even though you're whispering.'

'I'm old, Madeleine. Very old. Older than death. About your mother and Michael. They had an affair.'

I laughed. The sound echoed around the church. 'Sorry, old man. You're too late there. I've already worked that out. And frankly I couldn't care less. Good luck to both of them, I say.'

'Oh, there's something else. Something you will care about. Remember, you mustn't look round. When I've stopped, I will leave the church. You must wait for at least five minutes. If you don't do as I say, there will be no more contact. If you do, we'll meet here tomorrow at the same time. Can you hear me? Do you understand?'

'Yes.'

'They had an affair. Then he killed her.'

The kneeler creaked again. The door at the back of the church swung open. How could an old man have got there so quickly? I waited no more than a minute. I ran frantically around the churchyard, then into the hamlet, then back along the path I had taken from the coast. My lungs heaved and my breath came in agonising spasms. There was no sign of him.

TWELVE

May 1986

The day after my visit to the house, I was stepping out of the shower when I heard a loud knock on the door. I dried myself quickly, put on my dressing gown and went to the door. I glanced in at the kitchen clock as I did so. Eleven o'clock. Not an unreasonable hour for a visitor. But who could it be?

David stood there, in jeans and a red sweater, carrying a large, flat document case. I folded my arms and stood in the doorway. My anger with him from the day before had not abated. I had intended to find him on the headland and demand an apology. Now there would be no need to go to all that trouble. He could give me his apology there and then.

'What do you want?'

He did not reply but stepped forward suddenly, pushing past me into the hallway and through into the living room. I followed him. He put the case on the floor beside him.

'I don't recall saying you could come in.'

He sat in the armchair facing out to sea. I stood by the sofa opposite and stared at him for a full minute. He showed no sign that he was even aware of my presence. Then he turned to face me at last, his features wearing the same sneer he had worn the day before when he had looked me up and down in front of his uncle.

'I suppose you're disappointed I didn't come here to have sex with you. But no thanks. Why would I? With a fat, ugly old cow like you? Why don't you make us some coffee?'

I took a deep slow breath and coughed, wondering if anything would come out when I tried to speak.

'No, David. I won't do anything. But you will. Immediately. You will get out of my house and never come here again. And you can be sure I will speak to your uncle about your behaviour. Now, just before you go, and only out of curiosity, why did you come here?' My voice was shaking so much I barely recognised it as my own.

He shrugged his shoulders. 'All right. It's very simple. I need somewhere to work. Away from the house. Away from him.'

'Work on what?'

'My version of *The Assumption*. I told you about it.'

'Is it in there?' I pointed towards the case.

'Yes. Don't worry. I'm not going to move in. Uncle will think I'm sketching out of doors. I'll just come during the day.'

I shook my head, slowly, uncomfortably aware that I was unable to close my mouth. 'And tell me. Exactly what gives you the right to come round here and tell me what you're going to do in my cottage?'

'I told you. I need peace and quiet. I need to know there's no danger of him interrupting what I'm doing and interfering with it. I need solitude.'

'I see. So what do I do? Walk around the village?'

'Whatever you want. Except when I want you here.'

'And what would you want me here for?'

'That's the other thing. I will need a model, some of the time. When I need to be on my own, I'll tell you.'

I laughed, a note of near hysteria in my voice. 'That is really so generous of you, David. So kind and generous. Letting me be in my own house when it suits you. So tell me about this work. What does "Assumption" mean?'

'You are ignorant, aren't you? As well as fat and ugly. It's when the Mother of God was raised into Heaven. Only I'm not doing it that way exactly. I'm making a few modifications.'

'And apart from her, are there any other figures in the picture?'

'No other women.'

'Let's get this straight. You want me to be the model for the Virgin Mary? David, if you knew how funny that was—'

'But I do know. That's the point. You're the opposite of everything she stood for. As I said, I'm making some modifications. Reinterpreting it, if you like.'

'So you chose me because—'

'You're an ugly old cow and a whore. I could tell the former just by looking at you, of course. I was pretty sure about the whore bit, as well. I suppose I could have checked on that personally but I didn't see the point.'

I walked over to him and slapped him hard across the face. He grinned, stroking his reddening skin. Then he got up and pushed me back on to the sofa. He stood over me.

'Look, let's stop pretending, shall we? I know who you are and what you are. My uncle has no idea. Do you know why he's such a crap artist? He has no idea about people. He can't see through anybody. But nobody needs to see through you. You're all there on the surface. The way you were yesterday up at the house, smiling and flirting, wearing that dress showing your tits. You were turning it on for both of us. An old man and an obnoxious teenager. You don't care. Men are all the same to you, aren't they? You just turn it on automatically. Look at you now. You come to the door in that skimpy gown. You don't say, come back later when I've changed into something decent. Even now you've still got it on, though it hardly covers anything. I know you can't stand me. But you still let me come in. Has my uncle had you yet? Or are you expecting him later? I know what sort of woman you are. You've never been married, have you? Never had children, never been in a proper relationship. I'm right, aren't I? Don't you dare criticise me for being the way I am. You may be older than I am but you're not superior. All right, maybe I am an arrogant young sod, but you are a whore. You can slap me again if you like but that won't change the facts. Oh, you may not take money for it. Money isn't what you need. But you need something. And you use your body to buy it. Tell me I'm wrong. Tell me again to get out and I will. But inside you know I'm right.'

He turned away and sat down again in the same position, looking out to sea. I watched him, wondering what was happening to my own anger and the fear I had felt momentarily when he had stood over me. I knew I had to tell him to go. I had to tell Michael about him. But not yet. I had been angry with him since the day before. But how long had his anger been building up, there in that house, alone, no parents, no friends of his own age, with an uncle who, whatever his pride in him, would never understand him? Now he had at last found an object on whom to vent his anger. Would it make a difference? Was there another David underneath, one struggling to emerge from all that burning resentment? He had behaved appallingly. There was no denying that. But he was only nineteen. And he was right. I had no claim to superiority.

'My God, David, what a speech,' I muttered at last. 'And yesterday you couldn't put one word in front of another. All right. You're right. Everything you say about me. Shall I tell you about the bits you missed out? It hasn't just been sex. I've tried the lot. Alcohol, fags, drugs. Serious stuff, I mean, cocaine, heroin. Not just that pot rubbish I'm sure you tried at your highly respectable public school. I bet you thought you were so grown-up, didn't you? Work was another drug for me. Right now, it's a drink I need. And I don't mean coffee.'

I got up, went into the kitchen and poured out two glasses of whisky. I returned to the sitting room and handed one of them to him. He seemed, for the time being at least, to have nothing further to say.

'You know, David, it's almost a relief to meet somebody who understands me. Somebody who is totally and completely judgemental. Someone with a complete absence of sensitivity to anybody's feelings. Who holds nothing back. Who goes right for the jugular.'

He drained his glass, picked up the case and walked towards the hallway.

'Where are you going?'

'Home, of course. You did tell me to leave. And I can't expect you to model for me after everything I said, can I? It was a stupid idea, anyway. I'll take this stuff home and burn it.'

The sound of his voice was different now, weaker, even fearful.

'David, put the case back. I'll see you here tomorrow morning, ten o'clock.'

THIRTEEN

June 1995

'How do you know who I am?'

'I've seen you before. I read about your case. Your picture was in the papers.'

'That was years ago. I've changed a lot.'

'I recognised you. I knew right away who you were.'

'You don't seem the sort who reads papers. Just uses them to keep out the cold. When did you last have a wash?'

'I sleep under the stars while it's warm. In winter I sometimes go to a hostel for a bath and change of clothes.'

'Let me know when you're next due for a bath and we can meet immediately afterwards.'

'Didn't think you'd be too particular, after the places you've been in the last few years.'

'Explain what you said about Michael. You said he killed my mother. That's impossible. I know how she died.'

'You know the official verdict. We all know that. It was an

accident. She fell off the cliffs. Walked too close to the edge, in the dark and the rain.'

'He couldn't have killed her. If you want to kill someone you don't drag them up to the top of a cliff and throw them over. If he had killed her somewhere else and wanted to disguise it as an accident, he couldn't have hauled a dead body up there. The pathologist was definite. It was the fall which killed her. And say he had got her up there while she was still alive. There would have been the marks of a struggle. The police found no evidence of that. So, what proof have you got, and what was his motive?'

'No proof exactly. But enough to convince me. This.'

A hand in a ragged glove pushed a dirty piece of paper onto the bench beside me. I picked it up and read it. My mother's handwriting. There was no date or address at the top.

Dear Michael,

    It's been several years now. Things can't go on as they are. I only have a few days. I'm at the cottage, on my own. Where and when can we meet? Write to me here.

    Ceridwen

I pushed the paper back. He made no move to take it.

'Keep it.'

I scrunched it up and put it in my handbag.

'Where did you get it?'

'I stole it. Let's leave it at that for the moment.'

'I suppose the police never saw it.'

'No.'

'This is hardly evidence of blackmail.'

'Not blackmail as such. But she was putting him under pressure.'

'To divorce Celia and marry her? But Celia was ill and dying. Why didn't she wait?'

'Maybe she didn't know about Celia's condition.'

'Then why didn't Michael explain it to her? Tell her to be patient and wait a little longer?'

'What if she wasn't prepared to wait? What if she threatened to tell Celia? What if Michael no longer cared for her, if he ever had? What if all that mattered to him was to get her out of the way?'

'So he arranged to meet her at the top of the cliffs. Then took the opportunity to push her over. But it still doesn't make sense. You don't meet someone who might see you as a threat in such a dangerous place, and then stand so close to the edge that you're positively inviting him to push you.'

'I haven't been able to work it out in my head yet. All I know is that it's too much of a coincidence. She puts pressure on him, then she oh-so-conveniently dies.'

'And he helps arrange her funeral, looks after the inscription on the tombstone, does up her cottage. Not something you do when you've killed someone you were desperate to get rid of.'

'Why not? Maybe he really did want her dead but was stricken by guilt afterwards. That's why he did those things.'

'And why did he keep this letter? In his position, if I had done what you say, I would have destroyed everything that connected me to her.'

'That I can't explain. All I can say is that it wasn't the only thing of hers he kept.'

The notebook! She would have left it in the cottage. After her death he had gone and collected everything which might connect him to her. He might have glanced at the opening pages of the notebook and decided to take that as well. He was not to know then that it did not mention him. But he had not destroyed any of it. He had kept it all hidden in the house, even at the risk of the police searching the attics and finding it. The notebook he had left on the attic floor. The rest he had put into a blue folder which he had asked Megan to destroy. Megan had been unable to find it, because somehow it had come into the possession of this old tramp.

'Why are you so interested in all these things that happened so long ago?'

'I told you, Madeleine. I knew Michael.'

'You were a friend of his? What's your name?'

'No harm in telling you my first name. It's Alan.'

'Is that your real name? Where do you come from? Do you have an accent? I can't tell when you're whispering. Why don't you speak up? Nobody can overhear us.'

'I can't. Operation. Throat cancer. Too much smoking. Yes, it's my real name.'

'Michael never mentioned anybody called Alan. Were you an artist?'

'I dabbled a bit once. Wouldn't have a clue now.'

'How would someone like Michael know a tramp like you?'

'I wasn't always a tramp.'

'What were you?'

'No more for now, Madeleine. I'm going now.'

'Will we meet tomorrow?'

'Yes. Same time. Remember the rules. You broke them yesterday. I saw you. Five minutes after I've gone. Close your eyes. Stay there.'

Again I heard the church door creak open and clunk shut. This time I obeyed the rules.

FOURTEEN

May 1986

'How does this work?'

'You sit where I show you. Keep as still as possible. I'll make pencil sketches in the pad. Then I'll work them up into ink drawings. The drawings can stand alone. When I have one that's close to what I need for the larger picture I'll use that as a model. I won't work from life directly onto the main picture.'

'Where do you want me?'

'By the window. To catch the light.'

He moved the armchair so it was facing the sunlight streaming through the window. 'Take your clothes off first.'

I stared at him. 'Wait a minute. You're drawing the Mother of God and you want her naked? I may not know much about art but I'm sure it's not normally done like that.'

'That's right. I told you. This is not the normal version.'

'Are you sure you can face the sight of me this early in the morning, in this light? Yesterday, you told me I was an ugly old whore, or words to that effect.'

'I'm an artist, remember? I draw what I see. Beauty. Ugliness. All the same.'

I turned my back to him, took off my shoes, sweater, jeans, bra and pants, left them strewn untidily on the floor and walked over to the chair. David had opened his sketchpad on his knees. He picked up a pencil from a set of half a dozen he had spread on the floor beside him. He started to move it rapidly across the page.

'Look to the side, not straight at me. Keep still.'

He flicked the pages backwards and forwards, the pencil continuing to dash and dart. He was clearly working on several sheets at once. He did not erase anything. If something seemed to dissatisfy him, he shook his head and moved on to another page to start again.

'Spread your legs. Wider. Wider still.'

I forced them apart, my skin cringing before the merciless sunlight.

'Can I move my head? I've got cramp in my neck and shoulders.'

'Don't tense your upper body. Let yourself slump in the chair. Like a dead weight. Close your eyes if you want.'

After an hour he stopped and threw the pad on the floor.

'You can stand up now.'

I rose and stretched, feeling the blood flow back through my neck, legs and arms.

'Did you get anything?'

'Just outlines. All I was expecting to get at this stage.'

'Do you want to do any more today?'

'Later, maybe.'

'I'll go and lie down then.'

I walked stiffly past him and down the stairs to the

bedroom. I lay on my stomach, stretching out my arms and legs towards the four corners of the bed. After a minute I heard the steps creak. Out of the corner of my eye I watched him undress. I did not move.

'So this was your mother's place, was it?'

We were lying in bed, smoking, letting the ash fall on the sheets.

'That's right.'

'Uncle says her name was Ceridwen. Welsh. He says you're very like her.'

'I wanted to be like my father. He was a brilliant academic.'

'But you didn't end up like him, did you?'

'No. I was never anything like as clever. I was sure I could make money, though. I went into merchant banking.'

'What did your father think of your choice of career?'

'He never had the chance to think anything of it. He died when I was fourteen. What do you remember of your parents?'

'Nothing. I came over to England while I was still a baby.'

'I suppose Michael told you about them?'

'He told me my father was an engineer.'

'Weren't you curious to know more?'

'Not really. He said he would tell me the full truth about my parents, but not until I was older. On my eighteenth birthday he asked me if I wanted to know the whole story. I said I didn't. I've heard enough lies from him already.'

'Why lies?'

'I know when he's lying. I believe his brother and his wife died in a car crash. But if they were my parents why didn't he and Aunt Celia adopt me after the crash? I knew she wasn't well but I wouldn't have bothered her. I had a nanny when I first arrived and then I went to boarding school. I have some very vague memories of the time before I was brought here.

There were different women looking after me. I thought one of them was my mother. But then there was another woman, later on. She took over from the one I thought was my mother and handed me over to my uncle. She told me my mother died when I was a baby. I never really believed her either. I can see through people, you see. Tell when they're lying. I just have this impression that everybody's been lying to me all my life. So why should they stop now?'

'Do you have a girlfriend?'

'No.'

'But you weren't a virgin, were you?'

'I worked on a farm last year, to get some money of my own. There were two girls there helping out with the horses. Early twenties. Students. They had a bet as to which of them would deflower me first. In the end they decided to do it together. It was in the stables. All those grunting noises around. Like we were just three more farm animals.'

'You hate and despise women, don't you? You don't believe your mother died when you were a baby. You believe she couldn't be bothered to look after you. So she passed you on to another woman who passed you on to your uncle. You think your mother was a whore, don't you? And now you've found another whore. And you want to show the world what you think of women, and mothers in particular, by painting her as the Mother of God. As seen through your own distorted vision. Don't you think that's just a bit obscene, blasphemous, some might say?'

'Maybe. So why are you here? Why are you going along with it if you disapprove so much?'

'I don't know. Boredom, I suppose.'

With a sudden movement that startled me he threw the covers off the bed and rolled on top of me. He pinned me down by the shoulders, his face directly in front of mine. I closed my eyes.

'Open them. Open your eyes. Look at me.' I opened my eyelids a fraction. 'More.'

I groaned. This was far worse. An hour ago he had been behind me, nothing for him to see but an anonymous arrangement of hair, shoulder blades, vertebrae, buttocks. Now his staring eyes could see everything at a distance of a few inches, all the lines of age and pain etched on my face. I felt as if I were being flayed alive.

Afterwards, he dressed quickly and walked upstairs. Within a minute I could hear the scratch of his pencil. He was drawing a face, filling in an outline. He did not need me anymore that day.

'So how many's that you've done?'

It was three weeks after I had first modelled for him. He had come every day except Sundays, when Michael expected him to be home all day. The routine was always the same. He arrived at ten o'clock. By then I would have showered and put on my dressing gown. After coffee I would slip off my gown and take up whatever position he directed. He would work for an hour. Exhausted, I would go downstairs and lie on the bed. He would follow me down, undress and join me on the bed. Afterwards, we would sleep for an hour. Then he would either go home or order me upstairs for another session. From the time of his arrival to his always abrupt departure we barely spoke a word to each other.

This time I had ventured to ask him a question, hoping perhaps for a sign that his grim, relentless search for I did not know what would soon be coming to an end. The routine had been the same that morning. Except that after he had dressed and come upstairs he had neither left the cottage nor woken me for another session. That had never happened before. When I awoke and went upstairs I found him sitting at the table, leafing through his sketchpad. He was taking stock of progress. Now might be a good time to ask him. He gave no sign that he had heard me. I picked up my gown, put it on and sat down on the sofa. No point in repeating my question. Then to my surprise he pushed back his chair, yawned and spoke.

'Eleven complete ink drawings. About a hundred pencil sketches.'

'Can't I see them yet?'

'No.'

'Have you got what you need for the picture?'

'Not yet. Something's always missing. Maybe the next one.'

'Does your uncle suspect anything at all?'

'No. He's very trusting. Believes in me implicitly. Or in some image he has of me. I think I'll tell him. Everything we do. Every detail. I'd love to see his face.'

No!' I almost screamed the word. 'You mustn't tell him a thing. God knows what he'll do.'

'To me or to you?'

'What do you mean?'

'Why do you think he'd bother about us unless...'

'Unless what?'

'Unless you're fucking him as well. I suppose that's it. He's fallen in love with you. Sort of stupid thing he would do. He's a real romantic. Sentimental old fool. He'd be jealous.'

'David, I'm not fucking him. That's the truth.'

'You can if you want. I couldn't care less.'

'Just promise me you won't tell him. You want to finish your picture, don't you?'

'And I can't do that if he kills us. All right I promise. I'll go now. I'll be back in the morning.'

When he had gone I waited for a few minutes, then carefully opened the case which he had left on the table. The sketchpad was inside. Underneath were the ink drawings, on separate sheets of a harder, yellower paper. I leafed through them, shuddering. I took the pad and the drawings out and laid them on the table. Below them, taking up most of the dimensions of the case, was what I presumed was his sketch of *The Assumption*, a bizarre medley of pencil, ink, watercolour and crayon on a sheet of grey granulated paper. I took it out carefully and placed it on the other side of the table. The case was not yet empty. There were two colour photographs inside. They looked as if they had been torn out of a book. The first showed an altar in a gloomy, ornate church. The photograph seemed to have been taken from halfway down the nave. Above the altar, partly obscured at the bottom by candles, was a painting. At first I saw only three horizontal lines, the top enclosed within a curved arch, with two fluted columns on either side. As my eyes became accustomed to the shadows I could make out a figure in red in the middle of the three lines. Small white figures gathered around the feet as if bearing it up. The other photograph was a close-up reproduction of the same painting. I could now see the details of the three horizontal lines. In the centre, haloed in a blinding white light, robed in red, was Mary, the Mother of God, gazing upwards, eyes blinded by an ecstatic vision. Along the bottom were the apostles, clamouring and pleading to her as she was lifted from out of their midst. At the top was God the Father, borne aloft by two cherubs, meeting her gaze, drawing her up to receive her into Heaven.

I placed the more detailed reproduction next to David's sketch. I was puzzled. At first I could find no possible connection. What was it he had said? A reinterpretation. What exactly did he mean by that? He had written the title in small pencil letters at the top of his sheet. The three horizontal lines were there all right. But they seemed to be upside down and in the wrong place. They were at the top of the sheet. And there was no sign of any central figure being lifted up, no God the Father at the top. I turned the whole picture upside down. I put my hand to my mouth to stifle a cry.

He did not come round the next morning. It was three o'clock when he knocked at the door. When I opened it he lurched unsteadily in.

'Where have you been? You're drunk.'

'Thought I'd call in at the inn on the way.'

'The inn isn't on the way. I want to talk to you.'

'About what?'

'About that.'

We were in the living room. I was pointing at the large sketch, still on the table where I had examined it.

'You took it out. I told you not to do that yet. You fucking nosy cow. Might have known you'd have to have a peep.'

'I've looked at everything you've done here. I'm not bothered about your drawings of me. But I am bothered about this. I've compared it with the reproduction. I can see what you're doing. It's not just a blasphemy. It's a perversion. It's sick. You're sick. She's not going to be lifted into Heaven, is she? You've turned God the Father into Satan. And he's dragging her down to Hell.'

'That's right. The title's ironic, you see.'

'Yes, I see now. And what I see is that I want no more to do with this… this obscene nightmare.'

'Oh, you don't, do you? Well, I've got news for you. It's too late. You're in this with me, up to your neck. Yes, we are in a nightmare. And the only way to get out of it is to finish it.'

'And how are you going to do that? You've been trying for three weeks now. You still haven't got the image you want. How long can this go on?'

'Today, Madeleine. Today is when we finish it. You haven't given me the image I need because I haven't yet taken you where you need to go. Go downstairs.'

He followed me down, holding the railing unsteadily. In a corner of the bedroom was a full-length mirror on castors. He pulled it away from the wall towards the centre of the room, next to the bed. I was naked, already climbing onto the bed, about to take up my usual facedown position.

'Not there. Here. On the floor. In front of the mirror. Kneel down.'

FIFTEEN

June 1995

'Before you tell me anything else, tell me how you knew
Michael.'

'I was related to him. Very closely. I never knew
how closely until I found those papers he had been hiding.'

'What did you find?'

'My birth certificate.'

'How old are you really, Alan?'

'Really? It's funny how when you live rough you get to look
old, almost overnight. When you have a beard, and the sun
and wind crease your skin and the dirt gets into the creases
and can't ever be washed out, and you walk with a stoop
because you daren't look people in the eye because you don't
want to see their contempt, or worse, their pity, then you look
old. I wasn't really lying. I am old. Age and chronology aren't
the same thing.'

'So how old are you, in terms of chronology?'

'I'm younger than you.'

'And Michael…'

'He was my father.'

'I don't believe you. I would have known.'

'He never acknowledged me. But he was aware of my existence.'

'How did you find out?'

'It wasn't difficult. I came here to watch him. He didn't even see me.'

'Your mother?'

'No idea what happened to her. I was adopted. My adoptive parents are dead.'

'Did they tell you Michael was your father?'

'I said it wasn't difficult to find out.'

'When you came here, did you see his nephew?'

'You mean David? Oh yes. I saw him. I talked to him. Only he wasn't his nephew. He knew that. He told me. He was his son as well. My half-brother.'

'How did you feel about him?'

'About David? How do you think I felt?'

'I can imagine. He took in one son, brought him up, loved him as a son. But his other son he disowned and ignored.'

'That's right. Maybe I wasn't the only one out in the cold. Maybe he had lots of little bastards all over the place. But David was the only one he was remotely interested in. The only one who seemed to have inherited his artistic bent. The only one he thought he could make into an image of himself.'

'But, why… why did you talk to David? You didn't tell him—'

'Oh no. I never told him who I was. He would have been frightened. I couldn't do that to him. He had been ill. Gone a bit funny in the head. I didn't want to scare him.'

'What did you want to do to him?'

'Why don't you guess?'

I felt as if the weight of the church roof were pressing downing on me.

'You would have wanted him out of the way. You were insanely jealous of him. But you had won his trust. He thought you were a friend.'

'Yes. And friends can go for walks together. The coastal path is a popular place for walkers. And we were both very young. Young men aren't afraid to go near the edge. Or if they are they might dare each other. See who dares to go closest. Near enough to look over. No young man wants to look like a coward.'

I put my head in my hands. 'Oh no…'

'Oh yes, Madeleine. Another accident. Same place as your mother. Very dangerous spot, that.'

'They said he had been standing on unsupported earth. It had given way. So after you killed him—'

'I went back there at night to dislodge the earth. Easy.'

'You stole a torch from the house and left it to guide the searchers. They saw where the earth had fallen. They found the body at the foot of the cliffs. And in killing David you got your revenge on Michael as well. On the father who had pretended you never existed. You destroyed him. Please go, Alan. We must never meet again.'

'I'll go. But there's no need to be afraid of me. And you're certainly in no position to judge me. You, Michael and me. We have a lot in common. We're all killers.'

SIXTEEN

June 1986

'I've finished them. Both of them. The final ink drawing and the main picture.'

I was in bed, where I had stayed all day after taking a long, hot bath. I blinked open my eyes and gazed at him listlessly as he stood at the foot of the stairs. My whole body felt numb. My throat was raw.

'So what happens now?' My voice croaked.

'I don't know. I'll leave what I've done here. You can destroy it all if you want. I need to get away. I don't want to go his bloody academy. It'll squeeze the life out of me. I'll take off tomorrow. Go hitchhiking around Europe. He'll cut off my allowance. So when I get back I'll have to get a job. Move up to London, I suppose. In the meantime I'm going down to the inn for a drink.'

He stamped up the stairs. A few seconds later I heard the door slam. My eyes closed again.

After what seemed only a few seconds there was a loud knocking on the door. I struggled out of bed, put on my dressing gown and stumbled upstairs. I opened the door, half-expecting David to be standing there, having changed his mind about going to the inn.

'Christ, it's you.'

'Aren't you going to invite me in?'

'Of course. Come in. God, Michael, what's the matter with you? You look terrible. Are you ill?'

'I could ask the same about you. Did I get you out of bed?'

'Yes. I am a bit under the weather. Spot of flu, I think. I'd rather you didn't go through there… Michael, please, come into the kitchen. I've got private stuff in here.'

I had followed him into the living room. He was looking at the sheets David had left strewn on the table.

'So I see. Interesting work. Very rough but I think I recognise the style.'

'What do you want, Michael?'

'I want my nephew back.'

'What makes you think I've got him? You'd better sit down. Catch your breath. You look as if you're about to collapse. You didn't walk the coastal path, did you?'

'No. I drove. Left the car at the bottom of the lane.'

So the short steep walk up the lane, which a few weeks ago would have been nothing to him, had exhausted him. He almost fell onto the sofa. I sat down opposite him.

'And the answer to your question,' he continued, still struggling for breath, 'is that I have information from a reliable source. He's been coming here during the day. Drawing. Now I know what. Or whom. While I thought he was out on the headlands. And he hasn't just been drawing you, has he?'

'For Christ's sake, Michael, stop behaving like a Victorian father. The boy's nearly twenty now. What he does, who he sees, who he fucks, is none of your business. Anyway, he's not here. So at this moment I can't give him back to you, as you put it. And don't you think it is about time you stopped treating him like a personal possession?'

'I know he's not here now. I saw him going into the inn. He never drank before. He never did pornographic rubbish like that. Have you any idea, you stupid, deluded woman, of the damage you've done? David was the most naturally talented artist I have ever come across, and I've met many in my time. In three short weeks you've destroyed his talent, destroyed his character, destroyed his future. And you've destroyed me as well. I trusted you. And you betrayed me.'

I stood up. 'No, Michael, I'm not buying that. You can say anything you like about me. But you can't build him up and then just knock him down because you feel like it. I know what game you've been playing all these years. You've been trying to live through him. Trying to make him into the artist you never could be. Well, now he's his own artist and his own man. You may not like either of them. But that's just too fucking bad. The game's up now. And you just lost. David will come back to you if he chooses to do so. I certainly won't keep him here. But two things are certain. He will never be the sort of artist you want him to be. And he never was the person you thought he was.'

He stared at me, hollow-eyed, shaking his head.

'Madeleine,' he gasped. 'You have no idea... no idea at all what you have done. You and he together—'

'Oh, I see. That's what this is really all about. You're disgusted because I'm twice his age. For God's sake, do you think that has never happened before? Maybe if you hadn't kept him locked up in that prison of yours he would have grown up to be a normal boy and have a girlfriend of his own age. But what chance did you ever give him of being normal?'

He opened his mouth but no sound emerged. He rose and staggered towards the door, shaking his head. I slammed it behind him. I waited until I heard the gate close and his unsteady footsteps recede down the lane.

I waited for half an hour, then put on my coat and slipped out. On the sea front I turned right, in the direction of the inn. The yellow lights from the windows and the noises of laughter and shouting poured onto the road and the pavement. I ran past, looking straight ahead, seeking the darkness and the solitude of the beach lit only by a few early stars and a pale half-moon. I found the path above the beach and ran along it. After a hundred yards, I turned and ran down onto the beach. I stepped up to the edge and began to wade out, until I felt the still incoming tide pull and tug about my thighs. In front of me I saw grey shadows, hovering above the waves, floating silently towards me. I covered my eyes and screamed.

When I got back David was sitting in the armchair, staring at the play of bright moonlight on the water. There was a very strong smell of whisky. A bottle stood on the floor and he had a half-empty glass in his hand. On the floor beside him lay a flat, partly opened parcel. He shot me a glance, then looked away again.

'You're wet,' he muttered.

'I went for a walk on the beach. I was by the water's edge. The tide was coming in. I didn't notice it until it was nearly up to my knees.'

'I didn't go down to the inn straight away. I waited for a few minutes. Saw him go in.'

'That's right. He knows what time you usually leave. Waits for you to go. Then comes in for a quick fuck. Drives back so he's home before you. For God's sake, David, stop being so bloody stupid!'

'I found this. I was looking in your cupboard for another bottle.' His voice was heavily slurred.

He picked up the parcel and tore the remaining paper off it. He stood up and handed it to me. For a moment I was bewildered. Then I remembered.

'Yes, this is one of your uncle's. It used to hang above the stove. He took it away to repair the frame. Then he brought it back the day after I moved in. I never got round to hanging it back. Never even took it out to have a look at it. So you found it. So what?'

'I can see it's his, you idiot. That's his signature. So when did he do it?'

I studied the drawing for a few moments. It was the first time I had seen anything of Michael's. Only a body. No face. Just a few ink lines. Quiet, controlled, serene, so different in mood from David's savage portrayals of me.

'I have no idea. It could have been years ago.'

'But you weren't here years ago.'

'Of course I wasn't.'

'So it could only have been a few weeks ago. Just before we met, I suppose. You fucked him and he drew you. He gave you the picture. You hung it up. But when I came round here that first time you had taken it down. You didn't want me to see it.'

I stared at him, then at the picture, then back at him. I laughed.

'Christ, David, you think this is me! Is that it? Oh, you bloody fool! I have no idea who this woman is.'

'Stop lying to me!' He was almost screaming. 'Did you think I wouldn't recognise you? Of course it's you. I know your body. Better than you do.'

Slowly I placed the picture face down on the table. I sat down and took a deep breath.

'But not better than he does, is that it?' I said, quietly.

'That's the problem for you, isn't it? You always said I was a whore. You wouldn't have minded if there was a queue of men outside the door, so long as he wasn't one of them. Because he wouldn't see me the way the others would. Or the way you would. Anybody could fuck me. But only you could draw me. I was your possession. You thought you had bought me by putting me into your hideous drawings. You thought I was part of your sick vision of the world. You can't bear to think that I could also be part of his. That he could draw me like that. You were always operating in different worlds, weren't you? He with his traditions, you with your dreams and nightmares. And now you find you're in competition over the same model. The way he drew me undermines everything you've done with me over the past few weeks. That's what you can't stand. Because suddenly you've seen what a real man and a real artist can do, when he sees someone as a woman and not just as piece of flesh, to be pulled around and abused. All right. I admit. This is a picture of me. And he fucked me before, during and after. Are you satisfied now?'

He stepped up to me and slapped my face, hard. I gasped. My head jerked to the side. He rushed out of the door and slammed it behind him.

After a few minutes I went over to the table and picked up a notepad and envelope. I wrote on the notepad.

Dear Michael,

This is just to let you know that I am leaving Porthhella and do not plan to return. You will find the key outside in the usual place. I would be grateful if you would put the cottage on the market. I no longer wish to be the owner. What you do with the proceeds is up to you. I will leave with my solicitor an authority for you to act on my behalf in the sale. His address is on the back of this letter.

David is not with me now and I know he will not come back here. Whatever it was we had together is finished. I am sure he will come back to you soon, probably this evening, certainly by the time you get this letter. I know he does not wish to attend your academy and I think you should respect his wishes. He needs to take a break from his work and was talking of going to Europe for a holiday. I suggest you let him have some breathing space and find his own way in his own time. Do not destroy your own health and peace of mind over what has happened. It was an unfortunate episode but I am sure he will look back on it as part of growing up. I am not proud of my role in it. I did not wish you or him any harm. I am sorry for having kept the secret from you. I wanted to save you unnecessary anxiety, but it seems that in the event I unwittingly caused you a great deal. I hope you will forgive me in time.

Madeleine

I wrote Michael's address on the envelope, stamped it and put the note inside. I then picked up a letter which I had received a few days before and left unopened on the table. It was from my estate agent in London, telling me he had found a suitable buyer for my flat. The buyer had made an offer which he believed was a highly favourable one in the present state of the market. He asked for instructions to proceed with the sale.

I packed a small suitcase and placed it in the hall. Was there anything else? Oh yes, the drawings. I gathered them together and leafed through them. When I came to his version of *The Assumption*, I took it out and examined it closely, studying the newly added image of the woman from different angles. Was this really all, after so much desperate effort on his part and so much pain and humiliation on mine? He had achieved his vision at last and had not even wanted to keep it. I placed Michael's drawing next to it.

'So you think these are both me, do you?' I said out loud. 'Which do you think is the truth? Yours or his? I know what you think. You're right. You resent his drawing but only because you thought I was your exclusive property. Not because you think it is better or more truthful. You despise him as an artist. He doesn't even try to capture the face. But you, you put it right in the centre of your work. And that face, that screaming, distorted image of evil being dragged down to Hell, is the mirror of my soul. How well you understood me.'

I placed the drawings carefully in a folder, wrapped it in brown paper and sealed it with parcel tape. I walked down to the sea front and placed the letter to Michael in the post box there. I returned to the cottage and looked round for the last time. I returned Michael's drawing to its place above the stove. I stepped back to look at it.

She could have been anybody, of course. Any one of thousands of women with a figure like that, just a model, an assembly of lines and curves. He probably did not even remember her. But there was definitely something about it.

I collected my luggage and took it down to the car.

I slept on the sofa, fully dressed, and made a very early start the next morning. I arrived in Dover in the late afternoon. I found a small hotel and booked in for the night. The next day I made arrangements with a branch of my bank for the secure deposit of the parcel containing the drawings. I sent a letter to my solicitor nominating Michael to act on my behalf in the sale of the cottage. I rang the estate agents in London and instructed them to go ahead with the sale of the flat. I found a second-hand car dealer who was only too pleased to take my car from me at the price I asked. I bought a rucksack and packed some of my clothes and accessories in it. The rest I threw away.

That evening I took a ferry for Calais. I never expected to return, not to Cornwall, nor to London, not even to England. I had cut all my ties. I told myself I was free and alone. Only I knew that I was neither.

SEVENTEEN

I travelled aimlessly through Europe. In late summer I found myself in Paris. I rented a tiny room near the Jardins du Luxembourg. Every day I walked through the gardens, watching the little old ladies who hurried past, dressed in overcoats despite the summer heat, dragging their proportionately tiny dogs behind them on tight leads. In the evenings I drifted along the boulevards, stopping from time to time at the cafés and bars. Usually I went back to my room alone. Sometimes I let a man I had met in one of the bars come back with me. I never asked his name or gave him mine.

In the oppressive heat of late August I at last found Paris intolerable. I hired a car and drove down to Marseilles. The roads were clear. Paris had been almost abandoned by its inhabitants for the holiday season and the *rentrées* had not yet begun. Marseilles was too noisy and crowded. I drove on along the coast, looking for somewhere quieter. I found a secluded harbour and checked in at a dingy little hotel nearby. When evening fell I stepped outside. A small Moroccan café crouched by the harbour wall. The air was still, treacly with smells of oil, tar and brine. I sat down outside and ordered a coffee. It was strong, sweet, thick as mud. Waves slapped sluggishly against the base of the wall. Boats creaked at their moorings. The French of passing chatter, the lilt of the Midi intermingled here and there with the sing-song of North Africa, was like a foreign language to me, used as I was to Paris.

A man sat down opposite me. His face was deeply tanned. Wind and sea had furrowed his skin. He had a large white moustache, drooping at the corners. He wore blue serge overalls, the clothes of a deckhand. He waved to the *patron*, who was inside, wiping a row of tiny glasses. The *patron* nodded and came outside, bearing a tray on which were two glasses of brown liquid. He put them down on the table between us. The man smiled and pushed one of the glasses over to me. I sipped it and coughed noisily. It was a local brandy, burning the back of my throat like hot cinders. The man laughed. He spoke, a medley of harsh sounds in a language I could not identify. Not Greek or Turkish. Somewhere from the Balkans, I guessed. In French, then again in English, I told him I did not understand. He shook his head.

I looked over to where the shadows were hovering. They were the same shadows I had seen floating towards me that night I had run onto the beach and into the sea. I knew who they were. My father had told me about them. They were the Furies. The Eumenides. Older than Christ, older than Zeus. It was Mother Earth who bore them, from drops of the blood of Uranus, the First Father. They avenged crimes against nature. But why had they come for me? Whatever the reason, of one thing I was sure. They would pursue me to the ends of the earth and for the rest of my days.

They did not move. There was one unlike the others. Black while they were grey. He seemed to be their leader. Although he had no human shape, no body or head, I had the impression he was nodding at me, telling me that this stranger was the one for whom I had, without knowing it, been searching all along. I looked up at the stranger. Words were no use. My eyes held his, trying to tell him I understood. So, who was she? I bet you never asked her name. Where was it? A bar or a brothel in some anonymous port where you had taken shore leave. This very one, perhaps. You were lonely, desperate, careless. For the price of a few drinks you sought comfort in her body. Now you see her face in every woman you meet. You are a messenger of death, as she was. Soon, you will meet your own. I rose and walked slowly away, in the direction of my hotel. I heard his footsteps padding softly behind me.

The shadows stayed with me, of course, even after that night. But when I got back to Paris I sensed that their presence was less oppressive. I knew that in some way I had pacified them. They would not go away. But now they only watched, silently, from a distance.

With late autumn giving way to winter, I began to have a recurring nightmare. I was falling, endlessly, through swirling darkness and rain, to Tartarus. My father had told me about that, too. It was a gloomy corner of the underworld. From the earth it would take a falling anvil nine days to reach it. At first I was alone. Then my mother was with me. The smooth shiny rocks of the cliff face rushed past us. Then there was a third person, falling with us. I awoke, calling out David's name.

The nightmare persisted. On an impulse, and despite my resolution to put everything that had happened in Porthhella behind me, I wrote a letter to Michael, asking him how he and David were. I received his reply after two weeks. For hours I sat in my room, frozen with shock. Then I went down to the telephone in the hall and rang the airport.

EIGHTEEN

July 1995

B ack in my room in the inn I had a dream, the night after
that last meeting with Alan in the church.

I was him. I was stumbling along a rough path
between two granite headlands, my feet sliding on the
streaming stones, the rain driving through my thin sweater
and sodden jeans. I held a torch loosely in my slippery left
hand, the tiny puddle of faint light zigzagging drunkenly from
one side of the path to the other.

The crashing sound of the waves increased with every
step. The cliffs were very close now. I stepped off the path,
leaving my torch beside it. I groped my way through solid
darkness across saturated grass and gorse. For a moment a
distant flicker from the lighthouse was just enough to outline
the edge. I sank to my knees, pushing my hands in front of
me until I was lying flat on the ground. I crawled forward,
the tufts of slippery grass becoming ever smaller and sparser

until there was only sloping mud, crisscrossed by rivulets of rainwater. There was a taste of slime and grit in my mouth.

At last I felt my fingers grip the edge. I eased my body forward until my face overhung. I could hear the waves slap and boom against the rocks hundreds of feet below, sending up a salt spray like inverted rain. Centuries ago, the sea cut away the base of the cliff, leaving the rock above to hang over and at last to fall in a huddle of huge stones, now sculpted smooth and round by the endlessly swelling and retreating tide. At the top, right at the edge, a layer of earth only a few inches thick was left unsupported, where I was now stretched out. I eased myself back into a kneeling position. I started to push my hands into the soft mud. As I felt it yield I pushed harder, pulling my hands back and beating them against the ground with the weight of my body. Barely perceptibly at first, then with increasing momentum, the beaten earth began to give way. I sensed the tremor running through me as the long fissure spread out on either side. There was a rumbling sound, distant at first, then ever closer. I stood up and held out my arms towards the black void above and the abyss below. I screamed, the wind and rain bearing away the sound. The dislodged earth groaned and hurtled down.

I awoke with a cry. I had fallen asleep lying on the bed, fully dressed. I knew I would not be able to get back to sleep. I crept downstairs, past the bar and out the front door. As I passed the bar I could hear the loud voices of the three fishermen. Their complaints were the usual ones: the decommissioning of boats, the state of the harbour wall, the price of local cottages, the absence of their owners during the winter months, the presence of their owners during the summer months. But at least they were not talking about me.

I walked around to Brenda's cottage. There was still a light on. She answered the door in a dressing gown and nightcap, a mug of cocoa in her hand. She glared at me for a few moments before opening the door just wide enough to let me in.

'So you've taken to coming round to see me at night, have you? Do you know what time it is?'

'You weren't in bed, Brenda.'

'No. I hardly ever sleep. I don't know why I bother going through the bedtime rituals. What time is it, anyway?'

'Eleven o'clock. I don't come out during the day now. I stay in my room. Keep out of sight. I'm moving out at the end of the week.'

'Come on in. Sit down. Cocoa?'

'No thanks.'

We sat down. She sipped her cocoa and waited.

'So what do you do in your room?' she asked at last.

'Think. Try to work things out.'

'And what have you worked out?'

'That Michael and my mother had an affair. And you knew about it. You lied to me.'

'All right. I lied. I admit it. I lied because it's humiliating and painful for me. So what do you want from me now?'

'I want to know why you hated my mother so much, and why you hated me. Take your time. Start at the beginning.'

'The beginning? All right. If you really want to know. I come from Newcastle originally. I went to art school there. It's not the most inspiring part of the world for an artist. So I came down here. I had heard about the artists' colonies. I never thought I would be good enough to be part of them, but I wanted to be in the same surroundings. I wanted to see if the light and the scenery would stimulate my rather feeble creative faculties. I got a job in a gallery in St Ives. That was where I first saw Michael's works, and where I first met him. He lived in Penzance then. He was in the gallery supervising the hanging of one of his exhibitions. I showed him some of my work from art school and asked him if he would take me on as a private pupil. He did. He was a good teacher, patient and kind. I fell in love with him. He never noticed. We both realised early on that my talents were very limited and there was little he could do for me. I stopped going to him for lessons. But I was still working in the St Ives gallery and saw him from time to time. When he moved to the house on the bay, he visited Porthhella and saw the capstan house. It was in a very poor condition. He told me he was thinking of buying it and converting it into a gallery. I went to look at it. I pleaded with him for the opportunity to work with him on it. I got in the best local designers and contractors. When it was ready he asked me to run it for him. I was delighted. I enjoyed the extra responsibility. I enjoyed seeing more of him than I had in St Ives. He let me run it more or less as I saw fit, but he came down regularly to visit. I travelled around, looking for new talent. He was always pleased when I discovered a promising young artist whose career we could promote by mounting an exhibition. It was the happiest time of my life. I still loved him but I knew nothing would ever come of it. He had married by then. Even if I could have interested him in an affair I don't believe in chasing after married men.

'Then she arrived. She had no such compunctions. Ceridwen. Your mother. They met there. She was admiring the paintings in the gallery. He was admiring her. All I could do was watch. I had never met Celia but I wasn't jealous of her. I knew he had married her to improve his social standing. Her family were well-connected county people. It wasn't a love match. This was different. I was sick with jealousy. I started following them. They met up on the headlands, then at the cottage. I spied on them. I know it made matters worse for me but I couldn't help it.'

'I'm sorry if it made you unhappy. But it wasn't her fault. And it certainly wasn't mine.'

'You still don't get it, do you? Of course it wasn't her fault. That's the whole point. She was just doing what came naturally to her. Can you imagine what life is like for someone like me? Someone whose face and manner are somehow soured from birth, who could never have friends, who could fall in love but never attract either love or hatred in return? The worst thing was that Michael didn't hate me or despise me. He had very good reasons to be grateful to me. He admired me. He always said how efficient I was. But as for my other feelings... He never even knew! They lived somewhere inside me. They never reached my eyes or my lips. I didn't know how. I had never learned. God knows, I tried many times to tell him. The words just died in my throat. I wouldn't have minded if he had laughed at me. I'm sure he would have done. Laughed at me and despised me. I could have accepted that. Anything would have been better than just being regarded as an efficient assistant. Of course I hated your mother. She was everything I wasn't. She had never had to learn. She didn't have to try. She could just look at a man and that was that. I mean, you would think God would have withheld one little gift from her. Just one which he could have spared for me. But no. He gave her everything. More than she could ever need. She just looked at him and she had his love, his whole being, from that second onwards. All I wanted was his contempt and I couldn't even win that. I hated her just for existing.'

'So, when she died...'

'I felt at last that there was some justice in the world. She had had far more than she deserved but at least it was all over. I had something on her. I was still alive.'

'I see. Then I came along.'

'Yes. Ceridwen rising from the grave. The nightmare was

starting all over again. You were the image of her. I always thought it would be you and Michael from the start. If I were God that was how I would have arranged it. As the most exquisite punishment possible for my having wished her dead. When you took up with David, I was sick with relief. You were not like her at all. When it comes to the art of being a woman, Ceridwen was supreme. She was at her peak. She accepted everything about herself, every one of the years she had lived and grown and learned. Above all, she had taste. She knew the sort of man who was worthy of her. She chose Michael. A philanderer, maybe, but a gentleman. A man who never deserted his sick wife. A great artist, but one who was humble enough to know the limits of his gifts and generous enough to give the world the best of himself. But you... you could have had that man, when he was still in his prime.'

No, Brenda. Never. Precisely because he was a gentleman.

'But instead you chose David,' she continued. 'I could hate Ceridwen but I could never despise her. But I could despise you. You had never grown up. You had never accepted the passing years. You were trying to regain your youth by seducing a child. Thinking that opening your legs for a teenager would make you one again.'

'It wasn't like that, Brenda.'

'Then how was it? Don't tell me you loved him.'

'No. It wasn't love. I don't know anything about that sort of love. The feelings you had for Michael, I've never had anything like those. I've had a lot of affairs in my time, I admit that. None of those men meant anything to me. But David was different. He was special to me. I don't know why.'

'He was special. He was a genius, so Michael always said.'

'Yes. A genius. An abusive and totally self-centred genius.'

'As they often are.'

'Indeed. But I let him. I put up with it. I was thirty-eight.

He was nineteen and I let him use me like one of the rags he used to clean the paints off his brush. And yet he was violently jealous. He was convinced I was having sex with Michael. I encouraged him to think that so it would be easier to end our relationship or whatever you care to call it. I thought it would be better for him that way. If he really hated me rather than just despised me. I miscalculated. I didn't know he was so vulnerable.'

'So when you moved in with Michael, it wasn't because you loved him?'

'No. I was sorry for him. And guilty. I had destroyed both of them. But Michael was still alive. Just about. I could make things a bit easier for him, maybe. I owed him that. That was all.'

'I would have looked after him. But he would never have wanted me that close to him. Perhaps it was just as well it was you. You could give him what he needed. I didn't despise you anymore then. You had grown up. You weren't just thinking of yourself. I still hated you, of course. Because you were in my place.'

We sat in silence for a minute. Until I felt she was ready for my next question and I for the answer I expected.

'Brenda, I know this is an awful thought but… do you think Michael could have killed my mother? Because she was making things too uncomfortable for him?'

She shook her head violently. 'No, of course not. I know he loved your mother, but he couldn't leave Celia for her. Ceridwen was not the sort of woman who would just accept that and move on. She may have tried to pressure him. But I knew Michael. He wasn't a murderer. He could be a man of sudden passions. Maybe he could have killed in the heat of the moment, but we know that wasn't what happened. He couldn't have planned and carried out a murder in cold blood, working out exactly how to make it look like an accident, then carried his secret with him to the grave. That wasn't him. I know that. What gave you the idea?'

'I've been talking to somebody. There's this tramp hanging around. He's been following me.'

'I've seen him from a distance.'

'Only he's not just a tramp. He knows things. He showed me evidence that my mother was putting Michael under pressure.'

'Really? And does this well-informed tramp have a name?'

'He told me his name is Alan but I don't know if it's real or not. He won't let me see his face. He says he's Michael's son. Michael never acknowledged him. He discovered who his father was. Drifted aimlessly through life. Then at last he found a purpose. He met David and planned his revenge on him. Brenda, what is it?'

She was not looking at me. Her eyes stared into the empty fireplace, her face contorting. She was muttering to herself.

'No, it's impossible… It was all arranged. How could it…' She looked up and seemed to remember my presence. 'I'm sorry. You were saying. About this Alan. Did he give you any proof Michael was his father?'

'No.'

'He told you Michael killed your mother. Then he invented a son of Michael's who plotted to kill David. Well, I must admit it's a good story. One of the best I've heard. All right, he may have got hold of a piece of paper somewhere. But the rest is pure fantasy. Michael could never have treated a son of his like that.'

I stood up. 'All right, Brenda, maybe you're right. But hasn't it ever occurred to you that your image of Michael is rather biased? Isn't it at least possible that your views about what he could and could not have done might be coloured by your feelings for him? He may have had all the qualities you attribute to him. But he could have had other, less attractive ones as well. He could have killed my mother and he could have neglected and disowned one son in favour of another. He could pass one off as his nephew but not two. And it's perfectly possible that he never knew about Alan's existence, though Alan says he did. The fact is that neither of us really knows. All right, it could be made up. But Alan was so convincing. I really believed him.'

'Maybe he believes it himself. That's why he's so convincing. He suffers from delusions. He read about Michael's life. Became obsessed with it. He knows he's an orphan, but he has no idea who his parents were. He became convinced he was Michael's illegitimate son. He probably never met David but he dreamt of revenge. When David died, he convinced himself he'd done it. You've got to admit it's a possibility.'

'I suppose so.'

'What are you going to do? When you move out of the inn, I mean.'

'Am I going away? You'd like that, wouldn't you? No, I'm not leaving. I'm going back to the house.'

Yes, I nearly gave the game away there and then. By my reaction when she told me about Alan. After she had gone, I poured myself a glass of brandy. I was shaking with anger. The thought that Ceridwen had been playing me along all the time, that right from the start she intended to betray me. Of course, Madeleine could have been right. I took comfort from that thought as well as from the brandy. Michael planted his seed far and wide. Everywhere but in me. I could hardly blame the women, could I, not when I would gladly have borne him a bastard and hidden it away somewhere. Either this Alan was who he claimed

to be or he was a liar or delusional. Maybe there really
was nothing to worry about. But I needed to find out. I
decided to close the gallery for a couple of days. There was
somewhere I had to go.

B.R.

NINETEEN

'The doctor were with you for ages this morning,' said Megan, glancing suspiciously up at me after a long silence.

We were sitting in Megan's parlour in the late afternoon, drinking tea, she getting on with her knitting. It had become a fixed part of our routine, from the day I had moved back. We had the whole house to ourselves but preferred the cramped intimacy of the parlour. Neither of us ever went into the lounge facing the sea, except when Megan needed to go there to dust and polish the silverware.

'That's country doctors for you. They have so few patients. They like nothing better than to gossip. I told him I was fine. He listened to my chest and prescribed some pills. That took five minutes. The rest was just chatter, passing the time.'

I had spent the previous two days in bed with a chest infection. The doctor had come at Megan's insistence, despite my assuring her there was no need.

'Changing the subject,' I continued, 'I've decided I will sell the house, you'll be pleased to hear.'

She put down her knitting and beamed. 'There you are. I knew you'd make the right decision in the end. I'm really delighted. But it's not for my sake, is it? You're doing it because you want to. I told you you don't need to worry about me.'

'It's for both our sakes, Megan. But I'm not going to do it right away. There are things I have to think about first.'

'That's fine by me, my dear. You take your time. I hope you don't mind me asking but… I've been wondering, what with you being so poorly lately. Were it really very awful for you in that place? I mean, I were consoling myself with the thought that it were a hospital so they would be looking after you. But when you came back, well, it didn't look as if they had taken much care of you. You lost a lot of weight there. And you're always frowning, when I catch you on your own, as if you're trying to remember things. They didn't help you remember, did they?'

'No, they didn't. They had other priorities with me. I was a difficult patient at first. They needed to give me some injections. I had a panic attack when they first came to do it. I thought they were going to kill me. The nurse nearly broke my arm. They were better when I decided to behave. After a few months they were almost friendly. When they realised I wasn't a threat to them or anybody else. That was all they were bothered about. I can't blame them.'

She shook her head. 'Poor girl. What a dreadful business. And you still can't remember anything?'

'Yes, something. I must have known who Laura was. Because I know now and it came to me out of my own head. She was David's mother. Which of course means that Mr Wallace was his father.'

She stared at me. 'Are you sure? How did you find out?'

'I don't know. Mr Wallace didn't tell me, that's for sure.

But he might have told me to go and see her after his death for some reason. She did come to visit him once, here, late at night. I do remember that now.'

'I don't. I suppose I had gone to bed.'

'So had I. But then I got up again for some reason. I saw her from the landing. If I heard anything of their conversation I don't remember. Did you ever wonder about who David really was? I mean, it must have been a surprise to you, him just coming to live here like that.'

'No. I don't wonder and I don't pry. People choose to tell me things or not. It's up to them. Sometimes I believe them and sometimes I don't. He told me Master David were his nephew. It weren't my place to argue about that.'

'I can see you had your doubts. Do you believe me, about Laura being his mother?'

'I believe you believe it. But if you could remember how you found out, maybe the rest would follow. Did she tell you herself, when you went to see her?'

'Possibly. Though why that should lead me to do what I did, I don't know.'

'Couldn't it have been an accident? Or maybe nothing happened at all. She just died. People do. She was ill. Dying already. As for those bruise marks, I'm old now and my skin is frail and thin. Sometimes I see bruise marks on myself and I'm sure they just appeared.'

'But if nothing happened, why would I forget what we said to each other? No, I know you'll never believe me but I did it all right. I accepted that a long time ago. Megan, do you remember that first time Mr Wallace introduced me to David? It was in the lounge. You served us tea. It was the first time we had met since my mother's funeral.'

'Of course I remember. It was so lovely to see you again after all those years.'

'Did you ever hear anything afterwards, about David and me?'

'No. Village gossip never reaches here, and if it did, I wouldn't listen.'

'David and I took an instant dislike to each other. But we were drawn to each other at the same time. It was as if the only way we could dispel our feelings of animosity to each other was... Well, what I'm saying is that we met in secret. Mr Wallace found out. He came round to see me. We had a terrible row. I went away. After a few months I wrote to Mr Wallace to ask him how David was. I just had this bad feeling. He told me about his breakdown and how he had died. All those terrible things that happened were my fault. I could have stopped it before it started. I was older. I should have been in control.'

'Of course it weren't your fault, Madeleine. Master David... well, I'm not going to criticise the way Mr Wallace brought him up. That's not my place. But Master David were like a boiling pot with the lid on, ready to explode. I remember that time very well. One morning there were this woman in the house. I had been in the garden and I hadn't seen her come in. But they was having some dreadful words, her and Mr Wallace. I heard them from the hall. I went upstairs so they wouldn't come out and think I had been eavesdropping. I didn't recognise her voice. I heard the front door slam. Mr Wallace went out later that day. He looked as if he had seen a thousand devils. He ignored me when I asked him if he were feeling all right. Stupid thing to ask, really. It were obvious he weren't all right. Master David had already been out since the morning. I suppose that was when Mr Wallace went round to see you, to have it out with you about Master David. When you came back here, about six months later, I think it were, and decided to stay and look after Mr Wallace, you must have noticed how he had aged. His hair had gone white, he stooped, his back were bad, he had terrible angina. What you didn't know were that all that happened in the space of a few weeks. I never saw anyone fall off so quickly, from being a picture of health and energy. It were only you coming back that saved him.'

'After I'd gone away that time and David had come back here—'

'He weren't himself anymore either. It were as if we was total strangers to him, and him to us. I'm sorry, you wanted to ask me about Master David and I interrupted. Go on.'

'Did he meet up with anybody else, any friends from his past, anybody he might have met while he was walking outside?'

'No. I don't think so. What sort of person are you thinking of?'

'A boy, of about his own age.'

'No. Nobody like that. He had no friends like that around here. He had kept in touch with some school friends, writing to them and making the occasional telephone call, but they never came here and he never went to see them. Mr Wallace didn't encourage him to socialise. I'm sure he never met anybody after he came back. He were in a world of his own by then.'

'You never saw anyone like that hanging around the house, before or after he came back?'

'Oh no. Nobody that I noticed, anyway. Why do you ask?'

'Oh, nothing. I just wondered. Going back to what I was saying, about selling the house. There's something I need to do first. I need to spend some time here on my own.'

She put her hand to her mouth. 'But why, for God's sake? You, alone, in this dreadful old place, haunted by all that's happened here? After all you've been through?'

'That's the point, Megan. It is haunted. And I need

those ghosts to help me get my memories back. You've been wonderful about making me comfortable and at home, but it won't do. Not now. I'm stronger now, thanks to you, and I need to face the past. And I've been thinking that you need to get away for a while. I'm sure your niece in Truro would love to have you over for a few days. She's always inviting you, so you keep saying.'

She smiled and her eyes sparkled. 'And I suppose that's the deal?'

'The deal?'

'You don't do anything about selling the house and getting away yourself until I go away and leave you alone for a while.'

'That's it in a nutshell. I should have known I couldn't slip anything past you.'

'Megan, your taxi's here.'

I was waiting by the front door. After a minute, she shuffled through the door and down the porch steps.

'Here, let me take that for you.' I picked up her little suitcase and walked beside her. 'Are you sure you have enough things?'

'I don't have anything else to take. And if I need anything, Linda can get it for me. Are you really sure you'll be all right here on your own? I'm used to it, but for someone who's been through what you have… I'm still not at all sure it's the right thing.'

'I'll be fine, honestly. We've been through this many times. It's what I need to do. And it'll do you good to spend a couple of weeks away. I'll ring you at Linda's.'

'Every night?'

'Every night. I promise.'

'And if you want me back sooner you just let me know and I'll be here in two shakes of a lamb's tail.'

'I know. Now off you go. The meter's running.'

She shook her head, sighed, hugged me and lowered herself gingerly into the back seat of the taxi. I waved as the taxi disappeared round the bend of the driveway.

I walked back into the house and into the room which had served Michael as a library and writing room. Old books, mostly on art, philosophy and history, lined the walls from floor to ceiling, with spaces only for the windows and a huge open fireplace. If the books had been catalogued according to a system, only he had ever understood it. He always knew instantly where a book on any particular topic could be found. A rosewood cabinet contained his favourite brandies. I served myself a large glass and looked around the room. It was still exactly as he had left it, just like the rest of the house. Megan had preserved it like a museum.

Was it already a museum when David first came there, Celia's wheelchair installed in the hall as a permanent reminder of illness and death? Whatever Michael had expected of him, it could not have been the joy and laughter of a normal child. I tried to imagine his terror and grief on first coming to the house, trying to come to terms with its isolation and its dark, echoing spaces, facing a life without his mother, with a strange man whose voice and manner must have seemed so severe and distant.

And what about Michael's other son, the one he had scorned, whose very existence he denied? Had Michael spent the time I had lived with him there in fear of the knock on the door, of the spurned son's revenge? Had Alan hidden near the house, after David's death, looked through the windows into the study, watched Michael's head bend low with grief, his hair turn white, his body stiffen and waste away? If so, he would have known his revenge had been absolute.

TWENTY

January 1987

When I got back to England, after receiving Michael's letter, I wondered if I was doing the right thing. I wanted to go and see him. There were things I had to tell him which I couldn't put in a letter. But what effect would it have on him, seeing his old adversary again, after all he'd been through?

I booked into a hotel in London and stayed there over Christmas and the New Year. Then in January I made up my mind. I took the train to Penzance, then a taxi. It was late at night when I arrived. I knew Megan would have gone to bed. Perhaps he would have done as well. Even if he heard me it was unlikely he would open the door. I would go back to Penzance and call again the next day. I would telephone first and talk to Megan, sound her out, find out whether he would be willing to see me.

But the taxi had gone. The nearest phone box was miles

away. It was too late to try to walk to Porthhella and get a room at the inn. I decided to try the door. If nobody answered I would return to the main road and walk towards Land's End. I might be able to flag down a passing car and ask for a lift to the nearest phone box, or to a hotel that might still be open. If necessary I would walk to Land's End and back. It would be morning by then. My heart thumping, I approached the front door. There was a faint light through the stained glass of the library window. I pushed the bell. The noise seemed to echo through the whole building. I had decided to push it only once. I would wait five minutes. I was turning away when I heard slow footsteps shuffling through the hall, the inner door creaking open, sounds of panting and sighing, then the groaning of the bolts being pulled back, one by one.

He looked up at me, trying to catch his breath. His mouth hung open, a drop of saliva crawling from his lower lip down to his chin. I almost shook my head as if to say that I had come to the wrong house. Then in an instant I was aware how ridiculous that idea was. It had to be that house. So that shrunken, stooping figure with thin white hair had to be Michael, though all my memories of him told me it could not be he.

'Madeleine,' he whispered. 'It's really you? You'd better come in. You'll catch your death out there. Push the bolts back, will you? Come into the library. There's still a fire there. Sorry I took so long to come to the door. My back's so bad these days it takes me forever just to get up out of my chair. I'm always short of breath. Megan's in bed. She never hears the front door at night. I couldn't imagine who it might be.'

I followed him through the hall, very slowly, keeping my distance from him, letting him have the space and time he needed as he leaned on his walking stick and inched forward. Once in the library he sat down near the fire, the embers of which still glowed and crackled, wincing with pain, placed the walking stick across his knees and signalled for me to sit down opposite him. There was a half-full balloon glass of brandy on a small table next to his chair. He picked it up and sipped from it, his hand shaking. Despite everything he still kept up appearances. His shirt and trousers were clean and pressed, and he wore his favourite bow tie. I sat down, still unable to find any words to start our conversation. To my relief he spoke first, after a minute's aching silence.

'Thank you for writing to me from Paris. You hadn't heard a thing? It was in the papers here. Not over there, I suppose.'

'Nothing. It was a dreadful shock. I just wanted to know how you were. How both of you were. Then I got your letter back. Was it really the same place?'

'Yes. Exactly where your mother fell. It is truly an accursed spot. So, Madeleine, how long has it been?'

'About six months. I left last June.'

'Only six months? In that time I've aged twenty years. As you can see. You haven't aged. Not at all. I'm pleased about that.'

'Do you mind me coming? I didn't want to write again. I could never have found the words. I'll go away if you want. Right now. Just say the word.'

'No, no, of course not. You must stay. We should talk. It will be good to talk, after all this time. Good of you to come all this way to see a sick old man. You must have a brandy. Help yourself. I've still got this one. My brandy's all I have these days.'

'Thanks, I will.'

I went over to the cabinet and served myself in a much smaller glass than his. Then I realised I had made a mistake. Brandy should be drunk from a large glass, one like his, to appreciate the aroma, a man had told me once. I had not paid any attention. Brandy had never been one of my drinks. In the days when I had only drunk to achieve quick oblivion it had seemed a waste to drink something valued by connoisseurs. Now I had been afraid of giving myself too much of something so important to him, afraid of taking from a man I had hurt so deeply, a man who because of me was only a shadow of what he had been. But it was too late now. And I desperately needed a drink. Maybe he wouldn't notice the size of the glass, or if he did he would make allowances. I returned to my chair. I coughed as I took a small sip, then relaxed as I felt the warmth spread through my limbs.

'So where have you been? I sold your cottage. I never heard from you so I had no idea where to send the money. I've still got a cheque made out to you in the bureau. I didn't want to send it to your hotel in Paris in case you had already moved on.'

'I've been travelling around. Genoa, Venice, Verona, Paris, Marseilles, back to Paris. Michael, I am so sorry. What happened to David was my fault. As is what's happened to you.'

He shook his head. 'No, no. My fault. All mine. You did what I asked. You gave him up. I destroyed him. Over all the years before you ever met him. I put so much pressure on him. Tried to make him into the sort of artist he was never intended to be. Sent him to a school that was never right for him. At the time I told myself, an artist's life is tough. He needs to be able to cope. But he couldn't. I should have seen that.'

'That night after you came to see me in the cottage, I decided you were right. I had to get out of his life. I decided to leave. I was going to leave him a note. He returned and we quarrelled. Violently. He stormed out. I wrote you the note after that. I assumed he came straight back here to you.'

'He did come back to me. After a week.'

'A week! Oh my God.'

'I reported it to the police. They told me to wait a couple of days. I told them about you. I wondered if he had gone away with you. Thought your letter might just have been a trick to put me off the scent. They tried to contact you but couldn't find you. You weren't at the cottage. Your London flat had been sold. Your solicitor didn't have an address abroad for you. The police said they would keep a lookout around here, but they were sure he had run away with you. There was nothing I could do. I had forgotten to tell them that his passport was still here in the bureau. I'd forgotten that myself. When he came back he couldn't tell us where he had been. He had had a dreadful breakdown. He had lost his memory. He didn't know who I was. He could only have found his way back through some sort of homing instinct. He couldn't draw or paint any more. He had forgotten that he ever had. He didn't recognise his own works when I showed them to him. The doctor told me he was suffering from amnesia, probably induced by a severe shock. But he seemed very content, almost serene. He was far more affectionate than he had been, to me and to Megan. He didn't say much, but he would follow us around. He helped Megan to prepare and serve the meals, though he ate very little himself. He sat with us at mealtimes and smiled at us. He helped me go for walks outside. He wasn't the same person. He was easier to love, God forgive me. But it was impossible to know what was going on in his mind. He was a stranger.'

'How did the accident happen?'

'He started to go on long walks on his own. I watched him at first from the house, and Megan would follow him a little. But it seemed safe. He never went near the dangerous parts of the path. Sometimes I would follow him from a distance and find him sitting and looking out to sea. It was always the same spot. He was looking at a view he had often drawn. I thought it would help him to remember. He seemed strangely happy. I didn't want to disturb him by taking him away. I didn't want him among strangers, in one of those awful hospitals, drugged like a zombie. Now I wish I had taken him away. To somewhere where he would have been safe. Away from the sea and away from the cliffs.

'One day he went out in the morning and came back as usual. Then the next morning he was missing. He must have left in the night. He had never gone out in the dark before, so I hadn't thought to lock his room. He never knew whether it was morning or afternoon, or even day or night. We called the police immediately. They checked the coastal path. Just by where your mother fell they noticed part of the earth had fallen away very recently. There was a torch there. One of ours. I think he must have been standing there and the earth gave way underneath him.'

He fell silent, staring into the fire. His head was bowed. His shoulders shook.

'I'll go now, Michael. I wanted to come in person to say how sorry I was but I only seem to have made matters worse. I'd like to take some flowers, pay my last respects... Where should I...?'

'Take them to St Olave's. The family plot next to your mother's grave. His inscription is on the same stone as Celia's. There's still room for mine and that will be there soon.'

'I'll go there tomorrow. Stay there, Michael. I know it hurts you to stand. Where do you sleep?'

'Next door. It's my bedroom now.'

'Do you get any visitors?'

'I've no family left now. Sometimes an art lover with a long memory comes to pay his respects. I'm still something of a curio in these parts.'

'Do you want to go to bed now? Can I help you?'

'No, thank you. I don't sleep much. I go to bed about three in the morning. When the brandy starts to have some effect. Did you come by car?'

'No. Taxi.'

'Still there?'

'No. I sent it away. I didn't think about what I would do if nobody answered the door.'

'You can't walk out into the cold and dark like that. Stay here. I'll get Megan up to fix something up for you in one of the spare bedrooms.'

'No. Don't disturb her. I'll doze here by the fire, if that's all right. Leave in the morning. Go back to Paris, I suppose.'

'Is there anything in Paris for you? Or anybody?'

'No. It's just… where I ended up. So I might as well go back there as anywhere.'

'Of course. Why not? But stay here for tonight. Here by the fire, if that's what you want. Close your eyes now. You look exhausted.'

I was awoken by the morning light through the window, fragmented by the stained glass into a rainbow of colours which streamed across the carpet. I was alone. Somebody had put a blanket across my knees. Had he wakened Megan and told her about their unexpected guest? Very quietly I rose and stepped into the hall. Not a sound. I tiptoed to the door, eased back the bolts and closed the door behind me. I trudged up the driveway. A thin layer of snow which had fallen during the night crackled under my feet.

There was a bus stop near the top of the driveway. I looked at the timetable. There were only two buses a day but by luck one was due in an hour. There was no bus direct to St Olave's but this one would take me to a village within an hour's walk.

The bus was punctual to the minute. I was the only passenger. After the bus had dropped me in the main street of the village I walked round but could find nowhere to buy flowers. A few more weeks and early spring flowers would arrive from the Scillies. But not yet. I would have to go empty-handed. Perhaps I might find some snowdrops to pick in the nearby woodland.

An hour later I stood by my mother's grave. It was first time I had visited it since the funeral. The grave had been carefully tended. A bouquet of tiny white snowdrops in a vase had been placed there recently. I had intended after the funeral to ask Michael if he would arrange for the grave to be maintained at my expense. I had forgotten but he had done it anyway. He could have tended the grave himself, while looking after Celia's at the same time. But who had been coming there now Michael was ill? Who had placed the snowdrops there? Was it now part of Megan's regular duties? Or had they made arrangements with someone who lived locally?

I moved on to the white marble stone by the neighbouring grave and read the new inscription. I looked up and around the graveyard. The thin layer of sprinkled snow sparkled in the pale winter sun. My constant companions, the shadows who had come from the sea that night and stayed with me ever since, were only a few yards away, clustered under an oak tree whose lower branches seemed to gather them together in its grotesque arms.

'Is this why you are always with me?' I called across to them. 'Because I came between them? Or is it something else? Something from deep in the past, something I've forgotten? Something you want me to remember? Will you go away if I do? No, I know you'll never leave me. Do you torment Michael as well? No. His memories are all too vivid. He doesn't need you. He can see his guilt all too clearly. We belong together in that house. We're two of a kind. Two guilty creatures, waiting for death. I won't go back to Paris. I belong up there, with him.'

I caught my breath and whirled round, sure I had heard the crunch of a footstep on the snow. Nobody there. Nobody had overheard me.

TWENTY-ONE

Michael and I deceived each other. I told him nothing about my condition. He appeared to recover, at least in part, but I suspected he was only making an effort for my sake.

We knew it could not last. Time crawled along. It was as if we were locked into a perpetual winter. Finally, spring and then summer arrived, seasons he had never expected to see again. We could even go out for short walks. And sometimes, when we stopped to rest, he was in a mood to talk. Like the day he told me about Celia, and much else besides.

I helped him towards the bench set against the rock. He sat down gratefully, panting, placing his walking stick across his knees. Though it had been a very warm day, he wore his waistcoat, jacket and bow tie. We watched the sun until it settled on the water, scattering blood-reds among the blues, greens and turquoises of the water in the bay beneath us.

'You know, Madeleine, I used to think nothing of walking

along the coastal path all the way to Porthhella and back, sometimes twice a day. Now I can barely make it this far. It's not practical for someone in my condition to live around here. And then there are the memories. But I couldn't move away from here, not now. I'm bound to the place. Part of the landscape. And there are times when I feel as ancient as these granite rocks.'

'How did you first come to live out here?'

'I came to Cornwall after the army and art school. Other artists had discovered it long before me. There is a very special quality to the light here. I rented studio space in Penzance. I knew the town slightly. Two of my aunts had settled there and I visited them occasionally. I soon began to be noticed. I gave my first solo exhibition in the town hall. Celia and her parents attended. Her parents expressed an interest in buying some of my works. All the ones on display which were for sale had already gone. I told them I had more and promised to take them round to show them. That was how Celia and I got to know each other. We lived in Penzance when we first married. The marriage set the seal on my success. For generations her family were substantial landowners here. Her parents were widely respected for their work in the community. They were good people. They didn't remain aloof from the social and industrial changes around them. They set up charities for former tin-miners and fishermen and their families. They worked tirelessly to bring new industries into the area. They helped widows and orphans. Her father was mayor for a time. He disapproved of me at first, as a partner for Celia, I mean. Later he decided that he could make something respectable out of me if he could keep me away from my painting for long enough. He helped me to secure a seat on the council. I became involved with charitable work. I was appointed to various committees. My motives were not at all altruistic. My artistic reputation grew with my standing as a pillar of the community. Celia was a perfect social wife and hostess. She organised my exhibitions. She arranged press conferences and previews. To the outside world we were a couple who radiated success and prosperity.

'On the inside, things were rather different. Celia provided me with a social cachet which was very important to me. The life of a painter can be a lonely and difficult one. Even when there is critical acclaim, there is often social scorn. It is not considered an entirely respectable way of life. I yearned for respect as a member of society. When I became Celia's husband, it was awarded to me overnight. I enjoyed my new status. I used it to spread my reputation. I needed it and welcomed it. At the same time, I resented it. The price was high. I had to develop a social persona with which I was often uncomfortable and which interfered with my work. I bought this house to give myself the space and solitude I required to paint. We kept our house in Penzance as a base for our community activities. Soon we began to spend more and more time apart. She stayed in Penzance, maintaining the social fabric of our marriage. I stayed here.'

'You never had any children?'

'Her parents were anxious that we should have children soon, but it soon became clear that we never would. Our doctor carried out tests. The fault, if you can call it that, in medical terms, was Celia's. She became deeply depressed. Soon after that, he diagnosed in her the early symptoms of multiple sclerosis. Strangely, it was only then that I think I began to love her. She had done everything for me. I had felt resentful. Soon she would be dependent on me. We lived here quietly. Celia was still able to act as an efficient and charming hostess, though sometimes she would be exhausted for hours afterwards. Soon she would need to withdraw altogether from our social rounds. That prospect did not trouble me. I looked forward to it. I looked forward to the time when we could be alone together in this house and I would look after her. I had tired of the shallow society to which I had once yearned to belong.'

'How did you come to meet my mother?'

'It was like I told you at the funeral. I used to love to walk over to Porthhella from here and just wander around, soaking up the atmosphere. It was so relaxing after Penzance. I never knew who I would run into there. In Porthhella nobody knew me. I was fascinated by the old capstan house. When it came up for sale I bought it and converted it into a gallery. Brenda Rogers helped me, then she took it over. I met your mother there. I had gone over to see the work of some new artist Brenda had discovered. We met for coffee sometimes, your mother and I, in the café on the sea front. I think she was a bit lonely and enjoyed having someone to chat to.'

'Could you tell me about David's parents? If it won't upset you too much to talk about it?'

'I don't mind talking about it now. George was an engineer. He was a painter as well. A gifted amateur, you could say. He liked to experiment and try out new things. He had a very good feel for colour. He wasn't strong in the technical department. Couldn't draw to save his life. When I came to live here on the bay, George moved in with us for a while. He had been working in India. He was looking for somewhere to live. He had met a French girl in India, Sandrine. They had a relationship there, but she had broken it off. He came home. Sandrine returned to France and got in touch with him again. He went over to see her and they got engaged. They were married in France. David was born in Lyon. I hardly ever saw them. I was too busy with my life here. Celia was already sick. Two years after the wedding they died. They had been out to celebrate their anniversary, at one of those famous country restaurants. On the way back they collided with a lorry on a narrow road. They were killed instantly. David was with a babysitter. I went over to France to arrange their funeral and settle their affairs. That took months. Bloody French bureaucracy. Had to arrange for a nurse to take care of Celia. Her condition wasn't too serious at that stage. I brought David back to England, but with Celia getting worse all the time I couldn't move him in with us. He stayed with various relatives. When Celia died he came to live here.'

'I wanted to thank you for looking after her grave, by the way. My mother's, I mean. I had meant to mention it at the funeral but it slipped my mind.'

'It was hardly any trouble. Hers and Celia's being next door to each other. It was as easy to do both as to do one. Of course I couldn't do it anymore when I fell ill. Megan carried on, bless her, using the same taxi service every month. It's such a relief that I'm well enough now to go back there myself, with your help.'

'But you did my mother's before Celia died.'

'Why not? I wanted to help you. I also felt it was my responsibility. It was my idea that she should be buried there. And to tell you the honest truth, it was a relief to have an excuse to get out of the house. That's another reason why I looked after her cottage as well.'

'Didn't Celia mind?'

'No. I didn't tell her the whole story. I told her someone I knew in London had bought a cottage here and had asked me if I could find a managing agent. I said I had offered to do the job myself, to take up some of my spare time. I was with her day and night for most of the time. She couldn't object. Not when we had a live-in nurse to look after her clinical needs.'

'Well, thank you anyway.'

'Now I want to raise something with you. That's why I asked you to come out here with me today, not so I could talk about myself all the time.'

'Go on.'

'When you came back here that night and went away again I presumed I'd never see you again. You came back the next day, after you'd been to the churchyard. You said you'd been worried about me. You asked Megan to make you up a bed for a couple of nights. That was more than six months ago.'

'And I'm still here. Are you sorry I stayed?'

'Hardly. Look at me, for God's sake. Megan keeps saying that you pulled me back out of the grave. She's right. I thought I was dying. That night you came, I expected to live only a few weeks if that.'

'You're still very ill, Michael. You have to be very careful.'

'It wasn't me I wanted to talk about. You mustn't stay any longer. You're still young and beautiful.'

'And you're still a flatterer, Michael. A gentleman, but a flatterer.'

I knew the truth. Every day the mirror told me what Michael would not. I too was ageing rapidly. I knew when it had begun. That night in the dirty little hotel near Marseilles. And with each day spent in that house with Michael the process continued relentlessly.

'Sometimes you have to be one to be the other,' he said. 'But I'm not trying to flatter you. I was an artist, remember? I know beauty when I see it. You have your life ahead of you. Why don't you go off and live it? Away from here. Don't worry about me. My time will come when God wills. Don't waste yourself. You're so like your mother to look at. But there's something of hers you've lost. There was a wildness in her eyes, a vitality in her gestures, her walk, her laugh. Something flowed in her veins which is not there in yours. A moment in her company and you felt more intensely alive. That quality must have been there in you. And I'm stopping you from finding it again.'

I remembered that interview in the police station, the bag containing what was left of my mother's things.

'But was she always like that, when you knew her?'

'Why do you ask?'

'It doesn't fit in with what the police showed me when I went to identify the body. Her clothes were awful. All worn and shabby, much too big for me, and I was supposed to be just like her. She couldn't have been the way you describe. Not then. Not towards the end, I mean. Did you know her all the time she was here, right up to the time of her death?'

'Not really. Now I think of it, it had been some years since I had last met up with her. Of course I had to spend more and more time with Celia, as her illness got worse. So I can't really say what was happening to your mother then. But when I knew her, she certainly had that quality of life. It was so powerful I can't imagine anything which could have destroyed it. You must have it too. Go away from here and try to rediscover it. Get back to the Mediterranean. I always loved it there. The sun, the laughter, the people living for today. That's what you need. Forget what happened here. You weren't to blame for anything. You and David... that was outside your control. Leave me here to grieve for him. I can grieve for both of us. If you were trying to make it up to us you've done that. If you ever owed us anything you've repaid it a hundred-fold. You will think about it? Do you promise me?'

'All right. I'll promise to think about it. Now let's get back for tea. Megan's waving from the window. Give me your arm.'

Neither of us ever mentioned my promise again. We both knew it had no meaning. I could not leave. If he could not see the shadows which held me prisoner there, he must have come to sense their presence.

The months passed, the routine unchanged, except that his trips out of doors became ever shorter and rarer. Autumn and winter came again, though we were by then barely aware of the passage of time. The anniversary of my return to the house came and went, unnoticed and unmarked.

One night in early spring I was sitting with him until after midnight as usual. The fire was nearly dead. My eyes were closing, the words of the book I was reading no more than a blur. His glass slipped from his hand. He slumped forward as if struck from behind. Suddenly I was wide awake. I rushed over to him, eased his head back and felt his pulse. His mouth gaped and his lower lip sagged. His eyes rolled, unfocussed.

'It's all right, Michael, I'll get help.'

I ran out into the hall and picked up the telephone. Then I rushed up to Megan's room and knocked on the door.

'Megan, are you awake?'

There was a murmur from within.

'It's Mr Wallace. I've sent for an ambulance. I think he's had a stroke.'

'Who's that?' asked Megan, as we followed the coffin into St Olave's Church. Brenda was standing outside the church a few yards behind us, her face pale and drawn, her eyes red and swollen. I waved to her to join us in the church. Brenda shook her head and stood her ground.

'It's Brenda Rogers. Michael's former assistant. I wish she'd come in. It's so empty, just you and me the only mourners.'

'I recognise her now,' said Megan. 'She came to the house a few times, many years ago. Why won't she come in?'

'It's me. We've only met once. I think she hates me for some reason. Let's go in.'

We were glad to get inside. A numbing wind was sweeping through the little valley from the east, rattling the weathercock on the church roof. Apart from Brenda we had seen only a local reporter and a small group of hikers who had taken a diversion from the coastal path in the hope of securing some respite from the gale. No former students or fellow artists had come to pay their respects. The Royal Academy had sent a printed card of condolence. There was a short obituary in one of the broadsheets. In the history of the art of his time he had long since been no more than a footnote.

For the second time in my life I was forced to listen to a fulsome tribute from the Reverend Colm O'Brien, who had visited Michael only twice since I had returned.

'Michael Wallace was an adopted child of the West Country. He will be remembered as a skilful artist who drew inspiration from the wild landscapes which surround us, who was a model to his pupils and fellow artists of hard work and devotion to self-improvement. He was rewarded by a success which many would envy, though he remained clear-headed and conscious of his limitations. The other aspects of his life were less well known but give a far better indication of the real man. He sought no refuge in aesthetic ivory towers. With the help of his wife, Celia, he strove tirelessly to improve the lot of his fellow country dwellers, and to use the material wealth with which God had endowed him to protect them from the worst consequences of the decline in the well-being of their communities. When Celia became ill in the full bloom of her life, he nursed her devotedly until her tragic, premature death. Then, at a time when other men in that situation would have withdrawn into isolation and self-pity, he found a new outlet for his need to care for others. He took into his home his orphaned nephew, David, also a gifted artist. He shouldered the solitary burden of bringing him up, providing him with a good education, showing him by example how to lead a good and upright life, and using his own knowledge and experience to nurture his artistic talents. In Michael's final days, the shadows of three tragedies lay across his life. He and Celia had not been blessed with children. Her illness and death had affected him to the extent that he gave up the creative work which had been the core of his life and which had given, and continues to give, so much pleasure to others. Then came the final, cruellest blow of all. The nephew he had come to love as his own son had also fallen prey to illness and had met with a tragic accident, aged only twenty and barely at the threshold of his own artistic career. In the face of adversities which would have overwhelmed most people, Michael remained stoical and courageous to the last. He accepted without complaint his long and debilitating last illness, at the end of which death came with merciful speed. God had given him many blessings and, for reasons which only He can understand, had chosen to take some of them from him. Michael did not question those actions of God. He accepted His will. As we today must accept it as we remember Michael and give thanks to God for his life.'

As the coffin was lowered Brenda stood some distance away. When the final prayers had been said, I turned towards her but she had already left.

TWENTY-TWO

October 1995

I've just read through what I've written about my time with
Michael, his illness, his death and the funeral.

I've missed something out, of course. Or rather,
someone.

Laura. She came to visit Michael, a few months before
he died. I never spoke to her. She never saw me. But many
months later I went to see her and I killed her. I'm sure now
that Michael never mentioned her to me, never asked me to
visit her, never left any papers in the house about her. Why
should he? So how did I find out who she was and where to
find her?

Last night it came back to me. I made up the fire in the
library and sat there in my usual chair, opposite Michael's, as
I had each evening during his long and slow decline. I fetched
myself a brandy as I had always fetched his and mine. During
the evening he would drink three or four glasses, while I sipped

just a few drops, enough to be sociable. We rarely talked. We sat there, with each successive evening wrapping the shades of the house ever more closely around us, becoming part of its rotting fabric. I would choose a book for him and one for myself. I would pretend to read and glance up at him from time to time. I had long since lost the ability to concentrate on a book.

Last night, after half an hour, I moved over to his chair. I took his place. I went back in time to the evening he had sat there, waiting for a knock on the door, even though it was late, long past the time when Megan and I would be in bed.

Finally it came. Three sharp knocks on the front door. Not the bell. She had been told not to ring the bell. Megan would not hear it but I might. The hall and library doors had been left open to allow the sound of the knocks to carry to him but no further. But for some reason I was unusually restless that night. I couldn't sleep. I decided to go down to the kitchen and make myself a hot chocolate. I was crossing the landing when I heard the knocks.

TWENTY-THREE

November 1987

I caught my breath and stopped. After a few minutes, to my intense surprise, I heard the sound of the bolts being drawn back. Surely he would not be so foolish as to open the door to a stranger at that time of night? I moved quickly to the top of the stairs and was about to shout down to him when I saw the visitor. She had followed Michael into the hallway. She wore a thick, light-brown overcoat and a felt hat of the same colour. She was tall and upright. Her face was pale and strained. Her cheeks were sunken and her eyes bright. I judged her to be in her sixties, but illness could have aged her prematurely.

He took her hat and coat and hung them on one of the hooks just inside the hallway. They looked at each other. I stayed at the top of the stairs, my hand on the banister. Neither of them had noticed my presence.

'Well, Laura,' said Michael, after a pause which seemed to

freeze time. He was not smiling. 'It really is you. You still call yourself Laura, do you? You didn't change your name when you started your new life down under? Somehow I imagined you would.'

'I've nothing to hide. Unlike you. Laura James is my name.'

'You were Laura Peters when we knew each other.'

'You've obviously forgotten that James is my maiden name. I changed back to it when I went to Australia. I have no particular wish to remember my husband.'

'How long have you been back?'

'Four weeks. I'm staying with Naomi, my sister-in-law, in Portsmouth. She's on her own and doesn't mind company, even when the company's a sick old woman like me. We always got on very well. She never married, wise woman. Well, Michael? Are you going to ask me in or do I have to stand here in the hallway all night? Don't look so scared. You've nothing to fear from me. I'm not here to destroy you. It looks as if someone or something has already done that.'

'I'm sorry, Laura. I mustn't forget my manners. Please come on in.'

She walked slowly past him into the library. He followed her and closed the door behind them. He had obviously been expecting her and had arranged the visit for a time when he could keep it a secret. That was his business. There was nothing in her manner to suggest that she intended him any harm. I would leave them alone. But I was still intent on the hot chocolate I had promised myself. I trod softly down the stairs. As I passed the door I heard their voices. I paused, compelled to listen.

'You shouldn't have come back, Laura. We had an agreement, remember? You accepted the terms at the time. You agreed it was for the best. You went away. Nobody forced you. You should have stayed away.'

'So that's what you would call it. An agreement. It takes two willing parties to make an agreement. You lied to me, manipulated me, got what you wanted in the end. Call that an agreement if you want. I wasn't strong enough to stand up to you. I wish to God I had. I wish I had never gone away, and I wish I had never taken your money. I wish I had done what was right. But you weren't bothered about what was right, were you? You were worried about your precious reputation. You wanted to avoid a scandal.'

'You know there was more to it than that. All right, maybe that was my main concern at first. But later, things changed. I wanted to do the right thing by the child.'

'The right thing? We're talking about my child, Michael, mine. Not just yours. Don't you think I was the one who was in the best position to say what was right?'

'You can't do anything about all this now. It's too late for all of us. So why did you come back?'

'I intended to come a few years ago. Even though you had told me not to. I was never sure I could trust you. I wanted to see for myself. Then you wrote to me with the news. How he had lost his mind, fallen off the cliffs. There was no point in me coming. I fell ill soon after that. Then my sister died. I had no reason to stay there. I wrote to Naomi and told her about my circumstances. I was sick and alone, in a country I had never liked, where I would never have chosen to be. She invited me to come and stay with her. After I had been there a few days I began to think about you, now you were only a few miles away instead of on the other side of the world. So I thought I would drop by. Just out of curiosity. I wanted to see you before the end, see what had become of you.'

'Curiosity? Or revenge? Are you sure you didn't come to gloat?'

'No, not revenge. I'm sorry to see you like this. I've aged

as well, I know. That's the illness. I've fought it for years and now I've no fight left. I've brought you this as well.' There was a rustle of paper. 'It's what's left over from the money you paid me. Most of it's still there. I lived very frugally.'

'Keep it. I've no use for it.'

'No. I've waited all this time to be rid of it. It poisoned me, contaminated me. I could never look at it or think of it without thinking of what I gave up for it. Now I'm paying the price for what I did.'

'What are you going to do?'

'Nothing. What I know is of no interest or use to anybody now. You won't see me again or hear from me. I'll go back to Portsmouth. It won't be long now. The doctors have given me a few months, a year at most.'

I heard her rising laboriously to her feet. I padded carefully away from the door and up the stairs.

TWENTY-FOUR

October 1995

Yes, I had listened to them at the door. So that was how I found out that Laura was David's mother. I had heard it from her own lips. That was how I learned that Michael had lied to me about David's parentage and early life.

That poor woman! Sent to the other side of the world because Michael wanted her out of the way. She had only come back to die in peace. And I even took that away from her. How did I locate her? Through her sister-in-law. Naomi. Laura had said she had never married. Her name was Naomi Peters. As Laura's married name had been Peters. I looked up Naomi Peters in the Portsmouth directory. A few months after the funeral, I went to Portsmouth to see her. To see her, and kill her.

I went up to my bedroom and opened the cupboard. It was still there. The folder of twelve ink drawings David had made of me, together with his version of *The Assumption*. After I had moved in with Michael I asked my bank to forward them to me. I put them away unopened. I had sent for them because I knew I needed to feel their presence. But I was very anxious that Michael should not even suspect they were in the house. If he had asked I would have told him I had destroyed them. To my relief he never did ask and I assumed he had forgotten about them. As the months went by I forgot about them myself.

I pulled out *The Assumption*, forcing myself to look at it. I cried out and let it fall to the floor. I sank to my knees, gasping for breath. I could feel hands on my body, burning into my flesh, pulling me down. My fingers clutched at my throat as if trying to undo the grip of an unseen attacker.

After a minute I found my breath and struggled to my feet. I picked up the drawings and put them back into the folder. What had happened? It had felt like a nightmare from which I was trying to force myself to awaken. But I was sure I had been awake. Was it another returning memory? If so, was it the memory of a dream or of something which had really happened? Or was it simply a physical reaction to the drawing, a moment of terrifying identification with the scene for which I had served as a model?

As I put the folder down, I noticed another object on the cupboard floor. A spool of tape from an old-fashioned tape recorder. Only a museum now would have a machine on which it could be played. I had always kept the tape but could never remember who had given it to me or what was on it. I had only known that it was important and that I had promised someone to keep it. I had brought it with me when I first moved to Cornwall to live in my mother's cottage. It had accompanied me on my travels through France and Italy, resting at the bottom of whatever bag I was using as luggage.

Suddenly I felt overwhelmed by fatigue. I lay down on the bed and closed my eyes.

When I woke up the glimmerings of a grey dawn already hung around the room. I had forgotten to draw the curtains. I must have fallen asleep on the top of the bed, fully dressed. But I remembered having been in bed, between the sheets, in my new pink cotton nightdress. Not this bed and not this room. A single bed, in a tiny, reassuringly bright and cosy room. A room specially decorated for a child. Pink wallpaper with images of flowers. A room with no space for monsters to hide and frighten me in the night. Of course now I was thirteen I was no longer afraid of monsters. I had heard the footsteps outside. They didn't matter. I knew that in my room I would always be safe. I snuggled further down the bed until the top sheet almost covered me, hugging my pillow, breathing into it, feeling the fresh crispness against my cheek. I stopped breathing when I heard the voice.

'Are you awake, Madeleine?' Heard but did not see the handle turn, because I had screwed my eyes so tight shut that it hurt.

TWENTY-FIVE

---

*S*he came to me at last on the night of the storm, the worst
to hit that coast for years. Somehow I sensed that that was
when she would come, bearing within her all the fury of sea
and sky.

Earlier that evening I was looking at that wretched bracelet
again, turning it over in my hand, running my fingers round the
edge. And talking to her, even though she had yet to make her
appearance.

'So, Madeleine, how are you getting on up there, all on your
own in that dreadful place? I hear you sent Megan away. So the
deliveryman from the grocery tells me. He also told me you're
managing all right, still bearing up, or at least you were when you
answered the door to him the other day. Have you remembered
anything? Are you any closer to knowing what I did? When can
I expect your next knock on the door? Whatever you decide to do
to me, I'll deserve it. What did I get in the end for all my efforts?
This trinket I stole as a trophy. Trophy of what? She won in the
end. Even the way she died was a triumph. It guaranteed she would

always be remembered, even by people who never knew her. Who will ever remember me at all? Oh yes, she was that bitter old woman who ran the gallery and looked down her nose at everybody and died alone one night in her little cottage. She was always a bitter old woman. Even when she was young. What else did I get? Enough money to stay on here, not enough to let me get away and start a new life somewhere else. That pathetic little gallery. The contempt of my neighbours. What did I get from him? His grudging gratitude. And his final rejection. And the knowledge that my deeds set in motion a chain of tragedies that I was powerless to stop.'

I put the bracelet away and walked upstairs to my bedroom. I stared at myself in the mirror. There, staring back at me, was something else I had got. A face which with every passing year was more lined with bitterness and hate. If her death had really set me free I wouldn't have had to look at a face like that in the mirror every day. Yes, I wanted to be set free. But there was only one way that could happen. I had to confess. To her! To Madeleine, the woman I hated almost as much as the one who came before her.

I had to get out of the cottage. I wanted to find that tramp and talk to him. I had an idea where he might be staying, the observation point on the headland. A few days ago I had seen him in the distance, moving towards it, his step rapid and sure, too rapid for me to catch up. I would only get a chance to talk to him if I could confront him there. I clambered up the path and waited to catch my breath. Nobody around. No sounds from inside. I stooped beneath the low doorway and looked around. Plenty of signs of human presence. Cigarette ends, used matchsticks, sweet wrappers, empty lemonade bottles. And a newspaper. Greasy and dirty but quite recent. I picked it up gingerly. It was open at an article about her release. There was a blurred photograph of her face, barely recognisable, probably taken at the time of her arrest. There were other photographs, one of the house and one of the cliff where Ceridwen and David had fallen. I read through the article.

Over decades this wild beauty spot in the extreme West of Cornwall has lived under the shadow of a terrible curse. Nobody knows the original cause. Twenty-two years ago a woman called Ceridwen Williams fell from these cliffs to her death hundreds of feet below. Thirteen years later, David Wallace, nephew of famous local artist, Michael Wallace, fell from exactly the same spot. He had been suffering from amnesia and mental breakdown. Mr Wallace died soon afterwards of grief. But even then the curse had not run its course. The daughter of Ceridwen Williams, Madeleine Reed, had lived with Michael during the final stage of his life. After living on her own for months in that house of sickness, madness and death she too fell prey to madness, committing the senseless killing of a dying woman. Miss Reed has spent years in a secure hospital. This paper interviewed her on her release last month. She still cannot remember the killing or what drove her to it. She told us she was intending to return to the place where her mother and David died. Is some strange malign Fate drawing her back? Does the curse still have further to run, or has the evil finally spent itself? Only time will tell.

'So, I was right,' I said, addressing the spot from where I had picked up the paper. 'It's you, isn't it? You're the man who's been talking to her, spinning her stories. Nothing but an old tramp. This is where you've set up home. You found the paper, read the article and that started your imagination going. You came here. You recognised her and started to follow her. Or... maybe you really are who you say you are. There's something not quite right about you. I never knew an old man walk as quickly as you do.'

I stepped outside, looking out to sea. For early October it had been unusually hot and still for several days. Now it had turned *sultry. Over the horizon, just to the north of the Scillies, a black landscape of cloud was massing in bizarre towers like a demon kingdom rising from the sea. Another black cloud, this one flat like the underside of a huge alien spaceship, had settled directly overhead, moving from the land behind the village. The cloud masses faced each other across the intervening miles of water like opposing armies and stood their ground. The water was like glass. I had lived there long enough to know the signs of a brewing storm. I retraced my steps as quickly as possible.*

B.R.

TWENTY-SIX

It was the distant boom of thunder that woke me. I had fallen asleep in my chair in the library. The thunder came again, much closer. There was a pitter-patter of rain against the panes. I got up, stepped into the hall and stood there in the dark. My hand searched for the light switch. I found it and flicked it. Nothing. I swore. Always happens round here during storms. Bloody power cut. Then the knock on the door.

This time it was an insistent hammering. Nothing like Laura's almost apologetic knock that I had just been remembering. I ran to the door, pulled back the bolts and swung it open. Nobody. My bones froze. I was sure that what I had heard was nothing to do with my lost memories. It came from a time before I had ever seen the house. Why not? The ghosts from my own time were not the only ones to haunt it. But why now? And why had it responded to my presence, whatever it was?

Outside, by the side of the house, I heard running footsteps. Running onto the coastal path, in the dark and the rain. From here. Suddenly I knew.

'It was you, Mother, wasn't it?' I shouted. 'That's why I heard your knock just now. It was you. You came here the night you died. And you ran from here. Not from the cottage. From here. On a night just like this.'

I rushed outside, still in my pullover and jeans. I ran up the path, the rain and wind lashing against my face. I thought I could see movement ahead of me, but in the darkness it took no discernible shape. Then the wind brought a sharp cry to my ears. I ran on, here slipping off the path onto the grassy seaward slope, there grazing my knee against the rock on the other side. Now I was on level ground. I could hear the crashing of waves against the rocks. Then another cry. A seagull?

I turned off the path towards the sound of the waves, rainwater streaming down the inside of my blouse, my shoes squelching in the mud. Ahead, a jagged line, black against dark grey. The cliff edge. I could just make out two silhouettes. One was standing right on the edge. The other stood in front of the first, gesturing. It seemed to be trying to coax the other one forward, away from danger. The figure at the edge held out a trembling hand. My hand. My back was to the sea now, the cliff just below, my heels slipping in the mud, no earth left to support them. The figure in front of me was approaching, close enough to save me. He had only to stretch out his hand to take mine and pull me back onto solid ground. My hand sought his but found only air. I screamed.

I was still breathing. My hands could feel grass and slime. Rainwater poured into my open mouth. There were no sharp rocks, black and glistening with salt spray. The sea was still hundreds of feet below me. But I had felt everything. I even remembered the sensation of falling, the lurch of my stomach, my hands flailing helplessly, the cliff-top rushing up to the sky.

I pushed myself upwards and into a kneeling position, feeling the mud yield beneath me. I was still some twenty yards from the edge, from where I had seen the two silhouettes.

I stumbled on down the path in the direction of Porthhella. The rain was abating slightly. I kept my bearings from the distant glimmer of the lighthouse. The shadowy shapes of the sleeping village emerged at last, huddled beneath the cliffs as if taking shelter from the storm. I staggered to Brenda's door and knocked loudly.

TWENTY-SEVEN

'I've got to talk to you, Brenda.'

Brenda stood at the door. She was fully dressed. She nodded. 'Hello, Madeleine. I've been expecting you. You'd better come in and get dry.'

'I came by the coastal path.'

'Then you are still crazy. What are you trying to do? Follow your mother down the cliffs?'

'That's what I have been doing. Following her. Then, for a few moments, I was her.'

Brenda pushed me upstairs and into her bathroom and turned on the taps. 'Here, get those wet things off and have a good hot soak. I'll get you a brandy and some dry clothes for you. Mine will probably fit you. Your figure isn't as full as it once was.'

She cast a critical eye down my body as I undressed. I was too exhausted to mind the scrutiny.

'What are those marks?' she asked.

'What? Oh, those. I was in the hospital infirmary for a

long time. A chest and lung infection I couldn't shake off. The nursing was a bit primitive. I got pressure sores. They're not as bad as they were. Most of the time I'm not aware of them.'

I stepped into the bath. A few minutes later she returned with a glass of brandy. I was by then covered in warm water and foam; my eyes beginning to close.

'Here you are,' she said. 'I think you need it. We both do. Take as long as you like. Wash your hair under the shower and come and dry it in front of the fire. Use my dressing gown on the hook here until I can look out some proper clothes for you.'

An hour later, we were seated in front of the log fire, which she had refuelled. I was wearing a loose matching tweed jumper and skirt which she had given me. My wet hair was gathered in a towel. I unwrapped the towel and let my hair hang loose before the fire. Steam began to rise. I rubbed my hair fiercely with the towel, re-wrapped it inside it and sat back in my chair, looking into the fire. I was aware that she was staring at me. Finally, I looked up.

'You know, don't you?' she said.

I nodded.

'Thank God. You have no idea what a relief that is to me.'

'I came here tonight to get it out of you one way or the other. So go on. Tell me everything. I want to know what you and he did to her. First of all, I want to know how and when you knew that she was pregnant.'

TWENTY-EIGHT

'One evening Michael came to see me, just as I was closing the gallery. He was extremely agitated. Your mother was going to have a baby. There would be a scandal. He was a big cheese on the local council in those days. And he was on all sorts of important committees to do with the arts. And then there was Celia. She was of a nervous disposition and her health was delicate. She would be devastated. Her family would make sure his name was mud in all the high circles he was now moving in. There might be a messy and expensive divorce. His career could be ruined. He had to fix an abortion. He did not know how to go about it. He did not want word to get around that he was doing it, or that would be even worse. I told him to calm down. I would sort everything out for him.

'When I first went to live in St Ives I shared a flat with a girl who had been to college in Portsmouth. She had become pregnant there after a one-night stand and had decided to have an abortion. I was still in touch with her. I rang her and asked her for the name and address of the doctor who had arranged it. She laughed and said she was surprised at me. She thought I was much too straight-laced to get into trouble the way she had. I didn't disabuse her. She told me the name and gave me the number. Smith or Brown or something like that. Almost certainly not his real name. I didn't care. My friend told me he was the sort who didn't ask too many questions. That was enough for me. I rang him and explained the circumstances. He said he would be very pleased to help. He gave me details of the clinic where it would take place.

'I went to see your mother. I had been looking forward to it so much. I introduced myself. She had been to the gallery so we had already met and exchanged a few words. I had been polite to her but no more. She smiled and invited me in. That wretched picture of her was on the wall, where it still is.'

'It's definitely her? I was beginning to wonder, the last time I was in there. I never really noticed it before.'

'Oh yes, it was her all right. Drawn from life. Drawn in a way he had never drawn anybody before. She sat there, half-turned towards me, looking out to sea, ignoring me, feeling her belly from time to time, though it was still early days and there was nothing to show, looking all smug and serene. I was calm and business-like. There was no point in showing her how much I hated her. I was about to get my revenge. I was savouring every moment. I told her I was there on Michael's behalf. He had asked me to organise some things in connection with her pregnancy. It was a rather delicate matter so he could not come himself. In fact, he could not come at all. He could never see her again. I was sure she did not want to ruin both their lives by staying there and letting the pregnancy continue. So he had authorised me to offer her an arrangement which would be greatly to her advantage. He would pay for her to have the pregnancy terminated, at a clinic in Portsmouth. He would buy a house for her there, where she could go to live while she was waiting for the operation. Afterwards she could stay on there. Or she could ask him to sell the house and let her have the money so she could move somewhere else, so long as it was at least as far away. The only condition was that she must leave immediately and never return to Porthhella. I would give her one more day, so she could pack her things. I would fetch her the next day. She said nothing. The expression on her face never changed. I asked her if she had understood. She nodded. She was still sitting there when I left.

'When I went back the next day I thought I would have to explain it all again. But to my great surprise she was packed and ready to go. She smiled and got into the car. It was as if we were going somewhere for a day out. I had expected hysterics, at least a fight. This was almost too easy. I drove us to Portsmouth, where I had booked rooms in a small hotel. The next day, I took her to see my friend's doctor. There was another doctor there with him. I think he was Smith or Brown as well. They examined her and completed the paperwork. They asked her if she had ever been depressed. She said she had often been on anti-depressants when she lived in Oxford. Was that true?'

'I don't know. It's possible. She was unhappy. I realise that now. She was suffocating, married to an older man wrapped up in his researches, stifled by the petty social niceties of the life of a don's wife.'

'She gave them the name of her doctor so they could contact him to confirm it. They seemed very pleased about her having been depressed. They wrote down exactly what she said about it. They told us the clinic was comfortable and very discreet. Hygiene and clinical care, before and after the event, would be of the highest standard. I went there with her for her next examination. The clinic was bright and well-maintained. Not at all seedy. She seemed pleased with it.

'I spent the next few days looking for a house for her. She did not want to come with me. She stayed in her hotel. I found one I thought would be ideal. It was small and comfortable, in a quiet suburb. Nobody would pay any attention to her there. I took her the photograph and description the estate agents had given me. She agreed, without even seeing the house. I completed the purchase quickly on Michael's behalf. I did not want to draw attention back in Porthhella to what was happening by sending for the furniture from the cottage. I bought some for her locally. She showed no interest in coming with me to choose it. She said she had confidence in my taste. I was with her when she moved in. The next day I went round to ensure she had settled in. She seemed comfortable and relaxed. I told her not to worry about the operation. It would be quick and painless. Then the whole sorry episode would be over. She could get on with her life. She said she was looking forward to that. I asked her if she would like me to sell the cottage for her. She said she would send me written instructions. In the meantime could I look after it for her, for a regular small payment? I told her I would do it for nothing. When we parted we kissed each other on the cheek. Inside, I was crowing.

'I drove back to Porthhella. I told Michael everything was arranged. He was almost ill with relief. My reward and the price for my continuing silence would be a cash sum and ownership of the gallery. He was paying me off. I knew he didn't want to see me again. He did not want to be reminded of what I had done for him.

'The years went by. I ran the gallery and sold souvenirs. The authority to sell the cottage never arrived. She had given me a spare key so I could look after it, as I had promised. I was meticulous about that. I did not want her to have even the slightest pretext to come back. But she did. After seven years she returned. Without any warning.'

'How did she look?'

'Look? I didn't really notice. I remember thinking she had put on weight. That's all. I never looked closely. I didn't want her to see me. I had gone round there one Saturday to clean, as usual. I saw her through the window. Thought it was a burglar at first. When I had got over the shock I wondered if I should warn Michael. But he had made it clear he no longer wanted anything to do with me. And what was there to warn him about? She might have simply decided that after all those years there could be no harm in visiting what was still her property. I decided to tell Michael nothing. If she wanted to get in touch with him that was between the two of them. If I ran into her in the village I would ignore her. I never did run into her. It wasn't long after that that she died.

'Celia lived on for a few months. When she finally died I wrote to Michael to offer him my condolences. He wrote back and told me it would be nice if we could get in touch again after all those years. I went round to the house, and we drank some brandy together, to drown his sorrows. He was very lonely. With your mother and Celia both dead, I could be no danger to him now. I could come in out of the cold. I didn't mind. I understood why he had kept me away all that time. I was pleased to be back, on the fringes of his life. I knew I could never come any closer than that.'

'When did you find out she never went ahead with the abortion?'

She took a deep breath. 'Only recently. After the last time you came to see me. Even then I never found out for certain. But that was when I became sure in my own mind. When you told me about this Alan chap, who claims to be Michael's son,

I dismissed the idea at first. Then a thought occurred to me. Perhaps your mother had decided not to go through with it. Perhaps this Alan was her son by Michael. I went back to the clinic. It was a long time before I could persuade them to talk to me at all. I told them your mother had died recently and I was acting on behalf of a beneficiary of her will. She had also left money to a child who could not be traced and whose very existence was in doubt. There were several beneficiaries and potential beneficiaries who were disputing the will. There was doubt about her mental state. She had always acknowledged that she had once had an abortion at their clinic. Then remorse put her into a state of denial. She started to claim that she had the child after all and put it up for adoption. If I could just see proof that the abortion had taken place the matter would be settled. I was not seeking to see any confidential clinical records. I let them know that my client was a well-known journalist and dropped hints that if they weren't co-operative articles might appear in the press making dark hints about the clinic's rather shady past. They have a squeaky-clean image these days.

'In the end they gave in. They told me she had five appointments arranged, two preliminaries, one for the procedure itself, two for follow-up. They showed me their records. The trouble is, this was before the 1967 Abortion Act. The clinic took their share of the money but were careful not to accept any of the responsibility. That was entirely a matter for the doctors. They were just hiring the clinic's facilities. The case notes were never at the clinic. There was no way to confirm the appointments had been kept. And there was no way of tracing who the doctors really were. It's hardly surprising. The law in those days was very uncertain. Any doctor carrying out an abortion other than in an immediate life-threatening situation risked prosecution. They found ways to protect themselves, to muddy the waters, to stop the trail leading back to them.'

'It all sounds rather familiar. I had an abortion in those days. A couple of years before my mother did, or was supposed to. She never knew, of course. The place I had it wasn't as nice as the one you describe. Poor hygiene, inadequate back-up. They might have killed me. As it was they just made me sterile. So she changed her mind at the last minute?'

'Or she never intended to go through with it and was playing me along.'

'And now you think Alan is her son. My half-brother. It all fits, I suppose. My mother couldn't face bringing him up on her own. So she had him adopted. Somehow he found out about his father. I wonder if he knows who his mother was, and who I am. That might explain why he made contact with me.'

'I don't think he knows who you are. He has his reasons for following you. You're Michael's heir. And that's what he thinks he should be. He wants what's his. Real tramps never stay in one place. But he does. He's camping out in that disused observation point on the headland. I had a feeling he might be there. So I looked in earlier this evening. He wasn't at home. But there was stuff of his lying about. Not just the normal tramp's stuff you'd expect. There was a newspaper article about you. You'll know about that, of course. They interviewed you for it.'

She stood up and walked over to the sideboard. She took out a bracelet and handed it to me. I turned it over in my hands and looked questioningly at her.

'A present from Michael to your mother. When I came back to the cottage after getting her settled in Portsmouth, I found it on the bedroom floor. Perhaps she had dropped it there by accident. Perhaps she had thrown it there in anger, after hearing from me that Michael had rejected her. I should have returned it to him. But I didn't. He never mentioned it. Either he forgot it or he assumed it was still with her. I kept it. God knows what use I thought it would be. At the time it represented my victory over her. But the victory was always hers. Look at me. Look at the life I've led. Look at the person I was, the person I am now. None of this would have happened if I hadn't behaved the way I did. When your mother first came here, she was lonely. I could tell that. She tried to... not to make friends with me exactly but to make contact. I rebuffed her. She was never hostile to me, but I chose to hate her. I know it was Michael who wanted her to have the abortion. But I didn't need to help him. I could have told him to look elsewhere for an accomplice. It was nothing to do with me. But I didn't just help him out of loyalty for him and concern for his position and his peace of mind. I did it with such relish. I was so pleased at the chance to get back at her. To make her suffer for her pleasure. And look what happened. I had my revenge all right. She lived in exile all those years, her boy lost to her, not daring to contact the man she loved for fear he would reject her again. When eventually she plucked up the courage to return it was to meet her own death. I could have stood by her, against Michael's scheming. We could have defied him, together. She could have stayed here and had her baby. God knows she needed a friend then. All she found in me was an implacable enemy. And she had done nothing to hurt me.'

She sat down, her face in her hands. I turned round and peered into the blackness outside the window. After a few minutes I looked away again, my eyes travelling around the room, then to the door, then again to the window, everywhere except where she sat. She had nothing more to say. It was my turn.

'You weren't the only one who could have helped her but didn't. She had a daughter. I could have helped her. I was old enough for that. But I couldn't. Because I knew nothing about it. I keep asking myself why she didn't tell me. Now I think I know why. I found a notebook my mother had written in. It was up at the house. Michael must have found it in the cottage and taken it back there. She started writing it when I was still a teenager. As I read it I found it hard to believe what I was reading. I didn't recognise myself. I had persuaded myself that we had had a good relationship then, and only drifted apart after she came down here. But the truth was that I had withdrawn from all contact with her, from the age of thirteen. My mother obviously thought I was disgusted with her because she was unhappy and having affairs. A year later my father died of cancer. But that seemed to drive a further wedge between us. She had got over his death too quickly. That's what she thought I felt. So when she came here and had an affair with Michael and had a child, she decided to keep all that from me. She thought that if I knew I would judge her and despise her.'

Brenda looked up at last.

'I realise you must hate me very deeply.' Her voice was shaking. 'It's funny, isn't it? I was always the one who hated. I never thought what it must be like to be at the receiving end. Now I know. I'm not so stupid as to ask you to forgive me. Maybe one day you might forgive me for the way I behaved towards you. Though why on earth should you? But you can't speak for her. She's the one I most need to ask for forgiveness. But it's too late. She's gone. And I have to live with my share of the responsibility for that. Anyway, the choice is yours. We can decide never to see each other again. Or you can let me help you. If I can. Not to make me feel better or to make you feel better about me. I won't expect that. It's just that I'm beginning to sense how awful this must be for you. Trying to find the truth among your lost memories on the one hand and all the secrecy on the other. And you're probably wondering whether the truth is something you will be able to bear when you do know it.'

'I don't hate you, Brenda. I'm too tired to hate. And I'm too tired to carry on searching. You can't help me.'

'All right. You can leave now and we'll never see each other again. But maybe you want to think about it first. I think you do need help. And believe it or not, I'm on your side now. I want to know the truth. I want to know about Michael and your mother. I want to know who this Alan is and what he's up to. I want an end to the tragedies that have been going on around here for too long. I don't want anything more to happen to you, not after what you've already been through. And my story will have told you something about me. Not just that I'm a malevolent old bitch. I'm certainly that. But I'm also cunning and resourceful. Maybe you could use a bit of that. So before you decide to cut me out of your life, how about giving me a try? Stay a bit longer. Tell me everything you've seen and heard tonight. Tell me everything you're thinking about what happened here and what's happening now. Let's see what we can make of it between us.'

I smiled, weakly. 'All right. I haven't the strength to move, even if I wanted to. We can talk. Just while I'm here. First things first. How about a cup of tea?'

TWENTY-NINE

When she returned with the tea, my eyes had closed. They flickered open when she touched my hand and held the cup in front of me. We sat in silence for a few minutes. At last I found the energy to ask my next question.

'Did you tell Michael about David and me?'

'As this is confession time... yes, that was me.'

'You watched us? The way you watched Michael and my mother?'

She nodded. 'It was easy. I slipped through the front garden and down the stone stairs by the side of the cottage to the lawn by the front. I could see straight into your bedroom. You never drew the curtains. He was usually there during the day. I could see everything. There was no danger of either of you seeing me. Not with your face in the pillow and him behind you like that.'

'Like animals, you mean. So, did you enjoy the show?'

'No. You didn't enjoy it either, did you? It wasn't the way it was for your mother, was it?'

'Only you can say, Brenda. You're the only one who's seen both of us in action.'

'Me? I can't say. What do I know? I was never that interested in sex. There was only one man I would have wanted to teach me. When it was obvious that wasn't going to happen I never thought about how it might be with anybody else. I sometimes wonder what sort of pupil I would have made. Probably no better than I was as his art pupil. Your mother... she didn't need lessons, by God. I couldn't see them. Usually it was dark. If it was during the day they drew the curtains. I heard them, though. Mostly her. Like singing. No words, just voiced sounds. They seemed to be coming from deep inside her throat. It was almost a man's voice, though I knew it wasn't Michael's. Later there were words but I couldn't understand them. I'm sure they were Welsh. Very soft and low, soothing, caressing. He wouldn't have understood them but he must have loved the sound of them. It was never like that for you, was it? I might not know much about sex but I can tell the difference between sounds of pleasure and pain. He hurt you. Why did you let him?'

'If I knew that I might be able to explain a lot of things. So why did you watch us, if it wasn't for your enjoyment?'

'I felt I owed it to Michael. David was his life. I couldn't stand by and watch both of them being destroyed. I needed to be absolutely sure, to see with my own eyes. He refused to believe me at first. Said I was a gossiping bitch who was just jealous of people being friends. He told me he had introduced you and David to each other and you had only met in his presence. I had never seen him so angry. He became violent. He shook me by the shoulders and almost threw me out of the house. A few days later he rang to apologise. He said he would sort out the situation himself. When you left the village, I assumed he had paid you off.'

'You said you sometimes wondered if David was his son. Why did he go to such lengths to hide that fact, even after Celia had died?'

'Michael's world was built on flimsier foundations than most people realised. His family weren't wealthy. He never made much as an artist. At one time his larger works fetched high prices but there were few of them. He married money and social status. Everything he bought, the house, the gallery, the place for his academy in Portsmouth, was paid for by Celia's father and put into her name. None of it would come to Michael until after both Celia and her father were dead. I had to wait until then before I could be paid for what I did.'

'What about the house you bought in Portsmouth for my mother? That was his money.'

'A legacy from his aunt, paid from a separate account so neither Celia nor her father would know anything about it. When Michael decided he wanted David to move in with him he was playing a game with very high risks. If Celia's father as much as suspected that David was his son, that Michael had betrayed his daughter, he would have changed his will. And he would have done everything in his power to destroy Michael while he still had strength to do it. Once Michael had started the deception he had to continue with it. He could not tell David the truth until he had reached an age when he could handle it.'

'And by then David wasn't interested.'

'Earlier on, you said you had been following your mother tonight. What did you mean?'

I thought for a moment. Then I decided I had to tell her, despite the risk of her concluding that I was still insane.

'I haven't just been remembering things. I've been seeing them, feeling them. I think I know what happened on the cliffs, when she died. Michael didn't plan to kill her, and he didn't lure her up there. She came back because she desperately wanted to see him, to speak to him. She went up to the house. Perhaps he had refused to come to the cottage or meet her anywhere else.'

'And that was the one place where he didn't want her to come.'

'Because of Celia.'

'Precisely. Your mother would not have known how sick Celia was. How could she know? By then she was confined to a wheelchair.'

'Michael could never have left Celia. He told me. The more dependent she became on him, the more he loved her. A different sort of love from what he felt for my mother. What I don't get is where Laura fitted into all this.'

'Just a distraction.'

'From both of them?'

'No, just from Celia. God knows, he must have needed distraction from time to time. He must have met Laura before he met your mother. Maybe she was an old flame from his early days in Portsmouth. Before Celia became too ill for him to be away from these parts he used to spend a lot of time there, setting up his academy. He would have looked up old friends while he was there, revisited old haunts.'

'I'm still wondering why my mother was so insistent on speaking to him. Maybe she thought she could get Alan back if she and Michael were to marry. Perhaps Alan hadn't been formally adopted. Maybe she thought the courts might order him to be returned to her but only if she and his father were a couple. It's just the sort of crazy fantasy my mother would have pursued. But if she had known Celia was in a wheelchair she would never have gone there. Can you imagine the scene? Michael opens the door. My mother forces her way past him. Tells him that they have to talk. If necessary she will confront his wife. Michael is terrified. If Celia hears about the child, the one thing she had never been able to give Michael, it could kill her. So he takes my mother into the library, tries to calm her down. But inevitably voices are raised. Celia is in the next room. She hears everything. When my mother comes out she sees Celia, in the hallway. She is horrified. You never told me she was like this, she tells Michael. If I had known… She is overwhelmed with shock and remorse. She rushes out and onto the coastal path. By then it's very dark and raining hard. But she knows the path well. Or she thinks she does. Michael follows her, telling her it's not her fault, they can talk things over, sort something out. She is younger and stronger. He can't keep up with her. By the cliff-tops she loses her way, runs off the path and on towards the cliffs. Just in time she stops. Right by the edge. Michael runs up to her. She can't move. She's frozen with terror. Michael tells her to turn round slowly.'

'You saw all this, tonight?'

'Yes. At first I was following them. Then I was in her place. Not just in her place. I was her. I was a woman who had loved Michael, who had carried and borne his child. Those memories of pregnancy and childbirth were inside my body, the memories of holding the baby were in my hands and arms. They were her memories, not mine. My own child was aborted when I was seventeen, before I even began to sense its presence. But tonight I sensed Alan growing inside me, pushing out of me, clinging on to me. All those memories compressed into a few seconds. And I was standing in front of his father. I held out my hand so he could help me and pull me back. I started to fall. My hand was searching for his but it wasn't there.'

'Maybe he was just too late to reach her.'

'Or maybe he held back. He had seen something come between them, an image before his eyes. An image of Celia back at the house, the look of betrayal on her face which he knew would now never leave her. My mother was no longer the woman he had loved; she was the woman who had destroyed his peace of mind forever. So his hand did not meet hers. He dropped it. She fell.'

Brenda rose and started to pace about the room.

'Yes, of course. That's it. Now I understand it. Why he never drew or painted again. A moment's cold rage stopped him from saving her. Imagine the expression on her face as she fell. Where was the hand that was supposed to save her? That image must have haunted his every waking moment thereafter and stalked through his dreams at night. It all fits. That was the time he stopped drawing and painting. People said it was when Celia died. But I knew it was before that. It was when your mother died. How could he have carried on? Every time he tried to lift a brush or a pencil her final image would have been there. Of course, it's only supposition. What you saw and felt tonight could just be your imagination.'

'No. She was there, tonight. I know she was. She showed me what really happened. It explains why he seemed to be trying to make it up to her, arranging the funeral, taking over her cottage.'

She slumped down again in her chair. In less than a second an expression of intense fatigue had come over her face. After a minute she spoke, wearily.

'So, what are you going to do now?'

'Go back to the house.'

'Why, for God's sake?'

'I said before that I was too tired to go on searching. I am. But I know I have to carry on somehow.'

'You mustn't be there alone. I'll come with you. If you want to stay alone in your room I'll leave you to yourself. But you must have someone in the house.'

'I'm not alone. Megan's there.'

'And you're lying. I know you sent her away. I have my groceries delivered as well, you know. By the same man. He keeps me informed.'

'I won't deny that I'm scared. But I don't think the memories will return unless I'm on my own.'

'There's something else I'm worried about. I think you may be in danger.'

'Me? From whom?'

'From Alan. Because you're in his place. You inherited Michael's house and most of his money.'

'As far as I'm concerned, if he can prove who he is, he can have it all. I have enough money of my own. And I can't stand the house. And if he really is my brother, I need to help him to get back to some sort of normal life. If he'll let me.'

'He may not understand any of that. He's obviously paranoid. Thinks everybody has been plotting against him. If you tell him you're his sister he won't believe you. But he will believe it's a plot to take back a share of what he wants to take from you. He may decide that if he killed David he might as well get rid of you. He got away with it once, he might get away with it again.'

'He's no danger to me. I'm sure of that. I could sense it.'

'Look, I'm not trying to scare you. Just let me come to the house with you. Spend the rest of the night and tomorrow here. You need the rest. Then tomorrow evening I'll drive you back there and stay with you.'

'You can drive me back. I'd be grateful for that. But you must leave me there.'

'You can be stubborn when you want to be. All right. I agree.'

My eyes had already closed.

***

'What are you smiling about?' asked Brenda as she turned off the engine. We had parked in front of the house after a journey in complete silence.

'I don't know. Perhaps it's the thought of Alan being my brother. He's a dirty tramp. At best he's a fantasist and a paranoid. At worst he's a killer. Then I thought, I can't exactly be anybody's dream of a sister. Actually, we're ideally suited to each other. A tramp, a paranoid schizophrenic, and a killer. Does that remind you of anybody?'

'Come off it, Madeleine. There's no comparison. You had a bath last night.'

I stared at her for a few seconds. For a moment I could have sworn I saw the trace of a smile flicker across her face.

'If that's all you've got to say in my defence I'd better get inside. Thanks for the lift.'

'Are you really sure about this? You don't want me to stay with you? I could at least wait outside in the car until you give me the all-clear.'

'No thanks. It's best this way, honestly. I'm sure I'll be all right.'

'Have it your way.'

I got out of the car and waited outside the front door until I heard the engine start. Then I opened the door and stepped into the hallway. I flicked the light switch up and down several times. The power was still out. I groped my way up the stairs and into my bedroom. I heard a muffled sound behind me. Before I could cry out I felt a hand clamped against my mouth as the bedroom door slammed shut behind me.

THIRTY

There was a loud knocking sound at the front door. The hand pulled away from my mouth and pushed me towards the bed. The bedroom door opened and heavy footsteps clumped down the stairs. As I fumbled my way out of the bedroom towards the top of the stairs I heard a sharp cry. The front door slammed.

'Madeleine, are you all right?' Brenda's voice from just inside the hall.

'I'm up here. I'm all right.'

'Is there any light?'

'There was a power cut during the storm. I think it may still be off. I know where the fuse box is. You stay there.'

I crept carefully downstairs, my fingers tracing the top of the banister. I saw Brenda's bulky shadow near the front door.

'What happened?'

'There was someone waiting for me in my bedroom, in the dark. When he heard your knock he decided to leave.'

'I know. He nearly knocked me over as he ran out. Did you see who it was?'

'No. But it was Alan. I know his smell.'

'How did he get in?'

'He must have a key. Here we are. There's a torch somewhere… There it is. Could you shine it here, please? Inside this cupboard.'

I flicked a switch in the cupboard just inside the front door. Light flooded the hall, dazzling both of us.

'The power must have come back on,' I said. 'He switched it off deliberately so he could lie in wait for me. Why did you come back?'

'As I was turning out of the driveway I looked into my mirror and realised that I hadn't seen any lights come on. So I came back to check. Are you all right? He didn't hurt you? Don't say I didn't warn you.'

'I know, Brenda. You did warn me. And I didn't listen. Thanks for coming back.'

'And I'm staying. No arguments.'

'All right. But you must leave me alone. I'm going upstairs now. You can get yourself a drink in the library. You know where it is. And you know where the kitchen is if you need anything to eat.'

'Yes, I know. Off you go. If you need anything just shout. In the meantime I'm going to bolt the front door and check all the windows.'

I lay down on the bed. After a few minutes I sensed another person. Not Brenda. Not Alan. And not in the bedroom in which I had gone to lie down. I was in that other bedroom, with pink wallpaper with images of flowers. I forced myself to lie still, not to scream. He sat down on the side of the bed and started to speak, softly, with a Welsh lilt.

THIRTY-ONE

'You weren't asleep, were you, Madeleine? I could tell. I wanted to have a little chat with you. I hope you don't mind. I'm feeling a bit lonely, I suppose. Your mother's away again. Left us on our own. I don't mind. That's what she wants and that's what we want, don't we?'

He took a cigarette from a crumpled packet and lit it, slowly and deliberately. My heart was pounding. Underneath the bedclothes my hands were shaking. But I did not want him to go. I wanted him to continue talking to me, just to me, the two of us alone in that room. I loved his voice, but it had been so long since I had heard it just for me. I loved the sound of his words, like a Welsh harp, very soft, with a slight rise and fall, a cutting-off of the breath just before the end of each syllable.

'We were close once. Your mother and I. Or so it seemed. Two wild Celtic souls. That's what she called us. But that was her. It wasn't me. She saw a reflection of herself in me, God knows why. She was so young when I met her. Eighteen. I was thirty-two. She was one of my students, did she tell you that? Brilliant prospects. Then she got pregnant. Had you at nineteen. So we married. She never finished her degree. Then we found out how little we had in common. She hates it here in Oxford. Always has. Me, I couldn't survive anywhere else. I wondered whether our marriage had served any purpose at all. Whether it had not all been a dreadful mistake. But now, when I see what you are becoming, I know it wasn't. It had a purpose. The purpose was you. You know it as well, don't you? I've seen it, in the look in your eyes. You have them all. Your mother's eyes, your mother's face. Even your body is beginning to swell like hers. But you have my understanding. I can see it all now. Your mother was the conduit to you. That's all she was ever meant for. I don't care if she's throwing herself at other men. She doesn't matter now. Only you and I matter. She was made of the common clay of life. In you, the clay has been touched with a divine spark. I never noticed it before. The transformation is so gradual, you see. You are like a flower in bud, delicate, subtle and suggestive, not yet ripened and coarsened by the sun. We are two special souls. We are destined to be special together. There are certain rules in life, of course. There have to be. Every society in history has had them. But some people are destined to be above them, and so are we. How does that make you feel, Madeleine? I know how it makes me feel. It makes me feel like a bird on the wing, in full song. It's something I've never felt before. Sorry, I know I'm not making sense. Don't say anything. Go to sleep now.'

Such a way with words. Almost a poet. But what did he mean? I was not aware that I had looked at him in any special way. And what was that about my mother's body? Already, at the age of only thirteen? Of course I had been aware of the changes in my shape. They had disgusted me. I could hardly bring myself to look at myself naked in the mirror. Not that my mother was disgusting in any way. On the contrary. I had heard people speak of her as a real beauty, a complete woman. I had longed for my mother to notice me, to teach me how to be like her, how to accept the changes in me and the future which beckoned because of them. Now I realised that would never happen. It was too late. Despite my youth, my inexperience, my fear, my ignorance, I was to take my mother's place, to fulfil the role in which my mother had failed, to be my father's soulmate. We were to be special together. Whatever I learned would come from him and him alone. He would discuss his researches with me. Tell me about his new insights into classical mythology and history. We would pore together over his dusty old books. I would love all that. But the bit I did not yet understand was where my body came into it.

I would not understand that until the following night.

'I want to make it easy for you, Madeleine. It will be best if you don't see it. You're very young and it might frighten you. Take off your nightdress. That's a good girl. Now turn over. On your stomach. That's good. It might hurt at first. Try not to scream. Just relax. There'll be less pain that way. Please, Madeleine, don't scream. That's right. My Madeleine. So special. So very, very special.'

THIRTY-TWO

I pushed open the door and sat down opposite Brenda. I was carrying a folder under my arm. I placed the folder on the table next to some books which Brenda had just taken off the shelves and placed there.

'I heard you being sick,' she said. 'Are you all right?'

'Yes. I'm fine. I see you found some books to read.'

'Yes. I picked out a couple, from that shelf over there. Well, you know precisely where they were. I spotted them because they were not flush with the others. I could see you had taken them down and put them back, many times, perhaps. This one looks interesting. *The Kindly Ones.* By Dr Andrew Reed. What does it say about him on the back? "Andrew Reed is Tutor in Classical History at St Stephen's College, Oxford. This is the fourth book in his highly acclaimed series aiming to interpret the Greek myths for a modern audience. Dr Reed lives in Oxford with his wife and daughter."'

'Yes.'

'Your father?'

'That's right,' I whispered.

'What does the title mean?'

'It's a euphemism. The Kindly Ones were the Furies of Ancient Greece. They pursued people for unnatural crimes.'

'Unnatural?'

'Like Oedipus. Sleeping with his mother. That sort of thing.'

'That sort of thing.' She repeated my words slowly and deliberately. 'This inscription on the flyleaf. It surprises me. "To the one who is special, part of me, body and soul." That's very moving, Madeleine. A wonderful thing for a man to write to his wife or lover. For someone like me who's never attracted any sort of love it's almost unimaginable. I thought your parents weren't happy together. That was why your mother had affairs. That's what you told me. But to be loved like this... I don't understand it. But if this were dedicated to her you would think he would have addressed her by name. But there's no name. Unless...'

'Unless he was addressing someone else.'

'Was this in Michael's collection when you came here? Or did you bring it yourself?' I shook my head. 'All right, Madeleine. I know you find it difficult to talk about this. So let me help. Let's see, when was this published? I have trouble with these Roman numerals. Can you help me here?'

I looked up at her and swallowed hard. 'It was published in 1961.'

'Thank you. How old were you at the time?'

'Thirteen.'

'This is a first edition, isn't it? And he gave this one to you, with the dedication inside. When you were thirteen. You brought this book here, didn't you?'

'No. I'd forgotten all about it. My mother had a small collection of books, really awful ones, trashy rubbish. This must have got mixed in with them. I suppose she brought it with her when she came to live in the cottage. I never found it there.'

'Ah yes, I remember now. After your mother moved to Portsmouth I found her books and wrote to her to ask her if she wanted me to send them to her. She told me to leave them or get rid of them. She said they were trash. I left them there. I never looked at them. I don't go in for reading much. And I knew her tastes would not be mine.'

'Michael must have found that one when he sold the cottage for me. He would have known it was one of my father's. He already had some in his collection. He never mentioned it. He put it on the shelves with the others.'

'Did you look at it since?'

'No. I took my father's books down from time to time to browse through them. And I asked Megan to send them to me in the hospital. That one was part of the package she sent. But somehow I never wanted to open it.'

'Because it would have reminded you how you and he were special, part of each other, body and soul. But now you have remembered, haven't you? That's why you were sick just now.'

'Yes.'

'Did you tell anybody what was happening?'

'No, of course not. It was our secret. Our special secret.'

'Did it go on for long?'

'No. A few months. Then he became very ill.'

'Yes. Cancer. You told me.'

'No. Not cancer.'

'Why would you lie to me about that?'

'I wasn't lying. It was something I had made up to keep my memories buried.'

'But you remember the truth now.'

'Yes. Would you like to hear about it?'

'All right. If it will help you. What did he die of?'

'They came for him.'

'They?'

'The Furies. He had been writing about them while he and I were... It was as if he were defying them, provoking them. In the end they came.'

THIRTY-THREE

'Madeleine, do you see them? There, looking at me, pointing at me.'

'Don't be silly. There's nobody there. We're all alone. You must have fallen asleep. You were having a bad dream.'

We were in his room in college. As usual I had come straight from school to help him read the proofs of his latest book. For over a week now we had made little progress. He could not concentrate. He smoked continuously. His eyes were red with lack of sleep. He talked wildly, incoherently. He hardly ever came home, preferring to catch what moments of sleep he could in the armchair from which he conducted his tutorials. I always brought in some cakes and sandwiches, nearly always took them away again untouched. Sometimes he did not recognise me, mistaking me for one of his students. Once he had thrown me out of the room, calling me by my mother's name, calling me a slut and a whore. I urged him to see a doctor. He told me it was too late. I was becoming increasingly anxious. My mother was away and I did not know where I could contact her.

'No, I see them,' he whispered urgently.'Over there.'

'Who are you talking about?'

'The accusers. The Eumenides.'

'For God's sake, that was only a book! Your book. You brought them alive but only on paper and in your imagination. They're not real. They're mythical. You've been overworking, that's all.'

'No. Not mythical. Real. You should see them, too. Look, look. Over there.'

'I can't see anything.'

'I don't understand. You should see them. We both committed a crime, you see. Against the Gods. We defied them. Mocked them. Now they're taking revenge.'

He grasped my hand, so hard that I winced with pain.

'If you can't see them now, Madeleine, that means they will come for you in the future. That would be too horrible. What we did was very wrong, you see. We were special, not like other people. We set ourselves up against their laws. I kept expecting you to tell me that you were seeing them too. But they will come, unless we stop it. The guilt was yours as well as mine. It started with the changes in you. I didn't realise until I saw it in your eyes. I didn't realise what you were, what I was, what we had to be to each other, how we had to rise above the rest of common humanity. It was wonderful, wasn't it, to be up there together on the clouds? But it couldn't last. Our punishment had to come. You will understand it when we're together again. I dictated something, when I was trying to understand it myself.' He rummaged among the papers on the top of his desk.'Here's the tape. Should destroy it, really, but there's no time.'

'I'll destroy it if you want.'

'No, no. No time. It's discreet. It doesn't say what we did. If it fell into the wrong hands, nobody would understand. It'll be all right. Just lock it away. In the cabinet over there. Here's the key. Do it now. There's no more time.' He was almost screaming.

'There's plenty of time. But if it helps I'll do it now.'

I opened the cabinet, put the tape inside and locked it again.

'That's it, Father. Safely locked away. Rest now. It was just a dream, as I said.'

'No, not a dream. Madeleine, do something else for me. It's too dark in here. Go over to the window. Draw the curtain. That's my girl.'

I released his hand and walked over to the massive casement overlooking the quadrangle. Outside I heard the chatter and laughter of undergraduates, looked out and saw them running across the uneven paving stones, their gowns flapping, clutching armfuls of books and papers. Behind me I heard a drawer open, a sound like a clicking of metal.

'What was that, Father? I didn't hear you. What did you say?'

I was sure he had said something. Just a couple of words. But the noises from the quadrangle and the sound of the opening drawer had obscured them. I turned round. Then I was deaf. I smelt the smoke, saw the gun on the floor, saw the door open, people rushing in, mouthing at me, dashing over to the body slumped in the chair. I heard nothing.

THIRTY-FOUR

'Two months after his death, I was in a child psychiatric unit. My mother had discovered that I was mutilating myself. Nothing too drastic. Cigarettes stubbed out on my skin. Marks scored across my arms with a knife. It wasn't because I enjoyed the pain. I just felt this enormous sense of relief when the blood began to flow. I tried to be careful but one day she saw the marks on my arms. She was furious. Told me it was about time I got over my grief. If she had managed it, why couldn't I? She was sorry but she had no choice but to have me detained. When I was discharged after a few weeks I was cured, supposedly. All that meant was that I was out of immediate danger of suicide or serious self-harm. But I was hardly cured. I had affairs with my teachers. I became pregnant and had an abortion. A year later I was a heroin addict. I still needed the drugs, you see. The ones they had given me in hospital had suppressed my memories and my feelings. Once I was out I needed other drugs to keep them suppressed. I had to keep the lid on, to stop the memories breaking through again. In the end only the hard drugs would do it. Our doctor arranged for me to attend this very expensive private clinic.'

'Your mother must have been out of her mind with worry.'

'I didn't notice. All I felt was how disgusting, how repulsive I must have been to her.'

'Did the treatment work?'

'Oh yes. I kicked the habit. But by then I had the lid down really tight. Nothing could get through. I could function, but only as an automaton. I had been expelled from school, of course. I had planned to go to university but there was no chance of that. I went to London and got a job in a bank. Started at the bottom and worked my way up.'

'What I don't understand is why you and your mother didn't become close again as a result of what you were going through. Once you had got through the rehab successfully, why wasn't she there for you?'

'Because I had made sure she couldn't be. In the notebook she wrote about me screaming my disgust with her into her face. I remember what happened now. It was in the clinic. I had been there a few weeks. She used to visit but I wouldn't talk to her, wouldn't even acknowledge her. One day I turned on her. The doctor in charge of my case was in the room with us. I screamed at her, telling her to get out and never come back. She thought I was disgusted with her, because of her affairs. But it wasn't that at all. I couldn't bear her to look at me, even to be in the same room with me. I knew I had done something monstrous, something repulsive, even if I couldn't remember what. Even if she didn't know what had happened she would see it in my eyes, hear it in my voice. So I had to shield her from me. That was why I had been so distant from her, ever since she had returned home after it had happened the first time. So she went away and I never saw her again until the day I identified her body. That time at the clinic, when she had left, the doctor asked me why I had yelled at her, telling her she was disgusting. He had misunderstood as well. He seemed to think she had abused me, and that was the cause of my problems. He said he would make sure she would not visit again because it was obvious her visits were obstructing my recovery. By the time I got out she had moved down here and it was too late for us, too late to be mother and daughter again.'

'And you had really forgotten everything?'

'Yes. What he had done to me. What he had said before he died. I had even forgotten how he died, forgotten that I was there when it happened. I had no sense or image of myself. Not until David provided me with one. Here. Look at those.'

She picked up the folder and leafed quickly through the contents. Then she shut it and handed it back.

'I've never seen any of his work before. Thank God.'

'Michael said he was a genius. Far more naturally gifted than Michael ever was. I'm no expert. But when I first met him he was sketching something on the headland. He took it back home and made it into a watercolour. He showed it to me. I thought it was beautiful. He tore it up as soon as I praised it. Told me landscapes are trivial. He said he had more significant work to do.'

'Like this?'

'That's right. It was meant to be his first major work. Weeks of intensive effort. A hundred sketches.'

'And you as his model? Poor you. Maybe Michael was right about his natural gifts. But gifts need to be protected and nurtured, not abused. If this is genius it's in meltdown. His talent was destroying itself just as he was destroying himself. To me this isn't art. But then what do I know about art? Only what Michael taught me. And he was a traditionalist and much maligned for it. If you want to know what I think, I think they're monstrous. You should destroy them. Burn them.'

'What? Destroy the only proof I have that I exist at all? David was the only one, since him, who understood me, who saw into my soul.'

'These aren't about you, Madeleine. They're about him. I'll destroy them for you if you find it difficult.'

'No, I can't let you do that. I have to keep them.'

'All right. They're yours. It's up to you. Have you remembered everything now?'

'No. I still can't remember about killing Laura. But the other night I remembered how I found out she was David's mother. I overheard her talking with Michael, that time she came here to see him. He had paid her off, as I thought. She gave David up to him and went to Australia. She came back after she heard David had died. She was already ill by then.'

'And Michael never mentioned her afterwards?'

'No. I'm sure of that.'

'He never gave you a message for her?'

'No.'

'So it was your own decision to go and see her. You have to go back there. In your mind. Back to that room in the hospice. The same way you went back just now to that room where your father shot himself.'

I shook my head violently. 'I can't.'

'You must. You can't stop now.'

'All right. But I can't go to that room. Not yet.'

'You went to see her sister-in-law first. That's what you told me. What was her name?'

'Naomi.'

'That's right. How did you know where to find her?'

'Simple. I looked up her address in the phone book.'

THIRTY-FIVE

'Miss Reed? I'm Naomi. Come on in.'

Naomi was a plump, bustling woman in her sixties. Her smile was broad but did not disguise the lines of worry about her eyes and forehead. She wore an apron covered with flour, which she tried vainly to brush off her hands. I followed her into her living room. The furniture was old and shabby but the room was spotlessly clean and tidy. She had been keeping herself busy, cooking and cleaning, distracting herself from thoughts about her dying sister-in-law.

'Sit down, please. Cup of tea? And a scone? I've just baked some fresh.'

'That's very kind, but no thanks.'

'Well, Miss Reed, it's as I explained on the phone. She's been in the hospice for a few weeks now. It's only a mile from here. They call it a home for palliative care. They used to call it St Agnes' Hospice. But everybody still knows what it's for. They're very kind. They look after her better than I could here.

And the hospital can't do any more for her. It's a very peaceful place. If you still want to see her, it's best if I go with you. They know me there. What did you want with her, anyway?'

'I knew an acquaintance of hers, Michael Wallace. You may have heard of him. He's a well-known artist. Well, he was. He died recently. I think she would want to know. Could I ask you something? Michael never really told me anything about her. Did she have any children?'

'No. None that I'm aware of. She and my brother certainly didn't have children. She was only thirty when he died. As far as I know she never remarried. Nobody's come forward, since she's been ill. Not that she has any money or property to leave, even if they did. She's never mentioned anybody. She hasn't bothered with a will or anything like that. She's literally penniless so what's the point?'

'Does she have any other living relatives?'

'No. Her parents died when she was in her twenties. She had a sister. That was the one who went to Australia, the one she went to stay with when she went out there. The sister died, so Laura came back here. She was already very ill. The doctors had only given her a few months to live. They've been proved right. She's sinking fast. It really could be any day now. I was terribly shocked when I saw her. She just appeared on my doorstep. Said she had come back to die. I could see she wasn't joking. She was old far beyond her years.'

'Will she be able to talk?'

'I think so. I was there this morning. Her memory is still quite sharp. She might enjoy meeting someone new. She must be sick of the sight of me by now. I only hope they haven't given her too many drugs. Let's go now. I'll take you in there and introduce you but I won't stay. She's had enough of me for today. I'll come back here. Do you want to stay the night here, or will you go straight home?'

'I'll probably go straight home. Thanks anyway.'
'Fine. Let's go.'

Laura was in a private room. Naomi went in first. She came out after a minute.

'She's awake. The nurse is with her. I've told her what you said about why you want to see her. Laura's keen to meet you. I think it'll do her good. I'll go now.'

I went in. Laura was sitting up in bed. The curtains were drawn. I blinked until my eyes adjusted to the dim light. Perhaps sunlight disturbs her eyes, I thought.

I barely recognised her. Her cheeks were now deep hollows. Only the bright, staring eyes were familiar. Her gnarled hands lay on the blanket in front of her. An intravenous drip was attached to her arm. She looked blankly through me. I sat down and held her hand. The nurse nodded to me and told me she would wait outside. If she was needed there was a red emergency button near the bed. When the nurse had gone, I pulled a chair close to the bed and sat down.

'Laura. My name is Madeleine Reed. I was living with Michael when you came to the house. I saw you when he let you in. You talked with him about the past.'

'Yes.' She shifted and tried to sit up. I helped her to adjust the pillow. 'I remember. How is he?'

'He's dead, Laura.'

She coughed. I had the impression she was trying to laugh.

'Dead? The old bugger beat me to it. Sorry. I picked up some bad habits down under.'

'You were talking to him about your child. Do you remember?'

'I remember that was a private conversation. I don't remember anybody else being there.'

'I didn't mean to be nosy. I was just passing the room. I

overheard you. After Michael died, I remembered you, and what you said about a child. I wondered if you were all right. If you needed help. Michael hadn't mentioned you to me. But I traced you here, through your sister-in-law. Laura, would you like to talk? Would you like to tell me about you and Michael? I'd like to hear about it, if it wouldn't upset you or tire you too much. How did you first meet?'

'Here in Portsmouth. That's where we met. I come from here, born and bred. I met Harry, my husband, here and we married here. He ran a small garage. Always told me how well it was doing. Very impressive, he was. Sharp suits, flashy motor. Lots of charm. I fell for the lot. We bought a little house in a nice quiet area. He looked after all that. The house was in his name. I trusted him completely. Everything was looking rosy. It was only when he died I discovered there were several mortgages on the house. He had debts. Business debts, gambling debts. You name it. I inherited the lot. I sold the house to a landlord and rented it back. But I got behind with the rent almost immediately.'

She paused and closed her eyes. For a moment I thought she had fallen asleep. Then her eyes opened and she spoke again.

'If only... if only Michael hadn't seen the boy. It would all have been different. We would have struggled but at least we would have stayed together. He would have let us alone. But he saw him. While Michael and I were talking he came running into the room, to show me something he'd just drawn. I told him to go back and finish it off and not to disturb us because me and the gentleman were talking. Michael, well, he looked as if he had been struck by lightning. He asked him to show him what he'd been drawing. He told him not to be afraid of him, because he could see he was. Michael, well, he wasn't used to children, was he? He didn't have the right manner or voice. I could tell he was trying to be kind. Well, he looked at the drawing and said it was very good indeed. He looked at it for ages, holding it up to the light, turning it round at different angles. Then he asked me how much money I owed. He had seen the unpaid bills I had left on the table. All I ever did with them was shuffle them around to make space for new ones when they arrived. I told him. It wasn't much, really, but it was far more than I could cope with. He wrote me out a cheque on the spot. Told me there would be much more where that came from. He sent me more cheques from time to time. Small amounts but enough to keep me afloat. He insisted that I never got in touch with him and never told anybody about him or what he was doing for us. Later on… it was much worse. The things he made me do. But I was helpless.'

She was crying. I leaned forward and held her head in my arms. Then I poured some water into a glass from a jug by the bedside and held the glass to her mouth while she sipped. After another minute she continued.

'He wanted the boy to live with him under a new identity. So he could make a completely fresh start. That's what he said. I had to tell him his parents had been killed in a car crash when he was a baby.'

'What! You had to tell David he wasn't yours?'

'That's right. Michael had never even acknowledged him, not for the whole of the first six years of his life. Now he had seen him and decided he wanted him, just like that. So at first I told him he could get lost. He wasn't going to bribe him away from me by paying a few of my debts. Then he told me he could get custody. He could prove I had been in debt, that I was not a fit person to be his mother. He would employ the best lawyers. I had no money at all. Only what he chose to give me. I couldn't fight him. He was just too strong. Too powerful. I knew the court case would ruin me completely and I would lose anyway. In the end I gave in. I accepted a promise of money from him to go away to Australia. He bought my ticket for me. I delivered David into his hands. I surrendered my heart and soul at the same time. I never recovered them. After I had been out there a couple of years he sent me the payment he had promised. I had long since given up expecting it. There was a letter saying this was the final communication between us. But it wasn't. I got another letter from him, many years later. He told me how David had died. My sister died soon after that and I realised it was the end for me. There I was, alone, in a country on the other side of the world, a country I had always detested. I had nothing here either. I knew I was sick. I decided I couldn't die there. I came back while I still had the strength to do it. To die in the town where I was born. I went to see Michael to pay him back what was left of the money he had given me. For the first time I felt free. Now I'm waiting for death. I didn't hate him anymore. Not when I saw what had happened to him.' Her eyes began to close.

'Laura, I'm going now. I know it must have been awful for you. Losing your child like that. I'm sorry to have brought back such bad memories. But there must have been a time when you loved him. When you were together. When you were first pregnant with David. There must have been some happy times for you then. Try to think about those. Think about what Michael was to you then. Laura…?'

'What? I'm sorry. I didn't catch that. I thought for a moment… Come closer, will you? I can't see you properly. Open the curtains. Let me see your face…'

THIRTY-SIX

'Don't stop, Madeleine,' Brenda shouted. 'Not now. Why have you stopped? What happened next?'

'I can't.'

'What? You can't remember, or you can't bear to face the memory? So what did you come here for tonight? Go on. You have to. What happened?'

'Stop, Brenda. You're hurting me.'

She had stood up and moved behind my chair. Her fingers were digging sharply into my shoulder blades.

'Yes, and I'll carry on hurting you until you continue. For God's sake, breathe!'

My breath forced itself into my lungs with a harsh, whooping sound. I cried out as her fingers pressed harder and harder.

'She... she... For God's sake, Brenda... she... recognised me.'

THIRTY-SEVEN

'It's you! It really is. You've come back to me. You've come to say goodbye. Come here. Hold my hand.' Laura's face lit up.

'Laura, we've never met before. Who are you talking about?'

She stared at me, frowning. 'It is you, isn't it? But how can it be? She's dead. But you're the image of her.'

'Of whom?'

'Of my closest friend. Of Ceridwen. Yes, I remember now. She had a daughter. She told me. I had forgotten the name. Now I remember. Madeleine. I saw you outside the church. After Ceridwen's funeral. He wouldn't let us go inside until after the coffin arrived. And we had to leave before it came out. He didn't want us to see or be seen by anybody else there.'

'But I don't understand. You and my mother were friends? But how did you meet?'

'She moved in next door to me. Here in Portsmouth.'

'But that's impossible. She never lived here. She lived in

Oxford, until I went to London. Then she moved to Cornwall. She stayed there until she died.'

'No, my dear. She left Cornwall, came here to make a fresh start.'

'But why here?'

'I have no idea. All I knew was that she was on her own and needed a friend. I was lonely too. The baby was a real bond between us. We looked after him together, always popping in and out of each other's houses. When he started school we'd take it in turns to take him and then fetch him. It was like he had two mothers.'

THIRTY-EIGHT

'Wait.' Brenda was frowning, running her fingers through her hair. 'This doesn't make sense. She recognised you. She and your mother were friends. Your mother went to Portsmouth to have an abortion. You didn't know that then but you do now. We both know that. I was the one who arranged it, as I told you. In the end she decided to have the child. So we think. Michael's child. And Laura had Michael's child. So two women with his love-children end up next door to each other in a town hundreds of miles away from here and become friends. That's impossible.'

'No, Brenda. There was only one child. Laura only mentioned one child. Not two.'

'Fine. That means your mother did go ahead with the abortion after all. There was only one child. David. Alan is nothing to do with this, after all. Just a tramp who's trying to pass himself off as Michael's heir, as I always thought. Or maybe he's a love-child of someone else entirely, someone we don't know about. But you're still saying that two of Michael's ex-lovers from different parts of the world came by chance to live next door to each other. That's preposterous.'

'I agree.' I sighed. 'This isn't working. I can't be sure if I'm remembering things or making them up.'

She returned to her chair and thought for a minute. 'Wait a second. Your father's death. What was the date?'

'1962.'

She waved her hand impatiently. 'Yes, but the actual date. The day and the month.'

'I'm trying to think. I can't remember the day. It was summer. There were exams going on. Finals. June, probably.'

'Okay. June 1962. If your memories of your father's death are correct there'll be records. Newspaper reports. Reports of the inquest. Do you have a copy of his death certificate?'

'No. I never saw a copy. There wasn't one with my mother's effects. I suppose she had one but lost it or threw it away.'

'But there'll be the entry in the register. Did he leave a will?'

'Yes.'

'Who would have handled that?'

'Our family solicitor, I suppose. A Mr Wilson.'

'Do you have his address?'

'Yes. His card is in the bureau. What's this all about, Brenda?'

'What I'm getting at is that your account of your father's death is a memory we can verify, or otherwise. We'll know if you are recovering real memories or just fantasising. If you are remembering the truth we can take it from there. Find out what really happened in Portsmouth. Go to the house, talk to the people there now and the neighbours, things like that. See if anybody remembers. But first things first. Let's check what happened to your father. Go to the bureau. Write down everything you can remember about it. Every detail. I know it must be very unpleasant for you to go back over it again, but we need to have your own account in full before we can check other accounts against it. And get Mr Wilson's card.'

I went over to the bureau and started to write. Brenda left the room and returned twenty minutes later with two mugs of hot chocolate and some tiny white pills on a plate. I rose and handed her an envelope.

'I've written it down and put it in here. Mr Wilson's card is in there as well.'

'Thanks. Now, drink this and take these pills.'

'What are they?'

'Sleeping tablets. They have no effect on me but I take them anyway. Do you want to go up to your room to sleep, or would you prefer to stay down here?'

'I'll go upstairs.'

She watched me as I put the pills into my mouth. 'Good girl. Off you go. You look totally exhausted. And that's how I feel. Get a good night's sleep if you can. Tomorrow we'll go to Oxford. Pack a bag in the morning, in case we need to be away a couple of days. We'll collect some of my stuff on the way. You'd better ring Megan before we leave to say you may not be here when she returns.'

'Where are you going to sleep?'

'Down here. Just in case Alan comes creeping back. If he has a key and tries to get in by the front door the bolts will stop him. But I'll hear him. And old and frail as I am I'd love to have a go at chasing him and catching him. He'll wish he never came near the place.'

'I doubt if he'll come back tonight. I've been thinking about what happened. I don't think he meant to harm me. I think he just wanted to talk to me. He turned the lights off so he could talk freely without worrying about the possibility of me seeing him. He grabbed me so I wouldn't rush out and fall down the stairs. If he had wanted to harm me he had plenty of time to do it.'

She grunted. 'Well, maybe. But I'm not taking any chances. Goodnight, Madeleine. Turn off the light as you go out.'

'Goodnight, Brenda.'

In the bathroom, I slipped the pills out from under my tongue and flushed them down the toilet. I crossed over to my bedroom and sat on the bed for an hour. Quietly, I packed a small suitcase. I crept downstairs. Brenda was asleep in an armchair, snoring gently. Fatigue had at last caught up with her. She had left the envelope on a small table near her chair. I turned it over and wrote on the back.

Sorry, Brenda. I have to do this on my own. M.

As softly as I knew how I drew back the bolts and let myself out.

THIRTY-NINE

I heard footsteps behind me, crunching on the newly fallen crisp brown leaves. I looked round. My eyes met hers for a moment, then turned back towards the grave.

'I never came to the funeral,' I said. 'I must have been in shock. I suppose I was staying with a relative. I've never been here before.'

'Is that why you dressed in black today?' asked Brenda. 'To make up for not being there at the time?'

I nodded.

'May I look?'

'Of course.'

She stepped up beside me and looked at the gravestone. It was small, no more than waist high. She read the inscription out loud. '"In memory of Andrew Reed, beloved husband of Ceridwen and loving father of Madeleine."'

'Nothing more. Very simple. I expected much more. Nothing about his fame or success. His contribution to learning. Could be anybody. I'm sorry about running away like that, Brenda. How did you know where to find me?'

'I had Mr Wilson's card you gave me. I drove up yesterday afternoon. Found a hotel. I went to see him this morning. It's young Mr Wilson who runs it now, of course, as you know. But his father was there as well. Retired now. The one who handled your father's will. He was there because you had just been with them. Young Mr Wilson had called him in so he could tell you about your father's death. They told me, too, when I explained I was a friend who was anxious about you. Everything fits your account. They told me you had come on here, to pay your belated respects. They gave me directions. Well, have you?'

'Have I what?'

'Paid your respects. Or did you come here for another purpose?'

'I came here to ask for his forgiveness.'

'Forgiveness?' Realising she had shouted, she turned to apologise to anybody nearby for having disturbed the peace of the graveyard. But we were alone. 'Forgiveness? After what he did to you?'

'I remember something he wrote in one of his books. "Beauty in the young is a curse. It awakens evil." Those words kept coming back to me, all down the years since he went. I never understood what he meant. I understand now.'

'So do I. You had her beauty, all right. The beauty I hated her for. You already had it, even at thirteen. And it awakened evil in him. And you asked for *his* forgiveness?'

'The evil was in me too. It started in me. That was what he meant. Yes, I asked for forgiveness. Why not? If he had never had me for a daughter, or if I had behaved differently, none of this would have happened. He would have lived on. Still been alive now, maybe. He was quite well known by the time he died. But he was never really recognised as a great scholar. He never had the time for that. Never had time to become a professor, to be revered all around the world. Never had time to become a great man, proud and happy in his achievements.'

'He destroyed himself. And you.'

'No. I started it. I was alone, you see. Mother never noticed what was happening to me. I was terrified. I turned to him instead. It must have been the way I looked at him. My eyes must have asked him, what's happening to me? What must I do? What am I? Who am I? Not just my eyes. I used my whole body to call out to him. And he responded. He told me who I was. He told me I was special. He told me I wasn't alone. And he didn't just say it. He made me special. Part of him.'

'You accepted what he did because he made you special? But surely it was far more terrifying than being alone.'

'Yes. The first time, I thought I was going to die. I didn't understand why he wanted… the most disgusting parts of me. Why I had to display those parts to him, naked, on my belly, as if crawling in the dirt. Why he was breaking me into pieces. And all the time he was calling me special. Later, I understood. He was breaking me so he could remake me in his own image. So we could be together, above the rest of mankind.'

'As God remakes the sinner. But the sinner is made whole and taken up into Heaven. He wanted you in Hell with him.'

'Yes. That's where I belong.'

'And was it worth it? Once he had remade you, as you put it. Was it worth it, being a stranger to your mother, to the people who might have been your friends, your lovers? Was it worth it, going through life as a shadow because you had given everything away, heart, body and soul, when you were a child of thirteen to an evil man, a coward who could not go on living with what he had done, who could not face the consequences of his actions? But he left you to face them, didn't he? So look me in the eye and tell me it was worth it. Can you do that? And if not, what in the name of all that is holy are you doing here, asking for his forgiveness, when he should be screaming up from the depths of Hell to ask for yours?'

I turned to her. Before I realised what I was doing I had seized the lapel of her coat.

'Worth it? Of course it was. How could you, how could anybody possibly understand? When we were together, working on his books and articles. When he was trying to explain his thoughts to me even before he had formed them himself. When I felt that together he and I had the power to reinterpret the world, to make it afresh. After that, how could I be interested in anything anyone else might do or say to me, least of all the girls at school with their inane chat about boyfriends and make-up? So, what if they thought I was stuck-up and superior? What if they did hate me? What if I had no friends? What if I could do nothing but despise every man I met since, because it could never be with them the way it was with him? What if I had to live my life alone because what I shared with him could never be shared with anybody else?'

I lowered my arm and tried to turn away but she had grabbed me by the shoulder. 'What if, Madeleine? What if? I'll tell you what if. Because he took from you everything you could and should have been, that's what if. What would I have done with a fraction of the heart and the beauty and the intellect you were born with? You've wasted them all. You lost your mind, killed a woman who had done you no harm, spent all those years locked away, and now God knows what else is wrong with you and how much time is left. So what gave you the right to do that to your life? And what gave him the right to take all that from you?'

I pulled my hand away and stepped back. 'You're right about the life I've led. But it wasn't meant to be that way. The Furies came for him. And I betrayed him.'

'What are you talking about? They only came for him. Not for you. He was the guilty one. Not you.'

'You're wrong, Brenda. They did come for me. Later.'

'Because of you and him? Or something else? What was it you told me about the Furies? They pursue people for unnatural crimes. A mother and son. Or a father and daughter. Forbidden relationships. But there are others, aren't there?'

I smiled and clapped my hands, slowly. 'Well done, Brenda. You really are clever, aren't you? You worked it all out. You've solved the puzzle. Of Laura and my mother and the child.'

'Yes. I worked it out. On the way up yesterday. When did you?'

'The other night. Up in my room. While you were asleep in the chair. I'm afraid I never did take those pills you gave me. I knew I needed to keep alert. I went back to my conversation with Laura. I had heard her tell Michael that David was her child. My mother was next door and she and Laura were friends. Laura told me it was like David had two mothers. Two mothers, one child. And two ex-lovers of Michael living by chance next door to each other. That was the puzzle.'

'Tell me what she said.'

FORTY

'Two mothers, Laura? What a lucky child he was.'

'Yes. In those days he was a lucky child. We weren't rich but there was plenty of love for him. Lucky until his fate caught up with him. It started that time she went back to Cornwall. All the time she was away there was this feeling of dread in my heart. I wrote to her at the cottage, telling her we were well but missing her. I didn't hear from her. Then I saw it in the papers. I was in shock, wondering if I should go to the police because they were saying they didn't know who she was, this woman who had fallen from the cliffs. But I knew in my heart it had to be her.'

'But why did she go back to Cornwall?'

'To see his father, of course.'

'But why did she go? Why not you?'

'She said she had to go. She wanted him to meet his son, see what sort of boy he had become. Wanted him to leave his wife. But in case anything happened to her she had decided to make a new will. I told her she was just dreaming. But I couldn't put her off her plan. I wish to God I had managed to. I should have locked her up until the madness had passed. But I couldn't stop her.'

'But... I still don't understand. David was your child. So why didn't you go to Cornwall to see him?'

'He came to see me. Afterwards. I assumed he had come from the landlord about the rent. The posh suit and the fancy car, I supposed all that was to intimidate me. No point, I thought. You can't get blood out of a stone. I started to explain my situation, and he told me, no, he hadn't come about the rent. I still wonder about what he was going to say. Probably that he was a friend of hers who had lost contact and was trying to find her. That he had tracked down her address to next door, called there but got no reply. Did I know where she was, did I know who she had gone to visit? He must have seen the letter I had sent to the cottage. Got my address from that. Realised I was her next-door neighbour. He wanted to know if I knew about him. If she had left me his details. She hadn't. I didn't even know his name. If I had, I suppose his plan was to buy me off or find some other way to get me to stay out of the way. He didn't want the police finding out that she had gone to see him and then died in mysterious circumstances. This is what I thought later, when I began to suspect.'

'Suspect what?'

'That her death wasn't an accident, of course. But at the time I was completely in the dark. Anyway, he never did carry out his plan, if it was what I thought. He saw the boy and that changed everything. Up to then he had only wanted my silence. Now he wanted that and the boy. And that meant I had to disappear. I don't know if he worked all that out at the time. But he knew right away how to get to me. That was when he asked me how much I owed. Who the hell are you, I asked? He told me his name. I was none the wiser. Then he told me he was the boy's father, but the boy must never know. He said Ceridwen was dead. An accident. A fall from the cliffs. But how did he know it was her, I asked. According to the papers she hadn't been identified yet. He told me not to ask questions or he wouldn't give me the money. He handed over the cheque and left. His car was still outside, though, for another couple of hours after he had left me. I could hear him next door, in her house, rummaging around. Within a week he had the whole place cleared and up for sale. I had a key she had given me but I had to hand it over to him. I felt it was a sacrilege, him tearing all the memories out of her house like that. But I couldn't do anything about it. The house was in his name.

'When David died, all those years later, falling from the same cliffs, I was sure of it. Michael had killed her. David's death was divine justice. He had to live on with the knowledge of what he had done. If you can call that a life. May all their souls rest in peace.'

'But why should he want to kill her? David was your child. I overheard you say that, to Michael.'

'No, my dear. You misunderstood what I was saying because it wasn't meant for your ears. Michael and I knew what I meant. David was only mine because it was in her will and I had accepted responsibility for him.'

'Her will? But I know what was in her will. Everything came to me.'

'That must have been her previous one. Before any of this happened. She said she had to go to see him but that she had been having nightmares. She was afraid she might not return, might never see the boy again. I told her that in that case she shouldn't go. Why not just forget about the father and concentrate on bringing up the boy, if she was that concerned? While she was away I tried to keep my mind off what she had said, about being afraid something might happen to her. I took him out to play in the park, kept him amused, reassured him she would be back soon. But she never did return. David wasn't mine, my dear. Not in the way you thought. I never had children of my own. But I loved him as if he had been mine. When you heard me talk to Michael about my child, that was how it felt to me. She was already pregnant with him when she arrived. There was nothing to see then. But when it started to become noticeable I asked her about the father. She didn't want to say much about him. She said he had bought the house for them and sent them money from time to time. She hinted that he was an important public figure. He was married and needed to avoid a scandal. At first she was happy to stay out of his life and keep his identity a secret, for his sake. Later she changed her mind about that. Decided she had protected him for long enough. When she first admitted to me that she was pregnant she said, you don't think I'm a bad person, do you? You're not ashamed to be in my company? I told her not to be silly. I was never the one to go around judging people. I was delighted, in fact. As I said, it was a sort of bond between us.

'I was with her in the hospital when she had it. She always said she wanted a boy. She had her wish. I was so happy for her. She called him Hywel. After her father. David was the name Michael wanted him to be known by. Michael had a new identity ready for him for the time he would go to live with him. Still trying to avoid a scandal. Michael told me to tell him his real name was David and that his real parents had been killed in a car crash when he was a baby, like I told you. When I told him I don't think he really took it in. How could he at that age? But he took to his new name readily enough. I imagine he forgot his real name after a few years.

'Are you all right, my dear? You're very quiet. You're still there? I can't see very well. Is that you over by the window?

Come over here again. Close to me. That's right. I want to tell you about the will. She told me she wanted me to be her executor and Hywel's legal guardian in case anything happened to her and his father still refused to acknowledge him. Then there was you. She told me she had a daughter. You had gone to work in London and had done very well for yourself. Said you were the image of her. She sounded so proud of you. But she was very sad as well. I had always been able to tell she was sad about something, not just about not being with Hywel's father. Now I knew what it was. She said you had fallen out when you were still in your teens. She didn't say what it was about. Only that there had been some awful misunderstanding. In your eyes she had done something dreadful to you but she was never quite sure what it was. She hoped you would be reconciled one day. I told her, never mind about Hywel's father. Write to your daughter, make contact again, try to sort out what had happened between you. Maybe the two of you could be friends now. Then think about the father. No, she said. Not yet. Later. When I've seen him. I couldn't persuade her. But you were in her will. Half of what she had was to go to you and half to Hywel. She had a solicitor but he lived in Oxford. I knew a local one. He'd looked after Harry's affairs, in a manner of speaking. He agreed to act for her. He drew up the will, she signed it and I witnessed it. Before she left, she gave me Hywel's birth certificate, and other papers, school reports and stuff like that. For safe-keeping.

'After her death, Michael eventually agreed that we could go to her funeral. He refused point blank at first. I pleaded with him. In the end he relented. But only on condition that nobody else saw us. We had to wait in the churchyard until the coffin had gone into the church. Then we could go in but we had to stay at the back. Under no circumstances were we to talk to anybody. When he gave us the signal we had to leave.

As the service was drawing to a close he turned towards us and nodded. That was the signal to go. But we didn't leave the churchyard and go home, which was what he wanted us to do. I couldn't just go. Not like that. I wanted to watch her being lowered into her grave and hear the final prayers. So I could go up to it afterwards, when they had all gone, and say goodbye to her for the last time. So we hid, among the gravestones.

'Then you came out. I had seen you in the church. I knew right away who you were. I wanted to go up to you. To tell you she had always remembered you. That she had been sorry for what had happened between you. That she was sorry for any wrong she had done you. That she had intended one day to make it up with you. David ran towards you. Do you remember? I pulled him back. I lost my nerve. I thought, if Michael came out now and saw me approaching you, perhaps even speaking to you... God knows, the last thing I wanted was for him to take David away from me. But I knew he could provide him with a future. I persuaded myself I was going along with it for the boy's sake. I was sure that if I didn't follow Michael's orders he would cast both of us off. I would lose David anyway, I thought. How could I be a mother to him with no home and a mountain of debt? He would be taken into care. I wish I had been stronger. Told Michael to do his worst and tried somehow to make a life for the two of us. But there and then, at that moment in the churchyard, I lost my nerve. I pulled David back and we left. I never spoke to you. I lost my nerve and I never recovered it. If we had only managed to exchange a few words, if I had only been able to tell you who we were, what was going on, get you on our side... It would all have been different, wouldn't it? So very, very different. I'm so sorry, my dear. For everything. I wish to God I had been stronger.

'When I got back I asked my solicitor to let me have her will. I told him I wanted your solicitor to put it into effect, because he was the only one who knew how to contact you. But of course I never did get in touch with your solicitor. Michael had asked me if there was a will. When I told him there was, he told me to get it and give it to him. When I surrendered David to him I handed over the will and his birth certificate and all the other papers she had given me. I suppose he burned the will. I had told him I had a sister in Australia. She was ill and I had not had the chance to visit her there. In exchange for the boy, and my own heart and soul, I got a one-way air ticket to the other side of the world. And, later on, a few thousand pounds to make sure I stayed out there.

'When I came back to England my sister-in-law was shocked to see the condition I was in. I've come home to die, I said. She burst into tears. She's been good to me. Very good. I never told her what had happened. We had lost contact since Harry died. She kept telling me, you don't deserve this, Laura. You're a good person, she said. I know something happened after Harry's death to make you want to go away. But I'm not going to ask you what. All I know is that this is not what you deserve. That's what she said. But she's wrong. It's everything I deserve.

'That's all, my dear. There's nothing else to tell. I'd like you to go now. I'm very tired.'

FORTY-ONE

'So you and David...'

'Yes. Half-siblings.'

'What I saw you and him doing together... You were doing what you did with your father, weren't you? David was taking your father's place. Had you any idea at all?'

'Not consciously. I needed him because somehow I knew he would be the first since my father to give me a reflection of myself.'

'No, Madeleine. All they did was imprint a reflection of themselves on you. Why do you say you betrayed your father?'

'When you spoke to my solicitors, did they tell you there were two bullets in the gun?'

'No. How do you know that? It would be in the ballistics report, I suppose. But how did you hear about it? And what does it matter? He would have had more than one in case he missed with the first.'

'I didn't read about it. I just know. The second bullet was for him. The first should have been for me. But he couldn't bring himself to do it. So he told me to follow him. I didn't catch what he said at the time. Just two words. "Follow me." I only remembered while I was standing here, before you came. I was supposed to pick up the gun and follow him. He wanted me to die with him so we would be together and I would be spared the horror of the Furies. You see, he would never have wanted me to be here, in this world, on my own. Unable to be with him but remade in his image. Not fit for this world but not knowing how or when to leave it. He would never have done that to me. But I didn't understand. So they came.'

She put her hand round my shoulder, gently this time.

'Madeleine, when I couldn't find you in the house yesterday morning, I thought you had decided to kill yourself. I thought you had gone to the cliffs. I thought you couldn't live with the memories you had uncovered. When I found out you were still alive, and again when I saw you standing here, I felt sick. Sick with relief. Your mother's death is on my conscience. The thought of yours being there as well… If that sounds selfish, too bloody bad. And there's something else, too. Just as selfish. With you gone, I have no idea what I'll do with myself. I resented you coming into my life, when you were discharged. Now the thing I'm going to resent more than anything else is you leaving. And I don't like the way you're talking, about guns and not being supposed to be here and going to be with him.'

'It's all right, Brenda. I don't have a gun. And I'm not going to jump off the cliffs. That's not my way. I'm too much of a coward. There's no need for anything like that, don't you see? I am following him. I've killed myself already.'

She pulled her hand away and covered her mouth with it as she let out a little cry. Then she ran over to a nearby bench and sat down, sobbing. An elderly couple strolled by, carrying flowers. I smiled at them as I spoke to them, reassuringly. 'It's all right. She always gets upset like this when we visit her uncle. Even after all these years.' The couple smiled back at me, then at Brenda. She did not notice them. I walked over to the bench.

'I'm sorry, Brenda. I shouldn't have put it like that. I shouldn't have been so brutal. It was years ago. While I was abroad. Before I came back to live with Michael. It's not because I remembered what my father said. Not consciously. But his words, those final two words, must have registered somewhere. It's just taken a lot longer with me than it did with him, that's all. I know you realise that something is the matter. So I didn't think I would shock you. I'm sorry.'

She took a large cotton handkerchief out of her handbag and blew her nose noisily.

'But what if you're wrong about all this? What if you're horribly wrong about the whole business? What if you don't have to follow him? What if he was just an evil, cowardly man who shot himself and all that's in the past? That means it's not too late. Whatever happened in that room with Laura it was your final confrontation with the past. It's all over now. You did a terrible thing when you had no control over your mind or body. But you served your time. There's still a life ahead of you, if you can just believe it. For God's sake, can't something be done? There must be some treatment somewhere. What about America? I haven't got money, but you must have some left. What I do have is time and plenty of cunning. I'll help you. I have nothing else to do with my stupid little life.'

'No, Brenda. I've seen plenty of experts already. It's too late. I'm on borrowed time as it is.'

She blew her nose again. 'All right. I'm sorry. I won't mention it again. So long as you promise you won't do anything to cut short the time you do have, borrowed or not.'

'I promise. But there's something I want you to promise me.'

'What's that?'

'Don't tell anyone what my father did.'

'That may be difficult. But I'll try.'

'You must promise. Not before I go, and not after. You're the only person alive who knows. And you must take the secret with you to your grave.'

'All right. But why?'

'For a start, nobody would believe you. They'll ask where you got the information from. You'll say you got it from me. But she was crazy, they'll say. She was crazy from the age of fourteen. Officially diagnosed. That's why I could never have told anybody when I was alive, even if I had remembered. They'll think you're crazy too. But some mud may stick. The college set up a memorial fund in his name. He left a lump sum to start it off, plus a legacy, a percentage of the posthumous earnings from his books. There's a new lecture theatre named after him. I went there to look at it this morning. I paid a large sum towards the initial costs, anonymously, of course. More importantly, part of the fund goes towards scholarships for poor students. There are a lot of other sponsors, here and in the States. If there were rumours about his conduct, all that could be threatened.'

'All right. You have my word. None of that makes up for what he did, but it would be wrong not to let it continue. How are you feeling?'

'Tired.'

'Let's walk. I want you to tell me more. If you can. Then you can rest.'

'About what?'

'About why you went to see Laura in the first place. Come on, on your feet. The walk will do your good.'

I rose unsteadily. We linked arms and walked slowly along the path between the graves.

'After Michael's death I was desperate to settle his affairs and get away, anywhere. But I couldn't. He and the Furies kept me in the house.'

'When did they first come to you?'

'Before I went abroad. It was when David and I had finished whatever it was we had together. Everywhere I went on my travels they were with me. After Michael died, they were still there. But by then my father was with them. He had become one of them. He was the chief accuser. The only one who spoke. They were keeping me in the house until I confessed my crimes. My father was accusing me of something to do with David. But I didn't understand. My father died before David was born. What possible connection could there be? "The Furies avenge crimes against nature," he said. "Remember me telling you that? You are guilty of such crimes. First me, then David." "What do you mean?" I replied. "I had never been unnatural towards you. I had always loved you. No daughter could have loved a father more. If anything we were too close." "Yes," he said. "That was it. We were too close. Unnaturally close. Your love for me wasn't right. It was not natural." "I don't understand," I said. "What do you mean?" "You know very well what I mean," he said. "And your love for David was unnatural as well. When was it that the Furies manifested themselves to you? Only after you and David had joined your bodies together. They had held back the first time, decided that they would take me first. Now your time has come. You are just like me, corrupt and evil, through and through. Don't you know who he was? Don't you know who his mother was?" "No," I said. "You're wrong. You can go back to Hades and take those odious creatures with you. I can prove you're wrong. I heard her. Laura. The way she had spoken to Michael about David. My child, she had said." "But not her natural child," he replied. "She never said he was her natural child." "All right," I said. "I'll prove it to you. You can hear it from her own mouth. David was my natural child. I'll get her to say those words.'"

'So that was why you went to see her. Not to help her. To save yourself.'

'But she wouldn't say those words. I was doing everything I could to prompt her to say them. But she wouldn't. She couldn't. Because it wasn't true.'

'But surely you didn't kill her for that?'

'No. Why would I do that? But that's still the bit I can't remember.'

'Come on. Let's get away from all these graves. It's getting dark and I'm feeling quite spooky. Where are you staying?'

'Hotel just up the road from here.'

'Let's fetch your things, then mine.'

'Are we going back to Cornwall?'

'No. Portsmouth.'

FORTY-TWO

A pair of semi-detached thirties houses in a quiet suburban street.

Brenda parked the car on the opposite side. She pointed to the houses and nodded to me.

'Those two? Which was my mother's?'

'The one on the left. Number thirty-two. The one I bought for her with Michael's money.'

'It's very small.'

'Large enough for a woman on her own. And she didn't have to stay there. It was only meant to be a temporary arrangement. While she had the abortion and recovered. She could have moved away afterwards. I never thought she'd be here for more than a few weeks. She could have asked Michael to sell the house and give her the proceeds. She could have sold the cottage as well. I had promised to do that for her. She could have got somewhere a lot bigger, if she had wanted.'

'Yes. She could have moved anywhere, so long as it wasn't back to Cornwall. Or anywhere near.'

KEITH JACOBSEN

'That was the agreement.'

'But she stayed. Because she had a child. And a new friend next door. And hopes that one day she and Michael might be together again. She wanted to stay somewhere where Michael knew he could find her, if he changed his mind. I suppose Laura's was the other one in the pair.'

'I suppose so. There's a for sale sign outside.'

The front door of the first house opened. Two girls, about four and six years old, rushed outside and began to play with a doll in a toy pushchair. Then one of them noticed us in the car on the other side of the road. She ran to the door and shouted inside it. Their mother, a plump, red-faced young woman, came to the door and looked over at us, an expression of suspicion and hostility spreading over her face.

'Wait here a minute,' said Brenda. She opened the car and strode over the road with a brisk and business-like air. I watched for a few minutes as she engaged the mother of the two girls in conversation. The girls forgot their game and watched, fascinated by this unexpected arrival of a stranger. The mother smiled and disappeared into the house. Brenda came back to the car and opened the door.

'Come on. We're going inside. I told her we were supposed to meet the estate agents here but they've obviously forgotten the appointment. That lady has a key. She's going to let us in to have a look round. We're prospective buyers, don't forget. The place is for me. You're my niece, come along to help and advise me. I'll be enthusiastic while you pretend to be much more doubtful. Well, are you coming?'

I climbed out of my side of the car and followed her over the road. The other woman was already opening the door to the house which had been Laura's. She smiled broadly at us, clearly pleased at the prospect of a single respectable lady for a new neighbour.

257

'I'll let you go in and have a look round on your own. Then you can make up your own minds. Better than having all that sales chatter in your ear. It's been empty a while so it's a bit bare and bleak. But I'm sure between you you'll be able to make it homely again.' She glared at her children as if to warn them to be on their best behaviour and show what good neighbours they would be. 'When you've finished just knock next door and let me have the key back.'

We walked through into a lounge with a threadbare beige carpet and peeling wallpaper. In one corner of the wall all the paper had been removed, revealing mottled plaster beneath. The only furniture was a low cushionless settee with protruding springs. There was an air of chilly damp in the room.

'I wonder if this is her stuff,' said Brenda. 'What's left of it. I can't imagine anybody's lived here for years. Looks as if she started to decorate. Maybe that was when Michael sent her away.'

'It wasn't her house by then. She was renting it. Or trying to.'

'So the landlord came back and started to peel off the wallpaper. Then he decided not to bother. He put it on the market to get whatever price he can. No wonder nobody wants the place. So this is where Michael first saw his son. Maybe in this very room. Come on. There's somewhere else we have to go. Go and wait in the car. Here are the keys. I need to talk to the lady next door again.'

Twenty minutes later we were outside another building. We had driven away from the city centre and the inner suburbs to the fringe of the countryside. Detached, double-fronted houses were set well back behind tall hedges that bordered long, leafy avenues.

'This is the place, isn't it?' asked Brenda. 'You told me Naomi had said it was once called St Agnes' Hospice. I asked the lady who gave us the key for directions.'

'Yes. This is the place. I can't do this, Brenda.'

'Oh yes you can. Because you have to and you know it. Is it private?'

'Yes. Naomi paid for Laura's room with what little money she had left. Laura had none. Brenda, we can't just go in.'

'Yes we can. Private places need customers, don't they? And that's what we are. You're my niece, remember? And we're looking for a bed for my elder sister who's dying of cancer. The NHS can't do any more for her. And we don't like the conditions in the ward they've got her in. We want somewhere quiet and pleasant where she can spend her last days, don't we? I'll do the talking, don't worry. I'll be very convincing. You don't have to say a word.'

'But what if someone recognises me?'

'They won't. I don't want to be cruel but you have changed. Wrap that shawl closely around your head. Anyway, the chances are that nobody who worked here then is here today.'

A minute later we were standing in the reception area. I stood back, covering my mouth with my shawl, while Brenda talked to a young lady in a crisp grey suit carrying a black folder. The young lady smiled, nodded and disappeared into an office. Brenda ran back towards me and grabbed my arm.

'Come on. She's gone to get someone to show us round. When she comes back she'll think we've changed our minds and gone away. Now, which floor? Which floor, for God's sake?'

'First. Up those stairs.'

She frogmarched me up the stairs. 'Which room?'

'On the right. Just round that corner. Brenda, there'll be somebody in it.'

'If there is there is. We'll just have to see. It might be empty. This way?'

'Yes.'

'Are you sure?'

'Positive. I remember that nursing station we just passed. The nurse was there. I could reach her from the room by pressing a red button.'

'But there was nobody there. So maybe all the rooms along here are empty. It's very quiet here. No staff and no visitors. Which room?'

'That one.'

She knocked gently on the door, then pushed it open. The bed was vacant, the bedding stripped off, the equipment idle against the wall. She pulled me inside.

'Don't worry. If anybody comes in we'll say we lost our guide so we thought we'd look into some of the rooms. Where were you standing, exactly?'

'There. Just by the bedside.'

'This side, nearest the door?'

'Yes.'

'How close? Near enough to touch her? Show me.'

She lay down on the bed and stretched out. 'Was she like this? Where were you when she finished telling you about your mother and David and Michael? Show me.'

I moved towards the bed, stretching out my hands. When I was still a few feet away I pulled them back and clamped them over my mouth. She pushed herself off the bed and grabbed me by the shoulders.

'Madeleine, open your eyes. It's all right. You're safe. He's not here. It's only me. He was never here. You imagined it then and you did the same just now. But it was never real. Not then. Not now.'

I pushed her away and ran towards the door. I was outside

the main entrance and nearly into the street before Brenda caught up with me. She pulled me towards her and into her arms.

'Madeleine, look at me. Don't do this. You mustn't forget again. Not after what you've just done. It's safe now. You can remember. Just tell me. Tell me you remember where we were just now. Tell me you remember what we just did. Look at me. Concentrate. Madeleine, where were we? A few minutes ago? Come on. Talk to me.'

She shook me violently. Gradually, her features came into focus.

'Brenda?'

'Yes. It's me. Where were we just now?'

'In there. We went in so I could remember.'

'Thank God. And did you? Tell me you did, please, because I don't fancy going in and doing it all over again.'

'Yes. I remember. Everything. It's true. You were right. She wasn't there anymore. It was him. He was there in her place, on the bed. The Furies were there too. All around me. Pulling me down to Hell. Then he was gone. She was there again, in his place. I didn't know why I was there or what we had talked about.'

'There'll be time for all that. All that matters now is that you never forget again. Keep trying to remember what happened. Keep going over it in your head. Each time it will be less painful. Come to the car. We'll go back to the hotel now. You'll be in shock for a while. I'll take us back home tomorrow. You can stay with me and I'll keep an eye on you. You've done all you needed to. Just let me take care of you now. Come on. Don't be afraid.'

I was squirming in her arms, gasping, struggling to get away. She held me firmly.

'If you want to have hysterics I don't mind,' she continued, in a soothing voice. 'I'd quite understand if you did. I'm sure I would. But not here in public. You mustn't run away and you mustn't make a scene. I can't let you do that. You mustn't draw attention to yourself. Not here, of all places. Do you understand that? That's right. Come with me now. This is nobody's business but ours. You've been very brave. Far braver than I could have been. I really never thought I would get you to go in there and do what you did. You just need to be brave for a few more moments. Until we get into the car and get the hell out of here. Come on, this way.'

I resisted the tug of her hands. 'I'm all right. I'm not going to get hysterical. But you're not listening to me. I said he took her place. But that was only for a moment. I remember seeing her there again. She was looking at me as if I were crazy. What am I saying? I was crazy. I'm trying to imagine the expression on my face. She must have been totally bewildered. But I never went near her. I went no closer to her than I did with you just now, when you were lying on the bed.'

'What are you saying?'

'I'm not mad now and I'm not hysterical, though I don't expect you to believe me.'

'I do believe you. You imagined he was there for a moment. Then she came back. You thought it was still him. You pulled the pillow out and covered his face with it, to get away from him, to stop the Furies pulling you down.'

'Brenda, you're still not listening to me. The moment she told me who David was I stood up. I turned my back on her. When I turned round again, he was there instead of her, pointing at me and laughing. He had won and I had lost. The Furies had come for me, to take me down to him. I was terrified. I could never have gone up to him or touched him. I wanted to run away but all my limbs were frozen. I tried to scream. Then he was gone and she was there again. But everything had gone blank. I had no idea who she was or what I was doing there. I was still a few feet away from the bed. I was suffocating. All I knew was that I had to get out of there. I left. She was alive when I left the room, staring after me. I remember that now. That image of her staring at me as I left. As clear as you are now. Brenda, I didn't kill her.'

FORTY-THREE

'Did you ring Megan?'
We were in Brenda's cottage. Brenda called out from the kitchen, where she was making the sixth pot of tea of the day although it was barely mid-afternoon.

'Yes,' I replied. 'While you were out walking. Were those fishermen about?'

'Ex-fishermen. These days they wouldn't know one end of a boat from another. I didn't see them. I expect they were in the inn.'

'Good. Megan says she wants to come home tomorrow. Linda and her family are going on holiday so she can't stay any longer.'

Brenda returned to the living room, bearing a tray laden with biscuits and cakes, as well as the teapot, cups and sugar bowl. For a fortnight, since our return from Portsmouth, she had devoted herself to feeding me up, though my appetite was poor and she had had only limited success. We sat down near the fire.

'Do you think she believed you when you rang her last week?'

'About her having to stay away a bit longer because a prowler has been seen in the neighbourhood, which is why I'm staying with you? Yes, I think she believed me. But I'll have to go back tomorrow. Be there for when she gets back. I still think Alan is no threat.'

'Probably not. Just as a precaution I went to have a look inside the observation point while I was out. There's no sign of any of the stuff of his I saw there before. No sign of life at all. I'm sure he's moved on. Hardly surprising. Nobody in their right mind would stay up there now winter's setting in. I reckon he's moved away. Whatever strange ideas he had he's forgotten them. Whoever he is. We had him down as your half-brother. We now know he's not that, but that's all we do know.'

'I still think he's Michael's son. By another woman. Not my mother, not Laura.'

'And I still think he's just a fantasist. How are you feeling?'

'Much better. I'll be all right up at the house. Megan will keep an eye on me. And it really is about time you opened up the gallery again.'

'I'll open it the day after tomorrow. Not that I'm expecting many customers.'

'Why not tomorrow?'

'I'll come round to the house with you. I want to check it out, just in case Alan has moved in permanently. And then get some of the rooms heated and aired. After that, I'll leave you alone, I promise. In the meantime we need to talk about something. I've been waiting for you to recover a bit from what happened in Portsmouth. I think you're ready now. Don't worry. I'm not going to ask you to prove anything. I do believe you.'

'About what?'

'When you said you didn't kill her. So how did it happen that you thought you had?'

'I never admitted it. I told them I couldn't remember. They didn't believe me. They interviewed me for hours. Repeating the same questions but in a different order. Trying to trap me. Putting to me statements they said I had made but which I thought I hadn't but couldn't be sure. In the end they sent for a doctor. A psychiatrist. He had looked up my records. Found I had been detained when I was fourteen and treated in a clinic for drug addicts a few years later. When the police heard about that they changed tack. Kept asking me if I was still on hard drugs. If I made a practice of passing myself off as a relative or friend of hospital patients so I could steal their cash to feed my habit. That line of enquiry didn't come up with anything. I mean, why would I spend half an hour with a patient who didn't have a penny to her name? They called in the psychiatrist again. He asked me about my parents. Whether I had a happy childhood. Yes, of course, I said. My father had died young and I was sad about that. But my mother and I had been very close. I could tell he didn't believe me because he asked me why I had cut myself. I told him it was an accident. I was clumsy. My mother had overreacted. I believed what I was saying but he obviously didn't. So why had I then gone on to hard drugs? I had been young and stupid, that was all. I was experimenting. It just happened. I went to the clinic and sorted it out. He asked me about my relationships with men. I said I had lots of boyfriends and always enjoyed sex. I had just been too busy to settle down, that was all. I sensed all the time that he didn't believe me. Then he asked me why I was always looking across the room, away from him. I laughed. Of course, he couldn't see them. But I could. They were always there, watching me, pointing at me. Who? he asked. The Furies, I said. He had never heard of them. I told him about my father's book, about how they followed you for particularly vile crimes. Were they there because of Laura? he asked. No, I said. Not for anything like that. Other things. What? he asked. But I couldn't tell him.

'I soon put an end to our conversation. I attacked him. There was a particular word that set it off. A trigger. He found it by accident. He wanted to talk about relationships again. It was obvious he wasn't satisfied with what I had been saying. He asked me if there had never been anybody who was really special to me. That was the trigger word. Special. It was my father's word for me. He used it constantly. Especially when he was… Anyway, this psychiatrist said the word by chance and I went for him. There was a table between us. I was trying to climb across it to get to him. I was screaming at him. The door to the interview room was behind him. I suppose he knew from experience always to sit there, so he could escape. He got out of the door and closed it behind him. A doctor and nurse came in. They pinned me to the floor and gave me an injection. When I calmed down they took me back to my cell. The next day I saw the psychiatrist again. He asked me why I had reacted so strongly to that particular word. He was careful not to use it again. I said I had no idea what he was talking about. We never spoke again.'

'If only he had realised he had triggered a memory, momentarily. If only he had worked patiently with you to bring it back again.'

'He did realise, I'm sure of that. But it wasn't his job to cure me. It was to decide whether I was fit to stand trial. He had to make a report for the courts. He diagnosed paranoid schizophrenia with severe amnesia. He said I was obsessed with punitive figures from Greek mythology and had hallucinations that they were pursuing me for crimes I could not remember committing. He said I had a propensity to violence and was a potential danger to myself and others. I should be detained in a secure unit while receiving treatment, including therapy to help me recover my lost memories. They appointed a lawyer to act on my behalf. A young woman, very bored, very anxious to get on with something more interesting and lucrative. She told me what was in the report. She said I should plead guilty to manslaughter on grounds of diminished responsibility. The court would accept that. I agreed. I thought I had killed her. Everybody was telling me I had. So I believed them.'

'I know what I believe. We need another pot of tea.'

I rushed to the door when I heard Megan's knock. She stepped back in surprise.

'Why, Miss Madeleine, and I'm sorry to keep calling you that, but I'm so pleased to see you looking so much better. There's something like a touch of colour in your cheeks and I haven't seen that for a long time. Come here.'

Megan hugged me and we walked over to the taxi to fetch her luggage. When we returned Brenda was standing at the door, with Megan's feather duster in her hand. Megan stopped, open-mouthed.

'It's all right, Megan,' I said. 'Brenda isn't the new housekeeper, and she'll be delighted to let you have your duster back. She's been helping me get the house ready again. You remember I told you I've been staying with her in her cottage, because of the prowler who's been seen around here? She's the only other person I know in this part of the world.'

Megan stepped up and shook hands with Brenda. 'Come to think of it, I do remember you. You knew Mr Wallace, didn't you? You came here a couple of times although I only saw you enter and depart. Mr Wallace told me you had very private things to discuss so I weren't to bring you tea or anything.'

'That's right, Megan. I run the little gallery in Porthhella that Michael bought and did up. It is good to meet you at last. Madeleine is always saying how well you take care of her.'

'In that case I think you've been doing another of my jobs for me, she's looking almost blooming. Thanks anyway. And there were really no need to get the house ready, though I do appreciate it.'

'I've just made some tea,' said Brenda. 'Shall we have it in the lounge or the library? There's fires in both rooms.'

'How about the library?' I said.

'Fine by me,' said Megan.

We let Brenda walk into the library ahead of us. I was about to follow when Megan caught my arm. She whispered into my ear, 'That Brenda. I also remember her from somewhere else. She were at Mr Wallace's funeral, weren't she? Only she stood apart from the rest of us. Never came into the church. You said it were because she hated you. So what's happened since?'

'It's all right,' I whispered back. 'We talked things over. We're good friends now. Nothing to worry about. I'm safe with her. Honestly.'

Megan frowned as if she were not entirely convinced. Then she looked down at the floor by the front door. 'Just a moment. What's this envelope? Looks as if it's been pushed under the door. Addressed to you, Madeleine. Marked personal.'

'Go through to the library and start on the tea. I'll join you in a minute.'

I ran upstairs to my bedroom and tore open the envelope. The writing was familiar, as was the message.

St Olave's, tomorrow, noon. Usual arrangements.

FORTY-FOUR

'You're smelling a bit cleaner, Alan.'
'Thanks. I've had a bath and a change of clothes.'
'I thought the bathroom had been used recently.'
'I found the key to the attic. There were some clothes there that fit me.'
'David's? Your brother's? You kill him and then you wear his clothes. How could you do that?'
'He doesn't need them anymore.'
'Did you steal a key from David, to get into the house?'
'Yes.'
'Why did you attack me that time?'
'I didn't. I was having a look round and I heard a car coming. I turned the lights off.'
'To stop me seeing you.'
'That's right. When you came upstairs you nearly bumped into me. I put my hand over your mouth to stop you screaming. As soon as I got a chance I got out of there. I hope your friend's all right. I didn't mean to knock her over.'

'She's fine. She found out where you were staying. Said you had newspaper articles about me. So why did you come here in the first place? Why did you tell me all that about Michael and my mother?'

'I'm not new to these parts. I've been coming and going for a long time. I saw you with Michael. Looking after him. I wanted you to know what he was really like. The sort of man he was.'

'I know what sort of man he was. Whatever his sins, he was overwhelmed by grief and sickness. I had helped to make him that way. Anyway, it's none of your business.'

'Actually it is.'

'Oh yes, you say you're his heir. Well, if you can prove it you can have the house and the money he left me. I never wanted them.'

'I will prove it.'

'So you keep saying. I used to think I believed you. Now I don't. I don't believe you're Michael's son. I don't believe you killed David. I don't believe you ever knew him. You couldn't have known him. He had lost his mind, forgotten who he was. He would never have talked to you.'

'Why would I pretend I killed him?'

'I don't know. Because it makes you feel important, pretending that for once you had the power of life or death over someone.'

'Yes, I do know what that feels like. More than you could possibly imagine. No more now. Remember the rules? Same time tomorrow.'

'Bugger your rules.'

I turned round. But it was too late. The door had already closed. And I knew that if I ran outside as quickly as my legs would take me I would never find him.

FORTY-FIVE

When I arrived at the church the next day it was empty. I waited for ten minutes. I was about to leave when I noticed something. In the place where I had sat the day before was a blue folder, creased and dirty. On top of it was a piece of paper. A note had been scrawled across it in red felt-tip pen.

> *M. Go to Cove Cottage. Take the picture out of the frame and look at the back. Then come back here. Look at the inscriptions. Read them, don't just look at them. Read these papers. You will understand everything. A.*

I tucked the folder under my arm and walked to the phone box to ring for a taxi.

Brenda had given me a key to her own cottage the day after our return from Portsmouth. Asking the taxi to wait, I let myself in, took the key to Cove Cottage off the hook and walked round to the lane, keeping a sharp lookout for the fishermen. I had thought about dropping into the gallery to let Brenda know what was happening. But what would I tell her? That Alan was back and still playing games with me? She might still think he was a threat and try to persuade me to have nothing further to do with him. It would have been hard to argue with her. But I was too curious to back down now.

Why was he telling me to go to Cove Cottage? Had he been there himself? How did he know about the picture? He could have stolen Michael's key. Michael would have had his own while he was managing the cottage and might have kept it after he sold it. Alan might have discovered it in the blue folder or in the bureau in the library. But how would he have known what the key was for? Maybe there was a label with the address on it. But that still did not explain his interest in the picture or what he was telling me to do with it.

I entered the cottage quietly, holding my breath. It was spotlessly clean and tidy. Brenda was a thorough housekeeper. I shut my eyes as the memories began to crowd in again, David slouched in the armchair on his first visit, me sitting naked in the morning sunlight while he sketched furiously, Michael shaking with grief and anger at the sight of David's sketches. I tiptoed to the top of the stairs, looked down at the two of us naked on the bed, hearing those harsh cries and grunts, David striving desperately to tear from my face and body the images he needed for his nightmarish vision. Back in the upstairs room I saw what I had never seen in life, my mother looking calmly out to sea, aware of the new life growing within her, listening to Brenda's matter-of-fact plan for the destruction of that life.

At last I took the picture down and placed it on the table by the bay window. I saw that scene as well, my mother lying naked on the carpet, smiling at her artist lover, basking in his love and admiration and the skill and care with which she knew he was capturing her happiness, afterwards praising what he had done and insisting he frame it and give it to her, knowing few women were so privileged as to receive such a homage. I eased it out of the frame. I turned the fragile paper over. Some words were written on the reverse, in faded pencil.

For Ceridwen. This is the best of me. Without you I would never have known.

Of course. I had realised eventually that it was my mother. If I had only known Michael was in the habit of writing on the back of his portraits I could have proved it to David at the time and prevented that absurd misunderstanding. But what did this have to do with Alan?

What else did I need to do? Oh yes, look at the inscriptions. What inscriptions? The ones in the graveyard, presumably. No, not look at. Read. I had to read them. As if I hadn't already read them a thousand times. All right, I would humour him. I would go back and read them. Maybe he would be there and I could ask him what this was all about. Carefully, I restored the drawing to the frame and hung it back on the wall. I returned to Brenda's cottage and replaced the key. The taxi was still waiting.

I stood in the churchyard. I had read through them several times. What was it I hadn't spotted? I was on the point of giving up. If this was all a game I had had enough of it and I would tell him so as soon as I got the chance. Suddenly my breath caught in the back of my throat. When I was finally able to release it I swore, slowly and loudly. Then I heard the church door bang against the oak frame. My feet felt like lead. Very slowly I dragged them towards the door, pushed against it and nearly collapsed inside. My heart pounded agonisingly as I crept towards the figure in the front pew and knelt down immediately behind it. The figure did not move.

FORTY-SIX

'**Y**ou killed her. You killed Laura.'

There was a long pause.

'Yes.' The voice still rasping, though a little firmer than when he had spoken to me previously. Unmistakable now.

'And let me take the blame.'

'I killed two birds with one stone. Well, one bird was killed. The other went to prison.'

'Hospital.'

'You were still locked up. I bet it felt like a prison.'

'Go on.'

'What?'

'Tell me why and how.'

'Why? She gave me away to him. She was supposed to look after me. But she gave me to him. I saw her come to the house. She came during the day, more than once, looking round, trying to summon up the courage to ring the bell. Then she came late one night. Went straight up to the door and rang.

So I knew it must have been arranged. He was expecting her. After she had gone and he had gone to bed I broke in. I had done it before. The little window to the pantry in the back. I broke the glass the first time and nobody noticed for months. In the bureau drawer in the library I found a letter from her, asking him if he would agree to see her. There was a reference to me in the letter, and to how she had given me to him. So I knew it was definitely her. I couldn't be absolutely sure, just from seeing her. She had changed a lot. But now I had the evidence. I felt Fate had brought us together again and put the evidence into my hands. Did you ever find it, the letter, I mean?'

'No. He must have burned it.'

'There was an address in Portsmouth. I stole some money as well. He always kept cash in the bureau. I don't suppose he ever noticed any of it was gone. I took enough to get me a shave and a change of clothes, and to get me to Portsmouth and live cheaply for a while. I went to the address and made some enquiries around the neighbourhood. I found out she was in a hospice. Found out where and which room. It wasn't difficult. Then I became invisible. I'm good at that too. Who's the one person who never gets noticed in a place like that? That's right, the maintenance man, the odd-job gaffer. I borrowed some overalls from the maintenance room in the basement, and a clipboard and a box of tools. Drifted around the place trying to look busy. Nobody stopped me. Nobody gave me a second glance. I never intended to kill her. I just enjoyed popping my head round the door from time to time, watching her die. One day I would go in there, pretending to do a job, and take the opportunity to tell her who I was, tell her what I thought of her and what she had done. But it would need to be near the end. Just when she was trying to settle down to a peaceful death, come to terms with her past, make her peace with whatever god she believed in. I would take that away from her. I thought she had no right to that. So I waited.'

'Then I came to see her.'

'Yes. What a surprise that was. I couldn't imagine what you were doing there. If you're bringing some guilt money from him, you're too late, I thought. I saw the two of you coming along the corridor. You and that other woman. I had seen the other woman before, the one who came with you. Some sort of relation, I presume. When I saw you I nipped into an empty room, leaving the door open. After a few minutes I saw the other woman come past again. I came out and walked along the corridor, past the nurse, past the room. The nurse never saw me. She was on the phone, chatting. I looked in through the window in the door and saw you in there with her. I went on to the end of the corridor. There's a door there, leading to a fire escape. I saw you come out. I slipped quietly into the room. She was wide awake. I told her who I was. I waited to see that she understood, that she believed me. I mean, she wouldn't exactly have recognised me if we had passed in the street, would she? I held her hand. I asked her if she believed me when I told her who I was. Then I told her things only the two of us could have known. When I saw it in her eyes, the terror, the realisation, then I killed her. It was very easy. She went out like a light. Another day or two and she would have been dead anyway.'

'You could easily have been caught. Anybody could have come in.'

'So what? If they'd caught me with the pillow in my hand I would have said I was doing a job in the room and she had asked me for help in making her more comfortable. If they'd caught me pressing it down on her it wouldn't have mattered. That's the thing about being dead. You can do anything and you're not bothered about being caught.'

'Michael forced her to give you to him. It broke her heart. She had already paid. Did that never occur to you? No. You were like one of those avenging angels from the Old Testament. You said nothing afterwards, when they arrested me. You hated me as well.'

'I hated Michael. You had an affair with him. So I hated you.'

'I lied to you about that. To finish things between us. You were so stupidly jealous.'

'Then why did you go and live with him?'

'He needed somebody. I owed him. That was all.'

'He killed my mother. Don't you hate him for that? She was your mother too.'

'There's no proof he killed her.'

'I showed you that letter. How else do you explain what happened?'

'I think she may have come to see him at the house. To confront him about you. For some reason she rushed out onto the path. She lost her way and fell.'

'Possible. But you think there was more to it than that, don't you? I can tell by the tone of your voice. Maybe he followed her. That's what you think, don't you?'

'All right. I think he followed her. But I don't believe he meant to kill her.'

'Maybe he didn't try too hard to save her. It amounts to the same thing.'

'It would do, in your book. The book of wrongs done to you. The book you think gives you the right to sweep through the world with a sword of vengeance in your hand. Was it only because of Michael that you hated me?'

'You never told me who I was. That was really sick, letting me fuck you. I was your brother, for God's sake. I suppose you had tried everything else.'

'I didn't know.'

'He must have told you.'

'No. He was going to tell us both later, when we were friends. Not that there was much chance of that.'

We sat in silence for several minutes. At last he spoke again, nearly whispering so that I had to lean forward to catch his words.

'I never thought they would lock you up. I just wanted to cause you some grief. Kill two birds, as I said. I thought you would tell them she had been fine when you left. They might not have believed you. But with no motive I didn't think they would charge you. I wasn't to know you'd forget and they'd lock you up for being crazy.'

'But you didn't come forward.'

'Who would have believed me? I don't officially exist, remember. You can kill me if you want. I've got a penknife here. Not exactly a sword of vengeance but it would do. I'd let you. I'd show you exactly where to put it. We couldn't do it in church, of course. We'd have to go outside.'

'Don't be so bloody ridiculous. Do you think I'm like you? Do you think everybody is like you? Obsessed with taking revenge on everybody who's hurt them in some way? Do you really think I care now? I'm dying, for God's sake.'

'I was already dead. But that didn't stop me. Okay, have it your way. Don't say I didn't give you the chance.'

'After our quarrel, when you thought that picture was of me, and after I had gone, you went back. You knew where to find the key. You had remembered that when he used a live model he would sometimes put the name on the back. You expected to see my name there. Instead you saw hers. My image but her name. Like mother like daughter. Or two peas in a pod, as Megan used to say. Then you began to remember her. Images from your early childhood. I had reminded you of her, subconsciously. Of her and your hatred of her, for leaving you. What I discovered from Laura you found out from that picture. Michael was your father. You always knew that. But now you realised Ceridwen was your mother. And mine. Like me, you found that knowledge too much to bear. So you did what I did. You forgot. Did that happen right away?'

'I don't know. I wandered around, on the headlands, through the fields and woods, just walking. I slept under hedges. I was having a slow breakdown, I suppose. I forget to eat. In the end I think I forgot everything. I found myself by the house but I didn't know why I had gone back there. Megan saw me from the window. She seemed to know who I was. I was vaguely aware that I had a connection to the place but I didn't know their names. I didn't even know my own. Gradually it all came back. But I kept it from them. I didn't want to give him the satisfaction of knowing I had returned. I didn't want to give him the chance to take me over again and give me another bloody breakdown.'

'I can't believe I'm hearing this. You said he was a useless artist because he didn't understand human nature. Do you really think you do? Couldn't you see he was completely broken by what had happened? Did you really imagine he could behave in the same way again?'

'Maybe not. But I couldn't really be sure what would happen if he knew I had recovered. I couldn't take the chance. But what if I killed myself? He would have no power over me then. And that might really make him sorry. So I planned it, down to the last detail. Even the exact spot. I knew the earth was very thin there. You could see the overhang from the path on the other side. And I knew it was close to where she died. I thought that would make it more poetic somehow. The only problem was that once I was dead I wouldn't be able to see how he would react. Then I had a brainwave. I could stage my death and disappear. Come back and see. Haunt him like a ghost. Not many people get that chance. To see how other people react to their deaths. So I dislodged the earth. It was very dangerous, of course. I might have fallen. But that was my first plan, anyway, so I didn't care. When the earth fell but I was still there, I decided it was Fate again. I hung around and watched him. I enjoyed that. I saw you come back. I was so bloody angry with you for that. I wanted him to die alone. After I had disposed of Laura and they had taken you away I had no reason to hang around. I took to the road. Went up north. Did odd jobs here and there. Mostly I just walked and stole. Then I read about you being released. Thought I would come back and make contact. You know the rest.'

'So why did you decide to end your little game today?'

'I thought you would have guessed long before this. Then I realised you weren't going to, not unless I helped you. I also realised you were ill. I didn't want you to go while still believing you killed her. I hated you but not that much. And I wanted to say sorry. Not for killing her but for letting you take the blame. Give you the chance to take revenge.'

'And have you finished now? I mean, they're all dead, aren't they? All the people who did you wrong. Including me. Or is there anybody else I don't know about?'

'No. I'm finished. Just one more thing. What was she like?'

'Our mother? I hardly knew her. She wasn't like me, I can say that for certain. Only to look at. She was wild, impulsive, passionate, trusting, naïve. Things like that.'

'No. Definitely not like you. It was her fault as well, wasn't it?'

'What do you mean?'

'About us. She never told you about me. So when you came down here after her you didn't know she hadn't just left you a cottage. You didn't know she had left you a younger brother hanging around the place as well. So why didn't she?'

'We'd fallen out. We were leading completely separate lives. As I said, we were different. What will you do now?'

'I have a few plans. Nothing that need concern you. And no, nobody else is going to die or get hurt. You won't see me again. No more notes. No more secret meetings. I'll disappear again. Close your eyes.'

I did so. I sensed him rise and glide past me. With a single motion I pushed myself off the bench and into the aisle. I rushed towards the back of the church but he was already closing the door behind him. I pushed my weight against it but it would not move. I swore. I put my eye to the keyhole but could see nothing through it. I put my mouth to the hole and shouted, 'It's all right. I won't follow you. I won't look at you. I just want you to listen to me. For a few minutes. You won't have to say anything. Just stay there. I'll stay here. I won't try to open the door. I promise. Just knock on the door to show you understand.'

I heard him moving, his breath rasping, then a harsh grating sound. The key was in the lock. That was why I could not see through it. Now he was turning it, slowly, effortfully, finally forcing it into place with a heavy clunk. I turned round, leaned against the inside of the door and sank to the floor, the cold of the stone spreading through my body.

'All right. Have it your way. I don't suppose you intend to leave me locked in here. So I'll wait here until you unlock it. The door's heavy. By the time I get it open you'll be away. In the meantime I'll say what I'm going to say. You can listen to me or not. That's up to you. But I can't just let you go without saying it. You see, we are bound together. We're brother and sister. You can run away but nothing can alter that. You'll take me with you and leave yourself behind with me. So why do you keep disappearing? I won't look at you. I won't want to. I don't want to see the face I made. Any more than I can bear to look at my own. Can you hear me?'

I heard a slight scraping movement on the other side. He was sitting down as well.

'You were right to hate me,' I continued. 'But not for the reason you think. Not because of Michael. Because of us. You said you were sorry. Well, so am I. Sorry we ever met. Sorry I wasn't the one you needed. Sorry I wasn't the one who could see you were drowning and pull you out. I wasn't the one who would set you on the road to your brilliant, arrogant future, the one who would somehow prise you away from him without destroying either of you. You might have met someone like that. Instead you found me, an unknown sister on a lifelong mission to destroy herself. We each of us knew from the start it was wrong. We knew the only way ahead was madness. But we could do nothing about it, not once it had started. I could have prevented it. I should have suspected. I should have asked Michael what was going on, refused to put up with his lies and evasions, insisted on the truth. I should have made him tell me what he and our mother really were to each other, and who this so-called nephew really was. I didn't because I needed you. I needed you to help me finish off the task I had set myself. So I was blind, deliberately blind. I know you won't understand. I'm only beginning to understand it myself. I was beyond saving. But you could have been saved. So what right did I have to drag you down with me? Are you listening?'

Again there was a sound of movement, heavy, shuffling, fidgeting.

'I can tell you're still there. So I'll carry on. I tried to set you free in the end. I thought it might still be all right for you. That horrible stuff you did with me as a model... maybe you saw that as your first rebellion. Yes, I was really thinking that. Or trying to convince myself of it, against all my instincts. Perhaps you would move on, break with him altogether, find your own way. It was crazy, wasn't it? Because you knew something was wrong, terribly wrong. Of course you did. You knew we had both done something dreadful. Something neither of us could live with and stay sane. And soon enough you found out exactly what it was. How could you move on from that? I was still blind, still under the illusion you could be saved. When I heard you had fallen from the cliffs, I was shocked but I wasn't really surprised. I kept having these strange dreams. I must have known something had happened. I wrote to Michael, asking him how you were. Why would I have done that if I hadn't known, deep inside? I had tried to get away from you, from us, from our past. But I had taken you and all of that with me. Of course I had. I came back because I had to talk to Michael about it. When I looked after him it was a sort of attempt to make it up to both of you. As if I ever could.'

I heard him rise to his feet, clumsily. The key made a groaning sound in the lock.

'Wait a minute. Not yet. Don't open the door. I haven't finished. What you did to me wasn't important. I couldn't remember any reason for killing Laura. I couldn't even remember what happened. They would have locked me up sooner or later. You didn't do that to me. I did it to myself. And I was already dying, starting to rot away. Don't be sorry about letting me take the blame for her death. Be sorry about the ones you hurt who didn't deserve it. I am. Because I helped to make you what you are now, and that means I'm also responsible for the things you have done. Promise me it's all over now. Is it? Will you find some sort of peace, now you've seen them suffer, now they're all dead? You can really be free, now, can't you?'

I thought I heard a sobbing sound, followed by a metallic

grinding noise. The door yielded suddenly behind me and I fell backwards. When I had scrambled to my feet and turned round the porch was empty. As I knew the churchyard would be, and the hamlet, and the path to the sand dunes and the pilgrims' way across the fields. I knew that wherever I looked he would be nowhere to be found.

FORTY-SEVEN

———————————

Megan and Brenda were taking tea in the lounge, which had belatedly caught some of the weak late afternoon sun, when I walked in. I had the blue folder under my arm. I noticed that Megan had been crying. She was still dabbing her eyes when she looked up and smiled.

'I closed the gallery at midday,' said Brenda, in response to my enquiring glance. 'Nobody over the doorstep all morning. Thought I'd come over and talk to Megan. Tell her everything, as we agreed. I've just finished. She tells me she always believed you never killed Laura.'

'Which is easy enough for me,' said Megan. 'But what makes me so happy now is that you believe it, Madeleine.'

'I didn't leave out what I told you about me and your mother,' said Brenda. 'Now she knows what a monster I am, and she still made tea for us.'

'I don't judge people, Brenda,' said Megan. 'That's never been my role in life. And I'm happy to be friends with anyone who's been such a friend to Madeleine these past couple of weeks.'

Brenda looked closely at me and frowned. 'What's the matter with you? You look as if you've seen a ghost.'

I sat down and took the cup which Megan handed to me. 'You never said a truer word, Brenda.'

'What's that you've got there?'

'Some interesting papers. I looked through them on the way back here.'

'Back from where?'

'St Olave's.'

'Yes, you said you were going to visit your mother's grave. So where did you get that?'

Megan had said nothing but stared intently at the folder. Then she spoke. 'Just a minute, Brenda. Madeleine, I can see that it's a bit soiled and faded, but would I be right in saying that that there folder is blue?'

'Yes, Megan. Just like the one Michael asked you to destroy. Only you couldn't find it. Why? Because someone had removed it. And that someone has just given it back to me.'

'You didn't go to see the grave, did you?' said Brenda, disapprovingly. 'You went to see Alan again. That was what that note under the door was all about. The one you thought I hadn't noticed. So what did he have to say for himself this time?'

'First of all, just one question, to both of you. Did you know that no body was ever found?'

Brenda stared at me. It was Megan who answered.

'You mean Master David? Of course. They searched everywhere. All along the coast from here to Porthcurno and to St Ives in the other direction. That were the worst thing about it for Mr Wallace, not being able to bury him. The coroner refused to declare him to be presumed drowned because he hadn't been at sea when he disappeared. He said it were possible he were killed by the fall and his body carried out to sea on the next tide. But until the body were found he couldn't be sure of the cause of death, or even that he were dead. So Mr Wallace knew that unless the body turned up he would have to wait to have him declared legally dead. And he knew he would never live that long.'

'It was in the local papers,' said Brenda. 'But you were abroad at the time.'

'It's not that unusual, round these shores,' said Megan. 'Why, young Tom, the son of one of those fishermen, were lost in a storm off those headlands and never found. There've been about half a dozen such cases in my time here.'

'But didn't Michael tell you?' asked Brenda.

'When I first came back I think he was trying to, but I never gave him the chance. I asked where I should go to pay my last respects. He told me to go to St Olave's. That's all he said. I can well understand why he wouldn't want to talk about it afterwards.'

'So what has this to do with those papers?'

'Look.' I handed the folder to Brenda. She leafed through the contents, her jaw slackening, her breathing becoming increasingly laboured. Megan looked from one of us to the other, a bewildered expression on her face. At last Brenda put the folder down on the table.

'Bloody hell,' she said. 'I need a brandy. Anyone else?'

'Yes please,' I said.

'Megan?'

'What? Oh, no thanks, Brenda. Bit early for me.'

Brenda returned within a minute with two glasses of brandy and handed one to me. We looked at each other.

'Where is he now?' she asked.

'He's gone. He won't bother us again.'

'Hang on a moment,' said Megan. 'You were talking about Master David a minute ago—'

'No, Megan. I never mentioned that name.'

Megan sank back in her chair. 'That tramp you were just telling me about, Brenda? The one who claims he's Mr Wallace's son?'

'That's right,' I said. 'He was christened Hywel. Michael renamed him David. And he decided to call himself Alan.'

'Oh, my God,' said Megan. 'Three in one. A bloody holy trinity, pardon my French. Could I change my mind about that brandy?'

'You certainly can.' Brenda left the room again.

I turned to Megan. 'That folder Michael asked you to destroy. It contains some very interesting things. There are two birth certificates. One in French, issued in Lyon in 1967 in the name of David Wallace, the parents' names entered as George and Sandrine Wallace.'

'So Mr Wallace really did have a nephew.'

'Oh yes. He told me George and Sandrine died in a car crash. His story was that David was not with them. But according to the local newspaper article also in the folder, all three of them were killed instantly.'

'That's what I thought it meant,' said Brenda, returning at that moment with Megan's brandy. 'Only my French isn't as good as yours.'

'Michael was in France for some time, sorting out their affairs,' I continued. 'Presumably the deaths were not reported in the English press or the cuttings would have been in the folder as well. While he was there he must have had a lot of time to think. There was plenty to think about. He had a son who was David's age, one whose identity had to remain secret or it would cause a scandal. Not just that. If the news got out, it would hurt Celia terribly. She had never been able to have a child of her own. And Celia's parents would have withdrawn the financial support they had been giving to Michael. It would have been a disaster for him. But at that time he could not be sure he could keep it a secret.'

'You think he kept it from Celia and her parents that the real David was dead?' asked Brenda.

'Yes. He might have told them David had stayed in France, in the care of Sandrine's relatives. They would have had no reason to doubt the story. He brought his birth certificate back with him, having no doubt destroyed his death certificate. Already he was building a new identity for Hywel in case he needed it later. When he first saw Hywel, at Laura's house, he would have begun to plan the transfer of identity right away. In case Laura threatened to disclose who Hywel really was. It wouldn't just be his word against hers. He would have documentary evidence he was his nephew called David. But there was no danger of Laura talking to Celia or her parents. She knew nothing about them. She had no idea what a powerful weapon she had in her hands. If only she had and she had dared to use it. And a new identity would be essential for his longer-term plan, to bring Hywel, or David as he was by then, to live with him.'

'But by the time that happened Celia and her parents were dead,' said Brenda. 'He didn't need a cover for him.'

'That's right. But he wasn't to know that when he started to hatch his plans. And Hywel had already been told he was really David so Michael had to continue with the deceit.'

'What's the other birth certificate?' asked Megan.

I opened the folder and picked up a faded beige envelope.

'This contains Hywel's. The full name is given as Hywel Williams, mother Ceridwen Williams, no name entered for the father. Place of birth, Portsmouth.' I took out another piece of paper. 'This is my mother's final will, appointing

Laura Peters, née James, as her executor and legal guardian of Hywel Williams in the event of her death. There's also a letter from my mother to Michael, telling him she had decided not to go ahead with the abortion. Just imagine the shock of reading that your own father originally wanted you aborted. No wonder he hated him. What else? A letter from Laura to my mother, addressed to her at Cove Cottage, saying Hywel was well but missing his mother. Wanting to know when she is coming home.'

'Poor woman,' said Megan. 'She never did go home. Never saw her son again. And Laura, waiting for her all that time, wondering what had happened, wondering what to tell the boy.'

'I think Michael wanted you to destroy the folder for my sake,' I said. 'By the time he decided to do it he was too frail to get up to the attic on his own. And it was vital that I didn't suspect its existence. It wasn't until he was in hospital that he could talk to you on your own, without me being around, and swear you to secrecy. The secret he wanted to take with him to the grave was that the boy I thought was his nephew was my own half-brother. He did intend to tell us one day who we were. Then he found out what we had been doing together. That was the shock that destroyed Michael, even more than the fatal accident, as he supposed it.'

'I suppose he became Alan after that, when everybody thought he was dead,' said Brenda. 'A new beginning. Yet another new identity. You went up to the attics to look for the folder, Megan, but Alan found it first.'

'Michael got the will and Hywel's birth certificate from Laura,' I said. 'After my mother's death, he must have gone down to the cottage, looking for things he didn't want the police to find. I don't suppose he thought they'd suspect foul play. He just didn't want them to make the connection in case it all came out, my mother being his lover, their having a son. He found the letter from Laura. That was how he knew Laura's address. He went to see her to find out what she knew about him, and also to check out my mother's house in case there was anything there to connect her with him. When he was talking to Laura he saw Hywel. That changed everything. He decided he wanted him with him. He already had David's identity documents from France. To complete the transfer he took from Laura all the documents which could prove who Hywel really was. Some he needed to keep against the day he might want to restore Hywel's identity to him. Others he kept because he could not bring himself to destroy anything connected to my mother. Not until the end, when he saw it had to be done.'

'But wasn't he taking a risk?' asked Brenda. 'What if the police searched the attics?'

'Not really. The stuff was much safer here than in the cottage. They'd have needed a warrant to search this house, which means they'd first need to have reasonable grounds for suspecting he was involved in her death. He did everything he could to satisfy himself that nobody would connect him with my mother any more closely than he was ever prepared to admit. He contacted Laura to find out if he might need to buy her silence. He attended the inquest, to confirm that the police did not suspect foul play.'

'He could have done that by reading the verdict in the papers. Wasn't he taking a risk just by being there?'

'He had another reason to attend. He wanted to check that there were no family members around who might cause trouble by asking awkward questions. He must have had a real shock when he saw me. Almost as bad a shock as you had, Brenda, that time in the café when we first met. But he kept his head. He befriended me, saw I was out of my depth, took over the arrangements for the funeral. With my agreement he buried her where he knew he would lie beside her in his turn. He brought you, Megan, with him to the funeral, knowing you would help to put me at my ease. He must have been so relieved by what he saw of me. I obviously couldn't have cared less about my mother's death and I couldn't wait to get away. He knew it would be safe to rent out the cottage rather than sell it. I wouldn't interfere. I had my life to get on with, such as it was. Many years later, when that life had finished, I returned and became part of his plans.'

'You mean, to bring together two siblings who, through an unfortunate chain of circumstances, had up to then been unknown to each other,' said Brenda. 'A final link in the chain of restoration he had forged to make it up to your mother.'

'That's right. When he found out we had met and were in a physical relationship the only thing that mattered then was to maintain the secrecy to the end of his life and beyond.'

'Tell us what happened at the church,' said Brenda.

'I saw him there yesterday. I asked him why he had followed me and spoken to me. He told me he had watched me return to the house and look after Michael. He wanted me to think Michael had killed my mother, so I would realise what sort of man he was.' Megan gasped. 'I think he really believed it. The only evidence he had was a note from my mother to him, asking him to meet her. This was just before she died. He showed me the note. It must have been in the folder as well. It only proved that she had come here to put pressure on him. But he took it as proof positive that he had killed her. He also claimed to have killed the boy we all knew as David, out of jealousy.'

'And you never guessed who he were?' asked Megan.

'No. Don't forget, I always thought that David was buried at St Olave's. And as Alan he never showed me his face. He disguised his voice as well. With the life he's been leading, I probably wouldn't have recognised him anyway.'

'How did he say he killed David?' asked Brenda.

'You remember that the earth at the top of the headland was dislodged? Everybody thought he was standing on it and it collapsed beneath him. His story to me was that he dared David to go near the edge, pushed him over, then dislodged the earth himself to make it look like an accident. Which was all true, except that nobody went over. That wasn't the only revenge he got. He told me he saw Laura come here to visit Michael. He thought he recognised her as the woman who had given him away to Michael. He broke in and found some papers which confirmed his suspicions. He found out where she was spending her final days. He planned his revenge on her. He didn't intend to kill her at first. Just watch her die, after reminding her what she had done. Then he saw me visit her.'

Brenda's jaw dropped. 'My God,' she said at last. 'I never doubted you when you said you remembered leaving her alive in that room. But I couldn't get past the question, if you didn't kill her then who did? Who might have had a motive? The answer was always the same. Nobody.'

'Nobody living, certainly,' I said. 'But somebody we all thought dead had a motive all right.'

'And he admitted it?' asked Megan.

'Yes. He saw me visit her. He took the opportunity to kill her and let me take the blame, because of my involvement with Michael.'

Megan shook her head. 'Oh dear. I wanted you to be proved innocent. So your name could be cleared. But not to know it were him taking revenge on both of you.'

'And because he doesn't really exist, and nobody else but me heard him and nobody will ever find him again, we can't use his confession to clear my name publicly. But that doesn't matter to me now.'

'Well,' said Megan, 'I'll tell anybody who'll listen that there were someone who confessed, even though I won't be able to say exactly who. Brenda told me how you found out he were your brother. But did he know?'

'I was coming to that bit. Today there was nobody in the church when I went there the first time. Only that folder left for me, with a note to go to Cove Cottage. In the note he told me to take the picture out of its frame and look at the back. This was a picture Michael had done of my mother, only I hadn't recognised her. Before I left to go abroad David saw the picture, decided it was me and decided that I was also having an affair with Michael. Which I wasn't. I denied it at first. Then I admitted it, so we could finally put an end to a relationship that was destroying both of us. Today I looked at the back of the picture and there was my mother's name on it. I had realised it was her long ago. So what was Alan trying to do, leaving me a note telling me to look at the back? Then I realised he was telling me that that was what David did. Don't forget that at this stage I still thought they were two different people. David had gone back there on his own. I had gone. He was looking at a picture he was totally convinced was of me. But now he knew it was of my mother. He remembered that Michael used to put the names of his models on the back of his portraits. He took it out of the frame to prove it was me. He not only realised his mistake. He realised this was the woman Michael had loved. Another woman he remembered as a child. Remembered her hair, her laugh. He stood there, looking at a picture of his mother and his sister, two images in one. No wonder his mind broke.'

'He were a shadow of what he had been,' said Megan, shaking her head sadly. 'Didn't even know who we was.'

'So when did you realise who Alan was?' asked Brenda.

'Not in the cottage. I hadn't read the folder. I was just carrying it around. I still thought that he was telling me what David had told him. I couldn't understand why David would tell a stranger so much. The note he had left me in the church also told me to read the inscriptions in the churchyard. So I went back to do that. I realised when I read them properly for the first time. His is the only one on that stone that doesn't say "here lies". For him it's a memorial stone, not a burial stone. How blind and stupid could I be? I went into the church. He was there. That was when he told me he killed her. He said he was sorry for letting me take the blame.'

Megan was looking out of the window and scratching her head. Then she turned round, a little smile playing across her features. 'This picture you were talking about. I haven't seen it myself. Could you describe it?'

'Of course,' I said. 'It's an ink drawing. Nude. The face isn't visible. It's beautiful. Mr Wallace thought so too. On the back he wrote that it was the best of him.'

'Really? How big is it?'

I drew an outline in the air.

'That's really interesting. There's just the one like that, is there? No more?'

'No more. Just the one.'

Megan stood up. Her smile was now broad.

'Feeling fit, ladies? I'm going into the library to fetch the key. Then we're all going up to the attic. I've got a surprise for you.'

FORTY-EIGHT

The door at the top of the narrow staircase to the attics gave onto a small landing, beyond which there were two further doors. Megan pushed open the first door and stepped inside. We followed.

'Where did he hide the key, Megan?' asked Brenda.

'In a secret drawer in the bureau. There's a lever which opens it, hidden at the back of one of the pigeon-holes. You have to feel for it. It took me ages to find it. I thought at first it didn't exist. I wondered if he'd imagined it. This is the room where he kept his secrets. Just take a look at these and you'll see what I mean.'

We followed her to a corner where a pile of framed drawings had been stacked. Between us we laid them out neatly on the floor. We looked at each in turn, then at each other.

'Eleven,' said Brenda at last. 'All the same size as the one in the cottage. All framed in the same way. All ink drawings of a nude woman, her face invisible. Eleven and the one in the cottage makes twelve.'

'Did he frame them himself?' I asked.

'Oh yes. He was very skilful. I imagine there's still wood and glue and framing equipment in one of these cupboards.'

'That's right,' said Megan. 'That one over there. I searched through here like a fine toothcomb, looking for that folder as had disappeared from the face of the earth.'

Like David's drawings of me, I thought. Only these were tender and intimate. As eloquent of Michael's love as David's had been of his hatred. This room had been a shrine to my mother.

'You were right, Megan,' I said. 'It would have been unthinkable to destroy these.'

'Nothing else he did could compare with these,' said Brenda, almost to herself. 'To the world he gave admirable, meticulously crafted, lifeless artifices. But when love inspired him to real greatness at last, he hid the results away.'

'Except for the one in the cottage,' I said. 'He made a set of twelve. He chose one, his favourite, as a special present to the woman who had been his secret muse. One which he felt belonged in the cottage because out of the whole set it was closest to being a record of what they were to each other.'

'How come it's still there?' asked Megan. 'Why didn't he bring it back here, to go with the others?'

'He did,' I said. 'After her death. Then when I went to live in the cottage he decided it would be safe to put it back. It might even have been part of his plan to tell David and myself eventually about his affair with her. He brought it round the day after I arrived. I never looked at it. I left it unopened in a cupboard in the kitchen. David found it when he was looking for a fresh bottle of whisky, after he had finished off all the others I had.'

'But why didn't he take it back when he sold the cottage?'

'I can answer that,' said Brenda, standing up straight

and shaking herself. Up to that point, she had been lost in contemplation of the drawings, barely listening to us. 'Someone told the new owners I was in the market for cleaning jobs around the village. I went round to see them. I was surprised to see it still there, as you can imagine. I told them I knew Michael and I thought I had seen the picture in his house. Had he sold it to them? They told me he had offered it to them on long-term loan, on condition that it stayed in the cottage. He said it had a particular sentimental value but only if it stayed there. If they sold the cottage they had to return it to him. They had agreed but I could tell they were puzzled. They weren't bothered about pictures in general or that one in particular.'

'We have to bring them back together, as a set,' I said. 'Put them in your gallery, or sell them on to another one. Surely they'll force the art world to reappraise his work.'

Brenda stroked her chin. 'He's almost forgotten now. These really could put him back on the map. The loan agreement would have expired with Michael's death. So the one in the cottage belongs to you now. As they all do.'

I shook my head. 'No, Brenda, they're yours. They may be of my mother, but you're the one who knows how to make best use of them.'

'I'll try. About the one in the cottage. I don't think we even need to bother the owners. I'll slip it out quietly, without telling anybody. I've got a gouache of his of about the same size, a sunset, somewhere in my cottage. I'll put it in its place. They won't even notice. I'll need to think about what to do with the set. I could devote a wall to them in the gallery. But it's so cramped there. And it rather goes against the spirit of the place. It's always been about giving space to young artists at the beginning of their careers. While I'm thinking about it they can stay here. They're as safe here as anywhere.'

'What's in the other room, Megan?'

'Nothing much. Just rubbish, really. You can have a look if you like.'

We returned to the landing and Megan pushed open the other door. Within were two small rooms with a connecting door. One was a bedroom. It contained a single bed, two chairs, a wardrobe and a dressing table. All were covered with sheets. The other room was a studio. An easel had been placed beneath the skylight, a large sheet of white paper pinned to it. Faint charcoal lines swept across it. I stared at it. I could not discern any recognisable shapes. It was as if a child had picked up the charcoal to play with it.

'He was here too,' I said. 'Alan, I mean. Maybe he came in here after he had picked up the blue folder from next door. He drew these lines, wondering if they might show any vestiges of his former gifts. As David.'

'There's no trace of them, if he did,' said Brenda. 'He must have realised that. What did he feel, I wonder? Sorrow, relief, both at once?'

'I don't think he has any yearnings left for what he once was. He told me he had dabbled in art in the past but didn't have a clue now. That was his disguise speaking but I honestly think that is how he really feels about it.'

There were several cupboards in the room. I opened them while the others looked on. In one I found dried-out paints, crayons, inks, pens, brushes and paper. Another contained randomly stacked drawings and paintings. No toys or child's books. Not here. Not anywhere in the house. I noticed that Megan was crying.

'Let's go downstairs,' I said.

'He really loved her, didn't he?' said Megan. We were in the library. Megan had just returned the key to its hiding place. 'I could tell as soon as I saw them.'

'But you didn't know about her and Michael when you first saw them,' I said.

She smiled. 'Oh, I knew it were your mum he had drawn. That was why he wanted them destroyed. And why I knew I couldn't destroy them. I couldn't recognise her from the drawings, of course. Not directly. But I knew it had to be her.'

'You said you never met her. How did you know?'

'It's true I never met her. But she did come to the house.'

'Go on,' said Brenda, half-glancing at me.

'Well, as you know, my bedroom is at the back of the house nearest the sea. Once I've retired to bed there's no way as I'd normally hear if anybody came to the door. But that night there were a storm, and I were a bit scared, to tell the truth, with the wind rattling the windowpanes like a whole host of devils. So I came down again and went into my parlour and made myself a cup of tea. I must have dozed off in my armchair. That side of the house is sheltered from the sea winds so it weren't so noisy. Then I were woken up by this sound of knocking and shouting. A woman's voice. I were under instructions not to open the door at night if I ever did hear anything, so I stayed put. But I did allow myself a little peep out of the window. I saw her there. She had only a thin coat on top, nothing on her head. She were dripping with the rain, shivering, her hair plastered down, a wild look in her eyes. I heard Mr Wallace pulling back the bolts. He said something on the lines of God, it's you, what the hell are you doing here, I told you never to come here and all sorts of stuff like that.'

'Did he call her by name?'

'Yes. Ceridwen. I heard it as clear as a bell. She said she had to come. He had given her no choice, and she had to have it out with him and with Mrs Wallace if need be. Then they was in here and I couldn't catch everything they said. Later on the voices was raised so I could hear something. She were saying something about a child, their son, how he had a right to know his father. Then I heard the door slam, a lot of crying and shouting, and she had rushed out of the front door. I heard her footsteps on the gravel outside, leading to the coastal path. He said he were going after her and I heard his footsteps following her. I thought as they must be both crazy going out onto the path in those conditions. About an hour later Mr Wallace came back. Normally I would have gone to see how he were, got some dry things for him, made sure he had a good strong brandy so he didn't catch pneumonia. But I didn't want him to know I were not in my bedroom. I didn't want him to know I had heard. So I stayed put. Mrs Wallace must have been in the hall. He said there'd been an accident. That's all. I couldn't catch everything she said in reply. Something to the effect that whatever he had done his secret was safe. So long as he never mentioned... well, I'm afraid she used some rather bad language.'

'Go on, Megan,' we said in unison.

'So long as he never breathed a word in this house or anywhere else about that whore or her bastard child. Then Mr Wallace said he had to go out again, urgently. Over to the village. And the next day he would need to go to Portsmouth. She said something like, fine, do what you have to. Just remove all traces of her from the face of the earth. I heard him go out and slam the door. When I knew she had gone to her room I crept back up to bed. I never heard him come in again. By the time I were up the next morning he had left. He were away for a few days. When he got back he looked totally exhausted, but relieved at the same time. A few days after that he had recovered all his former energy. There were a spring in his step again. I would catch him almost running about the house, making notes and little drawings. It were like he were making plans for the future. But if he were, it were clear Celia were going to have no part in them. They barely spoke to each other, or even looked at each other. He had been so tender and loving with her for so many years. But now… it were like he blamed her for what had happened. There had been a nurse coming in every day to look after her needs. He got her to come and live in, so she could take care of her day and night. I helped out as well as I could. He took no part in her care anymore. She went downhill rapidly after that. She lasted less than a year.'

'And when David came to the house…'

'I knew it were him. Ceridwen's boy. Mr Wallace's son. He were proud of him as only a father can be. And hard on him as only a father can be.'

'Did Michael ever say anything,' I asked, 'about what had happened that night, when he followed my mother onto the coastal path?'

'Not a word.'

Brenda and I looked hard at each other for a few moments in silent agreement. Megan did not notice, her eyes still bent on the events she had just described. Now, thanks to Megan, we knew Michael had indeed followed my mother that night, as I had seen them in my vision. But there would never be proof of the part we suspected he had played in her death. Michael's memory was still dear to Megan. We both understood it would only hurt her to voice our suspicions.

'So, Megan…' I said after a further pause, 'all this means that when I told you about the affair between David and me, you knew then that we were siblings.'

'Yes. But I couldn't tell you what I knew. I knew it were what you were trying to remember and there were something stopping you. God knows what it might have done to you if I had just come out with it. And who says you would have believed me? I thought it best to let you find out for yourself in your own way and time. I hope I were right about that.'

'Yes, Megan. You were right. Thank you.'

Brenda stood up brusquely. 'Well, this has been fascinating,' she said. 'But I must get back now. Think about what we can salvage from all this. I'll talk to you about those pictures soon, Madeleine.'

'Before you go, I have to tell you both something,' I said. 'I have to go up to London. Tomorrow afternoon. I have a series of appointments. Some tests I have to have. And depending on the results I may need others. So I'll be away for a couple of weeks.'

'You mean, medical tests?' asked Megan, looking anxious.

I nodded. At the same time I glanced up at Brenda, who by then was standing behind Megan. Brenda shook her head. She had not told Megan about my condition, thank God.

'I realised as soon as you came back from the hospital that you wasn't well,' said Megan. 'I thought, I hoped, it were just the effect of all those years locked away. I hoped the sea air would soon put you to rights again. But you're saying it's something as needs a bit more than sea air to put right?'

'That's right.'

'And you'll be back in a couple of weeks?'

'Yes. And I haven't forgotten that I promised to look into selling the house. I'll do that as soon as I get back.'

'I'll take you to the station tomorrow,' said Brenda. 'What time shall I pick you up?'

'About three o'clock will do.'

'I'll help you pack in the morning,' said Megan. 'And I'll come with you to the station, if you don't mind bringing me back here afterwards, Brenda.'

FORTY-NINE

My first thought when I saw the fire was thank God we had all been out of the house. What a lucky coincidence that Megan had decided to come with us to the station to see Madeleine off. Later I realised it was not a coincidence. He had watched us leave and seized the opportunity.

It was the red on the water I noticed first. It was not the uniform blood-red from the setting sun. That had been and gone. This was a mixture of darting crimsons and flickering yellows. I stopped the car to watch from afar. The breeze was off the land, blowing acrid fumes into my eyes. Fragments of ash and cinder pinched and stung my cheek. Fire engines were already there, but even from that distance I could see it was too late.

Megan and I returned to my cottage. She was distraught, wondering if it was her fault, if she had left something burning on the stove. I told her that was impossible. She had not put anything on the stove that day. When the police came the next day and told us it was clearly a case of arson she was so relieved.

I was distraught myself for another reason, the loss of Michael's drawings of Ceridwen. Why had I not taken them away at the time and stored them somewhere safe? But it was too late for such regrets. At least we still had one, his favourite. I went round to Cove Cottage as soon as the police had left and did the switch.

The police asked if we had any idea who had done it. They had had reports of a tramp about the place. I had seen him, I told them, but I had no idea where he was now.

But I knew all along who it was. Of course I did. Confirmation came a few days later when I received a surprise visit from the Reverend Colm O'Brien. He had a large parcel for me, all neatly wrapped up. He was smiling when he gave it to me. I had the impression he knew what was in it but he wouldn't say anything about the contents or who it was from. He would not stay for a cup of tea. Said he had urgent appointments elsewhere. I almost cried with relief and delight when I brought the parcel inside and opened it up. All the eleven ink drawings were there, intact and completely unharmed.

So who, apart from the three of us, knew about those drawings? Only one person. For reasons known only to himself he had gone to the trouble of retrieving them before taking the spare cans of petrol from the garage, spreading the contents downstairs and putting a match to them. He had taken shelter with the minister and given him the parcel to bring to me. After that, God knows where he went. Certainly the minister would not know, or if he did he had been sworn to secrecy.

B.R.

FIFTY

November 1995

I rang Brenda yesterday from my hotel room. I told her I might need to be away for longer than I first thought. I did not tell her I do not expect to return. Time enough for that later, when I know for sure. Maybe I will be able to go back, despite what my doctor said. I have had periods of remission before. Only this time I sense that things are different.

She told me about the fire. I said I had seen something about it on the news. She told me Michael's drawings of my mother are safely in her hands. Those of me perished in the fire. She is pleased about that. So am I. She was right to tell me I should have destroyed them. What do I need those mirrors for, when soon there will be nothing of me to reflect? We didn't say anything but we both know who started the fire. His last act of destruction before departing, the ghosts and the memories consumed along with the shell that had contained them. But what had possessed him to save

Michael's drawings but not his own? The last bit is easy. Alan had rejected David and all he had done in that name. But he had always despised Michael as an artist. Was it simply that there was enough of the artist still in him to recognise that those drawings were different from the rest of Michael's work, that they had a life of their own which cried out to be saved? Nobody will ever be able to ask him. But I believe there was far more to it than a matter of artistic merit. In them, if he had opened his eyes to look below the surface, he might have seen a record of a love which could and should have blessed not only its protagonists but those who followed in their wake, including himself. Instead, a curse was laid on them all. As a man of the world Michael had, with terrible consequences, destroyed a love to which as an artist he had given immortality. It is a paradox which perhaps nobody will ever be able to explain, but at least the world will have the chance to contemplate it.

My doctor has carried out plenty of tests, though I suspect most of them were unnecessary. His expression the moment I first walked into his consulting room told me what he thought. The tests only confirmed his prognosis. At least he has been honest with me. They're admitting me tomorrow. It means I have a few more weeks at best. Maybe just a few days. Time enough to finish this. Time enough to take stock.

Stock of what? Of the men in my life. That man in the port near Marseilles. He was the Third. Of course there were more than that, if you count all the ones who fucked me. Not that I ever did. Count them, that is. What would be the point? No, there were really only three.

There was the First One, when I was thirteen. Then David. He was the Second. Then the stranger, the Third. They were a Holy Trinity, three in one. The Father, the Son and the Holy Ghost. The First made me, the Second forged my image so I could see myself and the Third was the envoy of the First, sent from Hades to bring me down to him.

The Trinity. High priests of sodomy. For them it was a sacred ritual, a solemn sacrament. They were putting me into their equivalent of a state of grace. It was a necessary precaution, said the First One, when I told him I had started my periods. We must not create a child who would be an abomination to the Gods, a child to whom I would be both mother and sister. As if what we were doing wasn't enough of an abomination already. For the Second One it was the means to get the image he needed for his great masterpiece. The Third One knew from experience that it was the most effective way to pass on the seed of death. Each of them told me not to scream. Even the Third. I knew that was what he was saying. I did scream, of course. They knew I would. That was the moment when they knew I was transformed, when the sacrament was complete.

I had been searching for the Holy Ghost all my life, without knowing it, ever since the Father had gone, like those disciples in the Gospel story who waited in fear and secrecy after the Crucifixion. This Holy Ghost did not give me the gift of tongues. I could not understand his words. But I could understand the burning hatred in his eyes. He knew nothing about me. It was enough that I was a woman. A woman had condemned him to die. So he would condemn me and as many others like me as he could find in the time left to him. He hoped we would transmit it to others. Maybe he had worked out that the same seed which had sentenced him might sentence thousands of others in the time it would take him to die. Maybe that thought gave him some comfort. But if he was thinking that about me he would have been disappointed to know that I did not pass it on. What he gave me stopped with me. One tiny glass of hideous, gut-wrenching local brandy and the deal was done. I left the café and he followed me. I never looked round. I walked back along the quay, through the pitch black of the narrow cobbled streets stinking of urine and rotten fish to my hotel, collected my key and went up to my room. All the time he was there behind me and I never turned to look at him. The room was filthy, infested with cockroaches. Why had I chosen it? I could have afforded something much more luxurious. It just seemed appropriate for what I sensed was going to happen in that place. I walked in and he closed the door behind us. I undressed and lay down on the bed, face down, in the sacramental position. He had not yet touched me. The first time I felt his flesh was when his weight pressed down on me. I could not be absolutely sure, of course, not until it was over. I might have got it wrong. He might not have been carrying anything. I might have misunderstood the nature of his hatred. He might just have been an ordinary strangler or stabber. But when he left immediately afterwards, without another word, I knew I had been right. He was the One.

I've already seen the ward. They took me up there so I could prepare myself, so they could show me how nice it is. The funny thing is that they're right. It is nice. It's not like a normal hospital ward at all. There's so much life and humour around. The patients are mostly young men, apparently in perfect health, apart from the drips they're attached to as they rush around, greeting their visitors, chatting to the doctors. I'm looking forward to it. With any luck I'll spend Christmas there.

So that's the whole story. I wanted to write it down so I could help myself to get my memories back. And to see if I could work out what really happened between me and my mother. But that's really quite simple. She went away to have her affairs.

One day she came back and found I had become a stranger. It was all over between us. She had a second go at love and motherhood. And look what happened.

Your tragedy wasn't that you died young, was it, Mother? It was that the two men you chose to father your children abused them in their different ways. And you could do nothing about it. Did you watch the child you had christened Hywel growing up, becoming David, turning into his own kind of abuser? And did you then watch helplessly as he and I found each other, the fruits of your womb coming together in one compound monstrosity? Now my body is rotting away, waiting to follow where my soul was taken all those years ago. And your son is a grotesque, despised creature on the margins of existence. That's hardly a great success story, is it? But at least you tried, which is more than you can say for me. At least you lived. One can admire a stranger and so I admire you. I admire your courage in living your life by the light of your illusions, right up to the end. I admire your love for Michael, that whirlwind of destruction that swept through both your lives. I admire the foolish honesty and credulous fidelity with which you held on to that love through all the desolate years when he betrayed you. You never betrayed him for an instant. Even at the moment on the cliffs when he let you fall, you still loved him, still trusted him to save you. Your passion lived then and it lives on now. It still haunts those wild places, screaming its defiance to the winds and the waves.

I've packed my bag. Not that I will need much. A change of clothes, a hairbrush. Not this one. It's already matted with grey hair now coming out in clumps every time I try to brush. No make-up. No point in that. Toothbrush and paste. What about the ointment for my sores? I won't need that. The nurses will look after that sort of thing once I'm in the ward. It won't be like that other place. This one is a proper hospital, where they take care of you. Tomorrow I'll take a taxi to the main entrance, go to the admissions reception, wait for the clerk to process the paperwork. Already a corpse, waiting to be buried.

FIFTY-ONE

_____

The following morning, I check out and hail a taxi in Sloane Square.

'Where to, love?' asks the driver, cheerfully.

'The Chelsea and Westminster.'

We crawl through the heavy traffic along the King's Road. At last he pulls up outside the main entrance.

'Here you are, darling. Do you need any help to get to reception? Hey, are you all right? You look as if you're having a fit. Do you want me to go and get a nurse or a doctor to help you inside?'

'I'm sorry. I'm fine. I just lost my breath for a moment. Must have been the thought of going in there. Then I remembered. I've got the wrong date. Stupid of me. I'm supposed to be in Oxford today. Can you take me to Paddington Station, please?'

Yet another taxi. This time from Penzance Station.

'Where to?'

Porthhella. No, not there. Not where Brenda or Megan or the fishermen might see me. Better to go from the house.

'Tregarnon House.'

'That's the place that burned down, isn't it?'

'Yes, that's right. I heard about that. I hear the site's for sale. I want to take a look.'

'Fine. Will you want me to wait and bring you back?'

'No thanks. I'm staying nearby.'

'There's nothing nearby. Wherever you're staying you'll still have quite a walk to get there. But you're the boss. Tregarnon House it is. Or where it used to be.'

No expressions of concern from this one about how ill I look. Thank God. I have my story ready, just in case. Food poisoning on the train. Can't trust railway caterers these days. I sit back in my seat, watching the familiar scenery unfold. The sky is clear. The hard frost from last night persists in shaded parts of the meadows and under the trees. The sunset will be spectacular. I will be there just in time. If my strength holds out.

The sun hangs blood-red on the surface of the water. I sit on a rock, still writing. There are a few walkers about. But in an hour it will be nearly dark and much too dangerous to be so close to the cliffs.

I am not sure of the exact spot. But I know it is where the old path has been roped off. The edge is closer now, since the fall of the earth. I am only a hundred yards away. I can crawl there if necessary. I have half-crawled much of the way as it is. I just need to finish what I am writing.

FIFTY-TWO

Those were not the last words Madeleine wrote. I will
come to the rest later. Now I will pick up the story myself
with that phone call from Mr Wilson, as Megan and I
waited in my cottage for news of her.
    B.R.

'Miss Rogers? Brenda Rogers?'
    'That's right. Who is this?'
    There was a crackle on the line which made his
voice hard to hear.

'James Wilson. Madeleine's solicitor. From Oxford. You
remember we met, when you came up here to find her. You
left your name and number in case we found her first.'

'Yes, of course, Mr Wilson. I remember. What can I do
for you?'

'It's about Madeleine again, I'm afraid. She came up here
yesterday to see me. She's very ill, as I'm sure you know, and
she came to sort out her will. The fact is, I hadn't expected to

see her here. She was in London, waiting to be admitted to hospital. We had an appointment for me to go to meet her there today, at the hospital. When she arrived here yesterday she told me her admission had been delayed by a week. So she thought she would come and see me first and get it all sorted. The fact is, I'm very worried about her. She barely had the strength to get through the meeting. I'm no doctor but in my opinion she needed to be in hospital right away. I have some contacts in the medical world here so I asked her if she wanted me to get her into the Radcliffe without risking the journey back to London. She was absolutely insistent that she would be all right. Frankly, I didn't believe her.'

'I did know she was ill, Mr Wilson. She left here a few days ago. She told us she was seeing a specialist in London to have a few tests done. She rang me yesterday to say she might have to stay up there a bit longer. Obviously they decided they would have to admit her. But what surprises me is that she didn't tell me about going into hospital. She rang me from her hotel but I never thought to ask which one.'

'I asked her that myself, in case I needed to contact her before her admission. She gave me the name of a hotel in Paddington. I rang them after she had left. She had checked out before coming here. She never intended to go back. I then rang the Chelsea and Westminster. She had lied to me about her admission being delayed. She was booked to be admitted yesterday, urgent priority. No delays on any account. When she never turned up, they tried to locate her. They rang her doctor in London in case he had referred her elsewhere and the message hadn't got through to them. But he had no idea where she was. He was horrified to learn she had not turned up at the hospital.'

My heart was pounding. I tried desperately to control my breathing.

'So I wondered if she had decided to return to Cornwall and had arrived back with you,' he continued. 'I mean, she would stay with you, wouldn't she? I had heard on the news what happened to the house. The fire, I mean.'

'Yes, she would stay with me. If she were coming back down here. But she would have told me if that was what she was planning.'

'I can't explain why she hasn't contacted you but I am sure she is returning to you. My father was here as well, yesterday. You know he's supposed to be retired but he can't stay away. And he's an old family friend. So he drove her to the station. He hung around to make sure she got on her train to London. She told him she didn't have a return so she needed to go to the ticket window. He waited nearby. She got a ticket to London all right. But he swears she also bought a through ticket for the journey on to Penzance.'

'What did the police say?' asked Megan.

'They traced the taxi driver who picked her up at Penzance. Definitely her. Fitted the description I gave them. Looked as if she was about to expire, so he said.'

'So where is she?'

'He took her to the house.'

'What house?'

'Her house, of course. Only there's no house there anymore. As she bloody well knows.'

'Maybe she's gone and forgotten again.'

'In that case he would have brought her here or back to the station or somewhere she could stay. No, she told him she wanted to see the site because she was thinking of buying it. And she didn't want him to wait. She went there deliberately. I have an idea where's she going. But it's nearly dark now and the coastguard won't come out until morning.'

'The coastguard? You don't think…?' Megan covered her face with her hands.

I guided Megan to the sofa and eased her into a sitting position. I put my arm around her for a few moments. Then I stood up abruptly.

'It's no use, Megan. I've got to do something. I can't just hang around here waiting. I'll get round there in the car and look around. No, wait a minute. I'll go from here. It's shorter though the path's much steeper at the start. There's a torch in the cupboard. Here we are.'

'Where are you going?'

'Up to the headland, to where her mother fell. That's where she's going, I'll swear it.'

'Brenda, don't, please. It's much too dangerous.'

There was a loud knock on the door. We both jumped.

'Who's that, for God's sake?'

'Maybe it's the police,' said Megan. 'Maybe they've found her. Oh, please God they've found her.'

I jerked open the door. Five men stood outside. I recognised Charley, George and Samuel, and John Foster, the manager of the inn. The fifth man was young, a rucksack on his back. I stepped back, startled.

'Hello, John. Gentlemen. What—'

'Brenda, I'm sorry to disturb you,' said John. 'I thought you should know. These gentlemen said you were friends with her.' The trio nodded. 'Madeleine, I mean. I had a call from the police in Penzance to say she might be missing and near the coastal path. They found an overnight bag near the site of the fire which they think might be hers. The sergeant said she was very ill and in no state to be up there. Then this gentleman came into the bar.'

The man smiled, stepped forward and nodded. 'Ladies. My name's Bill. I don't know her. Your friend, I mean. I'm just visiting round here. But I think I might have seen her.'

'Go on, young man.' It was Megan who spoke. She had come up behind me as soon as I had opened the door.

'I saw this lady struggling up the path on the other side, towards the bay. That was well over an hour ago. I offered to help her but she refused. I came on here. I'm staying at the inn. I decided I should go back. But it was getting dark by then and I thought it would be a good idea to get help. Mr Foster here told me someone of that description had been reported missing. He remembered her from the time she stayed at the inn. He offered to join me. Then these three gentlemen who were in the bar said they were locals who knew the coastline better than anybody and they offered too.'

'And I was about to go up there on my own,' I said. 'And bloody terrified at the thought. I hate going up there even in daylight. So I'm pleased to see you all. Gentlemen...' I addressed the fishermen. 'I'm surprised you want to help. After what I've heard of your behaviour to her.'

George stepped forward. 'I wants to apologise for that, Miss Rogers. On behalf of us all. Miss Megan there saw us the other day when she were out shopping and explained it all. About how someone else confessed to the killing. And how she's so sick now. We're all three of us very sorry. And we're here to help. I can find my way up to that headland blindfold. And so can my friends.'

'Come on then,' said John. 'We're wasting time here.'

'Hang on a minute,' I said. 'I'll get my coat and torch. I'm coming with you.'

We passed the spot several times before we saw her. She was lying on her back, close to the edge, as still as the surrounding rocks. Instinctively we laid our coats over her, although there was no sign of movement. I shone my torch into her frozen eyelids. No response.

'She's dead, gentlemen,' I said. 'We shouldn't move her. But we can't just leave her like this. We'll take it in turns to watch her. Three on, three off.'

'You go back and sleep, Miss Rogers,' said Charley. 'The three of us will watch. We've spent many a night on the decks of our boats in much worse weather than this. We've got hides as tough as leather.'

'All right. You other two come back with me. We'll be back in an hour with flasks of hot coffee.'

'Then Bill and I will relieve you,' said John.

'I'll ring the police and the doctor,' I said. 'They'll be here as soon as it's light. Just give me a moment alone with her.'

The men stood back. I knelt down by the body and fumbled underneath the coats, looking up every now and then to check that none of them was watching. Shivering with the chill which despite the covers seeped from the body into my fingers, I at last found her notebook. I prised it away and tucked it inside my jacket. I stood up and looked down at her. None of the others was near enough to hear me. Or if they could they would assume I was saying a prayer. Which in a sense I was.

'You used up every last ounce of your strength to come up here to die. So why did you do that? What were you thinking of? You can't tell me now. But maybe this book will. Goodnight, Madeleine. Rest in peace now. You died much too soon, never knowing the good you did, never knowing the life you restored to others, including to this shrivelled-up shell of a woman. So often my hate has stopped me from loving but in the end I did learn to love you. Despite the evil that was done to you, you lit a fire within yourself, a yearning for love and truth, which sustained you long after your poor sick body should have passed away. I swear to you that I will do all I can in the years left to me to take that fire into myself, to show the world or whoever in it can take the time and trouble to heed me what you were and what you did. There is no breath left in you now but your work is far from done, as long as I have anything to do with it.'

I knelt down and kissed her icy brow.

FIFTY-THREE

Megan did not come with me to the inquest. I was pleased about that. She was still so devastated by the news of the death that I do not think she could have coped with the impersonal nature of the proceedings. The verdict was death from natural causes. There was no discussion about her motives in going up to the cliffs in freezing weather and in such a serious condition. The pathologist said she had gone into a coma from which she never recovered. The immediate cause of death was heart failure. Her constitution had been severely weakened over recent months by HIV-related infections. I didn't tell Megan that. I told her she had a chronic heart condition from childhood. That was no more than the truth.

I could not leave Megan alone in my cottage for more than an hour or so. I would sometimes go out for a short walk along the coastal path, just as far as the point where it began to get steep. Indoors I passed the time reading through Madeleine's notebook and typing out a fair copy of what she had written.

The notebook had been her mother's. She had started where her mother had finished, after those few diary entries. There were plenty of blank pages left. Madeleine referred back to her mother's entries by date. I transcribed them into the appropriate parts of my own copy. I also added some contributions of my own, none of them exactly flattering to me, to complete the sequence of events. When I had finished I locked away both the notebook and my own typescript in the cupboard in my bedroom.

Why did I go to all that trouble when she had sworn me to secrecy, that time we met by her father's grave? Why create a narrative which nobody would see? I did not understand at the time. I only knew it was something I had to do, in her memory.

A few weeks after her death, when I at last felt I could leave Megan on her own for a few days, I went to Oxford to see Mr Wilson about Madeleine's will. She left far more than I had expected. She had earned a great deal in her years in the City without ever having the chance or the inclination to spend it. Her will was very simple. The estate was split between Megan and myself. Plenty for her to buy herself a nice little cottage of her own, near to mine so I could keep an eye on her. She was used to her independence. All in good time, of course. She would need to recover first.

After we had discussed the will I spoke to Mr Wilson senior about the time of Madeleine's father's death. I told him Madeleine and I had belatedly become friends but had had little time to get to know each other well. I was trying to continue our friendship beyond her premature death by finding out all I could about her story. I asked if her father had left a note. No, he told me, but he had left a tape, which the police had found in his safe but decided was not relevant to the case. Madeleine had been desperate to have it back and they had eventually allowed her to keep it. The mention of a tape reminded me. She had told me about it. She had promised her father to lock it away, just before he shot himself. She had always kept it with her, despite not knowing its contents. Now, of course, it had been destroyed in the fire. So that was that. But then Mr Wilson told me that the police had shown him a copy of the transcript they had made of the tape. Like the cautious lawyer he had always been, he had kept a copy. He would be only too pleased to let me have a further copy if I thought it might help.

I then decided while I was in Oxford to pay a call on someone else. It took me some time to find the grave again. By then the rain which had threatened all day had begun to fall heavily and I had forgotten my umbrella. However, there was one advantage to the weather. I could be sure of being alone. I could say out loud what I had come to say to him.

'Hello, again, Dr Reed. Remember me? Brenda. Madeleine's friend. This time it's just the two of us. Nobody to ask for your forgiveness or any nonsense like that. Only me, your accuser, the only one left who knows what you did. But I'm going to be fair, Dr Reed. I'm not going to rant and rave. Not your style and certainly not mine. I'm going to try to imagine how it all happened.

'First of all, your upbringing. A remote Welsh village. Your parents distant and severe. The only joy you could find was in your studies. At school you were withdrawn, a loner. You went to church, or chapel more likely, but you never believed in it. Am I doing all right so far? Up to this point I could be talking about the two of us. But from now on there are important differences. I never needed faith. You did. As you read and studied the classics you decided you preferred the harsh, capricious gods of antiquity to a merciful Christian

God. You could believe in them. You went to university, here in Oxford, got a first-class degree, then a doctorate. You were elected a Fellow of an Oxford college at a relatively young age. Your reputation grew. You published books. Your entire world was your research and your teaching and your writing. You were in your early thirties by now. But you looked older. You were happy enough, so you thought. Safe and secure in your sheltered world.

'You had never been particularly interested in the opposite sex. Then you met a young student, beautiful, vibrant, impulsive. You married. Maybe you sensed you lacked something she could provide. Maybe you felt that by that stage in your career you needed the security and status of marriage. Whatever the reason you never really loved her, never understood her. The two of you drifted apart. You buried yourself even more deeply in your work.

'Then something happened which shook your world to its foundations. We need to give this something a name. You could never have done that, because it was totally outside your experience, your view of the world. Let's call it passion, for want of a better word. I know a little bit about that. I know how it can take you over, just when you think you have your life completely under control. I know how it can give you a capacity for evil you never thought you had. A young woman came into your life. Of course she had been there before. But as a child. An inconvenience. A distraction. You had ignored her as much as you could. Now you were overwhelmed. There she was, the perfect embodiment of beauty in your eyes, innocent, lonely, fearful, trembling on the verge of womanhood with nobody to help her, her mother an absent stranger. She had had no time to build defences, to learn how to manipulate, to be cynical, to use others and avoid being used. She was a pure, perfect human being in your eyes. And beautiful. Beautiful in a way she could never have been before and never could be again. *Beauty in the young is a curse. It awakens evil.* She told me you wrote that in one of your books. Her beauty was a curse indeed. On both of you.

'The emotions which raged inside you were all the more violent for having been suppressed for so long. One thought tortured you above all others. She was not intended for you. Soon she would attract the attention of others. Boys, then men, fighting for her time, her attention, her smile, her words, her affections, her body. She would be corrupted by the world outside the two of you, that strange, messy, threatening, unknown world. You had to prevent that. So you took everything she had to give before she had a chance to give it, before she even knew what it was you had taken. You made her yours, forever, or so you thought. You had a new god now. Passion, ecstasy, the joy of possession of perfection, call it what you will. You knew the old gods you had once revered had prescribed punishments for what you were doing. But you defied them. You told them you no longer believed in them. But it didn't work. The old gods were jealous and outraged. They sent their agents of punishment to torment you. The Furies. You had even written a book about them, recklessly daring to consign them to myth and superstition. They came and took their revenge. They drove you to kill yourself.

'But that wasn't the end of it. You expected her to see them as well. You thought her as guilty as you were. You expected her to follow you. You assumed she would never be able to live on after you. In a way you were right about that. If she hadn't forgotten she would have killed herself. But she did forget and she survived, after a fashion. But if our lives are built on the memories of what made us who we are then she had no life. All she knew was that she was different, special, not like other people. Unaware of what was driving her, she sought out men to take your place. I can hear you laughing about that. Of course nobody could take your place. But she had forgotten you. You had to find her again. You had to pursue her, even after death. Of course you did. She belonged to you, didn't she? So you and the Furies drove her to seek out that final encounter, the last sacrifice of her body, the one which would ensure that in time she would follow you.

'Let's go back a little. I don't want to get ahead of myself. Let's go back to the time she was drifting through life, searching for the man who might show her once again the image of herself you had given her. At last she met such a man. A brilliant young artist, someone whose genius justified any amount of bad behaviour. Or an intolerably selfish and abusive young man. Whichever way you care to look at it. He made her feel special all right. They were brother and sister. Nobody had told them. But I think they each suspected, deep down. He focussed his hatred of women on Madeleine because of those deep-lying memories of the first woman who abandoned him, as he saw it. He was sure Michael was his father. He must often have wondered who his mother was. Madeleine must have told him Michael had known her mother. Maybe that made him wonder even more. But what finally broke him was seeing that picture, that image of his mother and sister in one, both of them the objects of his abuse. He looked at the picture and saw his own evil. He took refuge by forgetting, and later by killing off the person who had done those things and becoming Alan.

'She must have had her suspicions as well. The picture, Michael's actions following her mother's death, arranging the funeral, having her buried next to his own family plot, looking after her cottage, always denying he had known her mother more than slightly. Then David turning up out of nowhere, just the right age. Another relationship forbidden by the gods. So when it ended the Furies pursued her, as you had prophesied. Her moment of truth finally came when she spoke to Laura. But in the meantime the Furies had driven her to do something terrible. I know her illness was not just bad luck. She sought it out. Although she did not realise it at the time it was her way to follow you, as you had told her to. The shock of what Laura told her caused her to lose her memories, just as David lost his. And in the hospital where she served her time for a crime she had not committed, she protected herself by taking literally some words she had overheard Laura say, that she was David's mother. Conveniently that was all she remembered about Laura. And that delusion was enough to protect her when she came back to Porthhella and found out for certain that her mother and Michael had had an affair. It even protected her when she realised her mother had been pregnant, and that somewhere she might have an unknown brother. But the real truth was still there, trying to break through. And the one who embodied that truth was you. You were trying to reach her, trying to take possession again, your image, your words, your deeds, forming slowly through the fog of her lost memories. Although she wanted to remember, at the same time she was terrified because she knew that when her memories returned so would you.

'I never believed in ghosts, Dr Reed. How could I? A hard-headed northerner like me. But when you've lived down there by the Atlantic, looking out towards the Scillies over the drowned lands of legend that lie between, you maybe get less sceptical. You begin to sense that there are spirits around you. Madeleine sensed that too. She sensed you, trying to get through to her, trying to claim your own. But she also sensed someone else. Ceridwen came to her, her spirit one of those released that night by the storm to roam abroad and seek whatever they need to find peace, be it vengeance or reconciliation. That's how the locals there have it and now I believe them. Ceridwen showed her how she had died. And in so doing she was telling her they would no longer be the strangers they had become because of you.

'God knows, there was a lot in her life for Ceridwen to regret. So many wasted opportunities. But the biggest waste of all was Madeleine. She was telling Madeleine that what she regretted most was that she never saw her own daughter until it was too late. Never had the chance to take her by the hand, and say, we're going to make up for lost time, you and me. There's nothing we can't be together, nothing we can't do together, we can take the earth and the heavens by storm with the love that is finally going to grow between us. But she never had the chance to say any of that, did she? And the reason for that was you and what you did.

'Now, shall I tell you something, Dr Reed? You did not win. You lost. You always thought Madeleine was your possession. But in her last moments she was finally able to choose. And she did not choose you. How does that make you feel? She went up to the cliffs to die because she couldn't face dying in hospital, still not knowing. She knew her mother did not know at the time what you did. So how would she react if she did know, if she actually saw it happening? Would she agree with you that Madeleine was evil as you were? If so, you would have won. She would have accepted your right to take her down with you to Hell. She crawled to the edge, to the last place on earth where her mother had drawn breath. She was there to put that question to her.

'Madeleine had seen how she died. Not just seen. She felt the last seconds of her mother's life, inside her own mind and body. She was her, standing on that spot by the edge, falling to her death. I believe it happened again. Her mother was her again, took her eyes to see what happened, in her bedroom all those years ago when you went to her, took her ears to hear her cry for help. And what mother, seeing and hearing that, seeing her daughter lying there afterwards, alone, terrified, in agony, would tell her she was evil, that she was to blame, that she belonged to you forever? No, I believe that that cry for help from all those years ago was finally answered. If it had not been, she would have turned her face into the ground. The Furies would have dragged her down to you.

'But she died looking upwards, holding closely to her the book in which she had written her story. And there on the last page is the final entry. Just three words. Barely legible. I believe she wrote them at the very moment of death. I recognised them from Sunday School. From the Bible, the Book of Revelation. And I think I know what she meant by them. She had her answer. Her face was peaceful. The Furies had finally left her. And so had you. And now I'll leave you to howl down there on your own for all eternity.'

So how do I know Madeleine had heard her mother's answer? How do I know the Furies had left her?

Because of the one passage from her notebook which I have yet to reveal. This is what she wrote as she made her way to the place appointed for her death.

FIFTY-FOUR

W as Michael the reason you stopped writing to
me in this book, Mother? Was it because of him
that you forgot you had ever written to me, that
you left this to gather dust? Or did you think that once you,
Michael and Hywel were a family you might find me again,
make me part of your new life?

That could never have happened. You were too late, twenty
years too late. I've just read again what I wrote above about you
being a stranger, one I could admire from a distance. But that
was all nonsense, wasn't it? You're never a stranger to someone
you've betrayed as you betrayed me.

I remembered, just as I was about to go into the hospital.
I thought I had remembered everything. But not that. Not
the moment I knew I was lost. The moment you betrayed me.
He had told me to be quiet. But I wasn't. I cried out, to you,
for help. You weren't there. Of course you weren't. So I was
quiet, all through the rest of the agony and the terror. The next
day I went down early but he was already up. I think he had

been up all night. He looked at me. For a moment I think he was afraid, in case I would run away in fear or horror. He was wondering what he had done, not to me but to the two of us. I showed no fear, no repulsion. I was calm and self-possessed. Overnight I had grown beyond my years. I looked him in the eye and asked him if he loved me, if he would always be there for me. I was thinking of you when I spoke. He said, of course I love you. It's special, isn't it? Our special love. You don't need anybody else. He never betrayed me. You did.

That is why I have come here to the place you died. To accuse you of betrayal.

If you had been a stranger you would never have returned to me that night, would you, to show me how you died? So why did you? Were you telling me that you too had been betrayed? Was that supposed to make up for your betrayal of me? Why did you enter my mind, let me feel your last moments? I need you to do that again, Mother, now, before I die. I want to be you again. I want you to take my eyes, so you can watch me, doing those things with him. I want you to see my evil, accuse me of it. Then I will know why you betrayed me. Because you knew before it happened that I was evil and always had been. Because you had to get away from me, from both of us. Then I can go to him. I will lie with my face pressed into the earth until his hands rise up and pull me down. I'll go to the edge, now. That's where I'll find you. That's where you'll tell me.

Only traces of red on the water now. My hands are numb, my legs without feeling. My breath is slow and painful. Already the frost is hardening the mud and the tufts of grass. The waves below are no more than a distant swish in my ear. I wait and listen. I sense your presence. You haunt this very place. With my last breath I give you my eyes to see and my ears to hear.

He told me about it at your funeral. The minister. About the sea which divides. I didn't understand then. Now at last I do.

So now it ends. Only three more words. Already I feel myself falling, not as you did, but slowly and silently. Through this last, endless, blessed night.

NO MORE SEA.

FIFTY-FIVE

I walked slowly to my car, suddenly overwhelmed by a feeling of intense fatigue. Time to get back to Megan. I'd been away long enough. I settled myself into the driving seat, preparing myself mentally for the long journey ahead. I would stop and phone Megan on the way.

Oh, there was one other thing. The copy of the transcript of the tape. It was short. I would read it first, before I started the engine. Think it over as I drove. I took it out of my handbag, unfolded it and began to read.

I have always found the Christian idea of Hell inherently ridiculous. An eternity of torment for an instant of sin. Only a madman could invent something like that. The Greek myths offer more potent and credible forms which we can recognise from our own lives. What worse hell can anybody imagine than to be hounded to death by loathsome tormentors who follow you everywhere you go?

Mankind devises euphemisms for concepts which it

finds painful or frightening. The Furies were real enough to the Ancient Greeks for them to find such a euphemism. They were so afraid of them they never referred to them by their real name. They called them the Eumenides, or the Kindly Ones. I believe the Furies of ancient times are still with us, though they may no longer have serpents for hair, or the heads of dogs, or the wings of bats. We fashion them according to whatever image suits our purposes. As for the crimes they pursue, they too have changed to suit the evolution of our modern taboos. Maybe it is our consciences that call them forth, but they are real. I believe in them as many believe in God and the Devil. I can attest to the reality of the Furies as others have attested to apparitions of the Virgin Mary. Those who saw such apparitions were special, like Saint Bernadette, or the children of Fatima. Some say they were mad or were liars. They were not. They simply saw what others could not. You and I too are special, like them. But unlike them, our place is not in Heaven but in whatever dark corner of Hades has been set aside for us.

335

FIFTY-SIX

I stooped and laid the fresh shop flowers on the grave. What were those, laid on the same grave? The stalks were crumpled and the flowers, too self-effacing for any shop or stall, already wilting. I knew I had not put them there. Somebody's idea of a joke. I turned and walked back to where Megan was standing, looking at the three inscriptions on the neighbouring stone.

'I'm just reading her inscription, underneath her mum's,' she said. 'In memory of Madeleine Reed, beloved daughter of Ceridwen Williams. I'd have put on it that they was two peas in a pod but because of a careless cook they got separated into two different saucepans. Only that doesn't quite seem the right sort of language for a gravestone.'

'It sums it up pretty well, though.'

'I were just thinking back to the service. I still find it funny to think of those fishermen carrying her coffin in. All dressed up in their Sunday best.'

'The night she died they watched over her all night, up

there on the cliffs in the freezing cold. John and that hiker chap offered to relieve them but they wouldn't hear of it. So what possessed you to go and talk to them?'

'I were never planning to. But I were so angry about what you had told me about the way they'd behaved. And when I went down to the shop on the sea front that day there they was, large as life, sitting on that bench across the road. I knew it were them right away. So before I knew what I were doing I crossed over and introduced myself. Said I were Mr Wallace's housekeeper for over thirty years, and I were there all the time she were there to look after him. I said I knew her and they didn't. I knew she had a kind heart and a good soul which were more than could be said for them. I said someone else had admitted to the killing, though who it were were none of their business. And even if she had done it what right did they have to judge her, especially now she were so very sick. I turned my back on them and stormed away, wondering what had got into me.'

'Good for you. But you should have told me. You could have knocked me down with a feather when they turned up on the doorstep insisting on helping to find her. Megan, I wonder if you could do me a favour? Let me have a few minutes alone here.'

'Of course, dear. I'll go and sit in the church. It'll be cooler there.'

I stared at the stone, seeing only Michael's inscription. I looked round. I was alone. Best not to make too much of a habit of talking to people by the side of their graves. But in the case of Dr Reed and now Michael I knew I had no choice. I had had unfinished business with the one and now it was the turn of the other.

'Hello, Michael. I thought it was about time we had a frank talk. There are so many things I never said to you while you were alive. If I had... Well, maybe some things would have been different. Who am I kidding? It would all have been different. You had to carry a heavy burden in your final days. Well, that's mine. Knowing I could have stopped it all.

'You've dominated my life and my thoughts from the moment we first met. Not that you had the slightest idea, or would have given a damn if you had. You were far too busy elsewhere. But the awful truth is that it was an image of you I loved, or thought I loved. I never really knew you. Even when I helped you send Ceridwen away I was too obsessed with my own revenge on her to judge your actions as I should have done. I hadn't hesitated to judge her, had I? Or her daughter. Or anybody else who presumed to cross my path. But the one I should have judged, should have condemned, I excused, out of my own blindness.

'That wasn't the end of your crimes, not by a long chalk. You sent Laura away, separating her from the boy she had come to love as her own son. You took her place and his mother's. You tried to be his father. And what sort of father were you? You loved him. I never doubted that. But you never knew how to show a father's love. You couldn't find the right words or the right gestures. He grew up in fear of you. I never admitted this before, even to myself, but you got everything wrong. You sent him to that awful school so he could learn to stand up for himself in the world. That wasn't right for a child like him. He learned only to sneer at the world and take what he thought was his.

'Then Madeleine came along. His sister. You thought you could put everything right through her. Arrange for him to have the sort of love you had taken from him, the love you could never give him yourself. But you made one dreadful, catastrophic mistake, worse than all the others. You kept their identity a secret from them. Why in God's name did you do that? Did you think they wouldn't believe you? Did you want to see first if their natures were compatible? Did you want to spare them the shock of being told a stranger is a sibling? Or were you just addicted to secrecy, to the control you thought it gave you? Could you not bear to lose that control until the time came when you had to accept the inevitable? Was it you rather than them that you needed to prepare?

'Whatever the reason, you had it all planned, didn't you? I have to admit, it was a beautiful scheme. They were going to become friends at first, under your supervision. Then one day you would reveal all. They were really brother and sister. Their friendship could flower into sibling love. Madeleine was older. She could give him the sort of maternal love and guidance you could not. You could withdraw, leave them to it, proud of what you had achieved at last, satisfied with the way you had so exquisitely, so triumphantly made amends. Maybe they would set up house together, until he left to pursue his career, in Paris, or Rome, or Venice. He would get married and bring his bride home to show to his father and sister. Yes, Michael, it was a perfect plan, except for one thing.

'For God's sake, did you know nothing about human nature? Had you never heard of what can happen between siblings who are not brought up together, who then meet in later life? They may have hated each other but they were drawn together irresistibly. I saw the result with my own eyes. I told you and you never forgave me for that. I understand your reaction now. How could you ever have forgiven me? I believe what she told me, what her mother showed her, that you watched Ceridwen fall to her death when you could have saved her. I believe that image haunted you daily. Now another nightmare of your own creation came to haunt you. The physical union of a brother and sister you had brought together, each bound to the other until their minds and their hearts and their souls finally broke.

'Some people, like me, never love enough, Michael. They are too afraid, only half-alive. They bury themselves in places like this, sometimes allowing themselves a thought of how things might have been, if only... You were never like that. You loved too much and too widely, destroying here to nurture there. You dreamed of being surrounded by love and beauty. But you could only do that in art. And even there your art was flawed. I'm not talking about your technical deficiencies. You overcame most of those, through sheer hard work. I'm not even talking about your greatest fault as an artist, your inability time and again to realise the warmth and passion of your inner being on the canvas or the page. So often you hid yourself from the world when you desperately wanted to show yourself. Something stopped you from being the artist you should have been. Only in those drawings of her did you let your feelings emerge, and you never intended those for the world.

'No, I'm not talking about your failures as an artist. I'm talking about the dishonesty of art, all art, even the greatest. You taught me about that. A trick of line here, of perspective there. Illusion everywhere. All the great artists did it, you told me. But in real life beauty dishonestly formed gives way to ugliness and pain. Look at the pain you created in those whose lives you touched. Celia, Ceridwen, Laura, David, Madeleine. I was only spared because you cared nothing for me. You tried to create your idea of beauty directly in life rather than in art. But however terrible your mistakes, you paid for them. God made you pay by forcing you to see what you had done, to feel their pain as well as your own, to live long enough to see all the seeds of horror you had planted come to fruition.

'I have to live with what I did and what I omitted to do, as you had to live with the knowledge of what you had done.

I am content to be judged for my sins. But as the God who punished you is my witness I'm not going to judge you now. Rest in peace if you can, Michael.'

Megan was waiting for me by the door of the church. Very slowly we walked back along the path between the gravestones, arm in arm.

'He did some wrong things, didn't he?' said Megan. 'There's no denying that. But I can't think ill of him. All I know is that he were always very good to me.'

We sat down on a stone bench, near the stile.

'When I come here on my own,' I said, 'I sometimes imagine how it might have been if I had acted differently.'

'Is that what you was talking to him about just now?'

'That's right.'

'You didn't need to tell me what you did, Brenda. You know I don't judge people. These things are between ourselves and the Almighty. I know you've tried to make up for it since.'

'I wanted to tell you. I wanted to give you the chance to tell me to get lost. I wouldn't have blamed you if you had.'

'So what it is you imagine?'

'I imagine that when Michael asked me for help in procuring an abortion for Ceridwen I told him I would have nothing more to do with him. Then I went to see her. Apologised for rejecting her earlier overtures of friendship. Told her what I knew about her condition and offered to help. Looked after her when she had her baby. In time she would have told me about Madeleine. I would have got them together, made them talk about the past. Maybe Madeleine's memories would have come back there and then. Or I would have got her proper help in getting them back. They would have sorted everything out between them. She would have met her younger brother. He would have grown up very differently from the way he did, would have been a different sort of person, someone who knew how to love and trust. They would have been a family.'

'With Aunt Brenda bringing presents at Christmas?'

'Why not?'

'But that didn't happen. So why torment yourself with what never were and were never going to be?'

'Because I need to be punished too. That's why I never let myself forget what I did or how things could, just could, have been different for them. For them, not for me. I was never going to have a real life of my own. But at least I could have prevented myself from destroying others.'

'Well, you're taking care of me now and keeping me company, and don't think I'm not grateful. So let's get back to the car. You've got an appointment at the chiropodists, remember? Without me I think you'd forget your head sometimes.'

'Megan?'

'What?'

'How about a trip to the Scillies tomorrow? If the fine weather holds. We can get the boat from Penzance.'

'I don't know. I've never been there. Is it part of Cornwall?'

'It used to be, before the sea level rose.'

'I suppose that's all right then.'

EPILOGUE

May 2007

N ow at last the time for secrecy is over. No harm will be done to the living. Megan has gone. It would have hurt her terribly to know the whole story. I could never have put her through that pain. Dr Reed's posthumous reputation is fading with time and fresh discoveries in his field of scholarship. Charitable funds raised in his name have dried up. Other sources have replenished them which no breath of scandal will ever touch. All this has been carefully researched on my behalf. There are no obstacles now. And I will be there to vouch for the truth of it all, for as long as there is still some breath in this broken old body.

First of all I need to catch up with developments since I last wrote in these pages. Megan and I went into partnership to administer Madeleine's legacy. We set up two trusts, one to run a new residential home on the site of the burnt-out house and the other to administer the Michael Wallace Memorial

Gallery, as we had decided to call it. The old harbourmaster's cottage next door to my gallery had come up for sale. We converted it into an annexe into which we put the drawings salvaged from the fire. I had contacts in the art world who were interested in becoming trustees. We got together what we could of the rest of Michael's work. A lot of it was destroyed in the fire. We advertised widely to see if any of the private owners were interested in selling. In time we had enough for a fitting tribute to Michael's memory while still having space for work for new artists.

Today is Mayday. But my morning routine is the same. After breakfast I hobble to the bench which the thoughtful parish council have installed for me at the foot of the steep incline leading up to the headland. It has been years since I was last able to visit the place where Madeleine and her mother died. Shortly after Madeleine's death I went back to the exact spot where I found her body and marked it with a small pile of stones. Hikers, perhaps thinking the stones had been placed there to mark their route and keep them well away from the cliffs, have added to the pile as they passed until it finally grew into a large cairn, visible from where I am now sitting. But these days my legs can carry me no further.

I have spoken to them from here, many times. I no longer bother to check first to see if I am alone. Nobody in the village minds. They know my eccentricities well enough by now. As for any strangers passing through, no doubt they dismiss me as a local madwoman who has wandered away from one of the new nursing homes they've built above the village.

I rise and struggle slowly and painfully back to my cottage, past the gallery, which is now a branch of a much larger one in St Ives. These days I never go inside. New managers come and go, learning their trade. But the collection is unchanged. That was a condition of the sale.

It is just before opening time and already a queue is forming at the door. Will visitors cease to come here when the full truth about Michael comes out? I do not believe so. The art and the persona he presented to the world while he was alive were cold and controlled. Many were repelled by that. What now brings them to the gallery door is the spreading word of a different Michael Wallace, a man of violent passions, and of a story of intense, forbidden love behind the drawings dramatically saved from a mysterious fire. The full story, as Madeleine and I have set it out here, whether or not it is believed, will draw many more to see not just the drawings but the wild places where those passions were played out and where the spirits of the dead must surely still roam.

I spent several fruitless years in an effort to secure a posthumous pardon for Madeleine, an effort that drained too much of my rapidly dwindling stock of time and energy. I always knew it would be a hopeless task. I was treated with sympathy and kindness but in the end nobody believed me. And who could blame them, with only my word to go on? Megan had always told me there was no point. We were the only two people left who had known and loved her and we knew the truth. That was all that mattered. She was right, as always. But still I felt I had to try.

Before I finish I have to tell what happened yesterday. I have written above that of all who inhabit this story only I remain. That is true in every real sense. But on a particular day of the year the shadow of one of those inhabitants still lingers.

I had ordered a taxi to take me round to the church. I have long since given up driving. A local shop had already delivered the flowers I would take with me. Megan and I had followed the same ritual together, visiting the graves, changing the flowers, then going into the church to say some prayers. The last day of April was always special. It was on that day that we first noticed the flowers had been changed. I noted the date in my mind. To my astonishment exactly the same thing happened the following year. We took shop flowers with us, placed them on the grave of Madeleine and her mother, and found them replaced after we had spent time inside the church. Sometimes we watched and waited, but we never saw anybody else approach the grave. We never discussed who it might be, simply exchanging glances of understanding. But one thing neither of us could explain was why that particular date had been chosen.

For the last two years I have visited the graves on my own, Megan's now being one of them. It was very quick and easy. A sudden change in the weather, a cold, an attack of pneumonia, all at home, all within a few hours, me, her niece who had just managed to get there in time from Truro, and the doctor, all by her bedside.

Yesterday I thought again about the date. What did it commemorate? Madeleine's death had been in the depths of winter. Not her birthday; he probably never knew that. Then what else but the date they had met?

So what happened yesterday? I placed the flowers and turned towards the church. This time I waited by the porch instead of going in. After a few minutes I saw the tramp. He crept noiselessly around the corner of the building. He moved towards the graveyard, silently, almost gliding along the footpaths. A long, thin hand, wizened by sun and wind, moved the flowers to one side and replaced them with a crumpled, sweat-dampened bunch of wild meadow flowers. Then in a moment he had gone, moving like a ghost, over the stile, past the Saxon cross, along the ancient pilgrims' way.